The Nightingale's Melody

TARA CONRAD

HIS ONE HER ONLY PUBLISHING

Contents

HER NIGHTINGALE

His Melody

This book is dedicated to You. To the person who feels as though they've lost everything. To the person who feels unloveable. To the person who has scars from the past. To the person who feels broken. I see you. I hear you. You are treasured beyond measure. Your scars tell your story and make you strong. You are not broken. You deserve love. Don't stop looking for your melody.
~Tara

Prologue

VIKTOR'S GOODBYE

After I say goodbye to Natalie, I take a few minutes to pack my things and compose my thoughts before heading downstairs to meet with Alex. We need to talk. He deserves honesty about everything that's happened between me and Natalie, even if it changes things between us forever. Alex has been more than a boss—he's a friend. This conversation might cost me that friendship, but it has to be done.

When I get to the apartment, I find him and Misha having a late breakfast in the kitchen.

"Care to join us?" Alex asks, motioning to the spread. "Timur made enough for an army."

"No thanks. I only have a few minutes," I say, shifting my weight. "I was hoping we could talk."

Misha catches on and grabs his plate. "I have some work to do. I'll be in the office if you need me."

Once we're alone, I sit across from Alex. "You look better today." His color's returning, and he's already regaining strength.

"A good night's sleep and some food will do that." He studies me for a minute. "But I don't think you're here to tell me how good I look."

"No," I say, bracing myself. "I'm not."

Alex raises a hand to stop me. "Before you say anything. While Tommy was holding me, he showed me pictures and videos of you and Natalie together."

I go still, unsure how to respond. But he continues.

"What he didn't realize," he says slowly, "is that watching those videos brought me peace. It meant you were doing what I asked—making sure Natalie and Rose were safe and loved."

I'm stunned and at a loss for words. How do I tell him that being able to love his wife was the best time of my life?

Alex gives a slight nod. "I know how much you love her. I see it in the way you look at her. Part of me wonders if coming back into her life is even right. She loves you, Viktor, and Rose is bonded to you. Maybe they're better off without me."

"You're wrong," I say quietly. "Natalie does love me, but I'm her second choice. She'll never love me the way she does you. I want to keep her forever. God knows I do, but I can't. You're her heart. Her whole world."

My mind drifts back to the day we thought Alex died. The light in Natalie's eyes went out. I genuinely believe if it wasn't for being pregnant, she might've ended it then. Rose gave her a reason to keep going, but there was always an empty place in her heart. One I couldn't fill, no matter how much I loved her. That place always belonged to Alex. He's her destiny—her forever.

"I need to tell you everything that happened between Natalie and me," I say finally. "The parts you didn't see on Tommy's camera."

There's nothing easy about this. I stare down as I talk, unable to meet his gaze. Through it all, Alex remains silent. When I finish, he closes his eyes for a moment, absorbing it.

"I know that wasn't easy for you," he says, his voice rough. "It wasn't easy for me to hear. But I appreciate your honesty. That's why I chose you. I'll never forget what you've done for me."

I swallow hard, unsure of what to say.

"You needed to know everything before I leave."

He sits up, alert. "You're leaving?"

"I have to." I force myself to make eye contact, ready to accept whatever judgment he gives. "Alex, I'm in love with your wife. I can't and don't want to stop loving her."

"Does Natalie know?"

"Yes."

"And?"

"She begged me to stay. But there isn't room for both of us. She belongs with you."

"I see," Alex says quietly. "Words can't express my gratitude, Viktor. For the love you showed both of them. For... everything."

"There were days I hated you for asking it of us," I admit, "but I also want to thank you. I've never had a relationship like that. Loving her and having her love in return was an honor. She's an extraordinary woman. You're one hell of a lucky man."

"I'll never forget what you've done for us." He reaches out to shake my hand. "Please keep in touch."

I nod, gripping his hand. "Will do, boss," I say, though I know I won't. I need to make a clean break.

The elevator ride down to the underground parking is silent. When I step out, I spot Michael and the rest of the team waiting in the black SUV. I climb into the front passenger seat.

"You good?" Michael asks, glancing over.

I give a quick nod, afraid to speak. If I open my mouth, the dam holding back my emotions will break.

⁂

It's a long ride to the airport, and I spend it staring out the window, lost in thought. The landscape blurs past, but inside, my turmoil builds, each emotion fighting for space. The men in the back talk among themselves, but no one tries to draw me in.

When we arrive, Maxim's jet is on the tarmac, waiting for us to board. One by one, we climb out of the SUV, each man grabbing his luggage and heading toward the plane, eager to go home. But I remain by the vehicle, rooted in place, staring at the jet.

I'm at a crossroads, faced with the choice of boarding the plane and letting it take me to the other side of the world—away from the woman I love and the little girl who feels like my own. Or getting into the SUV, driving back to Natalie, and begging her to choose me.

"What's going on?" Michael's voice breaks through my thoughts. He stands beside me, watching.

I glance over. "Just debating my options."

"You know she's meant to be with him, Viktor. Your only option is to let her go and get on the plane. Set her free and give yourself permission to be free, too."

He claps a hand on my shoulder, then turns and heads toward the jet. His words linger, *set her free*. The truth hits hard. Natalie was never mine to keep. I close my eyes, take a deep breath, and steel myself. With one last look toward the horizon, I straighten my shoulders and walk to the plane.

Climbing the steps, I resist the urge to turn around, afraid that if I do, I won't have the strength to leave. Moments later, we're taxiing down the runway. The wheels lift from the ground, and New York City begins to fade beneath us.

As the plane ascends, the weight of my loss settles in. Tears slide down my face. I know I'm leaving a piece of my heart behind with a woman and a little girl who will always hold a part of me—no matter where I go.

Viktor

Set her free. I stare down at the diamond engagement ring I bought for Natalie, feeling a kind of hurt I never knew was possible. For ten months, I lived a life I'd never dared to dream of, and in a matter of minutes, it was gone.

I'm not a good man. Violence and death are woven into the fabric of my existence. Loving a woman is a weakness, But I would've kept her and Rose safe. I'd have given my life for them without a second thought.

What the hell kind of man am I that I wish Alex hadn't come back? That I could've had it all—the girl, a baby, a family of my own.

"Where are you running off to?" Dimitri's voice interrupts my thoughts as I make my way toward the back of the plane. "Being antisocial as usual?"

I can't deal with his shit right now. The best thing for both of us is for me to keep walking.

"Leave him alone," Sasha says, coming to my defense. "He's got a lot on his mind."

I don't wait to hear Dimitri's response before closing the door to the bedroom on Maxim's jet. I need to be alone to figure out how to piece together what's left of my life. To decide what my next step should be.

One of the problems awaiting me in Russia is Maxim. He's

expecting us to meet at his house for our next assignment. But I can't go back there. Everything will remind me of her.

Taking out my phone, I book a commercial flight to Belgorod. Then, I send a message to my boss.

Me: I'm not coming back to work.

Maxim: Where are you going?

Me: Home.

I power off my phone, lean back, and close my eyes. Sleep drags me under, and in my dreams, Natalie's in my bed. My ring's on her finger— she's mine.

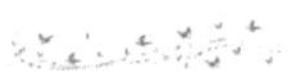

The wheels of the plane screech as we touch down on the runway. Thick clouds hide the moonlight, making it appear extra dark as we file off Max's jet. With their bags in hand, the team heads toward the waiting cars. But I walk in the opposite direction, toward the main terminal building.

"Viktor, where are you going?" Sasha calls out.

I don't answer, letting my silence speak for itself. Behind me, I hear the murmurs between the men. No one presses further, and no one follows.

Once again, I find myself alone.

Viktor

Compared to the flight from the states, the four-hour flight to Belgorod passes quickly. When I step outside the airport doors, I'm met by a shower and humid early morning air. The sun's just beginning to break through the remnants of night.

The taxi line stretches ahead, and I choose the nearest one. After tossing my bag onto the backseat, I slide in, give the driver my address, and settle in for the ride home.

Funny to think of it as home, I realize, almost surprised. This was the first apartment I bought while I was in the military, back in my early twenties. I rarely come back and barely ever think about it, yet somehow, it's always been here, waiting.

I've considered letting it go more than once, but somehow, I could never bring myself to do it. My gut told me I'd need it one day. Now, with nowhere else to go, it's all I have left.

"Are you from around here?" the cab driver asks, glancing at me in the rearview mirror.

"I grew up here."

"What brings you back?"

"A woman," I answer, not elaborating.

He raises an eyebrow. "Usually, when a man comes back for a woman, he looks happier than you are right now."

"I'm not coming back for her," I say flatly. "We aren't together anymore."

His face softens. "I'm very sorry."

"So am I," I reply quietly, turning to watch the city pass by, feeling the familiar ache set in.

I'm thankful when the cab comes to a stop in front of my apartment building. Inside my date, a bottle of premium Russian liquor waits.

"Thanks for the ride," I say, handing the driver a stack of rubles and reaching for the door.

The driver turns slightly in his seat. *"Inagda shto-ka kharosheye ne sluchayesta, shtoby maglo sluchitsa shto-ta luchsheye."*

"Khoroshego dnya," I respond, ignoring the sting of his words. Nothing will *"fall together"* for me. Natalie was my one shot at love. I won't make that mistake again.

The thought lingers as I unlock the door. Stepping inside, I'm met with a strange sense of unfamiliarity.

When I bought this place, I'd hoped my *babusya* would move here so I could care for her. It would've made things easier, but she refused to leave her small Ukranian village. Instead, I made the hour-long trip every week, bringing her supplies and spending time with her.

I toss my bag onto the counter and head to the fridge. It's fully stocked, just as I asked. I pay Zoya, my housekeeper, well to keep the place ready—an odd request, maybe, since no one lives here.

While I was on the flight from New York, I'd texted her to stock up, making sure she didn't forget the vodka. I pull out the bottle first, skip the glass, and drink straight from it, desperately trying to numb the ache in my heart.

Viktor

WARMTH FLOWS THROUGH MY VEINS AS THE VODKA BEGINS to work its way through my system. I close my eyes, and my mind drifts back in time.

My mother was a student at the Bolshoi Ballet Academy, one of the most prestigious ballet academies in Russia. Her dream was to become a premier dancer. At seventeen, she met my father, a *Serzhánt* in the Soviet army, three years older than her. Typically, the academy's students weren't allowed to date. However, because of his position, he received special permission to court her while she was still a student.

Six months after they met, she became pregnant and was kicked out of the academy. Her dreams of dancing professionally were over. In the 1980s, an unwed mother faced harsh judgment, so they married quickly. Not long after, Papa retired from the military, and they moved to his hometown—Belgorod.

My parents adored each other. One of my fondest memories is of them dancing together in the kitchen. Papa would come home from work and go straight to Mama. He'd take her in his arms and start humming a tune. She'd light up as he spun her around, completely lost in each other.

They were incredible parents. Mama gave me all her attention, and

Papa taught me how to be a man. I wanted to be just like him. Their only sadness was not being able to give me a sibling. They wanted a second child, but it never happened.

And then, their lives were cut short.

It was late December. Papa had planned a special trip to Moscow to take Mama to see The Nutcracker. I was thirteen, practically an adult in my eyes, and begged to stay home alone. But Mama insisted I was too young to be left alone for an entire weekend. Instead, *Babusya* came to stay with me.

"I'm going to miss you, Vitya," Mama said, pressing a tearful kiss to my forehead.

"Olena, he's no longer a child. He'll be fine," Papa assured her, placing a comforting arm around her shoulders.

"He'll always be my baby, Nikita," she'd replied, wiping her eyes. Then they turned to me.

"Mind your grandmother," Papa reminded me.

"Yes, sir."

"We'll see you in a few days."

I watched as Papa helped Mama into the car and loaded their luggage. Mama waved goodbye as they drove off.

Babusya and I spent the weekend preparing for Christmas. We baked dozens of *Pryaniki*, Ukaranian spice cookies, and got to work on their Christmas gift. She didn't believe in store-bought presents, saying a handmade gift had more value. So, we spent hours painting a set of hand-carved *Matryoshka* dolls that a village artisan had made for us. It was a painstaking process, but by the end of the weekend, they were perfect.

The night they were supposed to come home, I was in my room, finishing the wrapping. A knock on the door interrupted me. I heard the low murmur of voices followed by a blood-curdling scream. I rushed into the hallway to find *Babusya* on her knees, wailing, while a uniformed officer stood in the doorway.

"What's going on?" I demanded, my protective instincts kicking in.

The officer turned to me. "Are you Viktor Volkov?"

"Yes."

"I'm very sorry to inform you that your parents were killed in a car accident earlier this evening."

For a moment, I could only stare, convinced there had been a mistake. My parents couldn't be dead. They were on their way home to me. But the look on the officer's face shattered that hope.

Putting on a brave face, I helped my grief-stricken grandmother up from the floor and gently guided her to a chair. The officer explained there was a heavy snow squall. Visibility dropped quickly, and the roads because slick. An oncoming car had been speeding when they lost control and crossed into my parents' lane. They were hit head-on. The emergency responders said they died upon impact.

At thirteen, I became an orphan.

After the officer left, *Babusya* began preparing the house for the mourning period. Because my parents' death was sudden and tragic, a *bad death*, she followed tradition. She covered each mirror with black cloth and stopped all the clocks.

"Why are you doing this, Babusya?" I asked, confused by her actions.

"Mirrors are gateways to the land of the dead," she said quietly. "The first person to see their reflection will be the next to die."

"Why stop the clocks? How will we know the time?"

"Vitya, when a person dies suddenly, their soul lingers on earth for forty days," she explained patiently. "Because your parents' death was an accident, they will remain longer. By stopping the clocks, we help them transition to the afterlife quicker."

Later that day, mourners began arriving, bringing food and mementos to place in their caskets. They shared stories of my parents, memories I tried to listen to, but I was numb. I kept hoping to wake up from this nightmare. I was still expecting them to walk through the door.

But they never did.

Instead, we packed my belongings, and I said goodbye to my friends and the life I'd known. *Babuysa* took me to live in her small village. That's when I took her surname, Dobrow.

A few years later, another upheaval came—the fall of the Soviet Union. The village of *Bobrivka* was no longer part of Russia. We were now citizens of Ukraine, an independent country. I lived with her until I turned eighteen and finished school. After that, I enlisted in the Ukrainian army as a conscript.

That's when I met Dimitri. He had a similar story to mine. Originally from St. Petersburg, his father, a soldier in the Soviet Union, died during the battles that ended communism. Afterward, Dimitri's mother moved them to her home, which was now part of Ukraine.

We spent hours reminiscing about our childhoods in Russia. As kids, communism was an abstract concept. All we knew was that we had our families and friends. But then, we lost the people we loved, and our worlds were turned upside down.

Dimitri had family in Russia and planned to return to St. Petersburg after his service. "You should come with me," he urged. "My uncle promised me a job. We'll make more money than we could ever dream of."

And so we went.

I had no idea who Dimitri's uncle was or how my life would forever be changed after meeting Maxim Solonik. The skills we learned in the military translated well, and soon, we were making more money than any totally legal job could ever pay.

My first priority was sending money to *Babusya* to make sure she had everything she needed. She resisted, claiming she didn't need so much, and I suspected she gave most of it away. But I kept sending it anyway.

Then, I bought this apartment.

Which brings me right back to the present and why I'm drinking.

Natalie—the woman I'm in love with. The woman I had to give back to her husband. With each pull from the bottle, I try to forget the past and numb the pain of losing her.

Viktor

THE BRIGHT MORNING SUN STREAMING THROUGH THE window wakes me. My head throbs, and I realize I'm lying on the floor, though I don't know why—until I spot the empty vodka bottles beside me. Then it all comes rushing back.

Slowly, I stand, steadying myself as the room spins. I press a hand against the wall for balance and pull the heavy curtains closed, blocking the blinding sunlight that only worsens my headache. Once the room is dark again, I make my way to the bathroom, hoping to find something to dull the pounding in my head.

In the medicine cabinet, I find a bottle of Calpol. I pour three tablets into my hand and head back to the kitchen to find something to drink. I consider washing them down with more vodka. To spend another day in an alcohol-induced haze but settle for water instead.

After swallowing the pills, I step into a hot shower, letting the steam wash away the remnants of last night. I have something important to do today, and I need to be sober for it. Once I'm dressed and my headache has faded to a dull throb, I grab a quick bite to eat.

With my keys in hand, I head down to the parking garage and uncover my Harley. I bought her a few years back in the States and had her shipped here, though it's been far too long since I've ridden. The engine rumbles beneath me as I start her up, a low growl that reverberates through my bones. Then, I pull out of the garage and ride through the city.

When I reach the other side of town, I stop at a florist and buy eight of their finest yellow roses. The steady thud of my boots echoes along the brick path to the cemetery's entrance. When I reach the tall black wrought iron gate, I pause, almost losing my nerve. It would be easier to turn around, get back on my bike, and go home—like I've done so many times over the past fourteen years.

But not today. It's time to face my past. I pull open the gate and step inside.

Although I haven't been here since the day my parents were buried, I remember exactly where they lie entombed in the earth. It's a somber walk along the stone path that weaves through rows of headstones marking the resting places of others' loved ones.

I stop in front of their memorial—*Nikita Volkov and Olena Volkova*. Like so many others here, their faces are etched into the stone, digitally frozen in time. I stare at them, trying to recall the details of their faces and the sound of their voices. It's been so long. The realization that I can't picture them as clearly as I used to hits me hard, and I sink down onto the grass.

"Mama, I miss you so much." My voice is barely a whisper. "I fell in love with a woman. Her name's Natalie. You and she would've gotten along so well." I reach out and trace Mama's photo with my finger. "She has a baby girl, Rose. The baby isn't mine, but I was there when she was born. I loved her and learned how to take care of her. I know you would've loved both of them."

"I was going to marry her. But it was complicated. Almost a year after we were told her husband died in a tragic accident, we found out he was alive. And just like that, I lost everything." I stop to wipe away the tears that are falling freely now.

I'm a man. I shouldn't be crying, especially not in public. "I should've known better. I don't deserve someone as wonderful as Natalie. I don't deserve any woman. And I sure as hell don't deserve to be any child's father."

For so many years, I avoided facing my loss. I refused to face the fact that my parents were gone. That's why I took *Babusya's* last name. I wanted to fit in with my friends and have a *normal* family like everyone else. Whenever a schoolmate asked, I'd pretend that she was my mother. She never corrected me, letting me live in my made-up world. Now, I'm ashamed that I tried to erase my real parents from my life.

But as much as I miss them, there's a part of me that's relieved they're not here to see who I've become. Papa would never approve of the choices I've made, and Mama would be heartbroken that I'll never marry or give her grandchildren. As much as I miss them, their deaths spared them the disappointment of seeing the man I've become.

"Please forgive me, Papa," I murmur, staring at his image. "You were my hero. The man I wanted to grow up to be. I wish I could promise to change, to be someone you'd be proud of. But I can't walk away from the life I've built."

If only I knew when they left that night that it would be our final goodbye. I would have told them I loved them, held on a little longer.

I close my eyes, letting the silence envelop me as if hoping to hear their voices one last time. Praying for their forgiveness.

Finally, I lay the eight yellow roses, Mama's favorite, on their grave. "I love you both."

Viktor

"I'LL BE OUT OF TOUCH FOR A WHILE," I SAY, THROWING MY belongings into my bag as I speak.

"Where will you be?" Maxim asks.

"There's something I need to take care of. Someone I need to see."

"How long will you be gone?"

"I'll be in touch when I can." I end the call without waiting for his response.

With my bag slung over one shoulder, I head out, ready for the road ahead.

The rumble of my motorcycle draws attention as I pull into the tiny village of *Bobrivka*. Children stop to point and giggle, curious about the loud machine. No one here owns a car, let alone a motorcycle. I slow down, maneuvering carefully along the rough paths, until I see the familiar clay house with its thatched roof.

As I near, the wooden door creaks open, and a woman in a brightly colored *fuska* peers out. Her back is slightly hunched, and she leans on a cane. She looks much older than the last time I saw her. Her blue eyes, so much like my own, light up with recognition as I stop in front of her.

"Viktor, is it really you?"

"It's me, *Babusya*."

"*Miy onuk* has come home." She opens her arms, and I wrap her frail frame in a hug as she begins to cry.

"*Tak, Babusya*. I'm home."

Gently, I take her arm and lead her inside, wanting privacy for our reunion. Nothing in her modest home has changed. She's always lived a simple existence. The living room still has just a tattered sofa draped with a handmade blanket and a matching chair. I can almost picture *Dido* sitting there, smoking his pipe. Her kitchen is old-fashioned—traditional, she calls it, with an old wood stove and shelves lined with jars of preserved food. It's nothing like the modern houses I've become used to, but it's comfortable—it's home.

Like the other homes in the village, hers has no modern wiring or plumbing. A few years back, despite her protests, I gave her a cell phone and installed a small solar generator. I wanted to add some modern wiring to make life easier, but she refused. After many arguments, she relented and agreed to keep the generator solely to charge her cell phone —the one she never leaves turned on.

"Where is your love?" she asks softly.

I look away, feeling a familiar ache.

"*Vitya?* Why do you look so sad?"

"She's gone," I say, and we sit together on the sofa as I try to explain. Her eyes fill with compassion as she listens, and once again, I find myself struggling to hold back tears. This raw emotion is foreign and uncomfortable.

"I'm so sorry, my dear boy," she says, squeezing my hand. "You deserve happiness."

"No, *Babusya*. I don't."

She tuts, patting my hand firmly. "There will be no more talk like that. You are Viktor Dobrow, my beloved grandson who deserves everything good in this life." She offers a gentle smile. "Now, come with me. I need to bring in the laundry." She moves to stand, but her legs falter.

I rush to catch her, helping her settle back onto the sofa. "Are you okay?"

She reaches into her pocket, pulling out a small glass bottle. Shaking out a pill, she slips it under her tongue.

"What's that for?" I ask, alarmed.

"It's nothing."

"It's not nothing. Tell me, please."

With a sigh, she looks at me sadly. "I'm dying, *Vitya*."

The words hit like a punch to the gut, leaving me breathless. Dying? That can't be true. She's all I have left.

"What do you mean?" I ask, struggling to keep my voice steady.

"My heart is old and tired."

"I'll take you to a doctor." I pull out my phone, ready to call Maxim and find her the best care.

But she places her hand over mine, stopping me. "I've already seen one."

"Then I'll find you a better one."

"There's too much damage." She shakes her head. "I don't have much time left."

My grandmother explains that she had a major heart attack several months ago. Fortunately, she'd been visiting a neighbor, who called the village doctor. He stabilized her long enough to get her to a bigger hospital in Kharkiv.

"They poked and prodded at me for days," she says. "The tests showed there was much damage to my heart."

"There are surgeries, medications—"

She holds up a hand. "I'm an old woman, *Vitya*. Too old for surgery."

"Then come back to Belgorod with me," I urge, desperation edging my voice. "I'll hire a nurse. We'll find the best doctors."

"No," she says firmly, standing with difficulty. "I will not spend my remaining days in a strange place surrounded by doctors who treat me like a lab experiment. I belong here."

"*Babusya*, please—"

"There will be no argument, *onuk*. My decision is final."

Now isn't the time to push, so I try another approach. "Why didn't you call me? I would've come to take care of you." Guilt gnaws at me. She's my responsibility, and I've failed her.

"I have not been alone. Yelyzaveta comes every day to help me." She smiles, but I see the sadness behind it. "But not of that matters because you're here now."

Yelyzaveta. I haven't thought of her in years. Growing up, she was a year younger than me. Although western dating wasn't something practiced in the village, she and I spent all our free time together. Everyone in the village assumed we'd marry someday. But that was a long time ago. She's probably married now, with children of her own.

I follow *Babusya* outside to the clothesline, where she takes down her laundry, dropping it into the woven basket at her feet.

"Here, let me." I step in front of her, taking over.

"I'm perfectly capable of handling my own laundry," she protests, hands on her hips.

"As am I."

She mutters, "*Vpertyy khlopchyk.*"

"I learned to be stubborn from the best." I grin, carrying the basket back inside as she follows, grumbling under her breath.

"Put it on the table," she instructs, waving a hand, "then go get settled in your room. I'll fold it while I cook dinner." I open my mouth to argue, but she holds up a finger. "Do not argue with an old woman."

Shaking my head, I grab my bag and open the wooden door to what was once my bedroom. Everything looks the same. Untouched as if it were preserved in a time capsule. Handmade blue curtains hang over the window, faded with age. The bed is made with white sheets and the patchwork quilt *Babusya* crafted from pieces of my parents' clothing, so I'd always have them close. As a child, I never appreciated it, but now the familiarity brings a sense of peace. I sit on the edge of the bed, letting memories wash over me, before unpacking what few belongings I brought.

When I return to the kitchen, my grandmother is at the counter, rolling cabbage leaves around a meat mixture. I recognize it instantly—*holubtsi*, a favorite dish of mine from childhood.

"Did you grow the cabbage?" I ask, settling into a chair.

"Of course," she replies with a smile. "Now sit and rest. Dinner will be ready soon."

Her hands move deftly, and I watch in silence, grateful to be back in this small, familiar world, even if only for a little while.

Viktor

VIKTOR

Settling back into the village and returning to a simpler way of life has been an adjustment. There's no television or internet here, no rush to get from one place to another. Besides my cell phone, I'm fully unplugged from the digital world. Part of me finds comfort in the isolation, while another part craves my usual pace.

I've sent Babusya to rest while I rake out the chicken coop and gather the eggs. She works far too hard for her age.

"I can get those," a feminine voice says behind me.

"It's already done."

Carrying a bowl full of eggs, I step out of the hens' enclosure and find Yelyzaveta waiting. The beautiful woman standing in front of me is the grown-up version of the fair-skinned, hazel-eyed girl I once knew.

"I heard you were home," she says softly. "How is Anoushka today?"

"She's well." I start toward the house. "Babusya told me you come by daily to check on her, yet I haven't seen you in the two weeks I've been here."

"Mama thought you might want time alone with her. But I can start coming by if you'd like."

As much as I want to care for *Babusya* myself, there are things she needs help with that aren't appropriate for me to handle.

"I would appreciate that."

"I can look in on her now if you'd like."

"She's napping at the moment."

Veta's eyes brighten. "Would you take a walk with me? Like we used to?"

I set the eggs by the door. "As long as we're not too long. I don't like leaving *Babusya* alone for extended periods."

We stroll down the main path through the village. "It's surprising how little things have changed here."

She gives a small laugh. "What did you expect?"

"I thought maybe the younger generation would've brought in some modern technology—even basic things, like running water and electricity."

Veta shakes her head, smiling. "I don't think that'll ever happen."

We walk quietly until we reach the small lake on the edge of the village. Wildflowers line the bank, and frogs croak among the lily pads. I recall our childhood, how we'd race through our chores to come here on hot days, eager to jump into the cool water.

"Anoushka told me you met someone. Is it serious?"

"It was. But we're not together anymore."

"I'm sorry to hear that."

"What about you? Are you married?"

"No." Her reply is almost shy.

I look at her, surprised. "When we were kids, you always talked about marrying and having children."

She tucks a strand of honey-colored hair behind her ear. "I've had proposals. But I turned them down."

"Why?"

Veta hesitates, meeting my gaze. "Because none of them came from the man I'm in love with."

The intensity in her eyes is unmistakable. Before I can respond, an older man approaches.

"You must be Viktor." He extends his hand.

"And you are?"

"Volodymyr. I'm the village doctor."

I shake his hand. "Good to meet you. I've been wanting to discuss treatment options for my grandmother."

He glances between Yelyzeveta and me. "I can stop by the house later if that's more convenient."

"I'd prefer to talk now if you have the time. Every minute we delay feels like wasted time. I'm afraid if we don't do something soon, *Babusya* will run out of tomorrows."

Veta places a gentle hand on my arm. "I'll check on Anoushka before heading home."

"Thank you. I'll see you tomorrow."

Once she leaves, the doctor watches her go and turns back to me. "Old friends?" he asks, eyebrows raised.

"Yes, just old friends," I clarify, brushing off his curiosity.

He nods. "Understood."

"I want a more aggressive approach to my grandmother's treatment. Just managing her symptoms here in the village isn't enough. I want to take her back to Belgorod with me."

Volodymyr sighs. "Anoushka's a very stubborn woman. I doubt you'll have much success with that."

As we talk, he explains more about her health. "The only reason I managed to get her to Kharkiv was because she was unconscious most of the way. Once she stabilized, she was back to her usual self." He chuckles but soon grows serious. "Your grandmother's lucky to be alive, Viktor. The tests revealed significant heart damage. It took some coaxing, but she eventually admitted to shortness of breath and chest pain that she'd been experiencing for months."

Frustration builds as I listen. "I can get her the best doctors. Surely, they can—"

He shakes his head. "There's nothing more anyone can do. Even if the damage were fixable, she isn't strong enough for surgery. All we can do now is manage the symptoms and keep her comfortable."

I clench my jaw, barely containing my frustration. "Why wasn't I called sooner? She has my number on the cell phone I gave her."

"We tried. She refused to let anyone contact you."

"I don't care—"

"Viktor." Volodymyr's voice is firm but understanding. "I know you want to help, but she's my patient, and I must respect *her* wishes. I'll do everything I can to ensure she's comfortable and that when her time comes, she'll pass with dignity."

I hear his words, but I can't accept them. He may be a capable doctor, but he doesn't understand what's possible beyond this village. My connections can get the best doctors in the world. Until I've exhausted every option, I refuse to believe nothing can be done.

"I need to get back to her."

He nods, sympathetic. "I'll walk with you. She's on my list of patients to see today."

Viktor

Autumn is rapidly coming to a close. The last warm days are giving way to cooler air, a sure sign that winter is on its way. Unfortunately, as the seasons shift, so does *Babusya*. Every day, she grows weaker, her breathing more labored. She tries to hide it, but I see the strain.

For the past hour, I've been in my room staring at my phone with Maxim's contact pulled up. The doctor urged me to respect her wishes rather than spend our time fighting, but how can I sit by and watch her die when I have the resources to help?

"Are you ready to go?" *Babusya* calls from the kitchen.

"I'll be right there," I respond, tucking the phone away.

For weeks now, we've been canning vegetables from her garden. The village has a way of life that emphasizes family and community. Everyone contributes to their household and shares with neighbors. It's how they've not only survived but thrived for generations.

The elderly, like my grandmother, don't need to keep working, but she insists. It's part of her. I can't imagine her doing anything else as long as she's breathing.

Last night, after we finished the last of the work, I loaded the jars onto her wagon in preparation for today's deliveries. The decision on whether or not to call Max will have to wait a little longer. But I know I can't put it off much past today.

"You're finally ready," she says when I come out of my room.

"Sorry," I say, leaning down to kiss her cheek. "Be sure to put your coat on. It's chilly."

"My boy is trying to be the parent," she teases, though she grabs her coat with a small smile.

"No. I care about you and don't want you getting sick."

She pats my cheek. "You're a good man, *Vitya*."

Ignoring her words, I grip the wagon's handle. "Let's go."

Together, we walk through the village, dropping off food at each home. At every stop, her neighbors invite us in to sit and reminisce. This village is all they know. Their lives are woven together. They may not be connected by blood, but that doesn't make them any less of a family.

While they talk, I watch *Babusya*. Her happiness radiates with each home we enter. Understandably, she doesn't want to leave, but that doesn't make her decision right. Leaving wouldn't be forever—just long enough for her to get the care she needs.

When we step outside one of the homes, I take her arm. "You look tired, *Babusya*. Let's go home."

"We have one more stop."

"I'll do it tomorrow."

"No, we will go now," she insists.

I give in and help her to the last house—Yelyzeveta's family home.

The door opens before we even knock, and Veta's mother greets us. "Anoushka, you look well today. Please, come in." She turns to me with a smile. "Viktor, it's wonderful to have you back."

"Thank you, Ksenia." I lean in to kiss her on both cheeks.

"I just put tea on. Will you stay for a cup?"

"Maybe next—"

"Of course we will," *Babusya* interjects, cutting me off with a grin.

"Veta," Ksenia calls, "please set out two more cups."

"Who's—" Veta appears around the corner and freezes when she sees me. It only takes her a second to recover. She turns to my grandmother with a smile. "Anoushka, it's so good to see you out. And you too, Viktor."

The afternoon stretches on as we share tea and listen to Ksenia and *Babusya* recount stories from our childhood. They laugh about old pranks and retell memories I'd nearly forgotten.

"Yuri and I always thought Yelyzeveta and Viktor would end up married one day," Ksenia says with a twinkle in her eye.

"As did I," *Babusya* adds, not missing a beat.

Glancing at Veta, I notice a hint of sadness in her eyes. Did she believe it, too? I feel everyone's eyes on me as if they're expecting a response. A declaration of love. But there's nothing to offer.

"Mama, don't put Viktor on the spot," Veta murmurs, looking away. "That was a long time ago."

"It was, but love can span distance and time. You'll soon discover that," *Babusya* says with a knowing smile.

"We should start for home," I say, steering the conversation away.

"Why don't you stay for dinner?" Ksenia suggests.

Staying is the last thing I want, but I defer to my grandmother.

"Thank you for the invitation," she replies, "but I'm getting tired. Perhaps another time?"

"Of course. Yelyzeveta will let me know when you're up to it."

We say our goodbyes and begin the slow walk home at a pace much slower than before.

"I'm so glad you came home, dear boy," *Babusya* says between labored breaths.

"I still wish you'd called sooner."

"You're here now."

"But we could've had more time," I murmur.

More time. It seems that's become a theme echoing through my life. Always longing for more time with the people I love.

My parents. Natalie and Rose.

And now, these precious days with *Babusya*.

I can almost hear the clock ticking, each second reminding me that our time together is slipping away.

Maxim

Irina and I are at Jelena's Hope. Although Amelia is progressing well, she continues to attend therapy sessions once a week. Irina is visiting a few of our guests who are preparing to transition into community housing. I'm using the time to check on the construction team. We are expanding the building to accommodate more recovered persons. Most places would see an expansion as a success—yet here, it is a grim reminder of the evil that exists.

Our growth reflects the relentless spread of human trafficking. Some days, it feels as if dismantling one ring only gives rise to three more. It is discouraging, but it is a fight I will not give up. As long as I am breathing, I will continue to hunt these animals and take them down.

The construction foreman gives me a progress update when my phone vibrates in my pocket. Viktor's name appears on the screen. "Excuse me," I tell the foreman. "I need to take this." Walking a few steps away, I answer the call. "Viktor?"

"Hi," he says quietly.

I hesitate, noting the unusual tone in his voice. "How are things going there?"

"Not well," he replies, his voice tinged with sorrow. Viktor rarely calls unless it's about work, and I can tell this is different. "My grand-mother is dying."

His words catch me off guard.

"She won't let me help her. What do I do, Max? I can't lose her. Not now."

Viktor is not a boy, but the vulnerability in his voice sounds almost childlike. He has endured more loss than most in his thirty-two years, and even now, while he is home to recover from losing Natalie, he is facing another tragedy.

"Bring her here," I suggest. "I will arrange for the best doctors."

"I've tried," he says, sounding defeated. "She refuses to leave. Won't even let me bring anyone in. She's content to die."

"Anoushka has always been strong-willed," I say gently. "She was not afraid to challenge me head-on when you first came to work for me." I chuckle at the memory. "She raised you to be the man you are, Viktor. Now, it is your turn to care for her in the way she wishes."

"But I have the means to get—"

"No," I interrupt. "You must honor her wishes as she faces the end of her life. This will no doubt be the hardest job you have ever done."

He is quiet, then murmurs, "I don't know if I can do this, Max."

"You will find the strength." I pause, then add, "Alexander called, asking about you."

I had not planned on mentioning it, but maybe knowing someone cares will encourage him. Viktor and Alexander share a deep, if not complex, bond. I hope this knowledge prompts him to reach out.

"What did you tell him?"

"That you went home for some time off. And you are doing well."

"Does he know where I am?"

"No."

"Thank you. I need this distance right now."

"I understand you need the space, but think about calling him. Alexander values your friendship."

"I'm probably the last person Alex wants to hear from."

"Do not shut him out, Viktor. Just consider it."

"Yeah."

I do not press further. He needs his friends now more than ever, but pushing him might only drive him further away. "If there is anything you need, do not hesitate to call me."

We say our goodbyes, and I prepare to go in search of Irina. But when I turn around, she is already there.

"I didn't want to interrupt," she says softly.

"Thank you, *vozlyublenny*." I kiss her cheek. "It was Viktor. He is struggling."

She frowns in concern. "Where is he?"

"With Anoushka. It will be some time before he will be ready to return." I glance around. "Is Amelia ready?"

"Yes, she's waiting for us in the lobby."

"Let us get our girl and go home."

My heart is heavy, carrying the weight of Viktor's pain. I understand too well what it is to watch someone you love slip away, unable to stop it. My only hope is that he has someone by his side. But I know no one can spare him from the pain he will face shortly.

It is a road he must traverse alone.

Viktor

Drawn to the water, I walk to the stream at the edge of the village before placing the call. Talking to Max has brought up memories I haven't revisited in years—especially the day I left this place behind.

Babusya wasn't pleased when I told her I was going to Russia for work. My excitement was genuine as I shared a carefully crafted story about Maxim's involvement in clean energy and how I'd be working with him in this up-and-coming field.

But *Babusya* didn't buy my story for a second.

"Vitya, you know nothing about this energy business," she said, eyeing me shrewdly. "I may be an old lady, but I'm not dumb. You're up to no good." She wagged a finger at me, unimpressed.

I chuckle now, remembering how she'd planted herself in front of the door, hands on her hips, refusing to let me pass. I politely asked her to move, but she refused, glaring at me. I had to lift her up and physically move her to get out the door.

My work is dangerous, but Maxim has been very good to me. He's the closest thing to a father I've had in years. Hearing his voice was comforting, even though I didn't like his advice. He's right, though. I can't change what's happening—my grandmother is dying. There's no stopping it.

What really surprised me was hearing that Alex had asked about me. He graciously accepted my apology, but I figured he'd be relieved I was out of his and Natalie's lives. Still, a part of me misses our friendship.

The thought pulls me back to a place I'd been trying to avoid. I open the gallery app on my phone, scrolling through pictures of happier times. Selfies with Natalie. Stolen moments of Natalie with Rose, tender interactions she didn't know I was capturing at the time. Videos of baby Rose giggling and calling for *Friker*.

Natalie.

God, I miss her so much it physically hurts. During the day, the smallest thing, a scent or a sound, triggers memories of her. At night, she fills my dreams. I wake up reaching out, but she's no longer curled up next to me. Everything in me wants to call her to hear her voice. But I can't. She's no longer mine. Natalie is with Alex, where she was always meant to be.

Swallowing the memories back down, I close the photos and tuck the phone away. There are other matters that need my attention now.

When I return to the house, *Babusya* is sitting outside. Her cheeks are grayish, and her lips have a faint blue tint. Every day, her heart fails her a little more. But her cyan-blue eyes still light up when she sees me. I'm thankful I came home when I did. That I have these last precious days with her.

"Why are you out here?" I ask, reaching for her arm. "It's too chilly. You'll catch a cold."

She swats my hand away, scowling. "I asked Veta to bring me out," she says, pausing to catch her breath. "I wanted fresh air."

"Where's Veta?" My voice hardens. She should know better than to leave her alone in this cold.

"I sent her home."

"You know I don't like you being alone."

She waves me off, and I take a deep breath, steadying myself.

"I wanted to talk to you alone," she says firmly.

I sit down beside her in a rickety wooden chair. "All right, what is it?"

"You. And Yelyzeveta." She turns to face me. "You two were always meant to be together. Neither of you has married. Now, after all these years, fate has brought you back together."

"*Babusya*," I sigh, unamused by her matchmaking.

"She's a good woman and will make a fine wife. You can marry and have a family. This house will be yours. You can build a life here."

"How do I even know she wants that?"

"Oh, Vitya, my boy," she says, patting my arm. "Yelyzeveta has waited for you to return. She always believed you'd come back someday."

Waited for me? Why would she do that?

"You've been invited to dinner this evening as part of your courtship," she announces as if it's settled.

"I'm not leaving you alone," I reply, crossing my arms.

"Ksenia will be along to sit with me."

"I'd rather stay here with you." I stand. "Let me make you something to eat."

"No. I'm not hungry."

She's barely eaten anything for days now.

"You need to eat, *Babusya*. To keep up your strength."

She shakes her head, smiling faintly. "I won't be here much longer."

"Don't say that," I murmur.

Her hand rests on my arm, and I cover it with my own. Her skin is thin and fragile, cold to the touch. As if her body is betraying her and breaking down.

"I'm grateful for each day I wake," she says quietly, "but I do not fear death."

Death.

It's not death itself I fear—I've stared it down countless times. Confronted it. Brought it to many people. It's living in the silence it leaves behind. It's wanting to touch and talk to loved ones who are no longer here.

It's being alone.

We sit there, her hand in mine, watching her neighbors go about their daily lives. Women pull laundry off clotheslines while young children toddle at their feet. Older children run in the streets, laughing and playing. The men work in the fields, preparing for winter. Life in this village has stayed the same, as though they live in a time capsule.

And then, another realization settles over me. When *Babusya* passes, life here will go on—without her. Sure, there will be a mourning period, but afterward, people will return to their routines. She'll become a memory, just another part of the past. The thought is a sobering reminder of how quickly life moves forward.

Viktor

After getting my grandmother in the house, I make a cup of tea to warm her up. Then, I head to my room to change for dinner. A date is the last thing I want tonight, but I won't disrespect *Babusya* or Yelyzeveta by refusing.

My options are limited since I packed light—jeans and a T-shirt will have to do. I glance in the small mirror atop the dresser. It's been years since I've let my hair grow out, and my reflection feels oddly unfamiliar. I run a hand through the blond strands and shrug. Good enough. Grabbing my jacket off the bed, I return to the main room.

Ksenia is already here. She's sitting on the sofa with my grandmother. The comforting smell of soup fills the house, and I notice a pot simmering on the stove. Ksenia must have brought dinner. Hopefully, she can coax my grandmother to eat.

"You look very handsome this evening, *Vitya*," Ksenia remarks with a warm smile.

"Thank you, ma'am." I walk over to *Babusya*. "Please, try to eat something. I won't be late."

She waves me off with a smile, exchanging a conspiratorial look with Ksenia. "Take your time. Ksenia will keep me company."

I shake my head, bending down to kiss her cheek. "All right. I'll see you later."

"Enjoy yourself, Viktor," she says softly.

I nod, heading out the door. The sun dips below the horizon, casting a warm glow over the quiet village as I make my way to Veta's house. The streets are empty. Everyone has gone inside for dinner. Here, without electricity, the people follow the sun's rhythms—early to bed, early to rise.

When I reach her house, I knock. After a moment, the door opens, and Veta greets me.

"I'm glad you came," she says, stepping aside. "Please, come in."

"Thanks for the invitation," I reply, following her inside.

She leads me to the kitchen, where the table is set for two. The soft glow from the oil lamp casts a cozy light over the room, giving it a surprisingly intimate feel. It reminds me of the Valentine's Day dinner I once planned for Natalie—a bittersweet memory. I force myself to put that aside and try to remain in the present moment.

"You're a little early," Veta says with a small laugh. "Dinner won't be ready for a few more minutes."

"Can I help with anything?" I offer.

She chuckles softly. "No. You sit and relax."

I forget how old-fashioned the expectations are here. There have always been traditional views of men's and women's roles. Even though I'm more than capable of helping, she pulls out a chair, waiting for me to sit.

Veta's modest blue dress flutters as she moves gracefully around the kitchen. Several loose curls frame her face. Every now and then, she reaches up, checking the pins in her hair. Soon, she begins bringing dishes to the table. She reaches behind her to untie her apron, but as hard as she tries, it doesn't come undone.

"It seems I've knotted it," she says, glancing over her shoulder. "Could you help?"

My hands shake as I work to untie the strings. Natalie used to wear an apron, too, one with a ridiculous pumpkin pattern. She'd always wrap the strings around her waist and tie them in front to avoid this very issue.

"There, I got it," I say, stepping back.

"Thank you." She sets the apron aside and joins me at the table.

Dinner is delicious, full of fresh ingredients and flavors that only a home-cooked meal can offer. Conversation flows effortlessly between us. I find myself smiling and laughing more than I expected.

"What are your plans now that you're back?" she asks, glancing at me curiously.

"I haven't really thought about it," I admit. "Right now, I'm focused on taking care of *Babusya*."

"She hasn't stopped smiling since you came home."

Home.

Once upon a time, this place was my home. Compared to the rush of New York City, life here is slower, simpler—untouched by the chaos of the modern world. But can I really see myself staying here permanently?

"Viktor." Veta waves her hand in front of my face, pulling me back. "You seemed like you were somewhere else."

"Sorry," I murmur and stand up. "Let me help you clear the table."

"This is woman's work," she says, carrying the dishes to the sink. "Would you like something to drink?"

"No, thank you." I walk to the window, gazing into the darkness. "Veta, would you ever consider leaving the village?"

She turns and leans against the wooden countertop. "That's an odd question. Why do you ask?"

"I'm just curious."

"For the right man, I'd go anywhere," she says, moving closer. "But I'd want to come back someday. I love it here and want to raise my children in this village."

We linger in silence, caught in a moment that stretches between us. Then, she rises onto her toes and kisses me. I slide my hands into her hair, loosening it from its pins, then grip the back of her neck, deepening the kiss.

"Viktor, stop." Her hands press against my chest, creating space between us.

I let go immediately, taking a step back as I catch my breath.

"What was that?" she asks as she quickly pins her hair back up.

"It was a kiss," I say, struggling to hide my confusion. She kissed me first. But when I closed my eyes, it wasn't Veta whose lips were kissing mine. It was Natalie's hair threaded through my fingers. "Isn't that what you wanted?" I ask, confused.

"I wanted it, yes," Veta says softly, touching her lips.

"Have you ever been kissed?"

"Yes," she says. "But it felt wrong. Like you weren't thinking about me."

How did she see right through me? "I need some air." I turn and hurry out the door, with Veta following behind.

"What do you want from me, Veta?" I ask, keeping my gaze on the ground.

"I want you to allow me to love you," she says, reaching out, her fingers brushing my arm. But it's not the touch I long to feel. "I want you to love me in return. I want us to be married, to start a family, right here where we belong."

Meeting her hazel eyes, I will myself to feel something for this woman who's poured out her heart to me. But there's nothing. "How do you know that you'd be happy with me?"

"I've loved you for most of my life."

I shake my head slowly. "Veta, you don't know who I am. Or what I've become."

"Please, don't say no." A tear slips down her cheek. "We'll be good together." She cups my face with her hand. "I've dreamt about what it would be like for so many years. I know you'll be kind and gentle."

"Are you still a virgin, Veta?"

She looks down, her voice barely a whisper. "No. But please, don't tell Mama."

The weight of her words sinks in, but I keep my expression unreadable. In this village, tradition and reputation are everything. If anyone finds out she hasn't saved herself for marriage, her prospects will vanish. The men here value purity over character, and that disgusts me more than I care to admit.

"Your secret is safe," I say, my voice steady, though my gaze sharpens. "But understand this—I'm not the kind of man who handles a woman gently."

She hesitates, then lifts her eyes to meet mine. There's determination there, defiance even. "You can teach me," she says softly, stepping closer. Her fingers brush mine as she tries to grab my hand.

I pull away sharply, retreating before she can close the gap.

"We can go inside now," she continues, undeterred. Her voice takes on a pleading edge. "I'll show you that I can please you."

"Veta," I snap, my tone harsher than intended. Her lips part in surprise, but I don't stop. "This isn't a game. You don't know what you're asking for."

Part of me longs to take her up on her offer. To go inside and sink into her, all while envisioning she's Natalie. I want to fuck her until the pain in my heart is gone. But I can't. Veta deserves more than to be used by a man who's in love with someone else.

Her cheeks flush, whether from embarrassment or frustration, I can't tell. "I'm not a child. I know what I want," she insists, her voice trembling slightly.

"You don't," I counter, the steel in my voice leaving no room for argument. I take a deliberate step back, putting more space between us. "I can't do this right now."

"I understand." Her eyes shine with unshed tears. For a brief moment, I see the fragility behind her boldness, the cracks in the facade she's trying so desperately to hold together. "You've been so focused on Anoushka you haven't thought about your own needs," she says softly. "Please, let me take care of you." Her hands move to my pants, but I grab them first.

"This isn't about what you want." My tone softens just enough to temper the sharpness of my earlier words. "I have to go." I can't stay a second longer, or my willpower is liable to falter, and I'll do something I can't take back.

Viktor

WINTER IS SETTING IN EARLY. IT'S MID-NOVEMBER, AND snow has been falling for the past two days. Veta still comes by each day to help with *Babusya*. She's not said anything more about us, but I see the longing in her eyes. I feel it when she brushes up against me. But I don't return her affection.

Babusya's been clinging to life, but each day, she slips further away. I know our time together is almost up. She hasn't been able to get out of bed, let alone sit up, for over a week. She's stopped eating, barely drinks, and spends her days in restless sleep, murmuring for *Dido*.

I spend my days by her side, holding her hand and talking to her about all the memories she and I share—the warmth of her kitchen and the stories she told me as a child. And I tell her about Natalie and Rose so that when she passes, she'll become their guardian angel, protecting them in ways I no longer can. Above all, I need her to know she's not alone.

"Illya is here," she whispers suddenly. Her shaky hand points toward the door. "He's calling for me."

My chest tightens. I've heard it said that just before a person passes, they see loved ones waiting for them.

"*Babusya*, please don't leave me," I plead, the words tumbling out in a broken whisper. The tears I've tried to hold back stream freely now, unstoppable. "I don't want to be alone."

Her gaze softens, though it seems far away. "Your mama and papa are with him," she murmurs, her tone laced with an otherworldly certainty.

I draw in a shaky breath, forcing myself to be strong. She doesn't deserve to carry my pain into the next world. "I know you have to go," I manage, though the words threaten to shatter me. "I'll be brave. Just like you always told me to be."

My heart shatters, but I press on. "You don't need to worry about me. Please, tell Mama and Papa I love them. Go to *Dido*." My voice cracks, and I swipe at the tears blurring my vision. "I will always love you, *Babusya*." I lean in, pressing a kiss to her weathered cheek, my lips trembling against her skin.

"*Vitya*, my boy," she whispers. "*Ya tebe lyublyu.*"

Her chest rises and falls in a final, ragged breath. Then her hand goes limp in mine.

Her last words to me, *I love you*, are a comfort I cling to even as grief crushes me. She's gone, but her spirit lingers. I feel it, faint but real, in the stillness of the room.

I hold her hand, unwilling to let go, even though she already has. The ache in my chest deepens with every moment that passes. She was my last remaining family. And now she's gone.

This time, I'm truly alone.

As is tradition, *Babusya's* viewing lasts for three days. Villagers visit to pay their respects to the woman many viewed as their own grandmother. Her funeral takes place in the village's small stone church, which is overflowing with people. Some have traveled from neighboring villages. Every face in the crowd reflects the love and admiration they felt for her.

During the service, I take a moment to speak. The grief in their eyes is heavy, but I force myself to meet it.

"*Babusya* was born and raised in this village," I begin. "She raised my mama here, and after my parents died, she raised me here, too. When I found out she was sick, I begged her to go to a bigger city with me, but she refused," I pause, a faint smile breaking through the sorrow. "She was always stubborn."

A quiet chuckle ripples through the room.

"I was prepared to drag her away kicking and screaming, if necessary, until someone I respect very much reminded me that I had to honor her wishes. I owed her at least that much for the unconditional love she'd always given to me. I owed her the right to leave this world where and how she chose." I pause, trying to control my emotions.

I stop for a moment, gathering myself, my hands gripping the podium tightly. "The past few months have been some of the best and worst of my life. I spent every moment I could with her. She told me her stories one last time, and I committed them to memory. And even though I didn't want her to leave, I had the chance to tell her how much I loved her. I was able to say goodbye."

My voice falters. No longer able to contain my emotions, I nod to the priest and step back to my seat in silence.

After the service, *Babusya* is laid to rest beside her husband. I stand by her grave while villagers take turns saying their final goodbyes, each one leaving flowers on the freshly turned soil. When the last mourner departs, I linger, staring at the mound of earth that now separates us.

Back at the house, the emptiness is suffocating. The echoes of her presence—her voice, her laughter—are replaced by the deafening silence of loss. The walls hold only ghosts now, whispers of memories that refuse to fade.

I throw open my bedroom door and drag my bag out from under the bed. Pulling open the drawers, I toss my clothes into it haphazardly. I don't care about order. I need to leave. The ride back to Belgorod will be cold, but I don't care. Anything is better than staying in this hollow shell of a home.

Helmet in hand, I move toward the door, only to find Yelyzaveta standing on the other side. Her eyes flick to the bag in my hand, and her face falls.

"Are you leaving?"

"Yes."

"There are more feasts. The mourning period isn't over."

"For me, it is."

"I was hoping you'd stay." Her voice is soft, but there's a desperate edge to it. "That you'd give us a chance."

"Veta," I say, forcing my tone to remain even, "you're a beautiful woman. I'll always be grateful for the love and care you showed *Babusya*."

"I can take care of you, too," she pleads, following me as I step toward my bike. "Just let me. Please don't leave me again."

"I'm not the man for you, Veta." I swing my leg over my bike and get adjusted on the seat.

"But you are." She grabs onto my arm. "Stop for a minute. Try to remember all the good times we've shared."

I stop, staring at her for a long moment. "That was a long time ago."

"It can be like that again," she insists.

I pull my helmet on. "No, it can't."

"If you won't stay," she says, her voice desperate now, "then let me come with you. We'll be so good together. Just give me a chance."

I start the bike. The roar of the engine drowns out her voice. Her lips move, her tears falling freely, but I can't hear her anymore. And I don't want to. I have no more feelings. The last of them died with *Babusya*.

Pulling down the face shield of my helmet, I rev the bike and drive away. Veta's reflection lingers in my mirror. She's dropped to her knees in the snow, her arms wrapped around herself as she weeps. Good. Let her see me for the bastard I am. Let her hate me. It's better this way. She deserves someone who will choose her, someone who'll love her the way she deserves.

At the edge of the village, I pull my cell from my pocket and toss it to the ground. The bike's tires crunch over it with ease.

I don't want anyone from my past to contact me. No one to follow me. It's better for everyone if I disappear.

Viktor Dobrow no longer exists.
It's time to become someone else and go back to work.

Viktor

Six months. That's how long I've been living in Belgorod, undergoing a transformation. My hair, now shoulder-length, is a darker shade of blond thanks to a wash in color. Brown contact lenses mask my blue eyes, helping me disappear into the crowd.

I don't need the money. My time with Maxim ensured I never have to work again, but I can't stand sitting around with nothing to do. I'm not going back to work for Max. So, I'm on a job hunt. Men like me don't scroll job sites and email a polished resume. The kind of work I'm seeking is buried in the darkest corners of the internet.

I set up a profile under the name *The Nightingale*. To most, the bird is an innocent songbird known for its haunting melody. But it carries a darker mythology. Legend says when the Nightingale sings at night, it connects to shadows and danger. Enemies fear its song. I've felt connected to the bird for many years, and wear its image on my back.

Since setting up my profile, I've had several offers. But I'm in no rush. Run-of-the-mill hit jobs or vengeful spouses don't interest me. I'm waiting for something that feels right.

I'm in the middle of my daily workout when my phone buzzes. A notification pops up: a new request addressed to *The Nightingale*. My instincts stir—this is it. The one I've been waiting for. I slip my phone back into my shorts pocket, not wanting prying eyes at the gym to catch a glimpse. Quickly wiping down the equipment, I head for my apartment.

Once there, I open the email.

Nightingale,

The target: Saimir Hasani, second in command for a breakoff clan of the Kompania Bello crime syndicate. Reply to this message if you are interested.

John Smith

Sitting back in my chair, I run my hands through my hair as I process the name. The Kompania Bello—Albanian Mafia. Their reputation is brutal. Other criminal organizations steer clear of them for a reason. Too unpredictable. Too violent. There's an old saying in this world: don't fuck with the Albanians.

This is exactly what I've been waiting for.

Mr. Smith,

You've piqued my interest. What's the job?

Nightingale.

I'm halfway through making dinner when the next notification arrives. I wipe my hands on a towel and open the email.

Nightingale,

Duke Henry and Duchess Adelaide of Southerland live on a private island off the coast of Grenada. Recently, their daughter, Lady Clare, went missing while vacationing on the mainland. She vanished from a nightclub, and after weeks of searching, she was found—alive, but barely. She'd been raped, beaten, and drugged repeatedly.

The person responsible? Saimir Hasani.

Lady Clare remembers meeting him at the club. He invited her for a walk on the beach, to which she agreed. The next thing she recalls is waking up in a concrete cell. Hasani marked her body, kept her drugged, and planned to traffic her. The family found her before he could sell her, but the damage was done. She's home now, but she's not recovering well.

Hasani's still in the area, protected by his clan. This will not be a quick or easy job.

The bounty is $20,000,000.

Are you interested?

John Smith

A wave of cold fury surges through me as I read. Another predator who thought he could take whatever he wanted. Am I interested in wiping another trafficking piece of shit off the earth? Yes. I don't delay my reply.

Mr. Smith

I'm the man for the job. Send the details—I'm ready to leave immediately.

As for Lady Clare, tell her family to contact Jelena's Hope in St. Petersburg. Ask for Maxim Solonik. Let them know an old friend referred them. He'll make sure she gets the help she needs.

Nightingale.

Viktor

AFTER NEARLY FOURTEEN HOURS IN THE AIR, THE PLANE'S wheels finally touch down in Grenada. My passport reads James Anderson, a Canadian software engineer who's grown tired of bitter winters and is ready for life in the Caribbean. The cover story is simple. I'll be staying at Hasani's resort while I *look for an apartment*. In reality, I'll be hunting for the perfect opportunity to take him out.

Maurice Bishop Airport is smaller than I expected. Its simplicity reminds me of Northmeadow, the airport I flew into countless times with Natalie.

Stop, Viktor. I shut down the thought before it can take root. This isn't the time or place. James Anderson doesn't know Natalie. I need to focus.

As I walk through the single terminal, I spot a man holding a sign with my alias on it: James Anderson. Approaching him, I nod, and he silently takes my bag. We head to a waiting car, the quiet stretching until we're on the road.

Finally, he speaks. "Saimir Hasani owns the Island Spice Resort. You'll be staying in one of their private villas. The main resort building houses The Cinnamon Room, one of the most popular clubs on the island. It's also where Lady Clare was last seen before her disappearance." He glances at me. "Before you ask, Hasani also controls the local authorities."

"Saimir Hasani is the owner of the Island Spice Resort. You'll be staying in one of their private villas. In the main resort building is The Cinnamon Room, one of the most popular clubs on the island. Hasani is known to keep a strong presence there. It's the same club Lady Clare disappeared from. Before you ask, Hasani also owns the local authorities."

Keeping my tone neutral, I ask, "Where do I fit in?"

"Hasani is currently in the market for a new security system for his club. As an upstanding member of the community," he says the words with an edge of sarcasm, "he's appalled a young woman was kidnapped from his establishment. He's eager to ensure the safety of future guests."

"And you're expecting me to sell it to him?"

"During the day, the club doubles as a computer lounge for resort patrons. You'll have a series of well-timed phone calls regarding the security software you're supposedly developing. The goal is for Hasani to overhear and inquire about your services."

I raise an eyebrow. "You think he'll take the bait?"

"He's desperate," the driver explains. "He screwed up when he took Lady Clare. She wasn't his usual target—too high-profile. Her face and the club were plastered all over the news. His clan may protect him, but he's still scrambling to cover his tracks. You'll appear as an unsuspecting foreigner, completely unaware of his reputation. He'll see you as an easy mark."

I lean back, considering this. "Mr. Smith didn't mention my supposed career. I don't know the first thing about software."

"There's a laptop bag with your luggage in the trunk. It's preloaded with everything you'll need, including a state-of-the-art security system that you're in the market to sell. All you have to do is press a button during your 'demos,' and the computer does the rest. Use your charm to build rapport with Hasani."

"You make it sound easy."

The driver's tone turns dry. "Hasani's desperate, careless, and in over his head. Your villa's been stocked with everything you'll need to complete the job."

Something about his phrasing makes my jaw tighten. "You're not suggesting I open fire in the middle of a resort, are you? If that's the plan, turn the car around. I'm not putting innocent lives at risk."

He glances at me, his expression impassive. "Hasani occupies the entire top floor of the main building. He has a private outdoor space. Your options are a sniper shot from the ground or something close-range if you secure an invitation to his penthouse."

The car rolls to a stop in front of the resort. He shifts into park, then turns to me. "Let me grab your bags and show you to your room, Mr. Anderson."

I nod and step out, glancing up at the resort's facade. On the surface, this job seems straightforward: get in, earn Hasani's trust, and eliminate him. But the glaring omission in all this is the exit strategy. How do I get out alive?

Maybe that's the point.

Only someone with a death wish would take a job like this.

And that describes me.

Death would be an improvement to the hell I'm currently living.

Viktor

I could easily get used to this carefree lifestyle. I wake up just as the sun is peeking over the horizon. Most days, I swim laps in my private pool or run on the beach. I'm just a guy on vacation laying low and getting a feel for the place.

So far, everything's just as I've been told. By day, the Cinnamon Room is filled with businesspeople whose faces are glued to their laptops or cell phone screens. Men who should be enjoying paradise instead of being slaves to their jobs.

Today, I'll be among this group of overachievers. I'm sporting khaki pants and a white linen shirt. My hair is up in the proverbial "man bun." My reflection is unrecognizable to me. I guess that's a good thing. If I can't recognize myself, no one else will be able to either. Grabbing my laptop bag, I walk along the flower-lined path to the resort's main building.

The aesthetic of this place isn't lost on me. It's a clean, modern resort situated on the beautiful turquoise waters of Grand Anse Beach. There're several private units, like mine, with infinity edge pools that appear as though they're spilling into the sea. In addition, the main building is twenty floors high.

The villas are high-end for the resort's wealthier guests, while the rooms in the main building are the more traditional hotel-like rooms. On the main floor are several restaurants, and the place I'm headed—The Cinnamon Room.

When I open the club's door, I'm hit with a gust of cold air. It's stale compared to the trade winds that flow through my villa. No one bothers to look up. Each is engrossed in their digital world. I find a table in the corner where I can sit with my back to the wall, giving me a clear view of the room. Pulling out my laptop, I get to work—whatever that's supposed to mean.

I find an encrypted email program and a note from Mr. Smith welcoming me to the island and advising me that the first installment of my salary has been deposited into my account. I log into my bank to ensure the money's there.

Usually, I'd have Dimitri do some digging to find who's behind the mask. But since we're not in contact, I'm trusting in an unknown. This time, the money's where it's supposed to be.

I occupy myself searching for information on Saimir Hasani. He's the second in command of his clan and has a reputation for his cocky attitude and sloppy work. Despite that, the Albanians are tight-knit, and they protect their own. No matter how unpopular Hasani may be, his clan will defend his life to the death.

My first goal is to meet Hasani and get into his good graces. If the intel I have is correct, not a day goes by that he doesn't make an appearance.

A young, attractive waitress approaches my table. "Can I get you anything to eat or drink?"

"I'll take a coffee."

"Sure. I'll be right back." She smiles and sashays her hips as she walks away.

I return my attention to my computer and do some more reading about Hasani. Several minutes later, the waitress returns, placing a steaming mug on the table.

"Do you need anything else?"

"No. Thank you."

I spend most of the afternoon in the Cinnamon room, but there's no sign of Hasani. As each hour passes, the room grows emptier. If I stay too much longer, it may draw unwanted attention. I decide to follow suit and pack it up for the day. Tomorrow, I'll be back to do this all over again.

Viktor

I'm getting ready for another day in my makeshift office when I receive an email from Mr. Smith letting me know a real estate agent will be here shortly to show me some properties—we must keep up the ruse. Moments later, there's a knock on my villa door. Opening it, I find an attractive woman on the other side.

"Mr. Anderson?"

"Yes."

"I'm Bianca, the realtor. Are you ready to go look at some properties?"

"Please, call me James. And yes, I can't wait to see what's available."

As Bianca and I make our way through the main lobby, a man steps out of an office and walks toward us.

"Mr. Anderson. Allow me to introduce myself. I'm Saimir Hasani."

I find it interesting that he knows who I am and has chosen to make his presence known today.

"It's a pleasure to meet you." We shake hands.

"Are you planning on leaving us?"

"What do you mean?"

"You are with Ms. Bianca, one of the island's top real estate brokers. So, I assumed you were going to look at properties. Unless I've interrupted something else?" He doesn't hide his perusal of her body. She stiffens beside me. Clearly, his reputation precedes him.

"Although this resort is gorgeous, I'm in the market for permanent housing."

"That's a shame. I was hoping we'd be able to spend some time together. I've been informed you have a product I'm in the market for."

"I see," I say flatly.

"Perhaps you can alter your plans so we can discuss the opportunity?"

"That won't be possible. I promised my afternoon to Bianca. Maybe we can meet tomorrow instead?"

Hasani looks surprised that I've turned down his offer. I don't want to appear too eager—desperate. And I want to get Bianca out of here as quickly as possible.

"Ms. Bianca is more than welcome to join us."

"Mr. Anderson, if you'd rather—"

"Mr. Hasani, I'm sure you understand Bianca has cleared her schedule today to show me available properties on the island. It would be rude of me to waste her time talking software." I give her a smile and a slight nod of my head. "I am free tomorrow afternoon if that fits into your schedule?"

Although he appears to be keeping his cool. I don't fail to notice the vein pulsing in his neck. This man is not used to being told no. "I will meet you in the Cinnamon Room tomorrow afternoon."

"That should work for me. I'll see you tomorrow." I place my hand on Bianca's back. "Shall we?"

Although I don't turn around, I feel Hasani's eyes boring into our backs as we walk away from him.

Once we get outside, Bianca turns to me. "Do you realize who that was?"

"I've heard his name mentioned. He owns part of the resort or something."

"Saimir Hasani is not a man you want to cross or say no to."

"I'll make a note of that. Are you ready to look at apartments?"

Maxim

"There you are," I say as I walk into the indoor swimming pool room and find Svetlana just climbing out of the pool. "I've been looking all over for you."

"What's up?"

"Have you heard from Viktor recently?"

"No. We aren't exactly on speaking terms."

"Have you spoken to Natalie or Alex?"

"I talked to Natalie yesterday." Svetlana wraps herself in a towel and sits on one of the poolside chairs. "Why?"

"Did she say anything about him?"

"Why the inquisition about Viktor?"

"He's been out of touch for quite a while."

Svetlana rolls her eyes. "Viktor's a big boy. He can take care of himself."

I am a patient man, but my daughter and her flippant attitude toward everyone and everything is beginning to wear on my last nerve. I was hoping that by giving her some time and space, she would open up and tell us what was troubling her, but she has not. Rather than opening up, she is becoming more closed off.

I sit in the chair next to her. "When are you going to tell us the real reason you came home?"

"Because Brandon and I broke up." She sounds like a broken record. "I had my fun in the States and decided it was time to come home."

I study her closely, looking for any hint that could give me a clue as to what is troubling my daughter, but she gives me none.

Svetlana stands and puts her hands on her hips. "Why is it so hard to believe I wanted to come home?"

"We thought things were going well with you and Brandon. Then, one day, you show up at home with no explanation to him or to us."

"Everyone's always taking his side. No one cares about what I want or how I feel. Forget it. I can't do this again." She tosses her towel and storms out of the room.

I am left confused. I would love to know what my daughter is feeling. However, she refuses to let anyone in.

And I still have no answers as to Viktor's whereabouts.

Viktor

Bianca and I spend the afternoon looking at incredible properties. If I was really in the market, I'd have difficulty choosing.

"Do you want to see any more today?"

"You've given me a lot to think about. Let's call it a day."

"Would you like to stop and get a bite to eat? I can show you one of my favorite restaurants."

I've had quite an enjoyable day with Bianca. She's not only beautiful, we've not found ourselves at a loss for anything to talk about. In another life, I'd be crazy to turn this woman down. But I'm not looking for friendship or love—that would further complicate an already difficult situation.

I'm here for one reason—to kill Saimir Hasani. Anyone conceived as being connected to me could find themselves in the line of fire.

"That's a very kind offer, but I'll have to pass."

"Oh," she says quietly and looks down. "I just thought—"

"Bianca, I've had a great time with you this afternoon, but I'm engaged." I lie. "My fiancé stayed behind until I find a permanent place here."

"I'm so sorry. I had no idea."

"It's fine. No harm done."

Our driver pulls up in front of the resort. "I'll give you a call as soon as I make a decision."

"Thank you, James."

I get out and watch as the car pulls away. I saw the way Hasani looked at her earlier. I don't want her anywhere near this place.

When I walk inside, Hasani's standing in the main lobby talking with several men. I can tell the second I'm spotted as the group stops talking, and Hasani makes his way over to me.

"Welcome back, Mr. Anderson. How was your tour?"

"It's a beautiful island. Several places look promising. If you'll excuse me, I have some business I need to attend to."

"What time should I expect you tomorrow?"

"I have several phone conferences scheduled for the first half of the day." I purposely don't give him a definite answer. "I'll be down as soon as my schedule permits."

"I'm a very busy man, Mr. Anderson."

"As am I, Mr. Hasani. Now, if you'll excuse me, I need to get back to my room."

He steps aside, allowing me to pass. As I walk away, he and the men he's with begin speaking in what I can only assume is Albanian.

This is the first I've seen other Albanians hanging around here. Although I was able to get a good look at them, this could pose a significant problem for me. The more I'm outnumbered, the more difficult it will be to plan an exit strategy that gives me even a slight chance of survival.

With their faces fresh in my mind, I head back to my villa, hoping to identify the new characters in the game.

Viktor

I was able to positively identify two out of three of the men Hasani was talking with earlier. The first is Ismael Hasani, Saimir's younger brother, and the third in command. From what I read, those two are very tight. Although Saimir holds a higher rank, Ismael is the brains of the operation and often makes the more important decisions. Saimir is merely his puppet.

The second man is Elion Tehiri, the clan leader. Since Lady Clare's kidnapping, Elion has kept a more public presence.

The third man is a mystery. I can't find his picture or any information on him. I don't like having unknowns.

If it were almost any other mafia outlet, I'd look for the power-hungry man. The one who's willing to take out the person blocking their climb to the top. The problem for me is the lengths Albanians will go to protect one of their own. Ismael is both clan and blood. I'll never find an in there, and Elion would just as soon take me out before turning on Hasani.

I'm on my own. As long as I take him out first, exact justice on Hasani for what he did to an innocent young woman, I'll gladly take a bullet.

After rehearsing the script I was given to sell the security program, I

"

check the time. It's half past two. I figure I've made Hasani wait long enough. Sliding my laptop into its bag, I slowly walk to the Cinnamon Room. Hasani has thirty minutes to show. First rule of the game is that we play by my rules.

I pull the door open and take a quick look around. It's relatively empty today compared to most other days. I head to the table in the corner and settle in. The same waitress that's here every day smiles when she sees me and starts walking over, but I wave her off.

I pull out my laptop and get to work. My senses are on high alert. I'm uncertain how Hasani knew my name and about the security program. I have a feeling there's more going on than meets the eye. This is where working on my own is risky. I don't have Dimitri and his tech skills to fall back on. No one has my back. If I make it out of this alive, I'll have to form a new team, people I'll be able to trust.

"Mr. Anderson, I'm glad you found time for me today." Hasani catches me off guard. I need to be more careful.

"How can I help you?" I sit back in my chair and cross my arms.

"I've heard you are selling a highly sophisticated security program. Is that true?"

"Possibly."

"I'm in the market for that exact product." He waves over the young waitress. "Bring Mr. Anderson and I both a *Skrapar*."

"Yes, sir." She bows her head.

"I'll just have some water," I say before she walks away.

The girl looks to Hasani, who nods before she scurries away.

"Are you not a fan?" he asks.

"I don't mix alcohol and business." My gaze goes to the young girl pouring our drinks at the bar.

He glances over his shoulder. "She's an attractive little thing, isn't she?" Hasani turns back to me.

"She's a bit young."

"Young and moldable is my preference," he says deadpan. "Now, let's discuss your product."

I've rehearsed the script so many times I see it in my sleep. Right now, I'm thankful for that because my words come out confident and unhurried. I stop talking while the girl sets our drinks on the table and resume my sales pitch once she walks away.

"Your product sounds too good to be true." Hasani is nearly salivating.

"I assure you that is not the case." Before continuing, I look around the room. "I'm sure you already have a security system, and your business looks to cater to high-class clientele. May I ask why you would require such sophisticated software?"

"Several months ago, a young woman was kidnapped from my club." He looks me dead in the eyes as he spins his tale. "As you can imagine, that is not the reputation I wish for my resort to have. My responsibility to the community and my guests is to ensure nothing like that happens again. I intend to have the best security system money can buy."

"I see." I don't break his stare. If it's a battle of wills, I'll be coming out on top. And I do. Hasani is the first to look away. "Would you like to see a demonstration?"

"Yes." He sits up straighter, obviously excited at the prospect of moving forward.

While I show him the slides and explain the capabilities of my product, I also keep an eye on the people around us. During our meeting, the same three men Hasani was talking to earlier have each meandered in. They're seated at separate tables, laptops in front of them, facing our direction. It's clear I'm being watched.

"So, as you see, this product will take care of both digital security and video surveillance inside and outside your resort. The data will be transferred to an encrypted server that's impenetrable from cyber-attacks."

"How much will all this cost me?"

"Five million," I say flatly.

"That's a steep price." He raises an eyebrow.

I'm not willing to negotiate. "I understand if your guests' safety and your reputation are not worth that much." I close my laptop and start to slide it back into the bag. "It was—"

"Where are you off to in such a hurry? I didn't turn your offer down."

I set the bag aside, leaving the laptop on the table.

"Typically, I don't do business with people I don't know. In my line of work, you can never be too careful. And five million is a large sum of money." He taps his fingers on the table. "I'm having a little get-together with some friends and other business associates in my penthouse this evening. Why don't you join us? It'll give us a chance to get better acquainted."

"What time?"

"Seven."

This time, I put the laptop in the bag and stand. "I'll be there."

Maxim

I HAVE ASKED EVERYONE I THOUGHT MIGHT HAVE HEARD from Viktor and received the same answer. Nothing. Viktor has not been in contact with anyone. My texts have been left unread. His voice-mail box is now full. He asked for space, and I have given him that for over six months. But in our line of work, when a person is unreachable, it usually signals they are in trouble.

I did not want to resort to this, but I am left with no other choice. I must enlist the help of Dimitri.

"Hey, boss. What's up?" he asks when I enter the tech room.

"Have you heard from Viktor?"

"No. We're not exactly friends these days." He turns his attention back to his screen.

That is the same story I am hearing from everyone. It seems as though Viktor has not only physically disappeared but has also cut everyone who cares about him out of his life.

"Why do you ask?"

"He has dropped off the radar. I am unable to contact him. Can you locate him with your tracking software?"

Dimitri developed a tracking program that has been installed on the phones of all my employees.

"Sure."

He pulls up another screen. It is a database of all my employees. He clicks on Viktor's name and attempts to locate his phone. This kind of technology is not my forte, but I can tell something is wrong. Dimitri flips through several screens before spinning his chair around.

"There's no signal from his phone. It hasn't sent info in months."

I was afraid of something like this. "We need to find him."

"Is he in trouble?"

"I am not certain."

"I'll get right on it." Dimitri starts the process of locating Viktor.

If anyone can locate Viktor, it is my nephew.

Viktor

I'M STRESSED ABOUT TONIGHT AND NEED TO WORK OFF MY nerves. When I return to my villa, I change and go for a run on the beach. I don't know why this job is shaking me. It's an uncomfortable feeling. Things can go wrong quickly if I don't stay in the right head space. I don't have a team to fall back on. This is all on me.

After my run, I shower and put on some dress clothes. When I check the time on my cell, it's a little after seven. Show time.

When I arrive at the penthouse, I'm greeted by security, who pats me down for weapons and then checks my name off the guest list.

Hasani's penthouse is enormous and ornately decorated. People mill about, drinks in hand, while calypso music plays in the background. The entire front wall of the penthouse is made of several large sets of doors that allow easy passage from inside to the large outdoor terrace.

A server walks by carrying a tray with glasses of both red and white wine. I grab a glass of red wine. I won't be drinking much, but I at least need to look the part. I wander around the inside room, making mental notes of the placement of the security cameras before making my way outside.

I finally spot Hasani speaking with a small group of men. One of them is his brother Ismael. Two women are hanging on his arms, giggling at everything he says. I force myself not to roll my eyes at their desperation.

When Hasani looks up and spots me, he shakes the girls off his arm and makes his way in my direction. The girls don't seem upset. They move on to the next man.

"Mr. Anderson, welcome to my home."

"Nice place."

"Follow me. I want to introduce you to my brother." I follow him over to the group he was speaking with. "Ismael. This is Mr. Anderson, the software developer I was telling you about."

"Please call me James," I say to both men. "It's a pleasure to meet you, Ismael." I put my hand out.

Hesitantly, he returns the gesture. "My brother tells me you're from the Czech Republic. How did you end up here?"

"Your brother must've misheard. I'm from Canada."

"Your accent says otherwise." Ismael eyes me suspiciously.

"My family is originally from the Soviet Union. Before I was born, they fled from the communist regime and settled in Canada."

"I see. And how is it you ended up here?"

"I got sick of Canadian winters." I chuckle. "Since I work for myself, I can live anywhere." Realizing it's a test, I don't break eye contact. "How I ended up here is an interesting story. I was out with a few of my friends. Admittedly, we'd had a little too much to drink. They dared me to spin the globe and move wherever my finger landed—Grenada it was. I'm thankful I landed in a warm area. I could've ended up in Saskatchewan."

"You're a man not afraid of taking risks?" Hasani asks.

"I have nothing to lose." I shrug.

"You have no family?" Ismael inquires.

"My parents died in a car accident several years ago, and I've never married." I make a show of perusing the bodies of the women who have reattached themselves to Hasani. "I prefer to sample merchandise. I've not found anyone worth keeping after a night or two."

"We only offer the finest delicacies." Ismael's serious demeanor cracks. "I'm sure my brother can offer you a sample to try."

"Give me your requirements, and I'll ensure it's delivered to your door." Hasani smiles.

"Let's table this discussion for another time. I don't want to monopolize your attention this evening."

"If you gentlemen will excuse me," Hasani says. "I see another business associate I need to speak to. So I'll leave you two to get better acquainted."

Ismael watches as his brother walks away. "Saimir tells me you've designed an impenetrable security system." He wastes no time getting back to business.

I'm thankful the conversation has changed. The *merchandise* Hasani deals in is hanging on the arms of multiple men in the room tonight. It chills me to my core, knowing these women are not here of their own free will, and there's nothing I can do to stop it on my own.

"Yes, I have." I deliver my practiced speech with ease. Ismael, like his brother, hangs on my every word. "As you see, my program will give you the ability to have hidden eyes and ears on every inch of this property while ensuring the security feed is impenetrable."

"When can we see your product in action?"

"I can arrange for a small-scale demonstration this week. I'll need the club closed to guests while my team installs the equipment."

"I'll make sure the club is closed on Monday. Will that work?"

"I'll get in touch with my team and make the arrangements."

Viktor

Parties are not my scene on a good day. Knowing I was being tested and watched all night only increased the stress. When I returned to my villa, I was exhausted. Before I passed out, I sent a message to Mr. Smith to have his team here early Monday morning for a trial installation. I don't wait for his reply before I power off the phone and fall asleep.

Morning comes far too quickly. I wish I was the kind of person who could sleep half of the day, but that's never been me. I reach over to the nightstand and grab my phone to power it on. The reply to last night's text is waiting for me.

Mr. Smith: I'm impressed by how quickly you work. My team will be there Monday morning with the necessary equipment.

Nightingale: How many men should I expect?

Mr. Smith: Two.

So far, things are moving along smoothly—too smoothly. Which concerns me. When things go this easy, there's usually a problem. But from everything I see, there's none. The bio and history of James Anderson are solid.

A knock on my villa door interrupts my thoughts. I throw my legs over the bed and pad over to the door in my boxers. It's most likely housekeeping. I'll ask them to come back later. I'm caught off guard when I see it's the young waitress from the club, and she's holding a tray.

"I have your breakfast, sir. Compliments of Mr. Hasani."

"How thoughtful of him." I reach for the tray.

"I'm sorry, sir. I was told to bring it into your room." She picks up an envelope from the tray and hands it to me. "This is for you."

"Come in." I step aside, allowing her to pass. Inside the envelope, there's a handwritten note.

Mr. Anderson,

My brother spoke very highly of you. I look forward to working together in the near future. Please accept this complimentary breakfast. It comes with a sampling of the best delicacies we have to offer.

S. Hasani

It doesn't take much effort to read between the lines. The delicacy included with my breakfast is the woman who delivered it. When I turn around, I find her unbuttoning her shirt.

"Stop," I say. "What's your name?"

She looks up at me with expressive brown eyes. "Crystal."

"What's your real name?"

"I don't know what you mean."

"Are you here of your own free will?"

"Yes," she answers hesitantly.

"Please sit down." I pull a chair out from the table for her and then take a seat across from her. "Have you eaten today?"

"Yes, sir." She looks down at her folded hands.

"Whatever your boss told you will happen here today will not happen."

Her body goes rigid. She's clearly afraid.

"Look at me, please.".

Slowly, she lifts her head, and her gaze meets mine.

"I'm not going to risk your safety. I'll tell your boss how pleased I am. Will that help?"

She nods.

"Now, tell me your real name?"

She looks around the room nervously.

"There are no cameras in here." That's the first thing I checked for when I arrived.

"Jessica," she says quietly.

"How old are you, Jessica?"

"Twenty-three."

I run my hands through my hair. "Are you from Grenada, Jessica?"

She shakes her head.

"Where are you from?"

Jessica drops her gaze once again.

"I know that you have no reason to trust me. But I promise you I won't tell Hasani anything."

"I used to live in New York City."

Her words are like a dagger in my heart. Of all the places she could've been from, it had to be there. "How did you end up here?"

"It was four years ago, and I was in my second year of college and was offered the opportunity to study abroad—Paris. It was like a dream come true." The corner of her mouth lifts in a small smile. "I met a wealthy man. He was gorgeous and was so nice to me. We had a whirlwind romance." She shakes her head. "I was so naïve. I put my complete trust in a stranger. One evening, we went sailing on his yacht. I don't remember anything until I woke up here."

"Is that man still here?"

"He comes and goes. Mr. Hasani sends him to get the girls."

"Is he here right now?"

"No. He's been gone for a week or so."

"Dammit." I slam my hands on the table, startling Jessica. "I'm sorry. I didn't mean to frighten you." I take the lids off the plates. There's an array of both hot and cold breakfast dishes. Jessica can't take her eyes off the food. I give her a plate. "Eat."

"I can't."

"You were sent to please me, right?"

"Yes, sir."

"It would please me to see you eat."

Hesitantly, she puts a few pieces of fresh fruit on her plate. That's when it dawns on me that I'm only wearing boxers. "I'm going to get dressed. Take as much food as you want."

I go to the bedroom, where I shut and lock the door. I'm not taking any chances of this girl following me here so she can follow Hasani's orders.

Once I'm dressed, I sit on the edge of the bed and put my head in my hands. What the hell am I supposed to do? This girl's been trafficked. She'll be safe if she's with me, but I don't know if I can trust her. There's a lot of sensitive information going back and forth in this room. What's worse is knowing there are people who can help her, but I can't call them. Keeping her here is a risk, but sending her back is unthinkable.

"Fuck." The best I can do is keep her with me for the day while I try to devise a better plan.

When I return to the main room, Jessica has a plate full of fruit and a bagel. I sit back down and grab a piece of mango.

"We're going into town today."

"Mr. Hasani won't allow me to leave—"

"Let me take care of Hasani."

I call the number I have programmed into my phone for the Cinnamon room. It's no surprise that Hasani picks up on the first ring.

"Mr. Anderson, I hope you found breakfast to your liking?"

"Your brother was correct when he said you only serve the finest delicacies. I'm honored to have been gifted a sample."

"I'm surprised to hear from you." He chuckles. "I assumed you'd be occupied today."

"I plan to be. I'm taking Crystal into town with me."

"That's a rather unusual request. I normally don't allow guests—"

"It's not a request, Mr. Hasani. Your note said she was sent to please me. Going into town with a beautiful woman on my arm will do just that." I keep my tone flat. "We'll be late. If she bores me, I'll have her back to you tonight. If she manages to keep my attention, we'll discuss other arrangements."

"Do be cautious with her off my property. Whoever took the Dutchess is still at large. I wouldn't want any harm to come to Crystal."

"There's no need for worry. I won't take my eyes off her."

Jessica's body trembles as we walk out the resort's front doors. I hold her tight against me, making it look like we're much better acquainted with one another's bodies.

"Try to relax," I say quietly. "This is just until we're out of Hasani's sight."

"He has eyes everywhere," she whispers.

"There's our ride." I point to the car waiting for us.

We both slide onto the back seat. When I look out the car's window, Ismael stands just outside the resort's doors. I'm going to have to play today very carefully. There's no way Hasani's letting me walk this girl out of here without having us followed.

Maxim

"Boss," Dimitri pops his head in my office. "Do you have a few minutes?"

"Come in." It's been several weeks since I asked him to locate Viktor. I am hoping his presence here means he has some news. Dimitri sits in one of the wingback chairs across from my desk.

"That man knows how to cover his tracks." He sighs.

I do not like the sound of this already. "Do you have any information?"

"He's not good enough to hide from me." Dimitri laughs. "After he left us in St. Petersburg, it seems he went back to Belgorod."

"He has kept an apartment there for many years."

Dimitri looks surprised. Viktor does not like to talk about his past. Even though the men have been friends for many years, it seems there is much Viktor has not told his friend.

"I knew he used to have an apartment. I assumed he got rid of it a long time ago," Dimitri says. "Anyway, the most logical place for me to look after that was Bobrivka. And sure enough, that's the last place his phone had a signal."

"Yes, I knew he was there. He needed to spend time with his grandmother."

"I got in touch with his old friend Yelyzaveta. She's one of the only people in the village with a cell phone. Can you imagine living in today's society without—"

"Dimitri, please try to stay on track."

"While he was there, his grandmother passed away. Veta said he left shortly after."

"And I am to assume he did not tell her where he was going."

"Considering the tears on the phone call, his leaving was not how she saw their future. She said he took off on his bike without so much as looking back."

That sounds very much like Viktor. To this day, he remains haunted by his past. "So, we have hit another dead end."

"Well, not exactly. I was able to get into the security footage from the apartment building." Dimitri smiles proudly. "He spent weeks there." He hands me his cell phone. "Check these out."

I flip through the photographs. Viktor has changed his appearance. He no longer has a bald head but rather shoulder-length dark blond hair and brown eyes. "It does not even resemble the man I know," I say and hand the phone back. "Why would he alter his appearance so drastically?"

"That was my question as well. And, boss, I don't like what I found. Someone in his building had been prowling the dark web, searching for jobs. I accessed some emails from a Mr. Smith to *The Nightingale*."

I do not like the direction Dimitri's story is heading.

"If *The Nightingale* is who I assume it is, he's taken a job in Grenada going after Saimir Hasani from the Kompania Bello crime syndicate."

"Viktor is going after the Albanian mafia alone? What the fuck is going through his head?" I pound my fist on my desk.

Dimitri fills me in on the details of his assignment—it is a death wish. Viktor is one of the best at his job, but he obviously does not think clearly. Going after the Albanians with a group of men is dangerous, but going after them alone is suicide.

"Where is he?"

"Grenada. He's traveling under an assumed identity, Mr. James Anderson, but facial recognition software isn't fooled by a name." Dimitri pulls up another screen on his phone. "He's undercover as a software engineer and is in the middle of a lucrative deal with Saimir Hasani."

Dimitri further explains how Lady Clare's abduction is related. The puzzle pieces are now coming together. When her parents called, they told us they were sent by an *old friend.* There is only a small group of people who would advise them to use that term. Viktor is one of them. He's there to avenge the harm brought to Lady Clare by killing Hasani.

"He's in way over his head, boss."

"I know." I pause for a moment, thinking over my next move. "You are going after him."

"Me?"

"We cannot send more than one man without attracting unwanted attention," I say thoughtfully. "You have the skills to find him and bring him back. I will call my pilot. You can take the jet to Venezuela. I will arrange for a chartered flight to the island."

Saimir

"Have they left?" I ask Ismael when he walks into my office.

"Yes."

"I don't trust him." I lean back in my chair and tap my finger on my lip. "We're going to search his room while he's gone."

"Do you have someone following them?"

I push the chair back and stand. "You must think I'm *budallaqe*. Of course, I'm having them followed. Let's go."

We meet a member of my cleaning staff on the way. "Have you cleaned Mr. Anderson's room today?"

"No, sir," she answers quickly.

"Why not? He's a very important guest. I don't want him thinking we give any less than the best service."

"Umm," she hesitates. "Mr. Anderson has instructed us not to enter his villa unless he's present."

"I see." That's an interesting bit of information. "Carry on."

She hurries away. Ismael and I look at each other. "It sounds like our Mr. Anderson may be hiding something."

When we get to the villa's door, I instruct Ismael to stand guard. I don't want any surprises while I'm here. Then, I go about searching his room.

At first glance, nothing seems out of the ordinary. His bed is made, and the room is neat and clean. His clothes are hanging in the closet. I search each of the drawers in the bureau but find nothing other than perfectly folded clothes. On the desk is his laptop. Of course, it's password protected. I don't want to waste time there unless I have to.

"I have to be missing something." Looking around, I realize I don't see his luggage. When he checked in, he had a laptop bag and a rolling suitcase. I look in the other storage cabinet but only find his rolling suitcase. Opening it, I find nothing other than a pair of shoes. But I still don't see the bag.

The only place I haven't looked is under the bed. I get down on my knees and move the edge of the bedspread. "There you are," I say, pulling out the black leather bag. Unzipping it, I find a pair of earbuds and an extra charging cord in the main compartment. There are several smaller pockets on the outside. Most of them are empty. Inside the last pocket, I find his passport. It was issued to Mr. James Anderson with his picture. There are several stamps from countries he's visited over the years. Nothing seems amiss.

When I put it back, something dark and shiny catches my eye—a hidden zipper. I open it and pull out another passport. This one has a picture of a man who looks very much like Mr. Anderson, except he's bald with blue eyes. "Viktor Dobrow?" I read the name and then snap a few pictures before carefully putting it back.

Before I leave the room, I take a final look to ensure everything is exactly as I found it. I prefer to maintain the element of surprise.

"Did you find anything?" Ismael asks when I exit the room.

"It seems our Mr. Anderson also goes by Viktor Dobrow."

"When we get back to the office, I'll run the name and his picture through our system and see what we find."

Viktor

"Is there anywhere you want to go?" I ask the young woman sitting next to me.

"I don't know." Jessica looks out the window and then back at me. "I've never been allowed out of the resort," she whispers.

I pull out my phone and do a quick search for tourist activities. Quickly, I spot something that looks fun. I lean forward and show the driver where I want to go. "Can we stop at a shop first? Somewhere, we can get swimsuits."

"No problem," the driver says.

A few minutes later, we're pulling up in front of a store.

"Can you wait for us? We won't be long."

Opening the door, I step out first and look around. Sure enough, a car pulls into a spot not far away. I recognize the face of the driver. He's an employee at the resort. I lean down and take Jessica's hand. "We have some company, so we need to play the part, okay?"

She nods.

When she gets out, she threads her arm through mine.

"Where're we going?" Jessica asks.

"That's a surprise." I smile. "Go pick out a swimsuit and anything else you want."

Jessica gives me a quizzical look. "Are you sure?"

"Unless you want me to pick one out for you. There's a nice one there." I point to some sort of swimsuit with a dress attached to it.

Jessica laughs. "I think I can handle it." She walks over to the rack of women's swimsuits and starts looking through them. While she shops, I grab swim trunks, two beach towels, sunscreen, and a backpack.

Ten minutes later, we've checked out and are ready for our adventure.

It's a short drive to our destination. I've arranged for a private tour of the Seven Sisters Waterfalls.

"James?" A man in a tour guide uniform asks.

"Yes. And this is my girlfriend, Crystal." I don't want to risk saying her real name in case Hasani's man comes asking questions.

"I'm Joaquin. I'll be your guide today." We shake hands. "There are changing rooms over there if you want to put your swimsuits on before we set off on our hike."

We take the opportunity to change and then get on our way.

"This place is beautiful," Jessica says as we walk along jungle-like trails.

"Look over there." I point to a nearby tree. "There's a monkey."

"That's a Mona Monkey. They're native to our island," Joaquin explains. "You're lucky. We don't always see them on our hikes."

We walk in silence for a while until the trail opens to a breathtaking waterfall.

"I'm going to leave you two here to enjoy the water. I'll be back in about an hour."

"Thanks," I say and wait for him to walk away. "Want to go for a swim?"

"Umm..." she hesitates.

"I have no ulterior motives, Jessica. Just a swim."

"Okay."

After taking my shirt and shoes off, I go to the edge of the rock and jump into the turquoise-blue water below. After I resurface, I run my hands through my hair.

"Come on, the water is beautiful."

Jessica takes her shorts and shirt off and stands at the edge of the rock. "I'm scared."

I can't help but stare at her perfect figure in a two-piece swimsuit. Silently chastising myself, I course correct.

"I'm right here. I won't let you get hurt," I encourage. "You can trust me."

"I don't know."

"You can do this."

Jessica shrugs, still uncertain, but then takes the leap. She lands next to me with a splash. I grab her arms, helping her to resurface. When she does, she giggles like a little girl.

"I've never done anything like that. It was incredible."

We swim around for a while, enjoying the crystal-clear water at the bottom of the spectacular waterfall.

"Do you have any family?" she asks.

"My parents died when I was a boy, and I never married."

"I'm sorry," she says quietly.

"What about you? Do you have a family out there?"

"My mom died when I was five. My dad was alive, last I knew, but he won't be looking for me."

"Why not?"

"After mom died, he started drinking. Then, he started using drugs. He didn't pay any attention to me—I was invisible." She pulls herself up on a rock, getting out of the water.

I follow her onto the rock and sit next to her.

"I can't believe a guy that looks like you doesn't have a girlfriend." Her face turns bright red. "Unless you're—"

"I'm not gay if that's what you were going to say." I laugh. "I did have a girl and a baby."

"What happened to them?"

"It was complicated." I don't know what's come over me, but I find myself telling Jessica what happened with Natalie. She's a good listener.

There's no judgment on her face. Surprisingly, it feels good to get it out and tell someone who doesn't know either of us.

"Wow," she says when I finish. "That really is complicated. Is that why you came here?"

"Yeah. I needed to get away and clear my head."

A twig snaps, and I jump up, shielding Jessica.

"Did you two enjoy the falls?" Joaquin asks as he makes his way over to us.

I drop my guard and grab a towel, passing the other to Jessica.

"It was amazing. I've never seen anything like it."

"It's time we start making our way back."

Jessica and I grab our things and follow our guide back along the trail. The rest of the hike takes us by the other waterfalls in the area. When we arrive back at the parking lot, I'm relieved to see our driver is still there. I paid the driver well above what he would've made picking up other riders today so that he'd be here when we were done. We slide into the backseat.

"What's the best food around these parts?"

"I know a place." He smiles proudly and starts driving.

After a drive along winding roads, we pull up at a food truck.

"Best food on the island."

Jessica and I enjoy fajitas and crab back.

"Thank you for today, James." She looks at me with tears in her eyes. "I'll never forget it."

The sadness in her brown eyes is almost my undoing. There's no way I'm letting her return to Hasani.

Viktor

WE ARRIVE BACK AT THE RESORT AND ARE BARELY THROUGH the front doors when Hasani appears. Jessica tenses beside me.

"Did you two enjoy your day out?" he asks, displeasure evident in his features.

"Ismael's description of your merchandise didn't do it justice." I look over at Jessica, who's staring down at her feet. "How much to keep her for the rest of my stay?"

Jessica gasps.

"You've been very generous with your time and product, Mr. Anderson. I'll throw her in compliments of the resort. However, she'll still need to report to work."

"While she's with me, I want your guarantee no other man will touch her. I don't like to share."

"That can be arranged." Hasani grabs Jessica's hair, forcing her head up. "Can you be a good girl for my friend?"

"Yes, sir," she says quietly.

I grab her arm. "Let's go. I haven't had my fill of you today."

With a hurried pace, I lead her away from Hasani, who's behind us laughing.

When we get back inside the relative safety of my villa, I lock the door and pull the curtains closed. Jessica and I need to have a chat. I'm taking a considerable risk by telling her why I'm really here. I'm hoping if I do, she'll be willing to help me with information on Hasani.

She stands in the middle of the room, nervously playing with her fingers and avoiding eye contact with me.

"Sit down. We need to talk."

Jessica sits on the chair by the desk, and I perch on the edge of the bed. Her face shows no emotion while I explain who I am and what I'm doing here. Yet, even as I speak, I'm second-guessing my decision to trust her with this info. If I'm wrong, this move will cost me my life.

"In exchange for your help and keeping my secret, I'll make sure you're free from Hasani. Do we have a deal?"

Then, I wait.

Silence fills the room as Jessica continues to stare at me. My heart rate increases with each second that goes by.

"Yes, we have a deal," she finally says. "What do I need to do?"

"You need to do what you always do when you work, in addition to keeping an ear out for any conversations that might be of importance." I lean forward, resting my elbows on my spread legs. "I'll take care of the rest."

It's bright and early Monday morning when I get the text that the installation team is here.

"I have to go to the Cinnamon Room for a bit. Keep the door locked. Do not open it for anyone." I hand Jessica a cell phone. "My number's programmed in. If you need anything, call me."

"You didn't have to do that."

"Just promise you'll do what I said."

"I promise."

I grab my laptop bag and head into the main resort building. When I get to the club's entrance, the team's waiting outside the door. After exchanging greetings, we walk into the club. Ismael's sitting at one of the tables. A quick look around tells me he's the only one here.

"Good afternoon, Mr. Anderson. I take it this is your crew?"

"It is. Will your brother be joining us?"

"Unfortunately, he was called away on another matter. I'll be overseeing today's work."

I don't like this at all, but I school my features and instruct my team. "The first camera will be installed at the club's entrance to catch anyone going in or out, and we need several discreet cameras inside the club. The final camera will be installed at the back exit leading to the beach."

The crew wastes no time getting to work. I join Ismael at his table. "The wireless cameras allow for quick and easy installation. Your current system doesn't support security feeds outside the villas. My system will give you the flexibility to have your entire property under constant surveillance. The system runs on encrypted software that is impenetrable."

He nods.

"Your brother said I'd have access to your computer system to set up the software."

Ismael stands. "Yes. Follow me." We exit through a door marked *staff only* and walk down a quiet hallway until we come to the office. "After you."

"May I?" I ask as I motion to the desk.

Ismael again nods and sits on the black leather sofa along the office's back wall. I sit in the oversized leather chair and pull out my laptop to begin transferring the program.

While I work, Ismael pulls out his phone and appears to be texting. Something feels very off about this situation, but I'm too far in to turn back now. There's also the promise I made to Jessica. Failure is not an option. But I've never wished for Dimitri's presence more than I do right now. He can be a pain in the ass, but when it comes to tech skills, there's no one better than him.

Dimitri

"I'M JUST PULLING UP NOW," I SAY TO MAXIM, WHO'S ON THE phone. "I'll be in touch once I know something."

Strolling into the resort, I make my way to the check-in desk. I'm registered under an assumed name. Just a guy on vacation. Check-in is a breeze. Before I know it, I'm on my way up to the tenth floor to my room. The first thing I do is put the 'do not disturb' sign on the door. Then, I start setting up my equipment. I need to get a good feel for the security system and hack into it as fast as possible. Which isn't hard to do.

The next order of business is to check all the camera feeds and familiarize myself with them. I'm pleasantly surprised to find the cameras have audio capability. So, not only can I see what's going on, but I can also hear it—that gives me another advantage.

The Cinnamon Room has a flurry of activity going on. I watch for a few minutes. It appears new security cameras are being installed—bingo. Three guys are working on the setup, but there's no sign of Viktor. My monitor has all the security camera images running, so I sit back and wait.

A half-hour passes before I spot Viktor walking into the Cinnamon Room with Ismael Hasani on his heels.

"We're all good in here, boss," one of the men says. "We just need to install the camera on the back exit, and we'll be done."

"Excellent work as always," Viktor replies. "I'll be back tonight after the club opens."

"Of course, Mr. Anderson," Ismael says and shakes Viktor's hand. "I'm anticipating seeing your software in action."

Viktor leaves the club with the three men. As soon as he's out the door, Ismael makes a call. I'm hoping to hear who he's calling, but he exits the club through the same staff door. There doesn't appear to be any cameras in that area.

I make a call to give Max a quick update.

"I didn't expect to hear from you already."

"I was able to get right into the existing security system and found Viktor right away. He had a few guys with him that were installing the new system. He was with Ismael Hasani."

"What the hell is Viktor thinking?"

"Apparently, nothing." I continue watching the footage tracking Viktor's movements to the end of the main lobby, but then I lose him. With a couple clicks on my keyboard, I get into the resort's guest log. "I found where he's staying. He's in a private villa. He's expected in the Cinnamon Room tonight. Once I know he's gone, I'll get in his villa and make a copy of his security software."

"Be careful. I don't need the both of you in trouble."

"Careful is my middle name, boss." I laugh as I disconnect the call.

Over the next few hours, I continue to watch the feed. Ismael Hasani makes an appearance moments before the club opens. Viktor enters a few minutes later. The men go back through the staff door.

It's time to make my move.

The sun hasn't yet set, so I put on my cap and sunglasses as I walk through the main lobby at a leisurely pace. I don't want to attract unwanted attention. It's much busier down here now that the club is open. I glance in and see there are several people inside. A relatively small crowd, but it is a Monday. Then, I continue straight out the back exit. One path leads to the resort's private beach, and the other goes to the left, where the villas are located.

"Ginger Villa," I mutter as I walk up to the door. "They really took Grenada's reputation as the spice island to the extreme." Using my phone and the master key card I acquired, I let myself in.

"Viktor?" a feminine voice calls from the bathroom. "Did you forget something?" She comes out with a towel wrapped around her body. "Who are you?" She backs up against the wall.

I put my hands up. "I'm a friend of Viktor's. I won't hurt you."

She looks around the room, her eyes stopping on the cell phone lying on the bed. "Viktor doesn't have any friends here."

"My name's Dimitri. Viktor and I have known each other for years."

"How did you get in here?"

I hold up my phone, showing her the digital keycard.

"Where did you get that?"

"I made it." I shrug.

She moves to take the phone, but I grab her wrist, stopping her.

"We're not going to call anyone."

"Let me go." She struggles to get out of my grasp.

"Relax. I'm not going to hurt you."

"I said, let me go." She pulls out of my grasp, and her towel falls to the floor.

I know I should look away, but I can't. She's fucking gorgeous. The girl scrambles to pick up the towel to cover herself. I take the opportunity to grab the cell that was lying there.

"Why don't you put some clothes on, and then we'll talk?" Although I wouldn't mind talking without her clothes on.

"Give me my phone."

"Nope. Can't do that. Go, get dressed, please."

"Viktor will be back any second. If you don't want to get caught, you better get out of here," she says and spins around, returning to the bathroom.

"Viktor's busy. He won't be back for a while."

She doesn't respond except to slam the bathroom door.

I know I shouldn't be aroused looking at the woman who's with Viktor, but I can't help it. He certainly has good taste. While she's in the bathroom, I open the laptop and start searching. If I get Viktor out of here alive, the first thing we're doing is sitting down to learn about cyber security. Everything I need is in folders on his desktop. I stick my flash drive in, and in a matter of seconds, I have all the info I need. I close the laptop and sit on the bed to wait for the girl. Several minutes later, she comes back in shorts and a T-shirt, this time.

"If Viktor comes back here—"

"I plan to be gone before that. And you aren't going to tell him I'm here."

"Why should I trust you?"

"Because if you don't, Viktor's life could be at stake." I pat the bed next to me. "Let's start by you telling me who you are and why you're here."

She crosses her arms over her chest. "Because Viktor bought me for the week."

"Wrong. Viktor would never buy a woman. Try again."

She blows out a frustrated breath before explaining the story. I can't believe what she's telling me. I thought Viktor was smarter than this.

"He's gotten himself into a real mess." I stand and run my hand through my hair. "I have to figure out how to get Viktor out of here alive."

"Is he in danger?" she asks quietly.

"You and I both know Hasani is not a good man. I think you can answer that question yourself."

"What can I do to help?"

"First, you will not tell Viktor I'm here." I go to the desk and pull open the drawers, searching for paper and pen. "Here's my number. Memorize it and then destroy the paper. If you hear anything important, call me, but make sure you delete the call from the log. Viktor's life depends on this."

"Okay." She takes the paper from my hand.

"Remember, not a word."

She nods.

I leave quickly and head back up to my room. I'm trusting a complete stranger with not only my safety but Viktor's as well. This does not sit well with me.

Viktor

Saimir's been away on business all week. Jessica and I have made a few public appearances to continue the ruse, but other than that, it's been pretty uneventful.

So far, Ismael's impressed with the security system. Tonight's the big test, though. It's Friday night, which means the club will be packed, and Saimir is expected to be back. I'm told we'll be in the main office so I can show Hasani how to operate the software.

I'm hoping I'll come across some information to help me achieve my goal and get Jessica and myself out of here sooner rather than later.

Jessica left a few hours ago to get ready for work. I'm doing everything I can to protect her until I can get her to safety. I'd rather her not be there, but despite all my protests, Hasani insists she works for the club on weekends.

I step outside to get some air, hoping it will quiet my nerves. My phone buzzes with a text.

Mr. Smith: I haven't heard from you all week. I want an update.

Nightingale: The security system is installed. Hasani was away all week. We're meeting tonight.

Mr. Smith: This is taking too long.

Nightingale: You knew this wasn't going to be easy. Hasani doesn't leave much to chance. I'll update you in the morning.

I slide my cell into my pocket and head over to the club.

When I get there, people are already filtering in. Then, right on cue, Hasani comes through the staff door to greet me.

"Are you ready, Mr. Anderson?"

"Everything's run smoothly all week. I'm certain it'll be no different tonight."

"Hopefully, I'll be as impressed as my brother." He motions for me to follow him back to his office. Another young woman is there. "Tell Crystal to come to my office."

"Yes, sir," she says and hurries off.

Why does he want Jessica in the office? The hairs on my neck stand on end.

Once we get settled, I power up the program, explaining how it works to Hasani as I go. The video feed is crystal clear, and the sound quality is studio-perfect.

"My men have attempted to hack into the system several times this week," Hasani announces. "They were unsuccessful every time."

"I told you the software's impenetrable."

There's a knock on the door.

"Come in."

Crystal walks in wearing the tiniest bit of clothes. It leaves little to the imagination. My jaw tenses.

"Do you like the new uniforms, Mr. Anderson?"

"I don't like that she's on display for every man in here when we had a deal." I motion for her to come to me and pull her to my lap.

"No one will touch her, but looking wasn't part of our arrangement." He snickers.

"Consider this a warning if anyone so much as reaches for her. They will meet their end in a most unfortunate way."

Hasani shakes his head. "I think you're becoming too attached to *my* property."

"She's keeping my dick wet and my bed warm, but I assure you, she'll be forgotten once I leave." Jessica glances at me. She has no reason to believe my promise of safety, which is clear from the hurt look in her eyes. I pull her to me and kiss her deeply. "Don't worry, I'm not through with you yet," I try to reassure her.

"You are through for now. Crystal has a special assignment tonight. Room 1003 is requesting personal room service."

I raise my eyebrow.

"Not to worry, Mr. Anderson. She'll only be delivering his meal and any other mundane tasks he requires. Run along now." Hasani watches her until she's out of sight. "She's a hot piece of ass, isn't she?" He looks at me.

"Yes." I clench my fists under the desk.

"Now, where were we?"

I spend the rest of the evening watching the security footage. Hasani's in and out of the office all night. He keeps a strong presence in the club, especially on the weekends. He's pleased with our ability to successfully track the guests as they move about the resort.

The club finally clears out around three a.m. Between being with Hasani and worrying about Jessica, it was an exhausting night. She never returned to the club. I can only hope she's okay.

I'm shutting down my system when the office door opens, and Hasani walks in.

"Well, Mr. Anderson. I'm very pleased with your product."

"As I knew you would be." I lean back in the chair as if I own the space.

Hasani sits on his leather sofa. "I'd like to make you an offer on the original setup we discussed, but I want to expand it. In addition to the cameras we discussed, I want cameras placed on all the floors of the main resort building and in a few of my staff areas."

"That can be arranged for a price."

"No price is too great to ensure I have the safest resort on the island."

"Of course."

"And to celebrate, I'm hosting a party in your honor."

"Oh?"

"I have an exclusive beachfront area reserved for only my most important guests. We'll celebrate our new partnership there tomorrow night."

"That sounds good." I know the area he's referring to. It'll be the perfect place to take out my target while giving me an easy escape. "I'm assuming Crystal will be at my disposal for the party?"

"Of course. I'll have a suitable outfit delivered to your villa for her tomorrow."

I make my way toward the door but stop before I open it. "I found an apartment. This will be my last weekend at the resort."

"We'll be sorry to see you go."

Saimir

"Everything's set for tomorrow night."

"Yes, sir. We'll be ready."

"Viktor Dobrow has crossed the wrong man."

Viktor

I return to the villa expecting to find Jessica, but she isn't there yet. Where the hell is she? We only have tonight to get our shit together. Tomorrow's going to happen fast. She needs to know the plan. There's a knock on the door. When I look, I see it's a guard, and he has Jessica with him. I pull the door open quickly.

"It's about time you returned her."

The guard says nothing and walks away. I close and lock the door.

"Where were you?"

"The guest I had to serve was very demanding."

"Was it a man?"

"Yes. But he didn't hurt me."

"Did he touch you?"

"No." She moves into the room and sits on the bed. "I'm just exhausted."

I sit next to her and take a deep breath. "I'm getting you out of here tomorrow."

"What?"

I relay all the information about tomorrow night. Luck's on my side. This is the perfect opportunity to neutralize Hasani without putting the general population of the resort at risk. It's really a best-case scenario for us.

"I've already reserved a room in the main building. It's a late check-in, so I can skip the desk and go right up to the room." I stand and start pacing. "Hasani's having an outfit sent to the villa for you tomorrow. We'll get ready like we're going to a party so we don't draw attention to ourselves."

"What about all our stuff?" She looks around the room.

"Other than the clothes we're wearing, it's all getting left behind. I'll destroy the laptop before we leave. Once we get to safety, I'll have to call in some favors to get you identification so you can go home."

"Home?"

"You want to go home, right?"

"I don't have a home."

Jessica falls fast asleep, but I lay awake. I'm trying to imagine every way tomorrow might go. Trying to plan for every possible scenario. To consider everything that can go wrong. Before I know it, the sun is shining through the window.

"Good morning," Jessica rolls onto her side and rubs her eyes.

"Hopefully, it's a good morning. Breakfast should be here any minute."

The phone in the room rings.

"Hello?"

"Ah, good morning, Mr. Anderson."

"What can I do for you, Mr. Hasani?"

"Crystal's needed to work today."

"It's a weekday, and she's my date tonight."

"She'll be back in time for the party."

"I had plans for her today."

"Plans?"

"She's a woman. It's a party. I was treating her to a spa day."

Hasani laughs. "Crystal's a paid escort. A whore. She's not entitled to a *spa* day."

"While she's with me, she's entitled to whatever I choose to give her."

"That's where you're wrong, Mr. Anderson. Crystal remains my employee, and she'll do only what I allow. And today, she *will* be working. Make sure she's at the Cinnamon Room in ten minutes."

"We're just getting out of bed. She'll be there after we eat."

"Perhaps I haven't made myself clear. This is my resort, and Crystal is my property. It is I who calls the shots."

"We haven't signed the contract for the security system yet." I make the unspoken threat. "She eats before she leaves my room. And she'll return no later than five to have time to properly prepare for tonight. It's my arm she'll be on, and I expect a certain level of presentation from any woman with me."

"I'll make a concession this time."

"Good day, Mr. Hasani." I hang up the phone.

"Do you have a death wish?" Jessica asks.

"Why?"

"No one talks to him that way."

"I've dealt with much worse than him. He doesn't realize it, but his time on the earth is rapidly coming to an end."

Breakfast is delivered a short time later. We discuss the specifics of what will happen tonight while we eat.

Then, with much reluctance, I watch her leave the villa.

Dimitri

I PUT IN A SPECIAL REQUEST AND A SUBSTANTIAL SUM OF money to ensure Jessica's available whenever I call for her services. I spend the better part of the day watching and listening. Hasani's setting up for a party in his private outdoor venue. Other than that, things have been quiet. I purposely haven't requested Jessica's services, hoping that if she's hanging around with the staff and Hasani, she'll overhear something. It isn't until lunchtime I request she deliver my food and stay to tidy my room—it'll give us some time to talk.

While I wait for her arrival, Hasani shows up outside the Cinnamon Room. He's met by several other men who follow him inside. I sit up in my seat. "What's going on here?"

"Gentlemen, good to see you," Hasani says.

"Is everything set for tonight?" one of the men asks.

"My people are setting up the venue now." He motions outside. "I'll make sure you have access to my penthouse. When I call Dobrow onto the stage to introduce him, you'll have a clear shot," Hasani explains.

"What the fuck?" His cover's blown. There's a knock on my door. "Shit." I throw the door open quickly, knowing it'll be Jessica. "Hurry up and come over here."

"What's wrong?" she asks.

"Viktor's cover is blown." I point to the screen.

Jessica sits next to me while we continue to listen. The men are highly armed with sniper rifles and have a solid plan.

"Do you recognize any of these men?"

She points to the screen. "That's the man who brought me here."

The blood coursing through my body boils with rage.

The other men have their backs to the camera, making identifying them impossible. They talk for a few more minutes before going their separate ways, presumably to set up in Hasani's penthouse—where there are no cameras.

"Viktor's planning to kill Hansani tonight," Jessica says.

"What did he tell you?"

Jessica details everything Viktor told her. There's no way my friend is going to pull this off by himself. Hell, I don't know if either of us will make it out of here.

"Shit." I stand and start pacing. "Why the hell did he do this?"

Jessica stands and touches my arm, stilling me. "What do we do?"

"We? *We* aren't going to do anything. I'll handle this."

This girl is half my size but places her hands on her hips and stands up to me anyway. She's hot as hell, spunky, and intelligent. Why does Viktor get all the good women?

"Yes, I am. There's no way you're doing this without me, Dimitri."

I turn away from her. The last thing I want to do is include this girl in my plans. We're severely outnumbered, and the Albanians are crazy as fuck. If anything happens to Viktor's girl, he'll kill me. Our chances of getting out of this alive are getting smaller by the second. But I don't think I have another choice. I need her help. Turning back to face her, I ask, "If I could just contact Viktor. Do you have your cell on you?" It's time he finds out I'm here.

"No. It's too risky during the day. But I know his number."

I punch in his cell number, and it starts ringing. "Come on, Viktor. Pick up." I have to try to talk some sense into him. But the line just rings and rings. "He doesn't have voicemail set up?" I look to Jessica.

"I don't know. I haven't had to call him."

What do I do now? Think Dimitri. I can't go to his villa, and I can't ask Jessica to tell him I'm here—it's too risky. "I'm going to have to take out the sniper before they take him out. Here's what I need you to do."

I send Jessica on her way with my instructions. Then, I go back to watching the video feed. I hope to get some clues as to where Viktor is and how I can try fixing this mess he's made.

While I watch, I call Max.

"They know who he is. Hasani is planning on taking him out at a party tonight, and Viktor has some crazy plan that's going to get him killed."

"Where the hell is his head?"

"Somewhere back in New York City, I suspect." Do I tell him? What the hell? "It appears that he's moving on. He's had a girl on his arm the whole time I've been here. She works for Hasani. I had to ask for her help."

"Do you trust her?"

"Hasani stole her. She's very much into Viktor. Yes, I trust her." I have no choice but to trust her. I run my hands through my hair. "Boss, I have no idea how I'm going to get us out of here."

"I'll do everything I can from here."

"If we're still alive in a few hours, I'll be in touch."

Viktor

I'VE SPENT THE AFTERNOON CHANGING MY APPEARANCE. Gone is the hair I've spent the past year or so growing out. And no more contacts. When I look in the mirror, my reflection is once again familiar.

Using my burner phone, I make a last-minute reservation for an ocean-front room with a balcony on one of the top floors of the resort. It's off-season for this area, so getting a room was easy. The rooms in the main resort building use a phone app to open the room doors, so I don't have to worry about checking in. The room's placement will give me an unobstructed shot at Hasani.

It's five o'clock, and she's not here. Her dress arrived hours ago. I pace back and forth, hoping she shows up soon. Another hour passes, and still nothing. The party starts at seven. The phone in my room rings.

"Hello?"

"Mr. Anderson, it's Crystal."

"Where are you?"

"Something's come up, and I'm not going to be able to attend tonight's function with you," she says quietly.

"What are you talking about? Is it Hasani?"

"No, sir."

"What's going on?"

"It was a pleasure serving you, Mr. Anderson. I hope you have a lovely evening." She hangs up.

Immediately I dial the number to Hasani's office.

"Why the hell did Crystal call me and back out of tonight?"

"I wasn't aware she did."

"We just hung up. Her refusal is unacceptable. I expect her at my door in ten minutes."

"Mr. Anderson, perhaps she doesn't appreciate a man as *forceful* as yourself."

"Ten minutes or the deal's off." I slam the phone down.

Ten minutes pass, and no Jessica. I don't know what to do. Hasani is going to be dead within the hour. After I fire the shot, I won't have time to look for her. This place will be crawling with Hasani's men. If I make it out alive, it'll be a miracle, but I promised Jessica she'd get out of here. How am I supposed to make good on that if she's not here?

I wait as long as possible, but she never shows. "Fuck, Jessica. Why did you do this?" I double-check my weapon, then grab my tactical bag. It's now or never.

When I step outside, there's a thick cloud cover obstructing the moonlight. Finally, something's working in my favor. I can leave my villa and get to the beach, where I walk away from the resort. I keep walking past several other resorts before going through a parking lot, where I backtrack my steps.

Once I'm back at Hasani's resort, I walk through the main doors like every other guest and head straight to the elevators. The hallway to my room is quiet. As soon as I get in the room, I lock the door and try the phone I gave Jessica once more, but there's no answer. "Dammit." There's no time to waste. I have to get myself set up before they realize Mr. Anderson isn't showing up.

Saimir

Viktor thought he'd outsmart us by using an alias and shaving his head. Well, he was wrong. Clearly, he has a death wish. Tonight, I'll be his genie in a bottle—his wish is my command.

"There's been a change of plans," I say to my sniper. "Dobrow is in 1417. Keep one man in the penthouse, just in case. Then, adjust your position on the beach. It'll be a clear shot to the balcony of his room."

"Yes, sir. I'm on it."

Dimitri

There's a knock on my door. Jessica's right on time. Pulling the door open, I let Jessica in.

"We don't have much time," she says as she pushes past me.

"I know. I heard."

Viktor thought he could outsmart the Albanians by shaving his head and using a fake name. He's better than this. Now, I'm left to try to fix this mess without getting the three of us killed.

Jessica's already at the computer. When she demanded she be allowed to help, I had no idea she studied computer programming before being kidnapped. Jessica was in Paris doing an exchange student program. She has some wicked skills that she's acquired along the way—skills that are very useful right now.

"Saimir's assuming Viktor will be on the balcony of the room he booked. He's got men at the Penthouse and one on the beach." She points to the picture on the security feed. "He blends in with the rest of his security," she says and looks at me. "But I'm familiar with him. He's Saimir's best sniper."

"Fuck." I slam my fists on the desk, making Jessica jump. "I'm sorry. I didn't mean to scare you."

"We're not getting out of here, are we?" A tear drips down her cheek.

"Look at me." I cup her face in my palms and wipe her tears. "I'm getting us all out of here tonight."

Although she nods in agreement, her eyes tell a different story.

"Here's how this is going to happen," I explain the plan quickly while I grab my handgun and holster it on my side. Then, I grab the rifle from my bag.

"How did you get that on a plane?"

"I took a private jet to Venezuela and then a chartered plane here," I say while I work. "We don't have much time." The words no sooner leave my mouth when loud music begins to play.

"They're starting."

I stop in front of Jessica. "Are you ready?"

"Yes."

I pull on my night vision goggles and take a covered position by the balcony doors. I have the perfect view. Now, I just need to wait for a clear shot at the sniper.

A shot rings out. As I pull the trigger, a second shot sounds. I hit my target, and he falls to the ground.

"Now," I yell to Jessica.

Screams come from the beach, and then the resort goes black.

"Come on." I grab her arm and pull her along through the pitch-black hallway and into the stairwell. I push the rifle into her hand. "Stay right here, and don't make a sound."

I take the steps three at a time, racing to the fourteenth floor. Viktor's room is six doors from the stairwell. The sniper got a shot out a split second before mine hit him. I'm not sure what I'm going to find when I get into his room.

Thankfully, the resort employees still use old-fashioned keys to access the guests' rooms. Jessica often works in housekeeping and managed to slip a key out. I slide it into the lock and turn it. With a click, the door opens.

I run to the balcony and find Viktor on the ground, propped against the wall.

"Fuck. How bad is it?"

"Dimitri? What the hell are you doing here?"

"Saving your sorry ass. Where are you hit?"

"My shoulder."

He has his hand over the spot where he was hit. Blood pours from his hand.

"Can you walk?"

"I think so."

He leans his weight on me as I help him up. I peer out over the balcony rail. There's a flurry of activity down on the beach. Hasani's men are everywhere.

"We don't have much time," I tell him as we head for the door.

"I can't go. I have to find—"

"Jessica, I know. She's in the stairwell waiting for us."

"How did you—"

"I'll fill you in after we get out of here."

Viktor keeps up with me as we hurry down the steps until we meet back up with Jessica.

"He's shot. But we have to hurry. Grab my cell out of my pocket and use it for light."

"Oh my God. How bad is it?" She asks as she slides her tiny hand into my pocket, grabbing my phone.

"It hurts like hell," Viktor growls and takes the rifle from her.

"Let's go. We don't have time for this." The three of us hurry down the steps. Viktor's body is getting heavier as he trips his way down.

Finally, we arrive at the side emergency exit door. I push it open, not knowing what we'll find on the other side. I take a small breath when there's no one there.

"Come on. We're almost there." I see our ride waiting at the other end of the parking lot.

We're halfway across when the resort's lights go back on.

"There he is," a voice calls behind us, followed by a shot. I push Jessica down behind a car and pull out my pistol, firing a shot back.

"Jessica, run to the black car and don't look back. I'll cover you from here."

"I'm not leaving you two behind."

"Dammit, Jessica, do as he says," Viktor yells.

"When you get to the car, I want you to close the door and stay down.

With a last look, she takes off for the car. A shot is fired from behind us. It misses by a fraction of an inch, hitting the car next to us. Again, I fire back.

"I need you to run."

"I'm going to slow you down. Just leave me here."

"I'm not leaving you behind."

"Make sure Jessica is safe." He tries to pull away from me, but I don't loosen my grasp on him.

"Shut the fuck up and run." I drag him with me, firing behind us as we run.

Several more shots sound. Bullets ricochet around us. We're almost to the car when a bullet grazes my arm. "Shit."

"Are you hit?"

I pull the door open and shove Viktor into the backseat. "Go," I tell the driver as I jump into the car, avoiding more shots. Before I get the door closed, the driver's already peeling out.

"Now what?" Viktor asks.

"We need to slow this bleeding down." I pull my shirt off and use it as a compress over his wound. He's lost a lot of blood and is starting to look pale. "Maxim has a chartered plane waiting for us."

"Do you have my phone?"

"Mhm." She pulls my phone from her pocket and passes it to me.

"Keep pressure on this." Viktor winces in pain when we hit a bump.

I pull up Maxim's contact and tap the green call button. It rings several times before the call connects.

"Are you out?"

"We're on our way to the airport." I look over at Viktor, whose head is laid back on the seat. "He's been shot." I lower my voice. "He's lost a lot of blood, boss."

"I have some contacts in South America. I will arrange for medical to meet you at the jet."

"Thanks, boss."

"I would like to talk to him."

I hold the phone out to Viktor. "The boss wants to speak to you." Viktor shakes his head. "He doesn't want to talk."

Maxim's silent. He's not a man you say no to. I brace myself for the worst, but he surprises me. "How bad is he?"

"I'm not a doctor, but I don't like what I see." The driver pulls into the small airport bringing us to where our charter waits. "We just got to the plane." I was so wrapped up in the conversation I didn't realize we were being followed. "We're in trouble."

"What's wrong?"

"Hasani's men are here." The words barely leave my lips when two police cars block their path. "What the hell's going on?"

"I have ensured safe passage out of the country."

I watch as the men get out of their cars. They look to be arguing with the police, who've now drawn their weapons.

"How?" I shouldn't be shocked, but I am.

"Call me when you are on my jet." Max ends the call.

"Are you two ready to get out of here?"

Viktor

I LEAN HEAVILY ON DIMITRI AS WE WALK UP THE STEPS TO get into the small jet. The concerned look he and Jessica exchange doesn't escape me.

"Get your ass in a seat." Dimitri tries to keep his fear out of his voice, but I see right through him.

"Make sure she's safe," I whisper.

"You're going to have to do that yourself." He buckles me in as we start to taxi down the runway. Then, he turns to Jessica. "Are you buckled in?"

"Yes"

I feel the plane's wheels leave the ground. The pressure from our ascent increases the pain in my shoulder. My entire body begins to shake from the intensity, and blackness creeps into my peripheral vision.

"Try to take some deep breaths," Dimitri coaches me.

My mind immediately goes back to Natalie in labor with Rose. Except it was me doing the coaching while she was bringing a miracle into the world. The pain in my heart is riveling the pain in my shoulder —God, I miss that woman.

Dimitri

Finally, the plane reaches cruising altitude, and I throw off my seatbelt. "Jessica, will you grab the medical kit out of my pack and pass me the scissors?" I'm not a doctor or anything, but in my line of work, we're used to patching up a gunshot wound until we can get real medical help. "I need to take your shirt off so I can get a good look at this."

"Leave it be." Viktor swipes my hand away.

"Do you want to bleed to death?"

"It doesn't matter."

It doesn't matter? Does he want to die? Then it hits me. Yes, he does. Losing Natalie and the kid really screwed him up. He doesn't care if he lives or dies. Well, he's not dying on my watch. "Shut the fuck up and let me get this shirt off."

Viktor rests his head back while I make quick work of cutting his shirt open. Jessica helps me remove it. The blood oozing from the open wound doesn't even cause her to flinch.

"What do we do?" she asks.

"We're going to clean it up." Holding Viktor's arm, I pull him forward. "Let me see the back." He rolls his eyes, but he lets me move him. "Well, the good news is the bullet is not lodged in your shoulder. The bad news is the back looks worse than the front."

I get up and begin rummaging through my medical kit. Jessica comes over and stands next to me.

"He doesn't look so good," she whispers. "How long until we get to Venezuela?"

"Too long." I look over at my friend. The color is drained from his face, and he's shivering. He's going into shock. "I'm going to attempt to stitch him up. It'll at least stop the blood loss."

"Is he going to make it?" Her eyes fill with tears.

"I won't let him die."

Viktor's been like a brother to me since we were eighteen. We had each other's backs while we served in the military and all the years we've worked for Max. I'll be damned if I lose him now.

"Natalie," Viktor's voice cracks. "Where are you? I need to feel you." His arm reaches out.

I look at Jessica, startled. Hearing Viktor call out for the woman he was in love with in front of his new fling isn't going to go over well. "I'm sure he didn't mean to call for her."

"It's okay. He told me the whole story."

"He did?" Jessica doesn't appear phased. Instead, she looks at him with compassion.

"Natalie," he calls out again.

This time, Jessica goes over. "Feel me." She takes his hand in hers. "I'm right here."

"Hey, buddy," I say, lowering in front of him. "I'm gonna give you a shot of something to try to numb this. But I'm not going to lie. This is going to hurt."

Jessica holds his hand while I do my best to stitch his skin closed. At this point, I'm just trying to stop the bleeding. I wish he'd wince or yell, but his body fell slack when he passed out a few minutes ago.

"Hold on, Vik," I beg. "Don't die on me."

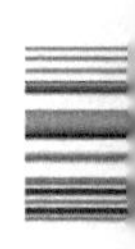

Viktor

I CALL FOR NATALIE, AND SHE COMES TO ME. I THOUGHT I'D lost her, but it must've been a dream because she's in my arms. Her hand caresses my face as she whispers to me. "I love you so much," I say. "And I love our baby, Rose." I may not have helped create her, but that little girl owns my heart. The three of us are a family—they're all I have.

But then she floats away. Coldness replaces the warmth of her presence.

I'm alone again.

I hear voices around me, but not the one voice I want to hear. I recognize the words spoken in Russian. The deep timbre's familiar, but I have to search the recess of my mind for its owner.

Maxim.

Where am I?

Slowly, I open my eyes. It takes several minutes before things come into focus and for me to figure out where I am. I attempt to sit up, but the searing pain in my shoulder forces me back down.

"Oh my God, Viktor. You're finally awake," Lana says.

"H-how did—" My throat is dry, making it hard to speak.

"You gave us quite a scare," Maxim adds. "It is nice to have you back."

"What am I doing here?" I ask and try to sit up again, but Max's strong arm stops me.

"Relax. Dimitri brought you back to us. Kazimir, my personal physician, had a heck of a time stitching you back together." Once I lay back down, he sits in his chair. "You lost a lot of blood and then developed an infection. It was touch and go for a bit."

"How long have I been out?"

"Almost two weeks," Lana says. "I'll be right back. There's someone who's been waiting for you to wake up."

I wait until Lana leaves the room. "Is she going to get Natalie?"

"Natalie is in New York. With Alex," Max says.

"She can't be. She was on the plane. I felt her. Heard her."

"You must have been dreaming. There was a girl on the plane. Your girlfriend, Jessica."

"Jessica?" The name sounds strangely familiar, but I'm not sure why. "My girlfriend? Everything's fuzzy. All jumbled together."

"Do not worry. Everything will come back to you now that you are awake." Max pats my arm. "I am sure once you see her, you will remember. She is a tenacious little thing." He chuckles.

"Viktor," a petite brunette says my name as she rushes over to my side. "You scared the shit out of us."

"It's about time you woke your lazy ass up," Dimitri says from the doorway.

I stare at the young woman at my side. She takes my hand in hers, but it feels wrong, and I pull away.

"I'm sorry," she says, folding her hands in her lap.

"We will leave you two to talk." Max walks toward the door. "Let us go, Dimitri."

"Right behind you, boss. Welcome back, brother."

I nod as I return my gaze back to the girl.

"Do you know who I am?" she asks quietly.

I search her face, looking for clues. Struggling to mix the familiarity of her face with my lack of knowledge. A switch flips. It's like a movie begins to play on fast-forward. I'm in Grenada. She's in my room. The dress. The party. The plane. "Jessica."

She smiles. "You remember me."

"You were supposed to come back to my room, but you called and said no."

"I did." She looks down at her hands. "Can I explain?"

"Please do."

She tells me how she met Dimitri and how they worked together. "I couldn't come to you because Dimitri needed my help."

Her eyes sparkle when she says his name. "Do you and Dimitri have something going on?"

She shakes her head. "He's barely said two words to me since we got here. This place is incredible, by the way."

"I don't remember you being so relaxed."

"Well." She looks around. "It's safe here."

"Did you call your family?"

"Yes."

"I'm sure they were relieved to hear from you." Carefully, I try to sit up but groan in pain. Jessica helps me and props pillows behind my back.

"I guess." She shrugs.

"That doesn't sound very positive." From having worked with Maxim for so long, I know not every family is overjoyed that their loved one has been found.

"Things are complicated with my parents, to say the least. I won't be going back to the States." She moves from the edge of the bed to the chair. "Irina brought me to Jelena's Hope to talk to a therapist. They're helping me deal with everything. And Irina said they'll help me start a new life wherever I want. I want to stay here. If everything works out."

For some reason, I sense there's much more to her story than she's telling me, but I won't push. When she's ready, if she's ready, she'll open up. Unfortunately, I'm starting to get tired already, and as hard as I try to hide it, a yawn escapes.

"You should get some rest. I'm glad you're going to be okay." Jessica heads for the door. She reaches for the doorknob but stops herself. Then, turning around, she asks, "Can you do me a favor?"

"I'll try."

"Can you tell Dimitri that you and I aren't together?"

I laugh. "Yeah. I think I can manage that."

Viktor

I CAN'T BELIEVE I LOST TWO WEEKS OF MY LIFE. TWO WEEKS that Hasani has continued to roam the earth. As soon as I get back to normal, I'm heading back to finish what I started.

Kasimir has come to check on me several times. The infection is finally cleared up, and my stitches are out. I have strengthening exercises to do every day to hopefully gain back the muscle tone I've lost. The most concerning thing is the residual numbness in my hand. The doc doesn't have an answer for me. It's a wait-and-see-what-happens kind of deal.

Meanwhile, I'm an animal stuck in a cage. Every move I make is done so under a microscope. Irina tells me it's for my own good, so I make a full recovery. Max has been quiet. Other than telling me Lady Clare's being cared for at Jelena's Hope, he refuses to discuss anything work-related.

I haven't seen much of Lana. Jessica said they are getting along really well, but I know Lana. She's usually the social butterfly bouncing from place to place. But since I've been here, she's been getting more reclusive.

I've just finished my physiotherapy in Max's gym. I'm heading to the indoor pool to swim a few laps before tonight's festivities. Amelia graduated secondary school last week. That kid's come a long way since we recovered her from Moreno's. She seems to be thriving as part of the Solonik family.

Last night, we all attended the traditional Last Bell ceremony and dance. It's an old Soviet-era tradition that, for some reason, lives on. The graduating class works diligently on perfecting a waltz that's performed for all the parents. Afterward, they pair up with an incoming first grader to plant Birch Trees. It's almost like a rite of passage for the graduate and the little one. Tonight, she's having a more American-style graduation party. The house will be crawling with teens. I plan on being in my room with the door locked long before that chaos ensues.

When I step into the pool room, I freeze. Amelia's sitting on a wicker chair, her laptop on the table in front of her. Natalie's image is on the screen. The two are deep in conversation and haven't noticed me walk in. I stay quiet for a few minutes, savoring the sound of Natalie's voice before clearing my throat to make my presence known.

"I didn't hear you come in. I'm sorry," Amelia says quickly as she looks back and forth between Natalie and me. "I can— Umm— I'll go somewhere else." She moves to pick up her laptop.

"No, stay here. It's okay." I can't take my eyes off the screen. "Natalie. How are you?"

"I'm doing well." Her smile lights up her face. "I'm glad to see you up and around. You gave us all a good scare."

"It's been a rough few weeks, I guess."

I can't take my eyes off her. My brain urges me to tell her everything that's happened, but my mouth refuses to utter a sound.

"Mama. Mama," Rose calls and toddles over.

Her sweet face is almost my undoing.

"Auntie Melia," she says. Then, her eyes open wide. "Frickter?"

She remembers me. I have to swallow over the lump in my throat. "Printessa, you've gotten so big."

"You come see me?"

"Frickter is at *Dedushka*'s house very far away. He can't come see you right now," Natalie explains.

"Oh." Her earlier smile is replaced with a frown. She pushes her bottom lip out just like she did when she was a baby.

She's grown so much this past year. Her blonde curls hang down to her shoulders like her mama's. Her big brown eyes are so expressive. They tell a story all their own. And those chubby pink cheeks. I remember how soft they were when I used to kiss her tiny face.

"Natalie, are you and Amelia still on the phone?" Alex asks as he comes into view of the camera. "Viktor." He looks surprised to see me. "We heard you were back. It's good to see you."

"You too." I have to get out of here. Now. The wounds I thought were healed are bursting open, threatening to pour out. "I forgot something I promised to do for Max. It was nice talking to you." I turn to leave.

"*Ya lyublyu tyebya,* Frickter," Rose says.

Her tiny voice nearly brings me to my knees. I close my eyes and try to push down the grief that's trying to claw its way to the surface. I can't speak. Can't turn back to the camera. So, I do the only thing I can manage. I walk away.

"I'm sorry, Viktor," Amelia calls.

I nod and get out of the room as fast as I can. I don't stop until I'm back in my bedroom. I lock the door and lean up against it to catch my breath. I can no longer hold back the tears that are wetting my face. My falling apart is something I don't want anyone else to witness. Although it's been over a year, seeing them brought back the pain as though it were just yesterday.

I should be happy they're together and well, but instead, I still wish it was me by her side. What the hell is wrong with me?

Maxim

"MY DAUGHTER, THIS BEAUTIFUL YOUNG LADY, HAS brought much joy into our family," I begin my toast in Amelia's honor. "And today we celebrate the completion of her secondary education as well as her being honored with the Outstanding Academic Success Gold Medal Award." Our guests applaud.

"Dad," she whispers, her cheeks pink.

Amelia is not comfortable being the center of attention, but right now, she deserves praise for every accolade she has earned. She has been through things no young woman, no person should ever have to face. Yet, she has come through it as a strong and self-confident young lady.

"Many of you know that Amelia is an accomplished pianist. Something first instilled in her by her biological family." I put my hand on her shoulder, knowing she often gets emotional talking about her parents. "Irina and I have been honored to be able to stand in for them and finish the job they began. Much to my dismay," I pause. "Amelia has decided to attend university in California to study music." Our guests laugh. I am certain remembering a very similar speech when Svetlana was going off to New York City. "Obviously, neither of my girls takes pity on their father's nerves."

"Look at it as a growing experience, Papa," Lana says and smiles.

"Irina and I will miss her very much, but we could not be any more proud of her accomplishments, and we cannot wait to see what the future holds for her." I raise my glass of champagne. "To Amelia and her future success."

The clink of glasses sounds around us as our guests toast my daughter. Then, the real party begins. Food is being served, and a DJ starts playing popular music—the kind the kids like. Irina and I make our way to the adult side of the party, away from the music and the splashing of teenagers in the outdoor pool.

I notice Viktor with the security team. "Excuse me, please," I say to the guests we are sitting with and go over to Viktor. "You are not working tonight. You are our guest. Come sit with us."

"Come on, boss. I'm fine to work."

"We will discuss your return to work tomorrow. Tonight, you will join us as a guest."

He rolls his eyes but follows me over to where we are sitting. As the evening progresses, he never lets his guard down. Never stops scanning for possible threats.

But when I look into his eyes, I see he is still lost. Amelia told Irina and me what happened earlier when he walked in on her conversation with Natalie. Even though a year has passed, his heart has not moved on.

When he arrived with Jessica, I thought perhaps there was a spark there. After observing them together, they function more like a brother and sister. The real spark is between Jessica and Dimitri. I am glad for him, but that does nothing to stop my concern about Viktor.

"I'm feeling pretty worn out," Viktor says. "I think I'm going to turn in early."

"Are you sure?"

"Yeah. It's been a long day." Then, without any further conversation, he walks away.

"He's still in a bad place, Max," Irina says. "I'm worried about him."

"As am I."

Viktor

Max invited me as a guest at Amelia's graduation party, but it feels wrong. I should be working security with the other guys. I feel useless. This afternoon didn't help. I'm still feeling the effects of seeing Natalie and Rose on the video call. The darkness of depression is beckoning me to come back and drown in its depths.

Despite being outside, everything begins to close in around me, and I quickly excuse myself from the party. On my way into the house, I stop by where Amelia is talking to a small group of girls.

"Congratulations on your graduation."

"Thank you," she says quietly.

Her friends giggle like little schoolgirls. Amelia rolls her eyes at their reaction.

"Are you leaving already?"

"I'm pretty tired. I guess I'm still recovering." I shrug and turn to walk away.

"Viktor." Amelia touches my arm. "I'm sorry about earlier. I didn't mean—"

"There's nothing to apologize for. Enjoy your party."

As I walk away, the girls continue to giggle and whisper loudly to

Amelia about me. One of them wants her to ask me if I'd be interested in going out with them.

Can you even imagine? They're barely eighteen-year-old children.

On my way back to my room, I pass Lana's room.

"You ditched the party early, too?" she asks when she sees me.

"Parties aren't my thing." I lean against her doorway. "Why aren't you out there? You're usually the life of the party."

"I don't feel much like socializing tonight."

"Just tonight?"

She shrugs.

"Why did you drop everything and come back here?"

"What do you mean? Why wouldn't I come back *home*?"

I don't miss her emphasis on the word 'home.' "You ditched everything and everyone. When Natalie's life fell apart, her best friend was nowhere to be found."

"She had you. She was fine."

I walk into the room and close the door so we don't attract unwanted attention. "She was fine. Is that what you think?"

"I know she was grieving, but it wasn't like she was alone. You were there with her. She didn't need me."

"Cut the shit, Lana."

She jumps up from where she's sitting on her bed. "Everyone's always worried about poor Natalie. Her husband died. Oh wait, you stepped right in and warmed her bed. She had a baby. You took the place of her father. Natalie had everything," she yells. "Did it ever occur to anyone that maybe not all of us are as lucky as Natalie?"

"Lucky?" I spit the word back at her. "Losing your husband, the father of your unborn baby, is such great luck. Maybe it's best you left. What kind of fucking friend is jealous of a grieving widow?"

Lana looks like someone's punched her in the gut. "I'm sorry. I didn't mean what I said." She sits on the edge of her bed. "I was going through my own shit. I would've only made things worse for everyone."

"Look, I know we're not close, but I'm here, and I can listen."

"It's in the past. That's where I'd like to leave it."

"What about Brandon?" The guy is lost and confused.

"He's better off without me."

"I guess that's your answer for everything."

"Let it go, please, Viktor."

"As you wish." I turn and walk out of her room with no more answers than when I went in. Clearly, she's not okay, but I'm not going to beg. If she wants to put up walls and shut everyone out, that's her problem. I've got enough of my own.

Viktor

I have to speak to Max, but I didn't want to bother him too early today. The party went on well into the night.

When I get to his office, the door is open.

"May I come in?"

"Yes," Max answers and sets aside whatever he's working on. "Is everything okay?"

I sink into the leather chair across from his desk. "Kasimir said I'm fully recovered. I want to go back to work. I have a job to finish."

Max rests his elbows on his desk and steeples his fingers. "That is going to be a bit of a problem."

"Oh?" I raise an eyebrow.

"It seems your shot hit Saimir Hasani in the chest. You narrowly missed his heart."

Dammit, I thought I killed the guy.

"Hasani's clan is out for blood."

"I figured as much." I shrug. "I'm going back to finish the job."

"Like hell you are."

"I was paid for the job. I need to see it through."

"I already took care of Mr. Smith. His money was refunded."

"How did you get that information?"

"Dimitri got into your system." Max laughs. "Your tech skills are lacking."

"I have a reputation to protect. I have to go back—"

"You are not going back." Maxim slams his fist on his desk.

I've rarely witnessed Max lose his temper. Anytime he did, it was never good for the man on the receiving end.

"You have no idea the concessions I have made to guarantee your safety—to spare your life." He stands and rounds his desk. "Going off on your own was reckless and sloppy. You had no one to watch your back."

What he's saying makes sense, but even as he says it, I feel nothing. It would've been okay if they killed me. I have nobody to live for.

"Viktor." Max's raised voice startles me. "Did you hear me?"

"Yes. I screwed up."

"That is all you heard?"

I shrug.

"Hasani put a price on your head. The two weeks you were unconscious, I spent not only worrying if you would ever wake up, but I was also bargaining for life in case you did." Max crosses his arms across his broad chest. "Reluctantly, and for a large payout, Hasani handed over the girls. He agreed to stay out of trafficking and to let you live as long as I arranged for a safe channel to transfer weapons—a more lucrative venture of his."

"You shouldn't have done that. My life isn't worth it."

"Enough." Max slices his hand through the air. "I know losing Natalie was hard."

"Hard?" I let out a sarcastic laugh. "She and Rose were everything to me. And just like that, they were gone." I walk over to the wall of windows that overlooks the front of Maxim's property.

"Her rightful place is with Alex," Max softens his voice. "What happened to both you and Alex was an unimaginable tragedy. You put your heart on the line, and it was broken. But you must make peace with it to move forward."

I turn my back on Max and place my hand on the window. "Move forward?"

"I think you should talk to one of the therapists at Jelena's Hope."

"I don't think so."

"Viktor," Max says and moves to stand next to me. "You are not alone. There are people who care about you—including Natalia and Rose. Do you think she would not care if something happened to you? That it would not break her heart?"

I've been a selfish prick. I never stopped to think about how she'd feel. The only person I've considered in all this is me.

"I was there and saw you two together. After you were shot, she called every day to check on your condition. Natalia loves you. A part of her heart will always belong to you. She knows that, and so does Alex— and he accepts that. He misses your friendship." Max puts his hand on my shoulder. "Natalia is just starting to be okay. If something happened to you, it would be more than she could endure."

"I don't know how to do this." I drop my forehead to the glass. "Everyone I've ever loved is gone. I have no one left, Max. Why? Why does everyone I love leave?"

"Talk to one of our therapists. If you cannot do it for yourself, do it for Natalia and Rose. Once they clear you, we can discuss a new assignment—far away from Hasani."

"I promise I'll go once, but there are no guarantees after that."

Viktor

I'VE HAD SEVERAL SESSIONS WITH GRIGOR, ONE OF THE MALE therapists at Jelena's Hope. The first few sessions were uncomfortable. We spent most of our time staring at one another. I'm not big on talking about my feelings or getting all touchy-feely. Grigor didn't force me to speak, but he also wasn't going to let me off the hook. He kept scheduling the next session.

Eventually, I gave in. It wasn't much to start with, but Grigor was patient and allowed me to wade through the muddy waters at my own pace.

I guess it's helping. I didn't want to feel anymore. Numbness was easier. But little by little, the numbness I've been living with has been dissipating, giving way to the emotions I was afraid to feel.

We've explored them, one at a time. The abandonment I've struggled with since my parents' deaths. Losing babusya. And most importantly, losing Natalie and Rose. I still don't know that I agree with Grigor that *I'm* not the problem, but I no longer wish myself dead. I've taken a step back and realized the effect it would have on the people around me.

I'm leaving Grigor's office when I see Amelia sitting in the waiting room, playing on her phone.

"What are you doing here?"

"Dad got called back home on business. He asked me to wait and get a ride home with you?"

"Where's Irina?"

"She's out of town with Lana and Jessica, remember?" Amelia stands up. "Are you ready to go?"

"I came on my bike."

A few days after I woke up, I knew it was time to sell my apartment in Belgorod. I put it on the market and had my bike shipped up here.

"Oh." She looks around. "Dad told me you'd bring me home. He's in an important meeting and told me I could only leave with you."

Max might kill me for this. "Are you comfortable with riding on the back of my bike?"

"Sure." Her face lights up. "I think it'll be fun."

Fun. That's what I was thinking, too. My boss's eighteen-year-old daughter, who he's massively overprotective about, is riding on the back of my bike. Sounds like a recipe for disaster to me, but I can't leave her here.

She follows me outside, and I hand her my black leather jacket. "Put this on."

"It's kinda hot for this, don't you think?"

"The heat doesn't matter. It's to protect your arms." I really wish she had pants and proper shoes on instead of shorts and strappy sandals. "It's going to be big, but it'll suit its purpose." I hold the worn jacket up, and she slips her arms into it.

I grab the helmet while she fiddles with the sleeves.

"Put this on too."

"What are you going to wear?"

"I'll be fine."

I help her guide the helmet on and buckle it, making sure it's a snug fit.

"It's really heavy," she complains.

I flick the visor down. "But your head will stay intact if it comes in contact with the ground."

"You're as bad as my father." She giggles.

I ignore her comment and throw my leg over the bike. "Get on behind me."

She easily climbs on. It's an odd feeling. I've never had a girl on my bike.

"You don't need to do anything except hold onto my waist."

"I think I can manage that."

I start up the bike. The engine rumbles beneath us, and then we're on our way. I stick to the speed limit and take as many side roads as possible. The last thing I need is to injure the boss's daughter.

Twenty minutes later, we're pulling up in front of Max's home. Amelia jumps off the bike, pulling the helmet off. She's smiling from ear to ear.

"That was amazing. Can we do that again sometime?"

"I don't think—"

The front door flies open, and Maxim rushes out. "What the hell do you think you are doing?"

"What's wrong?" Amelia asks.

"What is wrong?" He motions to the bike. "What were you thinking putting her on your bike? She could have been killed."

Maxim's level of protectiveness, where his daughters are concerned, is borderline obsessive. If it were up to him, he'd lock them in a tower and never let them out.

"Amelia told me she needed a ride home. I took my bike to the center. There wasn't much choice." I take the helmet from her and help her out of my jacket. "I took every precaution. I would never let anything happen to her."

"It was so much fun, Dad." Amelia walks up the steps and kisses his cheek. "I want to do it again."

"No."

She rolls her eyes. "You worry too much."

"Amelia," Max says, softening his voice and putting his arm around her. "If anything were to happen to you."

She looks over her shoulder at me. "Viktor wouldn't let me get hurt."

"I know, sweetheart. I trust Viktor. It is everyone else I do not trust."

"What will you do in a few weeks when I'm in California?" She smiles.

"I'm working on that."

When Amelia first moved in with Max and Irina, she was timid, like a frightened kitten. She'd been through hell at the hands of Moreno and the other sick bastards in Mexico. Amelia was wary of most men, but she seemed most intimidated by Max. Most days, she spent glued to Irina's side.

Watching the two of them today is amusing. You'd never know there were ever any obstacles in their relationship. This little redhead isn't afraid to challenge her father. I don't know how he'll manage when she's halfway across the world.

"You only have two weeks left," she says in a sing-song voice as she walks into the house.

"Don't remind me," Max says too quietly for her to hear. Then, he looks at me. "We need to talk."

"Now?"

"Meet me in my office in fifteen minutes."

Maxim

I walk back into the house and head to my office. That child is going to be the death of me. If I thought Svetlana gave me a hard time, Amelia has her beat. At least Lana was interested in the lifestyle, and I was able to set up some protection for her.

But Amelia is very different. She's aware of the lifestyle Irina and I share. At first, she was confused and frightened. Amelia asked Irina to be included in one of her sessions because she feared Irina was being abused by me. Although her parents had a healthy relationship, once they passed away, all she experienced was dysfunctional foster homes and then the depravity of Moreno's men.

Irina attended several sessions alone with Amelia before I was asked to join. It was difficult for me to hear Amelia's fears, but given her experiences, I understood their root cause. With words, I reassured her of my love for Irina and her and Lana.

But it took time for her to observe that my words matched my actions. That no matter what, I would protect the three of them—even if that meant giving my life in exchange for theirs. Little by little, Amelia warmed up to me. Eventually, she allowed me the privilege of earning her trust. Today, no one would ever question my spunky red-headed daughter, and I ever struggled with our relationship.

Now, it is my turn to struggle. Amelia trusts me, and she tolerates my men. I trust every one of them with her life. However, I will not force her to be uncomfortable as she embarks on this new chapter in her life.

At the same time, I cannot allow her to go to California without security. I have too many enemies who would love to get at me through someone I love, and Viktor just added to the list with the Albanians. We have come to an agreement, but I do not trust them. Trust is something to be earned, and it does not come easy in this business.

There is a knock on my office door. Igor pops his head in. "Viktor's here."

"Send him in."

The door opens wider, allowing Viktor to enter my office.

"Have a seat."

He sits across from me, a wary look on his face.

"How are you feeling?" I ask.

"I'm doing better." He lifts his hand and moves his fingers. "There's still some occasional numbness, but Kasimir says that should eventually go away."

Viktor is a lucky man. The bullet missed his major organs by a fraction of an inch. If Dimitri had not attempted to stitch up the wound, he most likely would not have made it.

"I know you have been anxious to get back to work, but the situation with the Albanians has complicated things."

"I screwed up. I'm sorry. I—"

I hold up my hand, stopping him. "We have already taken care of that. I have found a job that will keep you off the Albanian's radar while allowing you to get back to work."

"Oh?" He tilts his head. "What is it?"

"You will be accompanying Amelia to California as her personal security?"

"I'll be what?"

"No other members of my team are suitable for this job because of her comfort level. You are the only one Amelia feels safe with."

"Why me?"

"Because Natalie trusts you, and Amelia trusts Natalie."

"Oh." Darkness shadows his face. "When are we leaving?"

"Two weeks."

Viktor

I LEAVE MAXIM'S OFFICE, MY WHOLE WORD FEELING OFF-kilter. I've been waiting for a new assignment, but being put on security detail for Amelia was not on my radar. My phone just alerted me that the email from Max with all the info about the city, school, and house he's already purchased has arrived.

I head out back to the patio so I can sit and look through everything he sent me while I try to wrap my head around my new assignment.

Amelia wanted to live in the dorm, but Max wouldn't hear of it because she couldn't have security there. So, instead, he bought a four-million-dollar beachfront property. I click on the link he sent me and pull up an extraordinary home that is right on the shores of Long Beach, California.

Facing the water are two-story arched windows ensuring a panoramic view from anywhere inside the house. Max assured me the windows have already been replaced with bulletproof glass—he leaves nothing to chance. The interior is a modern three-bedroom, three-bath home complete with a kitchen that would be any chef's dream. "You never do anything small, do you?" I say and laugh.

"I guess he told you," Amelia says as she walks over to me.

"He did."

"Can you even believe him?" She blows out a frustrated breath as she sits in the chair next to me. "I wanted to live on campus and be like any other incoming freshman, but no. Dad has to go and buy me an outrageously expensive beach house. I'm not trying to sound ungrateful. I just wanted to feel normal for once."

I'm caught in that proverbial spot—between a rock and a hard place. I understand Amelia's desire to be like every other student. No matter how much she wants that, she's Maxim Solonik's daughter, and that association comes with strings attached.

"Try to see it from his point of view," I say, putting my phone on the small table next to me. "Maxim and Irina lost their daughter. Even with all of his connections, he was still helpless to save her. And all that happened right here. You want to go to the other side of the world— alone."

"But I'd be on campus with everyone else."

"I know, but that doesn't guarantee your safety," I explain. "Your last name now ties you to Maxim and everything, good and bad, that comes with what he does. He sees that he almost lost you before he got the chance to even know you existed. He's not going to let anything go to chance now."

Amelia sighs.

"It won't be as bad as you think. I'll keep my distance so you can have your space."

She looks at me with expressive brown eyes, "I'm glad Dad chose you."

I'm not sure how to respond. I wanted to return to work, but I wasn't anticipating this kind of assignment. "Yeah. Me too."

Amelia

"Viktor's less than thrilled about going to California with me," I say to Natalie on our video call.

"He'll come around," she reassures me.

I hope she's right. Otherwise, it's going to be a long, uncomfortable four years.

"Are you all packed?"

"Yep." I look over at my suitcases, and my eyes fill with tears.

"What's wrong, honey?" Natalie asks.

"I don't know. I'm happy, sad, nervous—everything all at once." I swipe at the tears that are now wetting my face. "I want to go, but at the same time, I don't want to leave."

"I completely understand. I felt that way when I first left for school, too. But, once you get there and make friends, you'll have a great time."

"I hope you're right."

"I am. You'll see." She smiles. Rose starts crying in the background. "She's ready for her nap. I have to go, but call me when you get there and get settled."

"I will. Love you, Nat."

"Love you too, Amelia."

I didn't get any sleep last night. Instead, I tossed and turned both from anxiety and excitement. As the hours tick by slowly, I take the time to look back over the past few years of my life.

I'll never forget that day in school. I was summoned to the principal's office. He was sitting there with an older woman whose hair was pulled back in a tight bun, a stern look on her face.

"Amelia Parker?" she asked.

"Yes."

"Amelia, come sit down," Mr. Walker said.

"Ms. Parker, your parents were killed in a car accident earlier today," the woman said. "I understand you have no other family."

She looked at me expectantly, as if I was supposed to be able to answer her question after she'd spit out words that changed my entire life. I didn't speak that day or for several weeks to come.

I left the school with Miss. Imogene and was put in my first foster home. It was also my last foster home.

The first two weeks were okay. The Harrisons were an affluent family. They had one child, a son, Seth. He was eighteen. They were so happy to have a daughter. I had my own bedroom with a beautiful canopy bed. Mrs. Harrison brought me shopping and filled my closet with more clothes than I'd ever seen. They enrolled me in a prep school and saw to it that I was able to continue my piano lessons. They would never replace my parents, but I started feeling safe and talking again.

Then, one night after I was asleep, Seth came into my room—into my bed. He put his hand over my mouth to keep me from calling out, and then he put his hand down my pajama shorts. I tried to fight him. I scratched and clawed at him, but he held me down. He told me if I ever said a word, he'd tell everyone it was me who sneaked into his room. Me who came on to him.

So, one night, when Seth was out with his friends, I climbed out my bedroom window and started running. I never looked back.

Living on the streets was preferable to spending another night in the Harrison's home, or so I thought. Three nights later, I was tucked away between two buildings. I was so tired. I'd only closed my eyes for a few minutes when I felt strong arms wrap around me.

"Don't make a sound," he said. *"Or you'll regret it. Do you understand?"*

I nodded.

"You're going to walk with me like a good little girl, and we're going to get into my car."

He squeezed my arm and dragged me alongside him. Then, he opened the backdoor and shoved me in. There was another man in the backseat. He held up a syringe. I tried to move. Tried to get away, but it was no use. I felt a prick and then nothing.

The next time I opened my eyes, I was in hell.

I was at Moreno's for six months when Natalie got there. She kept promising that her boyfriend would get us out of there, but I didn't believe her. Nor did I ever think I'd have a family—a place where I belong.

But I do have it. I have a mom and dad and a big sister. The past two years of my life have been more than I ever thought possible. And today, I'm willingly walking away from it.

My door cracks open. "May I come in?" Lana asks.

"Sure." I sit up in bed.

"I had a suspicion you'd be awake."

I yawn. "I didn't sleep much last night."

She sits on the bed next to me. "I remember the night before I left for New York City. I didn't sleep a wink. I was scared to leave behind the only life I knew, but at the same time, I was excited to see what the future held for me."

"That's exactly how I feel."

"It's going to be a big adjustment. There were days I wanted to call Papa to bring me home."

"Why didn't you?"

"Alex." Lana smiles. "He forced me to go out, meet people, and explore the city."

"I don't have an 'Alex.'" My heart sinks. I don't want to end up calling Dad to come back home.

"You'll have Viktor. He'll make sure you're okay." Lana gives me a hug. "I'm going to miss my little sister, though."

"California's only a plane ride away." I smile.

Amelia

I'VE NEVER CARED ABOUT THE MONEY MY PARENTS HAVE. IN the whole scheme of life, it's irrelevant. But right now, I'm thankful for it. Saying goodbye is proving harder than I thought. I haven't been able to stop crying—which is why I'm grateful we're in a private hangar.

"I'm counting on you to take care of my little girl," Dad says to Viktor.

"You know I will."

Viktor's a tough read. He's large and imposing. That alone is enough to scare most people. But underneath his tough exterior, I know there's a tender man. I've seen the way he was with Natalie and Rose. He used to look so happy until Alex came back. Now he's so closed off. He doesn't talk much, and he rarely ever smiles. But I know he's safe. That's what I'm hanging onto. Otherwise, the knowledge that he's going to be my roommate, the only person I'll know, is unsettling.

"Oh honey," Mom comes over and wraps me in her arms. "I'm going to miss you so much."

"Me too, mom." I sniffle and swipe at the tears pouring down my face.

"Are you sure this is what you want to do?"

"I'm sure." I try to sound as brave as possible.

"We're only a phone call away," she says and hugs me tight.

Dad pulls Viktor off to the side. It looks like they're discussing something important, but they're too far away to hear what's being said. Their conversation ends with a handshake, and then Viktor walks up the steps into the jet. Dad remains off to the side. Mom and Lana are busy talking with the pilot, so I make my way over to him.

"Everything okay?" I ask as I sidle up to him.

Dad puts his arm around me. "Yes. Everything is okay."

Guilt washes over me. "Would you rather I stayed here? I can find a school—"

"My sweet daughter, I am excited for you but sad for me. I feel like we have just found you, and you are ready to spread your wings and fly so quickly." He places a kiss on top of my head. "I will never allow my reservations to hold you back. I want you to chase your dreams."

"When I was in Mexico, I knew my days were numbered. But you gave me a second chance," I say quietly. "Thank you for everything you've given me. I promise to make you proud of me."

"Amelia Solonik, I am already proud of you."

My tears start falling again as I wrap my arms around my father's neck. "I love you."

"*Ya lyublyu tebya malen'kaya ptichka.*"

Before I lose my nerve, I run up the steps to the plane.

It's only a few minutes until the door is closed and the plane's engine roars to life. I wave goodbye through the plane's tiny windows, and then we're taking off to start my new adventure.

Viktor

Amelia's sobbing as the plane's wheels lift from the ground, and we take flight.

"You okay, kid?"

"Mhm." She nods.

I'm lacking in the feelings department. With Natalie, everything came so naturally, but I don't know what to say to this girl. She cries until she's fast asleep. I unbuckle and grab a light blanket from the bedroom. Carefully, I lay her seat back, and she stirs. Her eyes flutter open.

"It's okay. It's just me. I have a blanket for you," I say quietly and put the blanket over her.

"Thank you," she whispers, then cuddles up with the blanket and falls back asleep.

I pop in my earbuds and settle in for the long flight.

The flight attendant comes into the room to let me know we're approaching JFK. We have to land to refuel. I'm hit with an onslaught of feelings when I look out the window and see the New York City skyline lighting up the night. There are so many memories of Natalie attached to this place—this city.

"Amelia." I gently shake her shoulder. "You need to put your safety belt back on. We're getting ready to land."

Amelia rubs her eyes. "Already?"

"Already? It's been eleven hours."

She shoots up in her seat. "Are you serious?" She leans over me to look out the window. "I've never landed here at night. Look at all those lights. It's incredible."

"It is. Now sit down and buckle up, please."

Amelia slides back into her seat and buckles her lap belt. "How long are we going to be here?"

"Just long enough to refuel."

"Oh."

"Why?"

"I was hoping maybe I could see Natalie while we're here."

My heart stops beating. "We won't make it there and back in time. But you can call her while we're on the ground."

"Okay." Her shoulders slump.

The wheels of the plane touch down, and we taxi to a stop.

"I'm getting off with the pilot. I need you to stay on here with the flight attendant, okay?" I don't want to be around while she's talking to Natalie.

"That's fine."

"Are you hungry?"

"Yes, very."

"Do you want me to have the flight attendant make us something from the plane, or would you prefer some fancy airport food?

"A greasy burger sounds delicious."

"I'll see what I can find for us. You better be right here when I get back," I warn.

Amelia

AMELIA

Open mouth, insert foot, Amelia. Why did I ask Viktor if we could visit Natalie? That was the world's dumbest question. Of course, he's not going to want to see her. It's only nine o'clock. She should still be awake. I pull out my phone to call her while Viktor's gone. I tap her contact and wait for her to pick up.

"Hello?" Natalie's voice comes through a second before the video connects.

"Hi. I hope it wasn't too late to call."

"Not at all. Where are you?"

"In New York. We had to land to refuel."

"I wish things were different. I'd love to see you before you leave."

"Me too."

We talk for a bit longer. Rose makes a brief appearance with Alex before he puts her to bed. She's getting so big. I didn't realize kids grew so quickly. I tell her all about the house Dad bought and how nervous I am to start school.

"I think I better go. Viktor's on his way back."

"Okay, honey. Have a safe rest of your trip, and we'll talk soon."

We hang up right as Viktor enters the plane. He holds up a bag of food.

"I come bearing gifts." He grins.

"That smells like a burger and fries."

"It is."

My stomach growls, and I laugh.

"Sounds like I'm just in time."

Viktor pulls out the food, and we start eating. We've never really spent a lot of time alone together, so there are long, awkward pauses in our conversation. If this is how things are going to be between us, our living situation isn't going to work.

"You look deep in thought," Viktor says.

"I am." I struggle to look into his eyes.

It's something that was forbidden when Moreno had me. My therapist at Jelena's Hope worked on it with me for a very long time. It still doesn't come naturally, but I can do it most of the time.

When I do meet his gaze, my breath catches. His eyes are the most beautiful shade of sapphire blue. I've never seen eyes like his. It's easy to get lost in their depths and the stories they look like they hold.

"Everything okay?" he asks.

"Oh, yeah, sorry," I stumble over my words. "I was just thinking we're about to be roommates, and we really don't know one another."

"I'm sure it'll be fine. You'll be busy with school and your friends."

"I'm not big on social things. I'll most likely be spending a lot of time at home. So, we need to get to know one another."

"How do you suggest we do that?" he asks.

"We can ask each other questions." As soon as the words leave my mouth, I realize how juvenile they sound. "Never mind, pretend you never heard that."

Viktor chuckles. "How about we just let it happen naturally?"

"That sounds like a better idea." I smile.

"Excuse me," the flight attendant says. "We're about to take off again."

"Thanks." Viktor nods, and she goes back into the staff area. "Are you ready to become a California girl?"

Viktor

It's close to four a.m. when we step off the jet at LAX and make our way into a private hangar where the dark grey Audi e-Tron Quattro Max purchased for us is waiting.

"Wow." Amelia runs her hand across the hood. "Dad never does anything halfway, does he?"

"Never." I laugh.

An employee unloads our luggage from the plane, and I get it all into the car. It's a tight fit. The car is gorgeous but not made for transporting a lot of stuff.

"Ready?" I ask Amelia.

"I think so."

I open her door, and she slides her petite frame into the car. Then I round the car and get behind the wheel.

Thankfully, the traffic isn't as heavy as I'm told it can get on the highways here, and we make it to our new house in a little over an hour. I turn onto our palm tree-lined driveway and pull the car into the garage under the house.

"Viktor?"

"What's up?"

"Before we go in, can we go to the beach and watch the sunrise?"

The night sky is already giving way to the twilight of the early morning.

"I think we can manage that."

She rewards me with a smile. We walk out the door that leads us outside and to the entrance of our private beach. Amelia freezes when the ocean comes into view. I stand next to her.

"I've never been to the beach," she says quietly without taking her eyes off the water.

"For real?"

She nods her head.

"Come on." I take her by the hand. "Let's go down to the water."

Amelia follows me onto the sandy beach. I stop, take off my shoes, and roll my pants up.

"Take your shoes off."

"Why?"

"So we can get in the water."

"I don't know about that," she says, eyes wide.

"Why not?"

"There's so much of it, and the waves are so big."

The waves today are actually relatively tame. Wait until she sees the sea during a storm.

"Do you trust me?"

"Yes," she says hesitantly.

"Take off your shoes. I won't let anything happen to you."

She slips off her sandals and follows me to the water's edge. The water is warm as the waves lap at our feet. We stand there for a few minutes and watch as the sun peeks over the horizon. The sky becomes a canvas of pinks and purples as a new day is born.

I take a few more steps into the water. "Come on over."

"I'm scared."

"I'll hold onto you." I reach my hands out.

It takes a minute, but she finally places her hands in mine and takes tentative steps closer. I take a few more steps backward, the water nearing my knees. My pants are soaked, but I don't care. It's fitting that the first thing Amelia experiences is the ocean.

My back is to the oncoming waves, so I'm not prepared when a bigger wave crashes around us. Amelia loses her footing. I grab her by the waist, but it's too late. She's soaked from head to toe. I freeze, not knowing how she's going to react.

When she stands back up, Amelia laughs. A sweet, pure laugh. I can't help but join her.

"I must look like a drowned rat."

"You look fine." I tuck a curly red lock of hair behind her ear. "Do you want to go closer to the shore?"

"No. This is fun."

I keep her close to me while we let the waves splash around us and the sun lights up the sky. Once the vibrant colors give way to bright blue, we make our way out of the water. Amelia grabs her shoes and her cell. "Selfie?" she asks.

"It's the least I can do for getting you all wet."

She holds the phone out for our picture, but she's too short to get the both of us in the shot.

"May I?"

She passes me the phone, and I snap a few pictures.

"Thank you."

"It was my pleasure." We begin walking back to the house. "Why don't you go inside and get dried off? I'll get our stuff."

Amelia

THE OCEAN IS ENORMOUS. I FELT SO SMALL AND insignificant standing at the water's edge. Then, Viktor wanted me to follow him in. I was so scared. But when he put his hands out and asked me to trust him, something drew me to him. There was no way I could resist.

I flip through the pictures he took of us. We're both sopping wet. I'm grinning from ear to ear while Viktor barely cracks a smile. I'll have to get these printed and framed—our first moments in California.

Carefully, I make my way through the house, trying not to get everything wet and sandy. I go into the first bedroom I find and head straight into the bathroom to take a shower.

After I'm sure I got all the sand out of my hair, I turn off the water and grab a fluffy blue towel. Mom and Dad made sure the house was not only fully furnished but had everything in it so we'd feel at home when we got here.

I peek out of the bathroom and find my suitcases on the bed. I'm happy because I didn't consider needing clean, dry clothes after my shower. After I dress and comb my hair, I go back into the main room. I don't see Viktor anywhere, but this house is pretty big. So, I decide to go exploring.

There's a massive kitchen with granite countertops and stainless-steel appliances. "I sure hope Viktor knows how to cook," I say, knowing cooking is not my strong suit. The kitchen opens to an expansive living room with a fireplace. But the part I'm drawn to is the windows. They open fully, joining the house to a balcony overlooking the ocean. I slide them open, and it's as though there are no barriers between inside and outside.

Then, I decide to check out all the other rooms. I find a half bath in the hallway. The next door is another bedroom. I come to one final door and open it. Viktor's standing in the room wearing only a towel.

"Oh my gosh, I'm so sorry," I say, turning away as quickly as possible.

"It's okay. I should've locked the door."

"I didn't hear you in here. I should've knocked."

"It's okay, Amelia."

I close the door and hurry back to my room, completely humiliated. I flop on the bed and grab my cell to call home.

"I've been waiting for you to call," Mom says.

"Sorry. We went down to the beach to watch the sunrise before we came inside."

"What did you think?"

"Oh, Mom. It was incredible. Let me text you the pictures." I take a second to attach the pictures to a text and hit send. "You should get them in a second."

"Look at the two of you. You're soaked." Mom laughs.

"I've never been to the ocean. Viktor brought me into the water. And, well, a wave got us."

"You never told us you never saw the ocean. We would've brought you."

"That's okay. I was there today, and it was amazing."

Mom and I talk for a while longer.

I have one week before classes officially start. Freshman orientation is in two days, so I'll get to see the campus in person since we only did a virtual tour. Then, I need to pick up my books.

"You have the credit card. Use it for whatever you want."

"Thank you. I'll pay you back as soon as I find a job."

"You'll do no such thing," Mom says. "And you don't need to worry about working while you're in school."

Max and Irina have been more than generous with me since I met them. I know they have more than enough, but I don't want to keep taking from them.

"I know that, but—"

"No buts. This is your time to experience everything you can. You'll go to work soon enough."

"Yes, ma'am."

"I love you and miss you already."

"Me too."

"Dad and I will come to visit you soon."

"Okay." I yawn. "I think I'm going to take a nap. My body doesn't know what time zone it's in."

"Talk to you soon, *moya malen'kaya ptichka*."

Amelia

"Are you ready?" Viktor calls me for the third time. "If we don't leave now, we're not going to get there on time."

But I still don't answer. I can't answer. I'm sitting on the floor of my bathroom, knees drawn to my chest. I'm nauseous. My heart is pounding, and I'm unable to move.

Viktor knocks on my door. "I'm coming in." I hear the bedroom door open. "Amelia?"

"I'm in here," I say quietly.

Viktor stands in the doorway. "What's wrong?"

"I can't go." Tears begin pouring down my face.

He sits next to me. "What's going on?"I drop my head onto my knees.

"Hey," he says softly.

Slowly, I lift my head, and he wipes the tears from my face.

"What's wrong?"

"I'm having—" I struggle to take a breath. "A panic attack."

"Look at me. Let's slow that breathing down."

He inhales slowly, and I try to follow him, but my breath catches on a sob.

"That's okay, you're going to be okay. Just keep watching me."

I follow his slow inhales and exhales as he helps me through the worst of it. It takes a few more breaths until the fear starts to subside.

"Talk to me," he says. "What has you so scared?"

"I don't like the unexpected. I don't know what's going to happen today when we get there." I let out a breath of air. "I can't go."

"It's orientation, right?"

I nod.

"I'm guessing they'll take you on a campus tour. Show you where everything is. See if you have questions."

"What if there's a lot of people?"

"There might be. But I'll be with you."

"You'll stay with me?"

"It's kinda my job." The corner of his mouth lifts to a half smile.

I put my head back on the wall. "Maybe this was all a mistake? Maybe I should go back home?"

"You aren't going back home until you at least give this school a try. If you go and hate it, we'll talk about returning to Russia." He stands up, then takes me by hand, pulling me up. Then, he turns me to face the mirror. "Do you see that young woman?"

I nod.

"You are Amelia Solonik. You are brave and strong. You are going to crush this today. And I'll be by your side for every second of it."

I spin around and wrap my arms around him. It takes a second, but then I feel his muscular arms around my body. "Thank you, Viktor."

"No problem, kid." He lets go. "Take a second and get yourself put back together, and then we're out of here."

"Okay."

He leaves me alone in the bathroom. I rinse my face off and touch up the small amount of makeup I was wearing. Then, with a final look at myself, I leave the safety of my bedroom and meet Viktor, who's waiting in the kitchen.

Viktor takes advantage of the 'sport' in the sports car and drives far too fast, but we make it just in time. A large group of students and parents are gathered outside the campus's main building.

It looks like Viktor and I are the last to arrive, and all heads turn our way as we approach.

"Can we go home?"

"No. You've got this."

A girl with long brown hair wearing a shirt with the school's shark logo on it approaches us. "Are you Amelia?"

"Yes. I'm sorry we're late."

"It's okay. We're just about to get started with the tour." She looks up at Viktor. "Is this your father?" she asks, uncertain.

"No." I giggle. "This is Viktor, my—" How do I tell them he's my bodyguard?

"I get it. Your boyfriend," she whispers conspiratorially.

"He's not—"

"It's all good. We can call him your rich uncle." She smiles and heads back to the front of the group, leaving me shaking my head.

"Hi, everyone. My name's Kinsley. I'll be your student representative." She turns to face the rest of the group. "Let's get our tour started. Follow me." She walks to the front and leads everyone into the Student Center Building.

"Do I have to start calling you Uncle Viktor now?" I whisper.

"Would you have rathered tell them I'm your father?" He tilts his head.

"Point well taken."

We stay toward the back of the group as Kinsley leads us around the campus. Most of my classes are in the designated music buildings, so I shouldn't have difficulty navigating around. The tour concludes back where we started, and once Kinsley's answered everyone's questions, the group disperses.

"Do you mind taking a walk to the bookstore so I can pick up my textbooks?"

"Sure."

"So, when I'm at class, where will you be?"

"I'll be in the building close to your classrooms. Everything's been prearranged with the Dean."

"Oh." Part of me is relieved knowing Viktor will be nearby. The other part of me feels like I'm going to stick out from the crowd. "What am I supposed to tell people, for real, when they ask who you are?"

"It's up to you. You can tell them the truth or that I'm a friend. Whichever is easier for you."

"Don't you think they'll wonder why my *friend* follows me around campus every day?"

"Just tell them I go here too."

Seeing how every girl we passed couldn't stop staring at him, I'm sure whatever story I go with will cause drama. They'll be catty and jealous, or they'll be after me to set them up with him. Either way, it doesn't much matter. Making friends doesn't come easy for me.

Friends tend to ask about your family and your past. There's not much I can say about my adoptive family, and my past is something I'd rather not talk about—it's too painful. But really, who'd want to be friends with a girl that's been trafficked and raped? No one. So, it's easier to go to school, keep my head down, do my work, and come home.

Looking at it now, I guess Dad knew better than me about not living on campus. I thought it was something I'd try, but being here today, surrounded by people, reminds me why I need that quiet space. Next time I call, I'll have to apologize for giving him a hard time.

Amelia

Today's the first day of class. To say I'm nervous is an understatement. I spent last night trying on every piece of clothing I brought with me, plus the ones I bought here. Viktor was a good sport. He stayed patient as I showed him each one, hoping to get his opinion on what I should wear. In the end, he wasn't much help. He told me everything looked pretty, which was sweet, but I still didn't have an outfit to wear. I ended up going to my room and video-calling Natalie and Lana to get their opinions. Finally, the three of us settled on a soft pink sundress and a pair of sandals.

I got up early to make sure I had enough time to do my hair and put on makeup.

"Amelia," Viktor calls from outside my room.

"Come on in." He opens the door but stays in the doorway. "I made breakfast. Come and eat."

The thought of trying to swallow food makes my stomach turn. "I'm not really hungry."

"Wrong answer." He smiles. "You need to have something in your stomach."

"Fine."

When I get to the kitchen, I see he's made one of my favorite breakfasts. When my parents were still alive, we had several avocado trees on our property. My mom used to make avocado toast for me. My favorite variation has tomatoes and balsamic vinegar, exactly like what's on the plate in front of me.

"How did you know?"

"I have my ways." He grins. "Now, sit and eat."

Viktor loads the dishwasher while I have breakfast. "Aren't you eating?"

"I had an omelet. I'm not much for avocado anything."

"But you've never tasted this."

"And I never will."

"Come on, just take one bite." I bring a piece of my toast over to him. "If you don't like it, you never have to eat it again."

He leans down and bites into the toast. I watch his face as he chews. "Well?"

"It wasn't bad."

"Told you so." I smile and take the last bite.

I go to grab my plate and glass to load the dishwasher.

"I've got it. Go finish getting ready."

I touch up my lipstick, and then, with a final spin in front of the mirror, I'm ready to go. I grab my backpack and search for Viktor, who I find on the balcony, watching the waves roll in.

Setting my backpack on the couch, I join him on the balcony. For a few minutes, neither of us speaks. I'm enjoying the feel of the warm breeze and the cadence of the waves. It's almost hypnotic.

"Are you ready to go?" he asks.

"As much as I hate to leave this." I motion out toward the water. "I have to get to class."

I go to grab my backpack, but Viktor gets to it first.

"You don't have to carry it. I'm perfectly capable."

"You'll be lugging it around all day. The least I can do is bring it to the car for you."

"This car looks like so much fun to drive."

"It's not bad." Viktor smiles. "Do you want to drive when we get off the highway?"

"I'd love to. But I don't know how."

"You don't have your license?"

I shake my head. In Russia, Dad never let me out alone. Either he drove or one of the security team did. There was no need for me to have a license.

"Do you want to learn?"

"I'd love to, but I don't think Dad would approve."

"Let me handle him."

Amelia

Somehow, we still manage to get to campus early enough to park and take a leisurely stroll to the music building. Mondays are going to be busy days. First up is my History of Music class. After that, I have my private piano lesson, and then I have a U.S. History course. Viktor walks me to my classroom. That's where my brave façade cracks and I panic.

"I want to go home," I say quietly.

Viktor takes my hand and leads me to a quiet corner in the hall. "Keep your eyes on me and slow your breathing down. Today's going to be the hardest—the first day always is. But I'll be right out here." He points to a bench in the hallway near the classroom. "You have your phone. Text me if you need anything."

I nod, afraid if I speak, the tears I'm holding back will fall.

We breathe together for a few more minutes until I feel my heart rate slow and my muscles relax.

"Are you okay now?"

"I think so."

"You're going to do great."

"I'll see you after class." I manage a small yet uncertain smile and walk back toward the classroom.

A tall, bronze-skinned guy walks up to the door at the same time as me. He pulls it open. "After you," he says.

"Thank you," I answer shyly.

After a quick scan of the classroom, I decide on a desk in the back corner. The guy follows me and takes the desk next to me.

"I'm Mateo," he says.

"Amelia."

"You're not from around here, are you?"

"Nope. I'm from Russia."

He tilts his head. "A Russian with an Australian accent?"

"It's a long story."

"Gotcha." He smiles. "Do you live on campus?"

"No."

Thankfully, the professor calls the class to order, and our conversation is interrupted.

The first half of class is spent reviewing the syllabus's significant points. Then, the professor moves right into his lecture. I'm thankful when class is over because my hand is already tired from taking so many notes. I slide my notebook into my backpack and walk to the door.

"What instrument do you play?"

"Piano. What about you?"

"Guitar."

Once I get into the hallway, I look around for Viktor and find him leaning against the wall a few doors down. I can tell the second he notices Mateo's nearness to me. He pushes off the wall and walks toward me.

"It was nice meeting you, but I have to be going."

"Catch ya later," Mateo says with a smile. Then, he heads down the hall in the opposite direction.

"And you thought you wouldn't make any friends."

"I'd hardly call him a friend. He sat next to me, and we chatted a little."

"Looked to me like he was very taken with you."

"You're crazy. Did anyone ever tell you that?" I laugh.

"Many times."

"I have to get to my piano lesson. I'll see you later."

Viktor

She's only been to one class, and already, she has a guy interested in her. Part of me wanted to rush over and tell him to back off—like Maxim would've done. But I can't do that. I need to give her space while keeping a close eye. Amelia deserves to spread her wings. To build some confidence in herself.

I watch as she disappears into the music room. There's a bench across from the door that allows me to see inside the classroom. I grab a seat and pull out my phone to keep busy while she has her lesson. I'm told she's excellent, but I've never heard her play. Max ordered a piano for the house. It's scheduled for delivery next week.

Amelia warms up with some scales. Then she moves to a classical piece I recognize immediately. I set my phone down to listen to her play "Waltz No. 2" by Dimitri Shostakovich.

The song sparks a memory from when I was a boy. Papa converted part of our home into a studio so Mama could continue dancing. I close my eyes and see Mama in a flowy white ballet dress as she twirls on her toes. Waltz No. 2 plays on the record player in the corner of the room. She looks like an angel.

Of all the classical pieces, Amelia's playing one that holds such vivid memories for me.

After she goes through that classical piece several times, she switches to a modern song. I recognize it right away, "Scars to Your Beautiful" by Alessia Cara. Then, she begins singing. Her voice, the lyrics. It's as if the song was written for her. I walk over to the door to watch her closer. Her eyes are closed. She's fully immersed in the moment, and she's drawn me right into it with her.

Until the same boy from early comes up next to me and looks through the window.

"Wow," he says. "She's really good."

"Yes, she is." I return to my spot on the bench, and he sits beside me.

"Do you know her?"

"I do."

"Are you two *together*?" he asks cautiously.

"That's for her to tell you. If she chooses."

He nods and goes back to listening. After Amelia's lesson, she opens the door and steps into the hallway. Shock registers on her face when she sees the two of us sitting on the bench.

The boy pops up as soon as he sees her. "You sing and play perfectly."

"Thank you." Her cheeks turn pink. "What's going on here?"

"I don't know about him." The boy waves his thumb in my direction. "But I have a guitar lesson."

"Viktor, this is Mateo. Mateo, this is my friend, Viktor." Amelia introduces us.

"Good to meet you," Mateo says and reaches his hand out to me.

I stand but don't reciprocate the gesture. "Nice to meet you."

Mateo turns back to Amelia. "A few friends and I have a band. We're looking for a new keyboard player. Do you think you might be interested?"

Amelia glances over her shoulder at me. I shrug. This is up to her.

"I might be."

"What's your cell number? I'll text you the information." Amelia relays her number, and Mateo puts it into his contact. Her phone dings a second later. "Now you have my info, too."

"Thanks."

"I gotta run. I'll send everything after my lesson." With that, he disappears into the classroom.

"What do you make of that?" she asks. "I don't know that I'm good enough to play in a band."

"What are you talking about? You're amazing."

The sound of Mateo playing his guitar comes from the music room. Part of me hoped he was no good, so she wouldn't be interested in his band. But unfortunately for me, the kid is talented.

I won't mention this little development to Maxim until I'm sure it's a definite. Something tells me he'll lose it if he hears his daughter wants to play in a band.

Amelia

I'M FINISHING UP MY LAST CLASS OF THE DAY. SO FAR, THE music classes seem pretty easy. That's only because of the music education Maxim allowed me to pursue. It's given me an advantage over many other students, but I'm sure we'll all end up on an even playing field shortly. The U.S. History course, though, will take some extra studying.

When I get out of class, I look for Viktor and find him waiting at the end of the hall. It looks like he's just ending a phone call. He slides his cell into his pocket, his back to me.

"Ready to go?" I come up behind him and poke him in the sides.

Viktor spins around like he's ready to attack. "Shit, Amelia. Don't do that."

His reaction startles me, and the smile falls from my face. "I'm sorry."

He softens his features. "It's okay. I'm just not used to that." He reaches out and slides my backpack down my arm. "I'll take this. Your shoulder must be sore from carrying it around all day."

"It is a bit heavy."

We get back into the car and head toward home. The traffic's quite a bit heavier than this morning. These commutes back and forth are going to get old really quickly. Viktor's patient and doesn't seem bothered by it. But I'm thankful that some of my classes are remote, so we don't have to do this every day.

"I got the information you'll need to get your driver's permit."

"You did?"

The school needs to verify my student status with the state. Once that's done, I can apply for my permit online.

"I made an appointment to take care of the paperwork Wednesday between your classes. I hope that's okay."

"That's perfect. Thank you so much." I can't help the smile that spreads across my face. "Wait until I tell my parents about the band and learning to drive."

"Can we hold off on that for a little while?"

I laugh. "Don't want Dad to freak out and show up here tomorrow?"

"Exactly."

"I can live with that."

Viktor takes an unfamiliar exit off the freeway.

"Is this a different way to get home?" Maybe he's trying to avoid some of the traffic.

"I planned a little surprise for us." He glances at me. "Is that okay?"

The familiar feelings of panic start to rise, but I take a few slow breaths to keep them at bay. "Surprises aren't my favorite. But I'm safe with you." I say those words out loud more for myself than for Viktor.

"I can tell you where we're going if it's easier."

"No," I say quickly. "I can do this."

"If it gets to be too much, just say the word. I want this to be fun, not scary."

I wring my fingers in my lap, trying to quell the nerves that are causing butterflies in my stomach. Before too long, we're pulling into a parking spot at a marina.

"Have you ever been on a boat?"

"Nope."

"Good." Viktor smiles. "It'll be another first."

We get out, and I follow him toward a large yacht where a man is waiting.

"Viktor?" the man asks when we get closer.

"Yes, sir." They shake hands. "And this is Amelia."

"It's a pleasure to meet you, Amelia. I'm Gus, and this is *Serendipity*." He motions to the yacht behind him.

"She's beautiful."

"Are you two ready to go?"

"We are." Viktor smiles proudly.

Gus steps into the boat, followed by Viktor, who turns and offers me his hand. Cautiously, I step from the dock into the boat. A few minutes later, we're moving slowly as the captain maneuvers us out of the marina and into the open water.

"Come with me," Viktor says, leading me to what he explains is the aft, where a table is set for two.

"What's this?"

"We're going to be having dinner in a bit. To celebrate the big move and your starting school."

My heart melts into a puddle. I've never had a man treat me so kindly. We stand by the rail and look out over the water.

"Look. There's a dolphin."

It turns out to be more than one dolphin. A large pod of dolphins is swimming and playing in the boat's wake. Several of them jump out of the water, making a big splash.

I reach into my pocket to grab my phone to take a video. "I left my phone in my backpack. In the car."

"I don't have mine either. We'll have to do this again to get pictures."

I'm disappointed that I won't have any videos or pictures from this trip. But that quickly dissipates, and we live in the moment instead. The dolphins continue their private water show for several minutes before they swim away.

"Have you ever seen dolphins before?"

"I haven't," he says.

"Good. It was a first for us both." My stomach tingles with excitement, knowing we shared a first.

We're both watching each other, saying nothing when a server opens a door, breaking whatever spell we were just under. He sets two glasses of sparkling water on the table.

"Dinner will be served in a few minutes," he informs us and disappears behind the same door.

"Shall we?" Viktor asks and pulls out a chair for me.

Dinner is served over several relaxed courses, starting with a Caesar salad and then a small cup of clam chowder. The main dish, lobster tails, is served just as the sun is beginning to set.

It looks as if the ocean is swallowing the sun. The sky has turned from a beautiful bright blue to a canvas of bright purples, pinks, yellows, and oranges. It's truly breathtaking. I don't want to take my eyes off it, but I also don't want this delicious food to go to waste.

The last course is a refreshing sorbet with a side of fresh fruit.

By the time we finish eating, the sky's dark and is filled with millions of twinkling stars. I go back to the rail and look up at the night sky. When I turn around, Viktor's watching me from the table.

"Thank you, Viktor. This was amazing." He's made me feel like the most special girl in the world. I know this wasn't a *real* date, but a girl can pretend, right?

"It was nothing."

"It wasn't nothing to me."

"Well, you're very welcome."

While the boat continues to sail, we sit in an oversized lounger. The air is getting chilly, and I shiver.

"Are you cold?"

"A little bit."

"I should've brought a sweater for you. Come sit close." He puts his arm around me to keep me warm.

I feel safe and protected.

And like I'm falling for a man I shouldn't be falling for.

Viktor

I fought Max on this assignment. Coming to California with Amelia wasn't on my radar as far as a job and was the last thing I wanted to do. But I'm glad he persisted. It's been good for me to keep busy—to think about someone other than myself.

Amelia's not your typical eighteen-year-old. She's a hard worker and takes her schoolwork very seriously. She spends hours each day practicing the piano, something that's quickly become one of my favorite times of the day. She's also a lot of fun to be around. Turns out we make pretty good roommates.

I never attended college. Didn't have a reason to. Once I graduated, I never wanted to sit in a classroom again. Sitting in the hallway isn't much better. It can get pretty boring, but it does give me the opportunity to find fun things for Amelia and me to do. Since we're both new here, I try to plan one night a week where we explore the area.

Of all her school days, my favorites are the days she has piano lessons. Today, she's working on a piece I don't recognize. I enjoy the quiet and listening to her play when Mateo appears and sits next to me.

"Hey, Viktor. What's up?"

"I'm listening to Amelia practice her recital piece."

"She's amazing, isn't she," he says with starry eyes.

I stare at him without answering until he takes his attention off Amelia and back to me.

"I'd like to ask Amelia on a date. My sister's getting married. It's going to be an upscale event at the country club my parents belong to," he says without taking a breath.

"Okay."

"Does that mean you'd have to tag along?"

"What do you mean?"

He looks to the door and back to me. "Amelia told me you're her bodyguard or something. Said her dad's really overprotective."

"You could say that."

"So, if I took her on a date, does that mean you'd have to come too?"

"Yes."

"I don't know how I'd explain to my parents that my girlfriend and her bodyguard are coming?"

What's this kid talking about? To my knowledge, and I make sure to be aware of everything, Amelia has not consented to be this boy's anything.

"Your girlfriend?" I ask and raise an eyebrow.

"Well, I'm hoping she will be."

"Let's see what she says before you start calling her your girlfriend."

"Okay." Mateo takes a deep breath. "That was awkward."

I force myself not to laugh. If he thinks that was bad, he hasn't seen anything yet.

The door opens, and Amelia walks out. She catches my eye, and a smile graces her face.

Mateo walks between us and over to her. "I wanted to talk to you."

"What's up?"

He looks back at me. "Can we go over there and talk alone?"

"We're good here," she says. She's still timid around other people, especially guys.

"Okay. Well, I wanted to ask if you'd be my date for my sister's wedding next weekend?"

"Oh." She looks surprised.

"It's going to be a fancy thing, so you'd get to dress up and all that girly stuff."

"I'm not sure," she says and looks at me. "Can I think about it and let you know?"

"Yeah, sure. It's no big deal if you can't make it." Mateo acts unphased by her lack of enthusiasm.

"I'll text you later." She walks over to me. "Ready to go?"

I feel bad for the kid. He's left standing there, defeated, as we walk away. He has no idea about the issues Amelia struggles with. She doesn't say much on our walk to the car. It isn't until we're halfway home that she finally speaks.

"That was unexpected."

"A bit."

"What do you think I should do?"

"That's up to you." I am not the one to be giving dating advice. "Maybe you should call Lana or Natalie?"

"Maybe." She turns and looks out the window. "Do you think he's safe?" she asks quietly.

She doesn't know I've done a little research on Mateo. His father, Everett Hart, is a big-shot attorney to the stars in Los Angeles. His mother, Willa Hart, is a stay-at-home wife and socialite. He has one sister, Summer Hart, an aspiring actress who is poised to marry Christopher Darby III, a partner in Mr. Hart's law firm. Their background checks have come back clean. Mateo doesn't pose any known threat to Amelia.

"I think he's as safe as any other twenty-year-old guy."

"How do you know how old he is?"

"It's my job."

"You did a background check on him?" she asks, shocked.

"Yes."

She puts her head back on the car seat. "Please tell me you didn't call Dad."

"I didn't call him yet."

"Please don't say anything to him until I decide what I'm going to do.

Amelia

WHEN WE GET HOME, I HEAD TO MY ROOM TO MAKE A PHONE call. But not to who Viktor suggested. I love Lana, but we don't talk about guys. She doesn't know much about just regular dating, and I'm not interested in the lifestyle she lives. And I am not calling Mom. She'll give me great advice, but she doesn't keep anything from dad.

"Hi, sweetheart. You must be a mind reader." Natalie giggles.

"Oh?"

"I was going to call you this weekend. I have something to tell you."

"Really?" Sometimes, I worry I'm a bother to her, so hearing that she was going to call me makes me smile.

"Really. How's everything on the West Coast?"

"I guess it's okay."

"Just okay?" Natalie asks. "Is something wrong?"

"Not exactly. But don't worry about that. What did you want to tell me?"

"Nope, you first. What's going on?"

"Well, there's a guy, and I like him a lot."

"Oh my gosh, I'm so happy for you. Tell me all about him."

"He's gorgeous. Like not just good-looking, mouthwateringly gorgeous." We both laugh.

"Has Viktor checked him out?"

"He's been checked out. I'm safe with him." I mean, it's true.

"So far, so good."

"Most importantly, he's thoughtful and nice to me. He's always doing special things for me."

"That all sounds good."

"There's a problem, though."

"What is it?"

"I don't think he sees me as anything other than a friend." I sigh.

"I see," Natalie says. "The best relationships often start out as friendships."

"But how can I make it so we're more than just friends?"

"There's no real answer to that, sweetheart. The best thing you can do is continue to be friends. Keep getting to know one another, and don't try to force anything. If it's meant to be, it'll develop into more." She pauses. "You're in a new place with lots of different guys. If this guy is just a friend right now, don't be afraid to try going on some other dates. If he's really interested in you, he'll step up, and if not, maybe you meet the right one in the process."

"Yeah." That wasn't the advice I was hoping she'd give me.

"Just make sure Viktor checks everyone out first, please."

"I will. Now, what did you want to tell me?"

"I'm pregnant," Natalie squeals.

"Oh my gosh. Congratulations." My excitement threatens to bubble over. "Do you know if it's a boy or a girl? When are you due?"

"We just found out the other day. So far, only you and Lana know. And Alex, of course." Natalie says. "So, please don't tell anyone yet."

"I promise."

Finding out I'm going to be an aunt again distracts me from my problems.

"Is Rose excited?"

"We didn't tell her yet. I think she's a little too young to understand."

"She's going to be the perfect big sister."

Natalie and I talk about everything, baby. They're running out of room in their current apartment and are considering buying something roomier—whether or not to leave the city is a big consideration for them. When I look at the clock, I realize we've been on the phone for an hour.

"I should get going. I have a paper to write."

"It was wonderful to hear from you. Make sure you call me and keep me updated on this guy."

"I will. Can you not mention any of this to Lana and my parents? I'm not ready to tell them yet."

After we finish our goodbyes, I flop back on my bed. What answer do I give Mateo about the wedding? Viktor thoroughly checked him out, and he's safe, but Mateo isn't the one I want to be with. I think about what Natalie said. If I agree to go out with him, Viktor might get jealous and make a move. If not, at least I'll be having some fun with a nice guy.

Me: Is the offer still open to be your date for the wedding?

Mateo: It is, yes.

Me: I'd love to go

Mateo: Great. I'll pick you up at five on Friday. BTW- where do you live?

I don't know if I'm supposed to give that information out, so I go in search of Viktor. He's not in any of the main rooms, so I knock on his bedroom door.

"Come in."

I open the door and step into the doorway. "I told Mateo I'll go to the wedding with him next weekend. He wants to pick me up. Can I give him our address?"

"No. Find out where the wedding is, and I'll drive you."

"Can't we meet somewhere so he can take me himself?"

"No."

"You're as bad as my father, you know that?" I slam the door and go back to my room.

Me: I'm going to have to meet you there.

Mateo: Okay.

I can't believe I'm going on my very first date. I'm equally excited as I am nervous. My next problem is that I have nothing to wear. Viktor's going to have to take me shopping.

Viktor

AMELIA'S LAST CLASS OF THE DAY WILL BE OVER IN A FEW minutes. Then we're going shopping for a dress for the wedding. I've been holding off on telling Max about this Mateo kid. I was hoping he'd go away, but he isn't. I don't know what to do. Alex and I have been keeping in touch. He's pretty grounded and was Svetlana's keeper for a while. He'll know how to deal with this.

Me: I have a problem.

Alex: What's going on?

Me: Amelia has a date. I checked the guy out, and he's fine. But I haven't told Max. What do I do?

Alex: That is a dilemma. I'm going to suggest not telling him yet. You can let him in on it if it turns into more. There's no reason to alert him if it's just a one-time thing.

Me: Thanks. That helps.

Alex: There's something I need to talk to you about as well. Do you have a minute for a phone call?

Me: Sure.

What could be going on that Alex needs to talk to me? I walk to the end of the hall and find a quiet place. My phone vibrates.

"Hey."

"How's the West Coast treating you?"

"I got used to beach living very quickly." I chuckle. "How's Jelena's Hope NYC going?"

"Unfortunately, we keep busy. Somedays, it feels like a losing battle, but we'll keep up the fight as long as we need to."

"You're doing a good thing there, brother."

"Things aren't the same here without you."

"Yeah, well."

"There's something I need to tell you. I wanted you to hear it from me instead of someone else."

"Is everything ok?"

"It is." Alex pauses. "Natalie's pregnant."

I don't know what I expected Alex to say, but that wasn't it. I grab the wall for support while I let the news settle. This shouldn't surprise me. Natalie's a natural mom, and they're married. Of course, they'd want to extend their family. But in the world I used to live in, the one where Natalie and I were together, she'd be having my baby. This news puts things into a much different perspective. Natalie's moved on. I need to do the same.

"Congratulations. I'm happy for both of you."

"Thanks, Viktor. I really do appreciate it."

The classroom doors open, and students start filing out.

"I have to run. Amelia's getting out of class now."

"We'll talk soon."

I used the skills I learned in therapy. I felt the emotion and honored it for what it was. Now, I'm placing it in a neat box and putting it away. Life is moving on.

"Are you ready to go shopping?" Amelia's beaming.

"I can't wait." I laugh.

We find the boutique that was recommended to Amelia by another girl in her class. The sales lady, who introduced herself as Caroline, placed me in a cushiony chair outside the fitting rooms and instructed me to wait there. Then, she and Amelia disappear into the shop. When they return, Caroline has an armful of dresses.

"Time to try them on." She hasn't stopped smiling since we got here.

A few minutes later, Amelia comes out wearing a pink dress with puffy sleeves.

"What do you think?" she asks.

I glance up. "It looks fine."

She looks in the mirror, examining herself from all angles. "Nope. I don't like it."

She repeats the process with several more dresses. They all look the same to me, but she doesn't seem to like them.

"Last one," she says when she steps out of the changing area. "What do you think?"

I start to say it looks fine like all the dresses before, but when I look up, I'm speechless. Amelia's wearing a black off-the-shoulder dress that stops just above her knees. The dress hugs her curves. She looks grown-up and absolutely stunning, which is why she's not wearing this dress. "I don't like it. I think you should go with the first one."

"The pink one? Are you kidding?" She spins slowly in front of the mirror. "This is definitely the one."

I walk over and stand behind her, looking at her reflection in the mirror. "It makes you look far too grown-up. No."

She turns to face me, hands on her hips. Her ginger temper is about to make an appearance. "I'm not a child, Viktor. This dress fits perfectly." She runs her hands down her sides. "I'll be right back." She goes back into the changing area, where I'm hoping she removes the dress and puts something less—adult on.

When she comes back, she has her phone in her hand. She snaps a few pictures in front of the mirrors and attaches them to a text.

"Who are you texting?"

"Natalie. Why?"

Good. Natalie's sensible. She'll tell Amelia this isn't the right dress.

It feels like hours before Amelia's phone dings. She reads the text and smiles before turning the screen to face me.

Natalie: That's the one. It looks hot. You're going to have that guy eating out of the palm of your hand. (you won't be "just friends" anymore)

Great. Natalie's encouraging her. I don't stand a chance with the two of them on the same side.

"See. She thinks it's perfect."

"Whatever." I return to my spot on the chair.

Amelia rolls her eyes and goes back into the dressing room. When she comes back out, she's in her clothes. Caroline's carrying the dress.

"I need to grab a pair of shoes, and then I'll be ready to go."

Amelia

I skipped classes today to get my hair and nails done. Thankfully, Viktor didn't follow me into the salon. We need some space from each other. He's been in a mood all day. It's been nice to be alone and get pampered. My fingers and toes are painted a deep red, and the stylist is finishing my hair.

He hands me a mirror. "What do you think?"

Somehow, he worked magic with my unruly curls. The length of my hair is done in a French braid that's now elegantly pinned up in the back. Some of my corkscrew curls are hanging loosely, framing my face.

"It's beyond my expectations. Thank you so much."

"It was a pleasure, honey. I hope you have a terrific time on your date tonight."

After I finish paying, I leave the serenity of the salon and cross the sidewalk where Viktor's waiting by the car. I don't even bother to ask him what he thinks because I'll only get an unenthused *it's fine*.

Since there's already tension between us, I may as well tell him the rest of my news. It can't make things much worse.

"I told Mateo I'd join the band."

"What?" Viktor looks over at me. "You didn't even audition."

"He made a recording in the sound booth at school. The guys loved it."

"I see." Viktor narrows his eyes and grips the steering wheel tighter.

"I'll have rehearsal a few days a week, and they're booked every Friday and Saturday with different gigs."

"I need a list of all the venues."

"Why?"

"I have to check each one and make a decision on whether you can go."

"Wait a minute. You're here as security, not my father. I'm not asking for your permission."

"We're not having this argument while I'm driving."

"Fine." I turn to look out the window.

"Fine."

The rest of the drive is silent and tense. When he pulls into the garage, I don't wait for him to turn the car off before I grab my dress and get out. He follows on my heels.

"Amelia, wait."

"I can't. I have to get ready."

Viktor

I DON'T LIKE THIS TENSION AND FIGHTING BETWEEN AMELIA and me. I wish she'd realize I'm only doing my job. It's my responsibility to keep her safe, but I can't do that if she doesn't tell me what's going on.

So, it's a good thing that when I sent Mateo a text, he readily gave me their list of venues. We agreed it was best not to tell Amelia. He's a good kid and wants to make sure she's not only safe but feels like a normal person.

"Viktor," Amelia says quietly. "Can you help me with the zipper?"

She's nervous. I can see it written all over her face. I need to get over myself and make sure she stays calm so she can enjoy her date. I make my way across the room to her. "Turn around." My hands shake as I slowly slide the delicate zipper up her back. "There, all done."

She turns around to face me. "Do I look okay?"

She's breathtaking. My body responds at the sight of her. "You look very pretty," I say and walk away quickly so she doesn't see my arousal.

I don't know why I'm reacting this way to her. All I know is my body better cut the shit. She's not only eighteen, but she's also my boss's daughter—she's totally off-limits.

"Viktor." She comes up behind me, placing her hand on my arm.

"Can we please stop fighting? I don't like us being upset with each other."

"I agree." I turn around now that my dick is back under control. "Are you ready to go? I'm sure we'll hit traffic, and I don't want you to be late."

Mateo's waiting outside when we arrive at the country club. He's one of the groomsmen and is sporting a tux. The kid cleans up pretty well. I leave the keys in the car for the valet to park and make sure to get to Amelia's door before Mateo. Offering her my hand, I help her out.

"Thank you."

"Of course."

Mateo walks over. "Wow. You look hot."

I glare at him, but he doesn't seem to notice. He hasn't taken his eyes off Amelia.

"We need to go out to the garden. The ceremony will be starting in a few minutes."

He offers Amelia his arm and leads her to the wedding venue. I'm caught off guard by my feelings as I watch her walk away with him. You can't think those things, Viktor. She's not yours. She's allowed to date whomever she chooses. I silently repeat that, hoping it quells the jealousy that's stirring inside.

I leave a respectable distance, but I don't stray too far—Amelia is never out of my sight. It looks like she's having a great time. I don't think she's stopped smiling all evening. Finally, the DJ announces he's playing the last song. It's a slow dance. Mateo stepped away a few minutes ago, leaving Amelia at the table alone.

I'm just about to step in and ask her to dance when Mateo appears. He leads her to the dance floor. This time, he pulls her close to him. I see her tense up, but she doesn't pull away.

Then, he slides his hand down her back. She grabs his arm right before his hand lands on her ass. I can see her telling him something.

Lucky for him, he readjusts his hold. My nerves are on a hairpin trigger. It wouldn't take much for me to rush in there and whisk her away if he doesn't respect her.

The song finishes, and the wedding guests slowly begin to disperse. I shoot Amelia a quick text telling her I'm going out to get the car and I'll meet her there. I give the valet our ticket and wait for him to pull the car around. It only takes a few minutes, and Amelia and Mateo still haven't come out. Do I go in and get her? And embarrass her? I can't do that to her, so I get in the car and wait.

Although I have my phone out, I'm not looking at the screen. Instead, I'm watching as Mateo and Amelia finally make their way outside. He leads her off the path to a dimly lit area. When I see him leaning in to kiss her, I set my phone aside, ready to intervene at any second.

Amelia

Mateo's family is lovely. They made me feel welcome, and I had a wonderful time. But now the wedding's come to an end. Viktor lets me know he'll be waiting in the car. Mateo takes me around so I can say goodbye and wish the new couple my congratulations before he walks me out the front doors. I think he's taking me to the car, but then he tugs my hand and leads me to a darker area off to the side.

My heart begins pounding as panic sets in. Why do I keep feeling this way? Mateo leans in, his lips pressing against mine. Breathing's getting harder. He pulls me closer and uses his tongue to part my lips. I can't take it anymore, and I put my hands on his chest to push him away.

"What's wrong?".

"I can't do this."

"It's just a kiss." He seems genuinely confused.

"Mateo, my history's complicated."

"Is that why you have a bodyguard? Has a guy hurt you?"

"Yeah." That's a mild way of putting it. "I need things to go slow. I get it if that's not what you want."

"I can go as slow as you need. The last thing I ever want to do is scare you."

I study his face to see if I can detect any crack in his demeanor. Any sign that he's lying, but I find nothing. Then, I glance over my shoulder at the car and find Viktor watching us intently.

My heart's torn. Mateo's a nice guy. He's closer to my age. But he doesn't make me feel like I do when I'm with Viktor.

"I really should get going."

"I'd like to take you out again," Mateo says.

I'm not sure how to answer him.

"You don't have to give me an answer right now."

"Can I think about it?"

We walk in silence until we get to the car. "You'll be at band practice tomorrow, right?"

"I wouldn't miss it for anything." Then I do something Viktor told me not to do. "I'll text you my address so you can pick me up."

Mateo's face lights up. "Will Viktor be okay with that?"

"Probably not, but I'll take care of it."

Mateo opens the car door for me. "Goodnight, Amelia." He kisses my cheek.

"Thank you for a wonderful evening." I slide into the car, and Mateo shuts the door.

He gives a small wave as we pull away.

Amelia

Mateo will be here in less than twenty minutes to pick me up for band practice. But I still haven't figured out how to tell Viktor. I'm pacing back and forth in my room, trying to find the words, when the doorbell rings.

"Oh no." He's early.

I rush out of my room, but Viktor's already answering the door.

"Hi. Is Amelia ready?"

"What are you doing here?"

"Amelia told me I could pick her up. We have band practice."

"She did, did she?" Viktor stands with his hand on the door, blocking Mateo from coming in.

"Hey Mateo," I chirp. "Come on in."

Viktor steps aside and gives me a look, letting me know we will be discussing this when we're alone. "You didn't tell me you were going out today."

"I was just about to." I shrug. "The band doesn't have a show tonight, so we're getting together for practice instead."

"And where is this practice happening?"

"It's at Quincy's house." Mateo jumps into the conversation. "Tristan's in the car waiting for us."

"You brought someone else here?" Viktor raises his voice.

"Um, yeah. Tristan doesn't have a car. I always pick him up on the way to practice."

"I'll be okay, Viktor. You can follow behind us," I say quietly.

There's fire in Viktor's eyes as he grabs the keys but doesn't say a word to me.

"We good?" Mateo asks.

"Sure." I smile nervously and grab his arm. "Let's go."

Viktor

T HIS GIRL'S GOING TO BE THE DEATH OF ME. I SPECIFICALLY told her not to give out our address, but did she listen? Of course not. She did it anyway. Now, Mateo knows where we live, and so does his buddy. I don't think Amelia fully understands how many enemies Maxim has and the lengths they'll go to bring him to his knees.

And right now, tensions are high between Maxim and some of his new associates. Yes, I'm responsible for that, making giving our address even riskier. I don't trust the Albanians. Maxim made a deal with them, but that doesn't mean they've forgotten my transgressions. If they see an easy way to take me out, they'll take it.

I'm fuming as I follow Mateo's car to a house in what looks to be another affluent neighborhood a few towns over. He drives to the front of the house, and I pull in behind him.

"Is he coming too?" Tristan asks.

"They're a package deal," Mateo says.

"That must be fun when you two are—" The guy makes a lewd gesture, and I step forward, ready to punch him in the face. Talking about Amelia like that is unacceptable.

"Knock it off, Tris." Mateo elbows his friend.

Amelia looks uncomfortable but doesn't say anything.

"Come on, Viktor," Mateo says. "Practice is inside."

I follow the trio into the house. We walk down a long hall to another door and down a flight of steps.

"Quincy's parents converted this whole level into a studio for us."

That seems like a big commitment for a garage band.

"Amelia, this is Sparrow and Grayson." Mateo introduces her to the other members of the band.

"Nice to meet you both."

"You come highly recommended by Mateo here," Sparrow says.

"I hope I live up to whatever he's told you about me."

"So far, so good," Grayson adds.

Amelia tenses once again. I don't know if she's ready for this. She was doing great in Russia, but moving here brought back the panic attacks she used to suffer from. She has virtual sessions with her therapist at Jelena's Hope. It's helped. She's much more comfortable at school and at home. But being with four guys, three of whom are strangers, is a big stretch for her.

"Viktor, you can sit over there," Mateo points to a sitting area and then turns back to the group, "Let's warm up with "Two Steps Behind." You good with that one, Amelia?"

"Yep." She gets behind the keyboard, and I grab a seat off to the side.

I don't know what I expected, but this band is good. Like really good. And Amelia fits in as though she's played with them for years.

Gone is the tension from just moments before. Amelia's in her element. She looks genuinely carefree. I have my weekly call with Maxim tomorrow. It'll be a relief for him when I tell him she's found a good group of friends and is doing well.

Amelia

I'm finding it odd that the small group of friends I've amassed is a group of guys. At that first practice, I was a little unsure. Some of them were acting like jerks. But they've grown on me. I've even surprised myself with how comfortable I feel with them now. It feels like I have four older brothers looking out for me.

Mateo and I have been hanging out more. This is all new to me. I don't have the same feelings for Mateo that he does for me. But I decided it couldn't hurt to try Natalie's advice. So, I agreed to try out this dating thing as long as Mateo promised to go at my pace. Most of the time, he does a great job with that.

He knows I don't like being around crowds of people. Even though he prefers to be out in public doing things, he never complains when all I'm able to do is hang out at the house or go down to the beach for a picnic. He tells me I make him happy and how much he cares about me.

I think the best thing about Mateo is he treats me like a normal person. Would that change if he knew my history? Doesn't matter. We're not at a place where I'm ready to share that part of me. Right now, I'm enjoying our friendship. The problem is my eyes and heart are drawn to the man who's always present in the background.

Amelia

I'VE BEEN PLAYING THE PIANO FOR AS LONG AS I CAN remember. My earliest memories are of sitting on my dad's lap. I must've been only three or four. He'd take my tiny hands with his and teach me what each key was and how to make a song. He was an accomplished pianist and my very first teacher.

I knew my future would involve playing. I don't feel like a whole person without it. But I always pictured myself playing in an orchestra or something fancy. Being part of a rock band was never on my radar, but it's so much fun.

Death Rat, the crazy name for our band the guys picked, already has a great reputation and is in high demand at local venues. The guys are trying hard to get the attention of some A&Rs, who they tell me are basically talent agents that frequent some of the clubs and other places we play. If the right person discovers us, it could mean big things.

I haven't told my parents about it yet. I don't think they'll take the news that their daughter, who is supposed to be studying classical piano, is playing in a band called Death Rat. I can picture the look on Dad's face, and I laugh. I'll tell them eventually, especially if something big happens for us. But until that happens, I don't see any reason to upset my parents. I'm keeping this to myself and enjoying the ride.

Tonight's show was the biggest one we've played to date. Our audience was on fire, which really helped motivate us on stage.

My adrenaline's still running high when the show ends. The club planned a big afterparty for the band and our fans. They sold VIP admission tickets, and people are already gathering for it.

"You're going to stay for the party, right?" Mateo asks.

"I don't know. There's a lot of people."

"And they'll all want to see my girl to get her autograph and selfies. Please. I won't leave your side."

It's his eyes that get me every time. Sometimes, I watch him when he doesn't realize I'm looking. The grey turns dark and stormy. He doesn't show it on the outside, but I can almost feel the anger swirling inside him. Other times, they're a soft shade of grey that holds an immense sadness. But right now, they're sparkling with excitement, something I rarely see from Mateo.

"I'll stay for a little bit."

He gives me a huge grin and grabs my hand. "Come on. I can't wait to show my girlfriend off."

"Mateo, please don't introduce me as your girlfriend." Although I say the words, the music in the club is so loud he doesn't hear me.

On the way to the dance floor, we stop by a few people who want selfies and autographs. I think he introduces me to a few others. I smile since I can't hear what he's saying.

Finally, we make it to the dance floor. I try my best to relax and focus on Mateo, but there are too many people. They're dancing and brushing up against me. The loud music, the bass, and being touched toss me back in time—back to Mexico.

"I can't stay here," I say, not waiting for Mateo's response.

I rush off the dance floor and look around for Viktor. He's already coming to me.

"What's wrong?" He grabs my arms.

"There are too many people. I want to go home."

"Okay. Let's go." Viktor leads me to the door.

Mateo catches up and grabs my arm, making me flinch. "Where are you going?"

"Home."

"Why? Aren't you having fun?" Sadness has crept back into his eyes. "I wish you'd stay with me."

"I'm sorry, Mateo."

"I'll call you tomorrow." I grab Viktor's hand. "Can we go now?"

He nods, and although I was hoping he'd offer to leave with me, he doesn't move. Instead, he stays rooted in place, watching me go with Viktor.

The drive home is quiet. We don't even put the radio on. Viktor keeps glancing over at me. I'm sure trying to gauge my level of anxiety.

We finally pull up at home. The adrenaline's worn off, and I'm exhausted.

"Do you want a snack?" Viktor asks when we get in the house.

"I don't think so." I yawn. "I'm so tired I think I'm just going to go to bed."

He looks a little disappointed. Our regular after-show routine is to come home and have a snack. Sometimes we watch a movie or go for a walk on the beach, but tonight I'm spent.

"No problem. Sleep well."

I walk down the hallway to my bedroom and change into a night-shirt. I don't think my head hits the pillow before I'm asleep.

Amelia

I'm startled awake by the sound of someone yelling and banging on the front door. I grab my phone and see it's three a.m. I jump out of bed and throw open my door. Viktor's already in the hallway, gun in hand.

"What's going on?" I ask him frantically.

"I don't know. Get in my room and lock the door," he orders.

I'm frozen in place. The sound of yelling grows louder and more desperate."

"Amelia." Viktor shakes my shoulder, getting my attention. "Go. Now."

I run into his room and lock the door. Then, I tuck myself on the floor between his bed and the wall.

Viktor

THIS IS MY WORST NIGHTMARE COME TRUE. SOMEONE'S found us, and now Amelia's in danger. I wait until she's in my room, and I hear the click of the lock before I go to the door. With my gun in hand, I look through the peephole to see who's on the other side. My anxiety subsides when I see who it is, and I tuck the gun in my waistband before undoing the locks and opening the door.

"Mateo, what are you doing here?" I drag the obviously drunk kid into the house. "You're lucky the neighbors didn't call the cops."

"I came to see my girlfriend." He slurs his words. "Amelia," he calls.

"Shut the hell up." I take him by the arm and sit him down on the sofa. "Why do you want to see Amelia?"

"To tell her I'm in love with her."

"Mateo, you're drunk. You have no idea what you're saying."

"I might be drunk, but I still love her." He points a finger at my chest. "I know you do, too, but you can't have her."

What the hell is he talking about? Me? In love with Amelia?

"Mateo, you're drunk. You have no idea what you're saying."

"You can't have her because you're an old man." Mateo laughs. "Where is she?" He tries to stand up, but I push him back down.

"Sit here and be quiet." I pull out my phone. "I'm going to get you a ride. You need to go home and sober up."

"I want to see Amelia."

"Not tonight. When you're sober, I'll consider it."

Thankfully, it's only a few minutes until a car appears outside. I walk Mateo out and give the driver his address. I wait until they pull away before going back into the house.

After I lock up, I go to my room to let Amelia know everything's okay.

"Amelia, it's me. Unlock the door." There's no response, so I try knocking. "Amelia, everything's okay. Come open the door."

I wait, and still nothing. When I listen closer, I hear her crying. Dammit. If she's not going to open the door, I'm left with no choice. I kick the door in. The sound of wood cracking is loud. Her scream is even louder.

I rush across the room and find her curled up on the floor next to my bed. "It's just me. Everything's okay," I say as I slide down and sit beside her. But it's like she isn't hearing me. She has her hands wrapped tightly around her legs. She's shaking and crying. "It's okay, Amelia. I'm right here." I use my finger to gently turn her head to look at me. "See, it's just me. You're safe. Breathe with me. Remember how we do that?"

She nods slightly and keeps her eyes locked on mine while we inhale slowly and exhale together. It takes several minutes before she starts to relax and her breathing regulates.

"Are you okay now?"

She turns to face me. I think she's going to say something, but instead, her lips meet mine, and we kiss. It takes a minute for my brain to catch up and fully comprehend what's going on. When I can think straight, I take her arms and push her away.

"What was that?"

"I kissed you," she says quietly.

"I got that much." I stand and start pacing.

Slowly, Amelia stands and watches me, but she says nothing.

"Sit down." I motion for her to sit on the edge of my bed.

"I know I don't have a lot of experience. Do I kiss that bad?"

"Amelia, it's not that." I sit next to her. "It's just— We can't do that.

I'm too old for you, and most importantly, I work for your father. We can't have anything like that between us."

"Why not?" As soon as the words leave her mouth, darkness shadows her face. "It's because of what happened to me, isn't it?" She jumps up to get away from me. "You don't want me because Moreno took me, and his men raped me."

"No, Amelia. That has nothing to do with it."

"It does. I get it. I'm ruined, dirty." She wraps her arms around herself.

Shit. How the hell do I fix this? "None of that's true. I don't ever want to hear you talk about yourself like that." I get up and slowly walk toward her.

"Then, why don't you want me?" Tears stream down her face.

"I'm not a good man, Amelia. You deserve to find a good guy, someone closer to your age. Someone not like me."

"You're one of the best men I've ever met," she says quietly.

Her words go straight to my heart and leave an indelible mark. But no matter how much either of us might want this, it can't be. "I'm glad you think so, but you don't know me." I tuck a strand of hair behind her ear. "I'll always be here to protect you, but we can't—"

I don't get to finish my sentence before she turns and runs out of my room. I follow her into the hallway.

"Amelia, wait."

She doesn't listen. She goes into her room and slams the door behind her. I try to open it, but it's locked.

"Amelia, open up."

"Go away."

I stand there for several minutes, listening to her cries. I've just hurt her in the worst possible way. My heart's torn. I want to bust into her room, too. I want to wrap my arms around her and tell her I want her, too. Woah. Where did that come from?

This girl is so off-limits. I'm thirty-two, and she's my boss's eighteen-year-old daughter. She's innocent and sweet. I'm screwed up—damaged beyond repair. The last thing she needs is a guy like me. All I'd do is complicate her life and bring more danger into it. I can't fall for the woman I'm trying to protect again.

I know all that. So why am I sitting outside Amelia's door thinking about how good her lips felt pressed against mine? How right it felt knowing she was thinking about me—only me. And the only person I was thinking about was her. Then, the look of devastation on her face when I told her no.

I'm so screwed.

I stay outside her door until her crying stops. Then, I drag myself back to my room, where I lie awake in bed all night, picturing only one woman—Amelia.

Amelia

For the briefest of seconds, Viktor kissed me back. It was the most incredible feeling in the world. I'm sure he felt something too. But then he pushed me away—rejected me. Is what happened to me too much for him to look past? And how do I get him to see me as more than Maxim's daughter?

I grab my phone and call Natalie.

"How was your show last night?"

"It was amazing. There were so many people."

"I'm so happy for you." She pauses. "You know you'll have to tell your parents, right?"

"Yeah, I know. I'm working on that." It's going to have to happen soon. "I called because I need some more advice."

"About this mystery man?" She laughs.

"I kissed him last night."

"And?"

"It was perfect. Magical. Until he pushed me away."

"Why did he do that?"

I have to choose my words carefully. "He doesn't think the timing's right. We spend a lot of time together at school and band practice."

That's all true. "I think he might be afraid people won't be happy if we're together."

"That makes sense. Your bandmates would probably be concerned that the band would suffer if you and he broke up."

"Mhm."

"But you really like him and want to be with him anyway?"

"Yeah." I blow out a frustrated breath. "What do I do?"

"Maybe try some group activities. Something light and fun. A game night or pizza and a movie with some other friends," she suggests.

"That sounds like a good plan."

"If things do get more serious, you may have to sit down with the other band members and have an open and honest discussion. Listen to their concerns and address them the best you can."

"Right." Time for a subject change. "How are you feeling?"

"I have a whole lot more morning sickness this time around."

"Pregnancy does not sound appealing to me."

"You'll change your mind one day."

Will I? Although the idea of little brown-haired, blue-eyed babies makes me smile, I'm not sure I want children.

"Thanks for the advice. I have to get going."

We hang up, and I shower quickly before going to the kitchen to face Viktor. I'm nervous, especially after last night. But, when I get out there, Viktor's sitting at the table nursing a cup of coffee.

"Hi." My voice is barely a whisper.

"Hi."

"About last night. I'm sorry. I don't know what I was—"

"It's okay. It was a stressful situation. We're good," he says, never looking up from his coffee.

"Mateo and I are meeting with some friends to grab a bite to eat and catch a movie later."

"Is he picking you up?"

"No. I told him I'd meet him there." I reach into the cupboard to grab a cup and make myself some coffee. "You never told me who was at the door last night." I take my mug and sit across from Viktor at the table.

He looks confused. "Mateo didn't tell you?"

"Tell me what?"

"It was him. He'd been drinking. He was really drunk." She looks concerned. "I got him a ride and sent him home."

I didn't know Mateo drank. He's not twenty-one yet, but I don't have to remind Viktor. He already knows.

"It must have slipped his mind." I shrug.

I can't believe it's November, and we can still wear shorts. Back home, it's already snowing. But here, the sun's shining bright, and there's not a cloud in the sky. Viktor and I spend most of the afternoon on the beach. I didn't want to come in, but we have to get ready for my fake group date tonight.

I'm walking a fine line by not telling him the truth, and I feel guilty for lying to him. The truth is on the tip of my tongue while we're driving. But I know after last night, he never would've agreed to it.

"What do you think about starting your driving lessons now that you've got your permit?" Viktor asks.

Because I'm not a United States citizen, getting approved for a learner's permit was quite a lengthy process, but it finally came in the mail this week.

"I'd love that."

"How's tomorrow after school? Or do you have band practice?"

"We're off this week."

"Perfect." He smiles.

I love his smile. He has a dimple on his left cheek. His eyes used to be sad all the time, but lately, they sparkle. He looks happy.

We pull up at the pizza restaurant and go inside.

"I don't see anyone yet," I say and look around. "Should we grab a booth?"

"Sure. I'll sit with you until they get here."

We order sodas while we wait. After a half hour, no one showed up. It's not a surprise to me because no one was invited.

Viktor checks his watch for the millionth time. "Weren't they supposed to be here a while ago?"

On the way here, Mateo texted me to ask if he could come over tonight. I use now as a good time to respond.

Me: Tonight's not a good night.

Mateo: We really need to talk.

Me: Now's not a good time. I'll talk to you tomorrow.

"They aren't coming."

"What?"

"Mateo fell asleep. His buddy texted him, but he didn't hear his phone, so they figured we weren't interested. They changed plans and went to the waterpark instead. Mateo isn't coming either."

"He's just going to stand you up?"

"He said he isn't feeling well."

"Maybe it's the amount of alcohol he ingested last night," Viktor says sarcastically.

"I'm sorry you had to wait here with me for nothing. I guess we should pay for the sodas and go home." I drop my shoulders.

"I don't think so."

"What do you mean?"

"We're already here. There's no reason not to order a pizza and watch the movie."

"Really?"

"Sure."

We finish eating and make it to the theater just in time. The previews are starting. Viktor walks me to our seats and then goes back out to get snacks and drinks. The last preview is just finishing up when he gets back. He passes me a soda and a bucket of popcorn while he unloads several bags of candy from his pockets.

"It looks like you bought one of everything," I whisper.

"I didn't know what you'd want, so I got a variety." He grins.

I grab the bag of chocolate peanut butter candies. "These are my favorite."

While we watch the movie, we share the bucket of popcorn, our hands occasionally brushing against each other. My stomach does flip-flops each time they make contact. I sneak glances at Viktor to see if he's as affected as me, but his expression gives no clue to his feelings—or if he even has any.

Although it's late when we get home, the sky is clear, and the moon shines bright.

"I think I'm going to take a walk on the beach. Want to come?" I slide my sandals off and set them on the steps to the house.

"Give me a minute to go put this in the house." He holds up the candy. "I'll be down in a few minutes."

"Okay." I start walking away.

"Don't go in the water alone," Viktor calls.

"Yes, boss."

Viktor

I NEEDED A FEW MINUTES TO CLEAR MY HEAD. I KNEW FROM the start there were no plans with Mateo. He'd already texted me to apologize for last night and to let me know he was waiting to hear from Amelia about whether he could come over.

I was going to say something but decided not to. Why? Because I enjoy being out with her. I didn't want to share her with Mateo and his friends. But that's wrong. I shouldn't enjoy it. I can't want her, and I can't let that happen again.

I toss the leftover candy onto the kitchen counter and then open the glass doors. Stepping onto the balcony, I lean on the rail and watch her. The moonlight shines on her like a spotlight. Amelia's standing at the water's edge, her hair blowing in the breeze.

She doesn't realize how beautiful she is. How perfect she is for me. She consumes my thoughts. In another life, another time, we might be able to make something between us work. But in this life, if Max ever found out I have feelings for his daughter, all bets would be off. He'd likely hand me over to the Albanians himself.

Somehow, she got past my walls. She owns a piece of my heart. I stand up and sigh. As much as it hurts, nothing can ever come of it. I promised her I'd be down, so I leave the safety of the balcony and meet her on the beach.

"It's a gorgeous night."

She jumps. "You scared me."

"I'm sorry." We both stare out over the water, the waves barely visible.

Amelia steps closer, letting the water wash over her feet. "I have a recital coming up at school."

"You do? When?"

"Next Monday, before Thanksgiving break."

"Did you tell your parents?"

"No. I don't want them to feel like they have to drop everything to fly in for it. It's not a big deal."

"I don't think they'd agree with that. It's your first performance. They'll want to be here. You should call them."

Amelia pulls her phone out of her pocket and hits Irina's contact. She puts it on speaker. It rings several times before she answers.

"Good morning, sweetheart," Irina says. "It's been too long since you last called."

"Sorry, mom. I've been really busy with school."

"You must be by the water. I hear the waves."

"Viktor and I came for a walk on the beach. It's always so peaceful down here."

"Don't go in the water at night. I don't want a shark to eat you."

"I won't." She giggles. "The chamber music ensemble at school is having a recital next week. I wasn't going to bother you with it, but Viktor said I should call and let you and Dad know about it."

"Why would it be a bother?"

"I don't know." She shrugs. "The recital is only about an hour. That seems like not much for a super long flight. And I know you and Dad are busy."

"Amelia," Irina's voice turns serious. "We're never too busy for you. I'll speak to your father, and we'll make arrangements to fly in."

"Thank you, mom."

When they hang up, Amelia lets out a big sigh.

"I told you they'd want to be here."
"You'll still come, too, right?"
"I wouldn't miss it."

Mateo picked me up early tonight so we could go for dinner before the show. He brought me to my favorite sushi place. I asked Viktor to join us, but he declined as usual.

"When do you think he'll let me take you out without him tagging along?" Mateo asks, motioning to Viktor, who's eating dinner alone.

I watch Viktor for a minute before answering, "Never."

"Seriously?" Mateo cocks his head to the side.

"Yep. Viktor follows orders from my dad. And Dad says I have to have a bodyguard with me at all times."

"I can talk to your dad about it? I'll convince him I'm capable of taking care of you."

"Nope. That's not going to happen." I can't take my eyes off Viktor.

His shoulders are slumped, and he's scrolling on his phone. We always eat together. But here, he's alone.

"What happens if I marry you? Would you still have to have a bodyguard?"

His question catches me off guard. "Did you say marry me?"

"Yeah. Well, not right now. But maybe someday."

Mateo and I aren't even dating, and he's talking about marriage. I think he and I will have to have a serious discussion, but not here. "To answer your question, I'm not ready to talk about marriage, but yes, I'd still have to have a bodyguard."

"What exactly does your dad do?" he asks, setting down his chopsticks. In Russia, everyone knows who and what my dad is. I wasn't prepared for this. "He's involved in some cutting-edge clean energy things. I really don't understand most of it." I shrug.

"He must be really rich or something if you need all this."

"Something like that." I don't want to continue the line of questioning about Dad's job, so I change the subject. "Tell me more about what these A&R people do. How will we know who they are?"

"Are you ready for tonight's performance?" Mateo asks while we're sitting in the green room.

I've never been so nervous about a show before, but tonight's a big night for Death Rat. We're playing at the Viper Room. We also have confirmation there will be several A&Rs in the audience. If all goes well, tonight could be the big break we've been waiting for.

On top of that, Mateo and I are premiering the duet we've been secretly rehearsing in the soundproof studio at school. Our professor was nice and let us bring the other guys in to rehearse, too. But, outside of the four of us, no one has heard it yet.

"I'm terrified."

"Listen, Amelia. I'm sorry about last week. You know, coming to your house like that."

"It's no big deal."

"It is to me," he says.

"How did you get served anyway?"

"Getting alcohol is surprisingly easy when you're in the band. They don't even ask." He shrugs. "I don't usually drink that much."

"Why did you then?"

"I was jealous."

"Jealous?"

"Yeah. I saw the way Viktor was looking at you. When you left with him, you were holding his hand."

I'm really not sure what to say. I'm not going to apologize for leaving somewhere when I was uncomfortable.

"Amelia, I'm falling in love with you," Mateo confesses.

My heart stops. I had no idea he felt this way.

"Wow. Um," I stumble over my words.

"You guys ready?" Tristan asks as he walks by. "It's showtime."

I turn to follow Tristan onto the stage.

"Amelia, wait." Mateo grabs my arm and pulls me into him. "Please tell me you feel the same." He leans in to kiss me, but I pull away.

"Can we talk about this after the show?" My thoughts are spinning out of control.

"Of course."

I push my conversation with Matteo out of my mind and get situated behind the keyboard. It's surreal knowing we're about to play in a club that's nothing short of a legend, and it's packed. I scan the audience, and like every show, Viktor is seated right in front. We exchange glances just as the concert starts.

We play our full set to an enthusiastic audience. While the piano is rolled out for our last song, Mateo steps up to the mic and addresses the crowd. He talks about how he's fallen in love and makes no mistake about looking at me when he says it.

Mateo grabs his acoustic guitar and perches on the stool next to the piano. With a nod, I begin playing Pink's "Just Give Me a Reason." The first verse is my solo. I glance up and see Mateo watching me sing, but I avoid his gaze.

As we move into the chorus, my gaze goes to the audience. To a man with crystal blue eyes who's watching me intently as I sing about two people who bear the scars of their pasts but aren't broken. Two souls who've been drawn together to help one another learn how to love.

Our eyes remain locked on each other for the rest of the song. He has to know I'm singing about us. Tears drip down my cheeks and land on the piano's keys as I sing about the devastation in both of our pasts. About the parts deep inside that we thought were broken and the strength we share. The capacity we have to love again. It can't be denied. Viktor and I are one another's destiny.

We finish the song, and the room erupts in applause. We receive a standing ovation. Mateo approaches the piano and takes my hand, leading me to the center of the stage to take a bow. Then he wraps his arms around me, holding me tight against him. He's whispering something to me, but I don't hear what he says. All I see is the murderous look on Viktor's face and the clenched fists at his side. He makes an exit from the audience and heads for the stage door.

Backstage is pure chaos. Several of the A&R reps have made their way back. And there are women everywhere draping themselves over Tristan and Quincy. Thankfully, no one's interested in me.

I look for a quiet corner while I wait for Viktor. He knows I get overwhelmed by crowds, so he always hurries back. But it's taking him longer than usual because of how crowded it is back here. I make myself as small as possible while I wait. Then, finally, I see him heading in my direction.

"What did you think about the song?" Mateo appears from out of nowhere.

Viktor's eyes are locked on mine. "It was perfect. Amelia has a beautiful voice."

My heart's pounding. My body responds to Viktor's nearness.

Mateo steps in front of me. "I'd like to talk to you for a minute, Viktor."

"Go ahead."

Mateo glances at me and then back to Viktor. "It's private. Can we talk in the green room?"

"Are you doing okay?"

I nod.

"Wait right here. I'll only be a minute."

The two men enter the green room, closing the door behind them. I have no idea what's going on in there.

"Amelia, are you okay?" Quincy asks. "You're white as a ghost."

"There's a lot of people back here tonight."

"Where's your bodyguard?"

"He's in the greenroom with Mateo."

"That guy's got it bad for you." Quincy laughs.

"Viktor?"

"No, silly. Mateo."

"Oh yeah, Mateo." I manage a small smile.

"Want me to wait with you until Viktor comes back?"

"I'd really appreciate that."

Quincy and I exchange small talk while I wait for Viktor to come back.

Finally, the door opens, and they walk over to me. Mateo takes my hand in his.

"I got permission from your bodyguard to take you out tonight," he says.

"Only if that's okay with you," Viktor adds.

"I was looking forward to going home."

"The whole band was invited. I won't keep you out for long." Mateo rubs my hand with his thumb. "And you did promise we'd talk after the show."

We do need to have an important conversation. "As long as it's not for too long."

"Keep your phone on," Viktor instructs. "I won't be far away if you need me."

Amelia

"Where are we going?" I ask Mateo as we walk out to the parking lot.

"Tristan's having a party at his house. I can't wait to show you off to some of our other friends."

"How did you get Viktor to let me go with you?" I ask, looking over my shoulder at Viktor, who's walking a short distance behind us.

"I told him exactly how I feel about you." Mateo grabs my hand and threads his fingers with mine. It feels awkward—wrong." He said as long as he followed us and was inside the house for the party, we could go."

"Isn't that going to be weird? My bodyguard following us around?"

"Nah. It'll be fine."

Mateo opens the car door, and I slide in. I watch as he and Viktor talk for a minute, then Mateo gets in the driver's seat, and we're on our way.

"Can't we just go back to my house and watch a movie?"

"What do you mean?" Mateo glances in my direction.

"I'm not a fan of parties and crowds." We've talked about this. He puts his hand on my leg. "You'll be fine. I'm here."

"Mateo, I think we need to talk."

"I understand if you can't say the words back to me yet."

"Mateo, I—"

I stop talking when he pulls the car over in front of a house that's crawling with people and then shifts in his seat. "Don't say anything yet."

"I don't think—"

"Give me a chance to show you what we can be like. Let me make tonight special. We can talk about it later." His eyes plead with me to say yes to him.

I don't know what to do. I'm so confused. "Okay," I say quietly. I'm not comfortable ignoring this, but I also don't want to hurt him. He's a really nice guy. But he's not the one for me.

Amelia

Tristan's house is enormous, and people fill every nook and cranny. Mateo brings me from group to group and introduces me to all his friends. Some I've met, but most I've never seen before.

I smile and make polite conversation, but on the inside, I'm freaking out. Somehow, I have to keep it together because I refuse to have a panic attack in front of all these people. It takes all of my willpower to keep myself grounded. What's making me more nervous is that I don't see Viktor anywhere.

Mateo leads me to the kitchen, where pizza boxes are stacked high, along with several different selections of alcohol.

"Want a drink?" Mateo offers me a can of beer.

"Umm, no. And you shouldn't be drinking, either."

"Loosen up a little." He pushes the can into my hand.

I take the can but don't intend to drink it. I'll ditch it somewhere before Viktor sees it. It won't end up good for anyone. Mateo takes my free hand and leads me to a set of stairs.

"Where are we going?"

"Upstairs. It's a little quieter, and we can talk."

He knocks on a few doors until he finds a room that's not occupied.

"After you." He motions for me to go into the bedroom first.

"I'd rather go somewhere else to talk."

"It's quieter here. You trust me, don't you?"

So far, he's not given me any reason to distrust him. Maybe he's right. I can't look at every guy as though they're out to hurt me. That was my past. This is my present. I decide to give him the benefit of the doubt and walk into the room. Mateo follows behind me, shutting and locking the door.

"Do you have to lock it? Can't we keep it open?"

"It's okay, Amelia. I'm not going to hurt you. I don't want anyone barging in on our conversation."

I'm uncomfortable with this, but I know Viktor can't be far away.

Mateo takes the beer from my hand and sets it on the dresser. "Come sit with me." My body's tense. Something doesn't feel right. "I know you've had bad relationships in the past, but that's over. You have me now." He tucks a stray curl behind my ear before leaning in to kiss me.

I let him. I try to make myself feel something other than friendship. But there's nothing. Then, he grabs the bottom of my shirt and tries to slide it up.

"No." I push away and jump up from the bed, putting distance between us.

"Don't you want me?"

I know he's had a rough life. He's alluded to things but hasn't told me his story. I haven't pushed because I know what it feels like to want to keep a part of your life secret. I have hidden scars I'm not ready to show the world as well.

"Mateo, you're a really nice guy, and I enjoy hanging out with you."

"Please don't do this, Amelia." Tears fill his grey eyes.

"You've helped make my transition to California so much easier than it would've been on my own. I treasure our friendship, but I'm not in love with you."

He stands up and walks over to me. "You may not love me right now. Give me a chance. Let me show you how good I can make you feel. How good we'll be together." He grabs my hands and tries to lead me back to the bed. "Please say yes. I can't lose you."

Tears begin streaming down my face. "Mateo, I can't keep pretending. It's not fair to either of us. But you're not going to lose me. We'll always be friends."

"Friends." He wipes his face with the backs of his hands. "Is it because of Viktor?"

"No. Yes. I don't know." There are so many thoughts and feelings running through my head at warp speed that I can't manage to form a coherent thought. "I have feelings for him, yes. That's part of what I need to work through before I can move forward."

"He's a lucky man," Mateo says sadly. Then, he grabs his beer and walks out of the room, leaving me alone.

My whole body's shaking. I can't go back out there, so I sit on the bed. Every emotion I've experienced tonight rushes to the surface all at the same time. I don't hold back. I allow myself to feel and purge everything.

The door cracks open. I expect it to be Viktor, but instead, it's Sparrow.

"I thought I heard someone crying in here. Are you okay?" Sparrow asks as he walks over to me. "Never mind, that was a dumb question."

I manage a small smile.

"Wanna tell me what happened?"

"It's Mateo. He wanted to—" My voice catches on a sob. "He told me he loves me."

"Woah. I didn't realize you two were that serious about each other."

I'm glad Sparrow said that. It means I'm not the only one who missed it.

"I didn't either. I told him I didn't feel the same way." My tears start to fall again.

Sparrow grabs my shoulders. "Did he hurt you?"

I shake my head. "No, he just walked out. I don't think he's okay, but I can't go out there and look for him like this. I don't know where Viktor is. I want to go home."

"I haven't seen Viktor," he says. "But I can take you out the back way and bring you home if you'd like."

"Would you?"

"Sure. Come on."

Sparrow takes my hand and brings me down the hall to an elevator. "It's the staff entrance. No one will be back here."

He's right. The area's deserted.

"Are you okay with waiting here while I get my car?"

"Yeah. I'll be fine."

Within minutes, Sparrow's pulling up in a beat-up old Jeep. He gets out and walks around to open the door for me. "Sorry, it's not one of the fancy cars you're used to driving around in."

"I don't care about that." I smile.

Sparrow takes a narrow road that runs through the property until we reach the main road.

"Before we get too far, I need to text Viktor so he knows I'm leaving." I go to reach for my phone in my pocket. "My phone's gone."

"We can go back in and look for it."

I try to think back to when I last had it. "I put it in my bag that I left in Mateo's car."

"We can find him and get his keys."

"No. I don't think he wants to see me again tonight. I can get it another time."

Viktor

MATEO LET ME KNOW HE TOLD AMELIA HE LOVED HER before the show. He told me she was receptive to it, but that doesn't sit right with me. There was something else in her eyes when she sang that song. It was as if she reached inside me and pulled my darkest fears out, replacing them with her.

Could two people truly be destined for one another—even if everyone else will think it's wrong?

I agreed to let him take Amelia if she was okay with it. She was apprehensive, but she agreed.

I've been trying to keep my distance. I want Amelia to have the space to be an ordinary college girl. If something is up here, I'll know it. Kids have been coming in and out of the kitchen with pizza and drinks, so it didn't concern me when Mateo brought her in.

But that was over a half hour ago. There's no way they're still in there. So much for giving her space. I walk into the kitchen and look around. Empty pizza boxes are thrown everywhere. Beer cans and liquor bottles line the counter. But there's no sign of Amelia or Mateo. Where did they—

That's when I spot the back staircase. "If he touches her," I growl as I take the steps two at a time. The hallway's lined with doors. Much to the dismay of the inhabitants, I throw each door open in my search for Amelia, but she's not in any of them.

I pull out my cell to trace her phone. The location is just outside the house. Realizing I lost my shit for nothing, I take my time following the signal, which leads me right to Mateo's car. But there's no Mateo or Amelia. What the fuck? Her phone must be in her bag that's on the backseat. There's no way she'd leave here without telling me.

I search each floor of this oversized house but find no trace of Amelia. The last place I look is the backyard. There are kids everywhere. I check the pool area, but she's not there. My eyes scan the perimeter, and that's when I spot Mateo leaning against a tree.

I run over to him. "Where's Amelia?"

"I don't know," he slurs. "You're supposed to know that."

"Are you drunk again?"

He holds up a bottle of vodka. "I think so."

"What the hell are you doing getting drunk when you're supposed to be with Amelia?"

"Amelia's with Sparrow."

"Sparrow?"

"Yep." He nods dramatically. "She left with him." (he put her in his car and left out the back way)

I don't stand around to wait for any more info from Mateo. I break into a sprint. If anything happens to her, so help me.

"ARE YOU SURE YOU DON'T MIND TAKING ME HOME?"

"Not at all."

"How long have you known Mateo?"

"Since kindergarten." Sparrow chuckles.

"So, you know his story?"

"I do."

"I met his family at his sister's wedding. But that doesn't make sense because a few weeks after that, Mateo told me his dad died when he was little. That he and his mom aren't close. I know there's more that he's not telling me, but when I tried to bring it up, he pretended he didn't know what I was talking about."

"I'm surprised he said anything at all."

There's a long pause. Do I ask? Would Sparrow even tell me?

"I can see the look. You want me to tell you Mateo's story."

"I do." I need to hear it so I can understand the pain I see in his eyes.

"Mateo's old man, or at least the guy his mom said she thought was his father, overdosed when he was about four. His mom was also passed out. Mateo called 911."

Sparrow goes on to tell me when the ambulance and police arrived, they found Mateo dirty, malnourished, and living in a complete dump.

They tried to revive his father, but it was too late. He was already dead, but they were able to save his mother. Child Protective Services was called. They took Mateo away from his mom and put him in foster care.

"That's right about when we met. School was just starting, and he was in my class." Sparrow smiles. "He was smaller than everyone and didn't talk much, so some other kids liked to make fun of him. I don't know what it was. Something about the look in his eyes like he was lost made me want to stand up for him and protect him."

He was there for about two years while his mom got clean and eventually regained custody. After that, the boys lost touch for several years.

"Then, one day, we were in seventh grade, and he showed up again but was in rough shape. He refused to speak and flinched if anyone got too close. My need to protect him was even stronger."

It took some doing for Mateo to let Sparrow behind his protective shell. When he did, the things he described to Sparrow were nothing short of a living hell. His mom had only stayed clean for a few months—long enough for CPS to go away. That's when things went from bad to worse.

His mom prostituted herself out for drugs, and when that wasn't enough, she did the same with Mateo. She sat by while men raped him so she could get her next fix. What saved him was a broken collarbone.

"The last boyfriend was violent. His teacher saw him in pain and sent him to the nurse, who recognized he needed medical treatment. They couldn't get his mom, so they brought him to the hospital. CPS met them there, and he was put back into foster care. But this time, he wasn't going home. They found his mom dead."

"Oh my God," I say quietly. My heart splits in two listening to this story.

"The foster family he went to eventually adopted him."

"Mateo's adopted?"

"Mr. and Mrs. Hart adore him, even with his issues. Unfortunately, over the past few years, Mateo's been spiraling out of control. He's been drinking and doing drugs. I'm pretty sure he's high tonight."

That explains the change in his behavior tonight. Mateo was never that forward with me. He always respects the boundaries I put up. But tonight, it was like he wasn't listening to me—wasn't hearing me.

"Do his parents know?"

"I'm sure they do, but he's an adult. If he doesn't want help, their hands are tied."

Sparrow pulls up in front of my house. "Thank you for trusting me enough to tell me all that. I know I hurt him tonight. Can you go back and make sure he's okay?"

"I'll always look out for him. I—" Sparrow stops abruptly.

I can see in his eyes what he was about to say. "It's okay. Your secret is safe with me."

Sparrow looks at me. I know the look. It's the same one I have when I'm weighing someone's honesty. "Amelia, I'm gay. I'm in love with Mateo. I have been for years."

"Thank you for trusting me with that." I touch his arm.

"No one knows I'm gay. I don't know what my parents would do if they found out."

"Your secret's safe with me." I give him what I hope is a reassuring smile.

"It's nothing I can ever act on. Mateo's not into guys. He'll never return my love."

"I know a thing or two about loving someone who doesn't love you back," I say.

"Your bodyguard?"

"Is it that obvious?"

"To someone who's watching." I place my hand on his arm. "Your secret is safe with me."

Sparrow walks me to the door and sees me safely inside.

I reach out and hug him. "Thank you for the ride home. I'm only a phone call away if you need to talk."

"I'll keep that in mind."

I watch as he walks away and then closes the door. I make it to the couch, where I sit, stunned by everything I just heard. My heart aches for the little boy who was hurt by the adults he should've been able to trust. But I know from my trauma that he won't be able to have a healthy relationship until he's dealt with it.

I'm also sad for Sparrow. Being in love with someone who doesn't return your love is a difficult place to be.

I'm startled when the front door swings open. An imposing and angry Viktor steps in, slamming the door shut behind him.

"Why did you leave the party without telling me? You left your phone in Mateo's car and let some guy drive you alone. I had no idea where you were. And then I get here, and you don't even have the door locked."

I can't do this right now. Without a word, I stand and hurry to my room, slamming the door behind me. Then, I lay on my bed and cry.

Cry for Mateo.

Cry for Sparrow.

Cry for me.

Viktor

I DIDN'T MEAN TO LET MY DAMN TEMPER GET OUT OF control, but she had me scared to death. If anything happened to her, I'd never forgive myself.

Slumping onto the couch, I take a few deep breaths. Amelia's here, and she's safe. That's most important. As soon as I get my emotions under control, I'll apologize. And then we're going to have to have a talk about Mateo.

Heading down the hall, I stop at her room. I knock, but she doesn't answer. I knock again. "Amelia, I'm coming in." I'm prepared for the door to be locked, but it isn't.

Amelia's lying on the bed. Tears drench her face. I sit next to her.

"What happened? Did he hurt you?"

She shakes her head.

"I'm sorry for yelling at you, but scared the shit out of me."

"I'm sorry," she says and tries to catch her breath.

"Are you ready to tell me what happened?"

"Right before the concert, he told me he loved me," she begins. "At the party, he brought me upstairs. He said he wanted to talk."

The same feelings I had when he showed up here drunk to proclaim his love for her make their way back to the surface. Jealousy. Jealous that another man has feelings for Amelia.

"He started kissing me, and I let him. I thought I owed it to him to try," she says. "But then, he wanted more. He tried to take my shirt off."

"I'm going to kill him."

She reaches out and grabs my arm. "Please don't. He stopped as soon as I said no."

That sentence is the only thing saving that boy's life tonight.

"I told him we were just friends. That we'd only ever be friends."

"Why?"

"Because he's not the man I'm in love with. He's not you."

Her words hang in the air between us, and although I know I shouldn't, I lean in and kiss her. She opens her lips, allowing my tongue access. My hands tangle in her long hair. She lays back, and I place her arms above her head. Her chest rises and falls with her rapid breaths.

Our eyes remained fixed on each other as I remove her shirt, exposing her black lace bra. My hands explore her body and breasts before I lean over her and begin kissing her again. Her tiny hands take the hem of my shirt, sliding it up my chest. I sit up and pull it over my head, tossing it to the side. I need to feel her skin against mine.

She mewls in pleasure beneath me as our kiss turns more passionate. Her hands go for the button on my jeans, and that's when what we're about to do hits me. I jump back.

"We can't do this." I rub my hand over my head.

"Why not?" she asks breathlessly.

"This isn't right. I'm too old—"

"We're both adults, and we both want this," she says and sits up.

She reaches out for me, but I capture her hands. "Amelia, we have to stop. I'm sorry. I shouldn't have let it get this far."

I turn and head for the door.

"Please don't go," she cries.

I want so badly to turn around. To finish what we've started, but I can't. Without looking back, I walk out and go straight to my room, where I lock the door.

I sit on my bed and lean forward, my head in my hands. What the hell was I thinking? Why do I feel so drawn to her? She's eighteen years old. More importantly, she's my boss's daughter. Maxim would literally skin me alive if he knew I touched her.

I'm the last thing she needs. My past is dark.

I'm broken.

Everyone I love leaves.

Love.

I'm in love with Amelia Solonik.

Amelia

Viktor left so fast he didn't take his shirt. I pick it up and bring it to my face. It smells like him. My hands tremble as I pull it over my head. Why did he stop? I know he felt the same things I was feeling. I could feel how hard he was. He wanted me as much as I wanted him. And then he was gone.

I cry myself to sleep.

I was hoping I'd feel better after a good night's sleep. Maybe understand what happened last night, but I don't. This isn't going to be an easy phone call, but I have to talk to someone.

"Hi, sweetheart," Natalie answers the phone. "How was your show last night?"

With everything that happened last night, I practically forgot about the show.

"It went really well. The A&Rs were impressed." And hope I didn't screw up the whole band. "I need to talk to you about something."

"Anything. What's up?"

"It's about the guy I've been telling you about." I pause. "Last night, things started to get physical."

"Was it consensual?"

"It was perfect until he stopped. He told me he didn't think he was the right man for me."

"I'm sorry, honey. That must've been really hard."

"It hurt. Especially because I know he's the right man for me, and he knows it, too. He's just scared of our age difference and what Dad will say. But I don't care. I love him."

"I'm a little confused. I thought we were talking about the band guy. I didn't know he was so much older than you."

"It's not the band guy. It never was. Please don't freak out," I pause and take a deep breath. "I'm in

love with Viktor."

Viktor

I couldn't sleep last night. Instead, I spent the last few hours of darkness pacing. My brain and heart are at war with each other. One part, the sane part, knew to stay locked in my room. Far away from Amelia. The other part wanted nothing more than to go back to her room, tell her I'm in love with her, and finish what we started.

Hoping to clear my head, I took an early morning for a run on the beach. I've just returned, but my thoughts aren't any better than when I left. My feelings aren't any different.

I'm in love with a sweet, spunky, beautiful red-haired woman—the one woman I'm forbidden to have.

"I'm so screwed."

I need to talk to someone rational who'll tell me this is crazy and that I need to stay away from her.

Pulling my phone out, I dial the one person I can trust with this. It rings a few times before he answers.

"Hello?"

"Hey. It's me."

"Yes, it is." Alex chuckles. "What's up?"

"I need your help. Your advice about a woman."

"You met someone?"

"Yeah."

"You've been holding out on me. When did this happen?"

"I guess a few months ago."

"That's great."

"I'm not the right man for her. Nothing good will come of this."

"Viktor, you have to stop thinking you aren't good enough—"

"Alex, I'm in love with Amelia Solonik."

Love brought them together, but their journey is far from over. What comes next will change everything. Don't wait. Read *Her Nightingale* today.

Her Nightingale

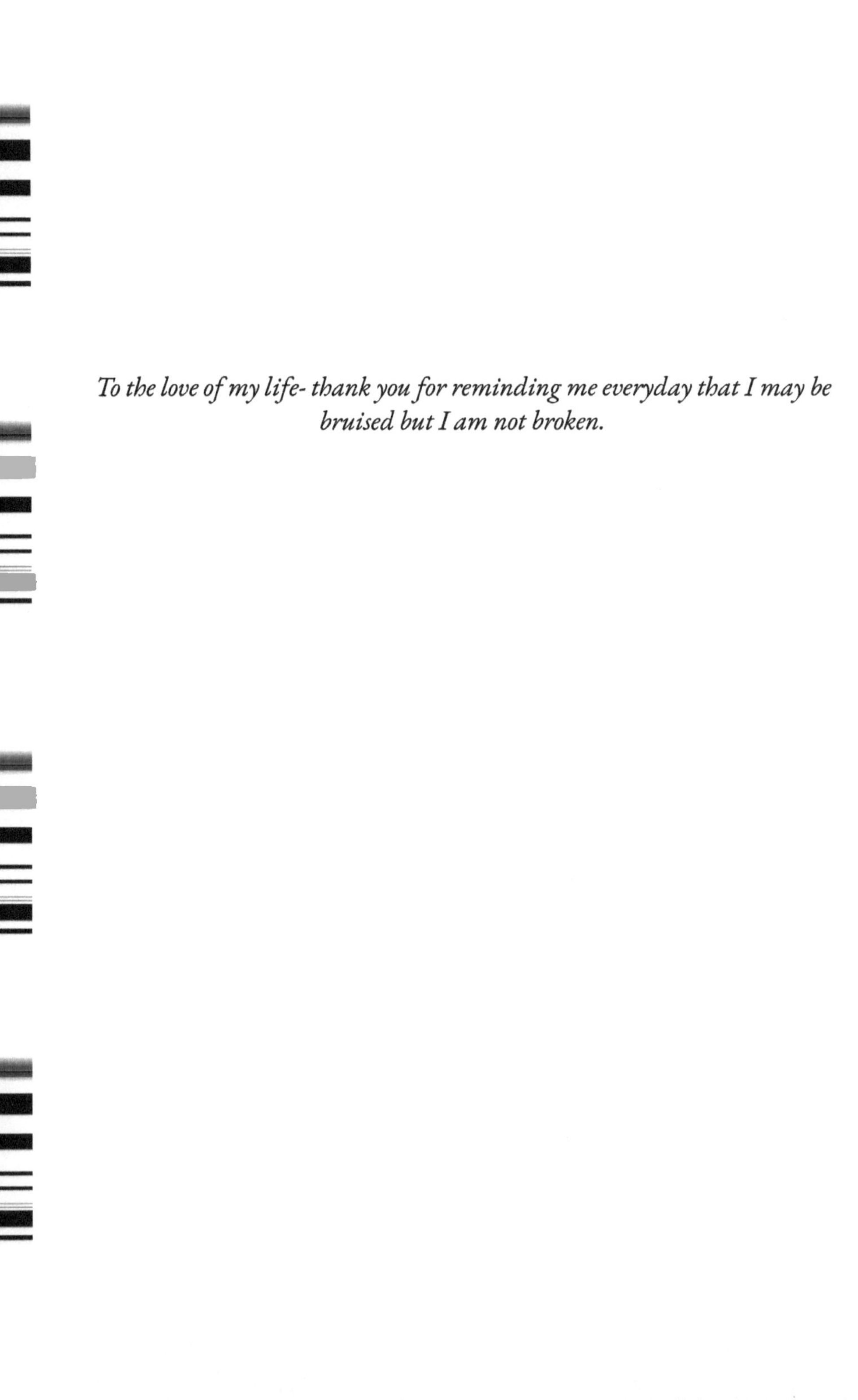

To the love of my life- thank you for reminding me everyday that I may be bruised but I am not broken.

Alex

VIKTOR'S PICTURE FLASHES ON MY PHONE. HE KEPT HIS distance for so long that I was afraid he'd never come around. I'm thankful we've finally been able to repair our friendship. "Hello?"

"Hey. It's me."

"Yes, it is." I chuckle. "What's up?"

"I need your help. Your advice about a woman."

My coming back caused him so much suffering. I'm thankful he's finally healing enough to move forward. "You met someone?"

"Yeah."

"You've been holding out on me. When did this happen?"

"I guess a few months ago."

"That's great."

"I'm not the right man for her. Nothing good will come of this."

"Viktor, you have to stop thinking you aren't good enough—"

"Alex, I'm in love with Amelia Solonik."

There's no way he just said the words *love* and *Amelia* in the same sentence. "Can you repeat that?"

"I'm in love with Amelia."

It's a good thing I'm sitting down. Otherwise, I would've fallen over.

"You are so fucked."

"Thanks. You're such an encouragement."

"Does she feel the same?"

"I think so. We haven't actually said the words, but we've—"

"Please tell me you haven't had sex with Maxim's daughter."

"Not yet."

I'm relieved knowing he hasn't done something he can't take back—yet.

"I don't know what to do. I've told myself this isn't okay. That I can't fall for my boss's daughter, but it's too late."

My first instinct, as a father, is to tell him to stay the hell away from her. He's thirty-two. She's eighteen. If that were Rose, I'd kill him. But that's not going to work. The heart doesn't care about age or rules.

I run my hands through my hair. Think Alex. Is there anything I can do to ensure Maxim doesn't kill him?

"She's young, and she's never dated. You two spend a lot of time together. It might be puppy love or infatuation."

"Right," he replies. "Infatuation."

My intent wasn't to hurt him, but the sadness in his voice is unmistakable. Amelia's young and inexperienced in the area of relationships. She'd never hurt him on purpose, but if he goes all in thinking this is a forever thing, he's going to be devastated again.

"I'm not saying that's what it is. Just keep it in the back of your mind."

"I appreciate your concern. But I want this—with her. What do I do?"

"Go slow. Really slow. Amelia couldn't have set her sights on a better man." I chuckle. "But Max is going to blow a gasket when he finds out."

"Which isn't going to be anytime soon."

Natalie

"HI, SWEETHEART," I ANSWER THE PHONE. "HOW WAS YOUR show last night?"

"It went really well. The A&Rs were impressed.." Amelia pauses. "I need to talk to you about something."

"Anything. What's up?"

"It's about the guy I've been telling you about." Amelia sounds hesitant. "Last night, things started to get physical."

"Was it consensual?"

"It was perfect, and then he stopped. He told me he didn't think he was the right man for me."

"I'm sorry, honey. That must've been really hard." My heart hurts for her. Relationships are all new to Amelia, and I can guess where her head went when she got rejected.

"It hurt. Especially because I know he's the right man for me. And he knows it, too. He's just scared of our age difference and what Dad will say. But I don't care. I love him."

"I'm a little confused. I thought we were talking about the band guy. I didn't know he was so much older than you."

"It's not the band guy. It never was." She pauses, and I hear her take a deep breath. "Natalie, please don't freak out. I'm in love with Viktor."

"Dobrow?" I ask.

"Yes," she replies, her voice barely above a whisper.

I'm in shock. Amelia's in love with Viktor. For months, she's been telling me about the sweet, thoughtful things her mystery man has been doing for her. It was apparent he cared about her but wasn't ready to take the leap. I assumed he was insecure. Knowing the mystery man is Viktor. It all makes sense.

"Natalie? Are you still there?"

"I'm here."

"I'm sorry." Amelia starts crying. "I just screwed up our friendship, didn't I?"

"Oh honey, it's nothing like that. I'm surprised, that's all."

And confused by the onslaught of emotions. Even though my heart and soul belong to Alex, I still feel possessive over Viktor. He was mine. I guess in the whirlwind of everything that's happened over the past year, I never really let go of him.

"I know how you feel about Viktor. I shouldn't have let this happen."

"Amelia, you've done nothing wrong. Yes, I'll always have a special place in my heart for Viktor. I'll always love him, but I'm not in love with him. My heart belongs to Alex—it always has."

"Are you sure?"

I wipe at my tears. Viktor and I were through so much together. He held me when my life shattered. I'll never forget what he meant to me, what he'll always mean to me. But it's time for me to let go of any what-ifs that may have been floating around in my head. Holding onto Viktor isn't fair to anyone.

"I'm very sure. Viktor's a wonderful man who deserves to be someone's first choice. That's something I could never give him," I explain. "Amelia, Viktor's had a difficult past. His heart's fragile."

"I know how hurt he was when he lost you."

"It goes far deeper than that. He's experienced a great deal of loss in his life. You need to be sure about this before you do anything with him."

"I know I don't have any experience with men. But I also know that

I want to be with him. I'll do everything I can to guard his heart. The same way he does mine."

I have no doubt Amelia will treasure him. Then another worry pops into my head—Maxim.

"Does your father know?"

"No. I don't know how to tell him."

"Carefully and from a distance. Because he's going to totally freak out."

"That's what I'm afraid of."

"Obviously, there's a lot you and Viktor have to work out. I'm assuming he's struggling with your age difference as well as what your parents are going to say."

"And my past."

"What do you mean?"

"I think he pushed me away because of what happened to me."

"That doesn't sound like Viktor," I reply.

Amelia listens patiently as I explain that I think Viktor's afraid of triggering her by doing anything sexual. He overthinks things and is most likely trying to figure everything out. We talk until I can't put Rose's dinner off any longer.

"You can call me anytime," I assure her.

"Thanks, Nat. I love you."

"Love you too, Melia-bug."

I scoop up my little girl and bring her into the kitchen to get settled in her highchair while I make her lunch.

Alex comes into the kitchen and sits next to Rose.

"Wow." He runs his hands through his hair.

"What's wrong?"

"I just hung up with Viktor," he says.

I give Rose her sippy cup. "I just hung up with Amelia."

"So, you know?"

I nod.

"Does she have feelings for him?"

"She's in love with him."

"Those two have one hell of a hard road ahead of them."

Viktor

Talking to Alex didn't do a damn thing to make this better. He was supposed to have the answers I needed, but other than going slow and wishing me luck with Max, he didn't have any other advice.

Amelia and I need to talk. After a quick shower, I go to find her. When I pass by her bedroom, I find the door open, but the room is empty. She's not in the kitchen or living room either. Where did she disappear to? Stepping onto the balcony, I spot her. She's in her swimsuit, lying on a blanket by the water.

I throw on a pair of swim shorts and head down to join her.

"You need to let me know if you're leaving the house."

"I needed some time alone," she says, pushing up on her elbows.

"We need to talk." I lower myself next to her. "What you said last night couldn't be any further from the truth."

"Then, why did you stop?"

"You were upset. It would've been wrong to take advantage of you."

"You weren't—"

"It wouldn't have been right. Not like that." I stare out at the water for a beat. "Amelia, there are so many things wrong with this. With us."

"But there doesn't have to be."

I wish that were true. That we lived in a world where we'd be accepted as a couple. Instead, we have everything going against us. Pursuing a relationship is crazy. The problem is, I don't want to walk away from this.

At the same time, I have no idea how to move forward. We're going to encounter a whole lot of hate. Hell, if Maxim finds out, and he eventually will, he's going to kill me.

Amelia studies me for a moment before she reaches out and threads her fingers with mine. "I want this. I want us."

Amelia

"I WANT THIS. I WANT US."

I know Viktor's scared. I am, too. The issues we're going to face won't be easy. Saying my parents won't be happy is an understatement. But I'm not a child. They don't get to tell me who I can be with.

"I called Natalie this morning. I told her everything," I confess.

"I called Alex." He cracks a smile. "I wish I was a fly on the wall. I can only imagine the conversation they had after talking to both of us." We share a laugh. "Seriously though, this—" He motions between us. "—isn't a good idea."

"What did Alex tell you?"

"That I'm fucked when your father finds out," Viktor says deadpan.

I guess that's one way to put it. Dad isn't going to be happy, that I'm sure of. But I think Alex and Viktor are being a bit overdramatic. I'm sure he and Mom will be surprised at first, but they're open-minded. They'll get over it quickly.

"He also told me to be careful and to go slow." Viktor brushes sand off the corner of the blanket. "How did your call with Natalie go?"

Knowing Viktor was in love with Natalie makes this conversation difficult. I don't want to hurt him or make this any harder than it already is.

"I know what you're thinking. Yes, I was in love with her. Natalie and I will always share a special friendship. But that's all it is. She's with Alex, where she belongs, and I'm where I belong."

His words calm my nerves. "I was afraid she was going to hate me."

"Why would she hate you?"

"Because of all this. But Natalie reassured me that she wasn't mad. Then she warned me to be sure of my feelings before going further."

"Amelia, I'm not sure there should be an us," Viktor says quietly. "There's a lot you don't know about me."

"So, tell me. I want to know all of it.

Viktor

Telling Amelia about my past terrifies me. Once she knows the things I've done, the people I've hurt, she'll never look at me the same. Maybe that's for the best. Scaring her away will keep her safe.

"My past isn't pretty."

"My life hasn't been a fairy tale either," she says softly.

"This is different. What happened to you wasn't your fault. My life has been a series of bad decisions."

"Trust me. Tell me, and let me decide."

Opening up, I lay myself at her feet, baring everything. I share the good, the bad, and all the moments in between—the people I've loved and lost, the extent of my work with Maxim. Finally, I tell her everything about Natalie, and for the first time, it doesn't feel like my heart is being torn apart.

When I finish, I'm left feeling vulnerable. Amelia's watching me, but she hasn't spoken. I knew my story would scare her away. I move to stand up, intending to go back up to the house to give her space.

"Where are you going?"

"Inside."

She adjusts her position to her knees. "Don't go."

"I figured you wouldn't want anything to do with me."

Amelia moves closer, straddling my legs. "You've experienced so much loss. You didn't deserve any of that, and I'm sorry." She presses her lips against mine. "But nothing you said changes how I feel." She kisses me again. "You're gentle and caring. You're kind." Another kiss. "You're safe."

"Amelia, my life is dangerous. I have enemies who'd love nothing more than to hurt someone I care about to get to me."

"There are many things in life that can't be controlled. You may have enemies, but I don't doubt for a second that you wouldn't do everything in your power to keep me safe."

"What if I fail?"

"You won't." She cups my cheek. "I'm willing to take that chance if you are."

"I want to try." I put my arms around her, pulling her closer to me. "But I'm scared."

"You've been my rock when I'm afraid," she says quietly. "Let me be strong for you now."

"I can't say no to you." I rest my forehead against hers. "I don't want to say no."

As the sun begins to set, we make our way back down to the water. Walking along the beach at dusk is a ritual we cherish, a moment of quiet serenity. The only sound is the rhythmic crash of waves against the shore, a soothing backdrop to our time together.

Tonight's walk is different. I'm free to hold Amelia's hand. To keep her close to me. We stay out until the sky turns dark, and we're treated to a sky full of twinkling stars.

"*Moya zirka*," I whisper and wrap her in my arms.

"What does that mean?"

"My star. You're my guiding light, the one who pulled me out of the darkness."

Viktor opened up to me last night and told me everything about his past. His glacier-blue eyes were haunted as he recalled his parents' deaths and how he went back home to heal from losing Natalie, only to face losing his grandmother—his only remaining family member.

We share a similar pain. When my parents died, I had no one. At fifteen years old, I was an orphan. My sixteenth birthday, one that was supposed to be a milestone, was a nightmare instead.

Both Viktor and I have dark pasts. We have scars. We've both shared moments where we were ready to give up. But we didn't, and we made it through. I believe we survived because we were meant to find each other —to love one another.

We've agreed to try at this—whatever *this* is. Neither of us wants to put a label on us. Instead, we're going to take it one day at a time and see what happens.

Right now, the only thing that's happening is we're straightening up the house before we leave for the airport to pick up my mom and Lana. They've flown in for my chamber music recital on Monday.

"You ready to go?" Viktor pops his head into the guest room, where I'm putting fresh sheets on the bed.

"As soon as I finish this, I will be." Viktor comes into the room and helps me finish making the bed. "Thank you." I wrap my arms around his waist.

He holds me against his chest. It's my favorite place to be. I feel safe in his protective embrace. Then, he leans down and kisses me. "One last kiss before your family gets here."

I'm going to miss this new normal we've been living. One where we're free to touch one another. Free to show affection. Viktor doesn't want to rush the physical side of our relationship, so he's placed limits on what he'll do, which is no more than holding and kissing me. He also insists we sleep in separate rooms. But each evening, when he kisses me goodnight at my bedroom door, it gets harder to let him go.

The closer we get to the airport, the more nervous I get.

"Amelia, you have to relax," Viktor says. "Everything will be fine."

I wish I had his confidence. I've never lied to my mom or kept anything from her. I don't like not being able to tell her about us. But it's too soon for that. I'm just afraid she's going to see right through me.

"What if they find out?"

"Then, they find out, and we deal with the consequences sooner rather than later."

"How are you so calm?"

"I have to be, moya zirka." He glances my way. "It's part of keeping you safe."

The ding of a text alert interrupts my worrying.

Lana: We're here. We landed early.

"It's Lana. They're already here," I tell Viktor before texting her back.

Me: Viktor just took the exit for LAX. We'll be there in a few minutes.

LAX is like a city within a city. There's an intricate system of roads leading to numerous terminals, hotels, and restaurants. It's crazy confusing. I'm impressed with the ease in which Viktor finds his way. I don't think I'd ever be able to drive in here.

Finally, we come to a private tarmac, and dad's jet comes into view. Viktor drives past it and pulls the car into the private hanger.

"Ready?" he asks.

"Do I have a choice?"

"Not really." He cracks a small smile. "We've got this."

Thankfully, he moves his hand just as Lana pulls my door open and nearly drags me out of the car.

"I missed you so much." She squeezes me tight.

I hug her right back, not realizing how much I miss my family. "Me too."

"*Moya malen'kaya ptichka,*" Mom says and wraps me in a hug. "The house is too quiet without you."

"I'm so happy you're both here."

"I see Viktor's his usual pleasant self," Lana says, motioning behind me where Viktor is standing by the car. "I don't know how you live with him. He's so moody he'd drive me crazy."

I look over my shoulder where Viktor's talking with Pyotr. "He's not that bad. We seem to do okay."

"You're a better person than me, little sis."

Viktor grabs their bags and gets them in the trunk.

"Are you ladies ready to go? The traffic's going to be terrible."

"How are we going to fit Pyotr?" Our car isn't that big.

"He's staying in L.A. The boss gave him a few days off."

Lana and I get settled in the backseat while Viktor helps mom into the front. Then, we make our way out of the airport and back onto the freeway.

"Are you hungry? We can stop for something to eat on the way home," I suggest.

"That would be lovely. Is that okay with you, Viktor?" Mom asks.

"Is there anywhere special you would like to go, Mrs. Solonik?"

"You can call me Irina. There's no need for all the formalities." Mom smiles and then looks back at me. "I don't know anything about the area. Where would you suggest, Amelia?"

"What about the restaurant by the bay we like?"
Viktor glances in the rearview. "That sounds perfect."

Viktor

Putting boundaries between Amelia and me is going to be more complicated than I thought. I already miss her next to me. Miss reaching out to touch her. I need to put distance between us, but we're stuck in the car in this ridiculous traffic. I thought New York City was bad, but it's nothing compared to the congested California freeways.

What should only be a half-hour drive takes nearly two hours, but finally, we're pulling into the parking lot for Bay Front Restaurant.

Once inside, I ask the hostess for two tables.

"You aren't going to eat with us?" Amelia asks.

"No."

"Oh." Her smile fades

Lana threads her arm through Amelia's. "He'll be fine. He's not great at conversation anyway."

"Thank you, Viktor," Irina says.

I watch as the three ladies are seated before I'm led to a separate table where I sit facing Amelia. Lana and Irina's backs are to me. A positive since they can't see me watching Amelia's every move.

The women laugh and chat throughout their meal, their conversation lively and animated. I can only imagine Amelia filling them in on everything they've missed. A pang of longing hits me—I miss being the one she talks to like that, sharing her thoughts and stories with me instead.

It's still light when we pull into our driveway.

"The pictures don't do the house justice," Irina says. "It's beautiful."

"It's been like living in a dream," Amelia says. "I can't thank you and dad enough."

"Forget the house. I want to go down to the beach," Lana says.

"I'd like to see the inside and get settled first." Irina overrules her daughter.

"Fine." Svetlana shrugs. "Come on, Melia. Give us the grand tour."

"I'm going to give Viktor a hand with the bags."

"No, you're not. Viktor's a big boy. He can handle it."

Amelia glances over her shoulder and mouths the words *I'm sorry* as Lana drags her away from me.

I've known Svetlana since she was a little girl. Despite being raised in a strict home where showing respect was expected, Svetlana often acts like a spoiled brat. When she was with Brandon, he kept her reigned in. But the longer she's been without him, the more out of control she's become.

It's going to be a long few days with her like this.

Amelia

I KNEW IT WOULD BE HARD TO KEEP MY DISTANCE FROM Viktor, but I didn't realize how difficult it would be. We've gotten used to being close very quickly. And now we're forced to act like two people who are no more than roommates.

"Here's your bedroom, Mom." I open the door to our guest room.

"It's stunning. And look at that view." She walks straight to the balcony doors I left open, allowing the ocean breeze to drift in.

"Some days, it's hard to peel myself away from it. Come on, Lana. I'll show you to our room."

"Our room? Dad said this place has three bedrooms."

"It does. The other bedroom is Viktor's. I didn't want either of you to have to sleep on the sofa bed. And I didn't think you'd mind sharing my room for a few days," I say, uncertain.

"That's fine. It'll give us a chance to catch up."

We pass Viktor in the hall. He nods politely and keeps walking.

"What's the deal with you and Viktor? You never seem to have a nice thing to say about him."

Lana flops down on my bed. "He's always there. In your face. You know what I mean?"

"Umm. Isn't that kinda his job?"

"I guess. But most of the other guards hang back and give you some personal space. You would've been better off having Igor here. He'd give you much more freedom than Viktor ever will."

"He's not that bad." I sit cross-legged on the other side of the king-sized bed.

Lana grabs my pillow to prop her head on. "What's this?"

She holds up Viktor's t-shirt that I sleep with every night.

"Nothing." I reach out to grab it, but she pulls it away. "Let me have it. It should be in the laundry."

"It smells like a man's shirt." Lana raises her eyebrows. "Does my little sister have a boyfriend she's not telling me about?"

"No." I pull the shirt out of her grasp and toss it into my laundry basket. I'll have to get another one from him.

Lana tilts her head as she studies me. From the look on her face, I know she doesn't believe me.

"Didn't you want to go to the beach?"

"Smooth." She grins. "I need my bag so I can get my swimsuit."

I open the door to go in search of her bag and find it waiting in the hall outside my room. Viktor mustn't have wanted to interrupt us.

"Here ya go." I wheel it in and set it on the bed. "I'll grab my swimsuit and get changed in the guest bathroom." Anything to get out of here.

I change into my favorite black two-piece, which I know always gets Viktor's attention. Then, I slip my shorts on and grab a few towels before heading out to the living room, where I find mom and Viktor sitting on the sofa chatting. Viktor stops speaking mid-sentence when I enter the room.

"Looks like you and Lana are going down to the water," Mom says with a smile.

"We are. Are you coming down with us?"

"Not this time. I'm exhausted from the flight."

"What about you, Viktor?"

"I'll stay here and keep Irina company."

"Don't be silly." She pats his arm. "I'll be fine. Go with the girls. The ocean makes me nervous."

"Ready?" Lana asks when she comes into the room.

"Yep. Let's go." We start walking toward the door. Viktor gets up and follows us.

"You're kidding, right," Lana says sarcastically. "Amelia can't even go to the beach without you tagging along?"

"I asked him to go with you," Mom says, not giving Viktor a chance to respond.

"It's a private beach. We'll be fine," Lana complains.

"You know how I feel about the water," Mom says.

Lana rolls her eyes and walks out the door. I look at Viktor and smile, glad he's coming with us.

Amelia

THE WEEKEND SEEMED TO FLY BY, AND TONIGHT'S CHAMBER
Music Recital is upon us. We're all enjoying a late lunch at the house
when my phone dings with a text alert.

Mateo

We need to talk. Can I pick you up for the recital tonight?

I read the text and set the phone face down without replying. I
haven't heard from Mateo since the disaster at the after-party the other
night, but Sparrow and I have been keeping in touch. He told me Mateo
had a few bad days after the incident, but he's slowly moving past it.

"Who's that? Could it be the owner of the T-shirt under your
pillow?" Lana waggles her eyebrows. Viktor and I exchange a questioning glance. I don't think he knew I kept his shirt.

"It's a friend from school. He wants to pick me up for the recital
tonight."

"Have you met someone special?" Mom asks. "I'd love to meet him
while I'm here."

"It's nothing serious. We're just friends, really."

"Since when do you sleep with a *friend's* shirt under your pillow?"

"Svetlana, don't embarrass your sister."

I've created quite a problem for myself, and I don't know how to explain my way out of it. If I introduce Mateo to my mom, it'll send mixed signals, and I don't want to do that.

"I'd prefer you didn't ride with him." Viktor comes to my rescue.

"Seriously? Amelia's allowed to date."

"It's a complicated situation, Svetlana. One I'd rather Amelia not get involved in."

"I'm assuming you've run a background check?" Irina asks.

"I have, and there's nothing apparently wrong."

"But?"

"Overall, he's a nice guy. But he's dealing with some major issues," I interrupt. "He'd like to be more than friends, but I'm not interested in him like that." I pick up the phone to text him back.

Me

I'm sorry. My family's here from Russia. We're going to ride there together.

With that disaster averted, I push out my chair and stand. "I'm going to go start getting ready. We'll have to leave early if we're going to get there on time."

Lana follows me into my room and sits on my bed. She watches as I go into my closet and return, holding the black dress I wore to the wedding.

"I hate that you and mom have to leave tomorrow," I say as I go into the bathroom to get changed.

"A lot is going on at Jelena's Hope. It's been keeping her very busy. But you'll be home in a few weeks for Christmas break."

Once I'm dressed, I walk back into my bedroom.

"Holy shit. The pictures didn't do the dress justice. You look hot."

My cheeks heat from embarrassment. "Viktor gave me a hard—" I stop as soon as I realize what I'm saying.

"Gave you a what? A hard time?" Lana cocks her head to the side. "What's really going on between the two of you?"

"What do you mean?" I turn around and pretend I'm checking out the dress in my mirror.

Lana gets off the bed and stands between me and my reflection. "I see the looks you two exchange. And that T-shirt under your pillow smelled strangely like his cologne. I think there's more going on here than you're letting on."

"You're crazy." And way too perceptive. "We're friends. He's the only person I really know here, so we spend a lot of time together. That's all."

"Mhm." Lana disappears inside the closet before I can respond. She returns a few minutes later with her clothes in hand. "I'm going to take a quick shower."

My hands shake as I try to apply my make-up. They can't find out about us yet. It'd be a disaster. I finish my make-up in record time, hoping I can talk to Viktor before Lana's done with her shower.

I find him in his favorite spot—the balcony. "Viktor, we need to talk." He spins around to face me. My breath catches. Viktor's dressed in a black suit and a blue tie that matches his eyes. I've never seen him dressed in a suit. Oh my God, I didn't think he could be any more gorgeous, but I was wrong. "Wow." I take a few steps closer. "You look amazing."

A smile spreads across his face, making my insides feel all tingly.

"And you, moya zirka, look stunning. Although I'd still rather you not wear this dress out in public." He leans in, placing a gentle kiss on my lips. "I'm sorry, I couldn't help myself."

"We need to be more careful. Lana's on to us."

"What do you mean?"

"She was questioning me about the T-shirt and the way we are together. She suspects something's going on."

"What T-shirt?" He asks, a playful smile on his face.

"After everything I said, you're only concerned about what T-shirt?"

"Don't worry about Lana. She's all about the drama. If we don't give her a response, she'll drop it."

"Are you sure?"

"I'm positive." Viktor runs his knuckles down my cheek.

"Aha," Lana exclaims. "I knew it."

Viktor

Amelia's eyes go wide, and her face turns ghostly white. I'm afraid she may pass out. Shit. I should've known better, but I couldn't not touch her.

"There's nothing to know," I say, hoping to control the situation before it gets out of hand.

"It's not what it looks like," Amelia spins around. "I was about to have a panic attack. Ania's worked with Viktor on ways to ground me—to avoid a full-blown panic attack. One of the techniques is physical touch." Amelia's speech is hurried, giving away her nerves. She pauses and looks back at me before returning her attention to Svetlana. "My face is the most sensitive and grounds me quickly."

"What's going on out here?" Irina appears in the doorway.

This is the moment. Lana's either going to call us out or at least pretend she believes the story Amelia came up with.

"Amelia's really nervous about the recital," Lana says, not taking her eyes off me. "Viktor and I were just telling her she's going to do terrific." She smiles at Amelia, and I breathe a sigh of relief.

"Of course, she's going to do great." Irina walks over to Amelia and embraces her. "I'm so proud of you, sweetheart."

"Thanks, Mom. I have to get my shoes, then I'll be ready to go." Amelia hurries off down the hall.

"She responds so well to you," Irina says, her eyes filling with tears. "Maxim and I are very grateful you're here."

"If my presence makes this transition a little bit easier for her, that's the least I can do."

"It looks like she's flourishing to me. I can't wait to tell Maxim. He's been so worried about her."

"I'm ready," Amelia announces as she walks back into the room. "Mom, why are you crying?"

"Look at you." Irina dabs at her eyes. "You look so grown up."

Amelia kisses Irina's cheek. "That's because I am."

"Enough of the kiss and cry," Lana says and rolls her eyes. "If we don't leave, we're going to miss Amelia's recital."

Irina and Amelia walk out the door together. I move to follow, but Lana steps in front of me.

"Don't think you two are fooling me for a second, Dobrow. You do realize she's only eighteen, right?"

"I'm aware of her age."

"And that my father's going to kill you if he finds out something's going on between you."

"Then we're in luck. There's nothing for him to find out." I move to walk around her, but Lana grabs my arm.

"I love my sister." She softens her voice.

There's no sense in continuing to deny this. Svetlana clearly knows what's going on. "That makes two of us."

"Don't do anything to hurt her, and I won't say anything."

"I give you my word."

***

Once we arrive at the theater, we bring Irina and Lana to the main entrance. Amelia was able to secure front-row seats for her family. As soon as they're safely inside, I escort Amelia around the back of the theater building to the stage door.

She places her hand on my chest, stopping me from following her inside. "This is where we say goodbye."

"I'm not leaving you."

She hands me a ticket and then stands on her tiptoes to place a gentle kiss on my lips. "The stage door locks from the inside. And unless you're on his list." She points to the young man standing outside the door with a clipboard in his hand. "You don't get access. I'll be fine. I want you to sit in the audience like any normal boyfriend-type."

I can't help the smile that spreads across my face. "I've never been anyone's boyfriend before."

"I'm glad."

"Promise to keep your phone on and text me if you need anything?"

"I promise."

"Break a leg."

I watch as she disappears behind the stage door. Then, I make my way back to the theater's main entrance, where I'm handed a program on the way to my seat.

"You aren't staying with her?" Irina asks when I sit next to her.

"Nope. She refused to allow me backstage." I shrug. "She wants me to be in the audience to enjoy the recital."

Irina studies me—too closely. It's as though she's peering into my soul and extracting all my secrets. I struggle to keep a neutral outward appearance. Because inside, I'm terrified she'll see right through me.

"She's a special young lady. Always thinking of others."

"Yes, she is."

Thankfully, the house lights dim, and a gentleman I recognize as Amelia's music professor steps onto the stage, announcing the start of the performance.

When the curtain opens, my eyes are immediately drawn to the young woman behind the grand piano. Like every Death Rat performance, she searches the audience until she spots me. I know the second she does because a beautiful smile graces her face.

Before I knew Amelia, I had never been interested in the arts. This is the first time I've been to an event like this. When I was young, my mother encouraged me to listen to classical music and to appreciate ballet. But I never gave it a real chance. Teenage boys didn't do such things.

Now, I wish I had cared less about my friends and more about the gift my mother was trying to give me. Because tonight, I find myself enthralled with the music being produced by this small group of talented musicians who are playing selections from various composers. Some songs are vaguely familiar, yet I couldn't tell you their names. Others I've never heard, but all are entrancing.

After the last song in the program, the conductor turns around to address the audience.

"Ladies and gentlemen, on behalf of myself and my students, we hope you've enjoyed our performance this evening." The audience's applause interrupts his speech. "This year, our university has had the pleasure of welcoming a very talented student who comes to us from St. Petersburg, Russia." He motions to Amelia, whose cheeks turn as red as her hair. "Ms. Solonik is majoring in classical piano with a minor in vocal studies. She's agreed to perform a classical piece from her country. I hope I say it correctly, "*Dve Siyayushchiye Zvezdy*—Two Shining Stars."

Amelia, accompanied by the rest of the chamber orchestra, begins playing the familiar song. Everything and everyone disappears when *moya zirka's* angelic voice fills the auditorium.

"Viktor," Irina whispers. "Did you know about this?"

I shake my head, unable to speak.

When the song finishes, Amelia receives a standing ovation from the audience.

While the audience is still applauding, I excuse myself. "I'll meet you outside the main doors," I say to Irina. I need to get to the box office before the audience makes their exit. The people inside have their backs to me, so I knock on the glass. A woman turns around, and I point to the bouquet of flowers on the table. She grabs them and motions for me to meet her at the door.

"Viktor?" she asks.

"Yes, ma'am."

She passes me the beautiful bouquet.

"Whoever's getting these is one lucky young lady."

"She's extraordinary."

With the flowers in hand, I step outside and wait for Irina and Lana to make their exit from the auditorium.

"Wow," Lana says when she sees the flowers. "That's a little over and above your job, isn't it, Vik?"

"Oh, Lana, leave him alone."

"It's her first recital. I wanted to make it special for her."

"I think it's a lovely gesture."

My heart feels like it's going to explode while we wait for Amelia. I struggle to keep my emotions in check, afraid I'll give away our relationship.

Amelia

"AMELIA, WAIT UP," MATEO CALLS AS I HEAD FOR THE DOOR. "Can we talk?"

I know we need to talk, but this isn't the time or place. Right now, the only thing I want is to get outside to Viktor and my family.

"I'm kinda in a hurry."

"Dad's going to be contacting everyone, but I wanted to be the one to tell you." Mateo runs over to me. "The A&R rep called. We got an offer."

"What does that mean?"

"We've been offered a contract to go on tour this summer with Zapped Euforia."

"Oh my God, that's so exciting. What happens next?"

"We have a meeting with our agent and attorneys next Monday afternoon. Can you be there?"

"I should be able to. Text me the info."

Mateo's smile fades. "Amelia, I'm sorry about what happened at the party. I want to explain—"

"Now isn't a good time."

One of my classmates walks around us and opens the door.

"There she is," Lana says excitedly.

"I have to go." I hurry outside.

Lana rushes over and throws her arms around my neck. "You were amazing."

"Thanks, Lan."

"Is this your sister?" Mateo asks.

I was hoping we didn't have to do this, but there's no avoiding it now. "Svetlana, this is my friend, Mateo."

"It's nice to meet you. Amelia's told me a lot about you," Mateo says.

"I see." Lana looks at me with a raised eyebrow.

"There's my girl," Mom says, wrapping me in a hug. "You were incredible."

"Thanks, Mom."

"Hi. I'm Mateo. I'm one of Amelia's band—"

"Mateo's in the chamber orchestra with me."

"It's a pleasure to meet you," Mom says.

"Congratulations." Viktor hands me an exquisite bouquet of flowers.

"Thank you." I bring the fragrant bouquet to my nose. "They're beautiful."

We stand in the middle of the walkway, facing one another. Several people grumble because they're forced to walk around us.

"We should all go and grab a bite to eat somewhere," Mateo suggests.

"I don't think—"

"That would be lovely." Mom smiles and slips her arm through mine. "You didn't tell us you met a boy," she whispers to me as we walk down the sidewalk.

"Mateo? He's just a friend."

"The way he's looking at you says he likes you as more than that."

And that's a problem because friends are all we'll ever be.

Mateo sidles up next to me. "How about we go to Snack and Shake?"

I look at him, eyes narrowed. "I'm kinda tired and would prefer to go home."

"Amelia, it's our last night here. I'd love to get to know your friend before we leave."

"You can ride with me—"

"No," Viktor and I say in unison.

Mateo raises his hands in surrender. "Can't blame a guy for trying."

The four of us squish into one of Snack and Shake's small booths. Once again, Viktor chooses to sit in the booth behind us.

"Do you and my sister have classes together?"

"Yep." Mateo takes a bite of his burger. "We have a few classes together."

"What instrument do you play?"

"Guitar."

I'm finding it hard to eat the loaded fries I ordered. Instead, I push them around on my plate. Viktor watches me carefully from his seat. I know Mateo won't do anything to hurt me, but I'm still uncomfortable. I see the game he's playing, and I don't like it. He's hoping to get my mom to think we're a couple or at least have promise as one. And she's falling for it.

When he's done eating, Mateo slides his arm around me. My body stiffens in response. His move puts Viktor on high alert. He meets Mateo's stare, but Mateo doesn't back down. He's playing with fire, and he's going to get burned.

"What do you want for dessert, Mel?" Mateo asks.

"I'm not feeling well. I want to go home," I say loud enough for Viktor to hear.

He jumps from his booth. "I'll settle the check, and we'll get out of here."

After the bill is paid, we walk out to the parking lot.

"It was nice meeting you, Mateo," Mom says, hugging him.

"I'm really happy I was finally able to meet Amelia's family." Mateo smiles. Although I believe his excitement is genuine, the whole situation feels wrong.

"I enjoyed spending the evening with you, too." Mateo turns to me. "Text me about next week, okay?"

"I will." I get into the car, but Mateo grabs my hand, stops me, and kisses my cheek. "Good night, everyone." Mateo gives a small wave as he turns and makes his way to his car.

"He seems like a sweet boy," Mom says.

"He's nice. But we're only friends."

"Some of the best relationships start as friendships, dear," she says as she slides into the car.

"What was that all about?" Lana asks quietly.

"It's a long story."

"And once we get home, you'll have all night to tell me everything."

Amelia

THE RIDE HOME IS FILLED WITH MOM ASKING ALL SORTS OF questions about Mateo. She assures me Dad's going to insist on meeting him. Once she's satisfied with my answers, she moves on to quizzing Viktor about Mateo's background check. Fortunately, he leaves out the parts about Mateo's drinking and drug use.

As soon as we pull into the driveway and Viktor turns the car off, I jump out. "I'm going for a walk."

"By yourself?" Mom asks.

"I'll come with you." Lana links her arm with mine.

I was hoping Viktor would join me, but I know Lana and I need to talk—away from Mom.

"Give me your flowers. I'll put them in water for you," Mom offers, and I pass her the bouquet.

"Be careful," Viktor adds. "I'll be watching from the house."

Lana and I ditch our heels on the steps and make our way through the cool sand until we get down to the water.

"Are you ready to tell me what's going on?"

"I could ask the same for you?" I give her a cheeky smile.

"Give it up, little sis. I already know something's going on with you and Viktor." She stops walking. "What I can't figure out is where this Mateo kid fits in."

I allow the warm ocean waves to lap over my feet while I consider how much information I should divulge. "Do you promise not to say anything to mom and dad?"

"Do you really think you have to ask me that?" Lana puts her hands on her hips. "Now, spill it."

I take a deep breath and start telling her the saga of Mateo. In her defense, she listens quietly and withholds any judgmental looks or comments, especially when I get to the part about how I fell for Viktor.

"He came into my room to check on me after the whole Mateo mess. Things got pretty heated between us. Nothing happened that night. Viktor put a stop to it. But that's how I ended up with his T-shirt."

"Wow. You've been busy."

"It wasn't anything we planned." I shrug. "It just happened."

"I don't want to sound all preachy, but you do realize how much older Viktor is, right?"

"Yes, I can count." I roll my eyes.

"Ha ha," Lana mocks me. "I'm just worried—"

"Worried that my past is going to cause problems."

"Yes and no." Lana splashes her foot gently in the water. "Viktor has a lot more experience with life in general. You're just starting out. Especially in the world of relationships."

"I understand your concerns, but my life hasn't exactly been sheltered. I'm not into parties or dating around. Heck, I never thought I'd trust a man enough to let him near me." I stop and look up. A thick cloud cover is blocking the usually star-filled sky. "Lana, I love him."

"Dad's going to lose his shit when he finds out."

We both share a laugh.

But on the inside, I'm terrified of just how bad Dad's reaction will be.

Viktor

From my spot on the balcony, I have an unobstructed view of the girls who are standing at the water's edge. Part of me is jealous. Walking on the beach at night is our thing—Amelia and me. But I know she needs time alone with her sister.

A short time later, Irina joins me on the balcony. "It's nice seeing the girls together. I think Svetlana misses Amelia more than she expected."

"Yeah." I don't take my eyes off them.

"Now that we're alone, I'd like to get your real thoughts on that Mateo boy. Something tells me you disapprove."

Despite being in Max and Irina's lives for most of my adult life, I've not spent much one-on-one time with Irina. I'm surprised at how perceptive she is. "His background check came back clean."

Which is true. However, it left out a lot of important information. I hated having to call in a favor, especially since our friendship was on rocky ground. But I didn't want to miss anything that could put Amelia in danger.

Dimitri agreed to do it since it was for Maxim's daughter. But, when he dug deeper, he uncovered Mateo's adoption records that his hotshot attorney father had buried so deep the average person wouldn't find them.

"Amelia only sees him as a friend, but the kid doesn't take a hint too well." I feign annoyance.

"I'm glad she has you looking out for her."

"I'm just doing my job."

"You're going to think I'm crazy. When we got here Saturday, I saw a look you and she exchanged. For a minute, I wondered if something was going on between you." Irina laughs softly.

I freeze, afraid she'll see the truth.

"I realize what a silly notion that was. She feels safe and is able to let her guard down with you. Amelia's obviously not ready to enter the world of dating yet. I'm not complaining. It's one less worry."

"Whatever she chooses, I'll look out for her safety."

"Maxim and I both appreciate what you're doing." Irina pats my arm.

A gentle breeze blows from the water, and I return my gaze to the girls. They've been down there for nearly an hour.

"I can't wait for them any longer." Irina stands up and yawns. "I'm going to head into bed."

"Goodnight."

I'm left alone with my thoughts. Thoughts about the beautiful girl who's finally walking back toward the house. A few minutes later, the door opens and closes.

"I'm heading to bed."

"I'll be in shortly," Amelia replies. Then she steps out onto the balcony. "Do you mind company?"

"From you? Never."

She starts to sit in the chair next to me, but I stop her and pull her onto my lap. She nestles her head against my chest.

"I miss being alone with you."

"Me too." She draws circles on my chest with her finger.

"I hate when you wear this dress, you know that?"

She picks her head up. "I thought you liked this dress?"

"I do."

"But?"

"I don't like other men looking at you in it." I lift her chin with my finger and kiss her.

She adjusts her position so she's straddling my legs. Her dress slides up, exposing too much of her. But I don't care. No one apart from me can see her out here. Our kiss quickly becomes heated.

I pull back, breathless. "We need to stop."

"Why?"

"Your mother and sister are in the other room."

She sighs. "I guess."

I lift her from my lap and adjust my prominent erection before standing. "We should get some sleep. Tomorrow's going to be a long day." She threads her fingers with mine as we walk into the house. "What do you have to text Mateo about?"

"Oh my gosh, I almost forgot. The band was offered a contract to open for Zapped Euforia on their summer tour."

"For real?"

"Yes. For real."

I want to be happy for her, but this news only further complicates an already very complicated situation.

"You know we'll have to tell your parents about Death Rat?"

"I know." She sighs. "I don't want to say anything while Mom's here. I'll wait until she's home and then call them. They're not going to be happy that I won't be home for the holidays. Hopefully, they'll understand why."

"Here's hoping." We stop outside her doorway. "This is where we part ways, moya zirka."

She stands on her tiptoes and places a gentle kiss on my lips. "Goodnight. Sleep well."

Amelia opens the door a crack and slips into her room. I wait until the door closes softly behind her before going to my room.

I'm glad Amelia had a good visit with her family. I know she's missed them. Unfortunately, the timing wasn't ideal. We're just beginning to figure out whatever this is between us. It'll be nice to be alone again to continue exploring our feelings for each other.

Amelia

"I'M SORRY WE COULDN'T STAY FOR THANKSGIVING," MOM says. "Jelena's Hope has been so busy. I can't be gone for too long."

"It's okay. We weren't really planning on doing anything special. Were we?" I look to Viktor for an answer.

"Whatever you want to do is fine with me." Viktor shrugs.

"Come here, let me hug you once more." Mom squeezes me tight.

"You're going to break her," Lana says. "It's not like we won't see her again. She'll be home in a few weeks."

Viktor and I exchange a knowing glance.

"I'll be counting the days." Mom dabs at her eyes.

"Are you ready to board, Mrs. Solonik?" Pyotr asks.

"Yes." He takes her arm and leads her up the steps into the plane.

"Are you coming home during break?"

"That's a long story. But there's no time for it now."

Lana gives me one last hug. "The flight home is over eighteen hours. Text me your *long* story." With one final goodbye, she disappears inside the jet.

Viktor and I walk back to where our car's parked. We watch the jet taxi down the runway, gaining enough speed to safely lift from the ground. A few stray tears spill from my eyes. Viktor puts his arm around me, and I rest my head against him.

"Are you up for a little adventure?"

"What are you thinking?"

"I had an idea about something fun we could do while we're up here." He opens the car door for me. "You game?"

"Sure."

Viktor grins as he rounds the car and slides into the driver's seat. He starts the drive out of the airport, but instead of heading south, he gets on the freeway to go north.

"Do I get any hints?"

"Nope."

While we're on the road, my phone dings with a text message.

Mateo: Do you have plans for Thanksgiving?

Me: I think we're just going to hang out at home.

Although we're living in the States, with neither of us being American, it's not a holiday we typically celebrate.

Mateo: My parents asked me to invite you to our house for dinner.

Me: Please thank them, but I'm going to have to pass.

Mateo: We still need to talk.

Me: Soon. TTYL.

I turn my phone off and slide it into my pocket. I want my full attention to be on Viktor and me.

We're pulling into a parking lot almost an hour later, and Viktor's surprise is revealed.

"Santa Monica pier," I exclaim. "I wish I brought my swimsuit."

"You did. I packed for us while you were busy with Lana and your mom."

We get out of the car, and Viktor grabs the bags from the trunk. Then, we find a public changing room.

"I'll meet you back here."

"Where do you think you're going?"

"To get changed." I point to the ladies' changing room.

"I don't like the idea of you going alone."

"It's not like you can come in with me," I say and roll my eyes.

Viktor doesn't move, but I see the wheels in his head spinning.

"Go get changed. I'll be out in a minute." I don't give him a chance to say anything before I disappear into the changing area.

I find an empty changing area and go in. Opening the bag, I see Viktor packed my black two-piece. There are also towels and sunscreen. Being fair-skinned with red hair, I burn easily. I change into my swimsuit and cover-up and go back out to find Viktor.

He's waiting for me a few steps away. Seeing him in only his swim trunks causes unrecognizable feelings to come to life.

"Oh my God. Check out the guy." Two girls stand next to me, talking to one another. "He's gorgeous."

"I know what I'd like to do with him." They both giggle.

That green-eyed monster called jealousy rears its ugly head. Now I know how Viktor feels when he says he can't stand if another guy looks at me. It takes a lot of self-control to not say anything rude to the girls. Instead, I walk over to my man, who puts his arm around me as we walk away.

"Was there a problem back there?" Viktor asks in a playful tone.

"Yes. I don't like it when other girls look at you."

"Are you jealous, *moya zirka*?"

"Very."

"There's no reason. I have eyes only for you."

We stop at the car to put our extra bag in. Then, hand-in-hand, we walk down the boardwalk and grab some fried food.

After we eat, Viktor rents an umbrella, and we find a spot on the beach. While Viktor digs the umbrella into the sand, I spread our blanket.

"Come here. Let me put sunscreen on you." I slide my cover-up off, and Viktor ensures every inch of my skin is properly protected before he puts his own on.

"Turn around. I'll get your back."

I squeeze some sunscreen into my hand and rub it over the taught muscles of Viktor's back. "What kind of bird is this?" I run my finger over the bird tattooed on his back.

"It's a Nightingale."

I move around to his front. "What does it mean?"

"Most people think of the bird as a shy bird that sings a beautiful song," he explains. "But when it's dark, the Nightingale sings its most beautiful melodies—ones that scare away its enemies."

I study his beautiful face for a moment. "That's you," I whisper. " My Nightingale."

He stands, offering me his hand. "Come swim with me."

I place my hand in his and follow Viktor into the cerulean blue ocean water. He leads us to where my feet can no longer touch the sand beneath us. But he never lets me go. Viktor pulls me to him, and I wrap my legs around his waist. I feel his arousal as he holds me against his body. Everything else fades away. It's just him and I riding the waves together. We stay in the water until the tips of our fingers are wrinkled before we make our way onto the sand.

Using my towel as a pillow, I lay back and relax. Viktor remains sitting.

"Lay down with me."

"I'm good."

I lean up on my elbow. "Don't you ever relax?"

Viktor looks down at me. "When I relax, people get hurt."

"That can't always be the case."

He doesn't answer. Instead, he returns to scanning the beach. Between the late night and the long drive today, I'm exhausted. Knowing my Nightingale is watching over me, I let my eyes close and drift off to sleep.

Viktor

I'm thankful Amelia isn't weighed down by the scope of the potential danger that's always lurking in the shadows. I don't want her to live in fear, always looking over her shoulder. I want her just as she is—relaxed.

The late afternoon sun is now shining directly on Amelia, who's still sound asleep on her back. I put my towel over her exposed skin so she doesn't burn. A wave of fear washes over me while I watch my sleeping angel.

People I get close to have a habit of getting hurt or, worse, dead. Because of my inability to keep them safe, they end up leaving me. I brush a lock of hair from her face. I will not allow this woman to get hurt, but do I really have the power to stop it? Somehow, I must do better than I ever have. I have to prove to myself and everyone else that I'm capable of keeping my loved ones safe.

"Hey," Amelia whispers. "What's wrong?"

"Nothing." Which is true. At this moment, everything's right in my world.

She sits up. "Your face tells another story."

"Does it now?" I tilt my head. "Tell me what the story is."

Amelia adjusts her position to face me and studies my face closer. "There's worry and sadness. Fear."

"Why?"

"What do you mean, why?"

"Why so much fear?"

Where do I start? Most people look at me and see a heartless killer. Few people have cared enough to look past the façade. To see the man behind the mask. The man who also experiences normal human emotions and feelings. In one sentence, my soul's been ripped open and bared before her. I don't know if I should flee in fear or bow at her feet for actually seeing me.

"*Moya zirka*, we have so much to be afraid of."

She reaches out and takes my hand.

"Don't you see? As long as we're together, there's nothing that can hurt us."

With everything I am, I want to hold onto her words and pretend they're true. But I know they're not. In addition to the danger of being connected to Maxim, we also face a certain amount of danger from Maxim himself.

Lana finding out was one thing. She challenges her parents at every turn. Lana's never opposed to fighting her father for what she wants. My concern is whether or not Amelia will be able to handle Maxim's wrath when he finds out about us.

"Are you dry?" I ask in an attempt to lead the conversation to a different topic.

"Yes."

"Good, let's go get changed."

"We're leaving already?" Amelia pouts.

"No. We're just on to the next part of our adventure."

"What is it?"

I point to the pier's amusement park, where the lights start to turn on as the sun begins to set.

"We're going on the rides?"

"As long as you're okay with it."

"Yes." Her smile spreads across her face. "Lana took me to my first amusement park, and I loved it."

Together, we pack up from our afternoon on the beach. After we change out of our swimwear, we stroll down the boardwalk in search of the ticket stand, where we purchase several books of tickets.

"Can we ride the roller coaster first?"

"We can do anything you want."

We spend the next few hours riding all the rides, including the famous solar-powered Ferris wheel. Unfortunately, it's already late, and we still haven't done everything I had planned.

"How about we spend the night?"

"Really?"

I nod. Amelia's smile and happiness are infectious. They spark unfamiliar feelings inside me.

This dating thing is new to me, too. I've been with women, yes, but never for more than a few nights. I never met anyone worth keeping around until Natalie. And as much as I cared about her, in my heart, I knew she'd always belong to Alex. She would've learned to love me, but I'd always be her second choice.

But with Amelia, I'm her first choice. Something I see reflected in her gaze. Feel in her touch. All she wants is me. I hope she sees those same emotions reflected back at her. She's my future—my forever.

After a quick internet search, I find us an oceanfront room at a hotel a few beaches down. It's not too far out of the way, but at the same time, far enough from the pier that we won't be disturbed by the noise from the boardwalk.

This place is magnificent. Although it's a modern hotel, the chosen décor makes the rooms feel more like a bed and breakfast. We don't have direct beach access, but the open floor-to-ceiling arched windows allow the cool night breeze to flow through the room.

The dark walnut four-poster bed is on the wall across from the windows, so the first thing we'll see when we wake up is the glistening water of the Pacific Ocean. A cozy sitting area with two Chesterfield chairs and a small accent table is off to the side.

"Wow," Amelia says as she explores. "This is stunning." She opens the door to an attached bathroom with a large glass-enclosed walk-in shower and a huge soaking tub. "This is the only thing our house is missing." Amelia runs her hand along the tub. "I miss taking a long, hot soak."

"Why don't you do that now, and I'll order room service. I'm starving."

"Dinner sounds good."

"Is there anything special you'd like me to order?"

"I'm not picky. If you choose it, I'm sure I'll love it."

"Don't drown in there, okay?" I grin and close the bathroom door behind me.

Amelia

I turn the tap on and adjust the water until it's pleasantly hot. Then I pour in some of the lavender vanilla-scented bubble bath that's on the sink. While the tub fills, I strip out of my clothes and rinse the sand and sunscreen off them in the shower. I leave them to dry on the retractable clothesline.

With the tub nearly full, I lower myself into the bubbly water and practically moan in delight. Nothing beats soaking in a tub. I rest my head back and relax. Today's been so much fun.

"Amelia," Viktor calls from the other side of the door. "Dinner's here."

"Okay, be out in a minute." Regrettably, I let the water out of the tub and dry off with one of the soft, fluffy towels. Then it hits me. Viktor only packed for the day and the stuff I was wearing is currently still dripping in the shower. I slide on one of the hotel robes and join Viktor in the main room.

"Umm. We don't have any clean clothes."

"I didn't think about that. If you don't mind, we can wear the same outfits tomorrow. We spent most of the day in our swimsuits anyway."

"I don't have a problem with that, but I rinsed my clothes off." I hesitate. "I have nothing to wear to bed."

Viktor's eyes sparkle with mischief. "You can wear my T-shirt if you want."

"That'll work."

He pulls his shirt off, exposing his chiseled muscles. Part of me wants to forgo dinner, but my stomach grumbles in protest.

"Let me throw this on quick, and then we can eat."

Once again, I disappear into the bathroom. His T-shirt is soft and worn in, but the best part is that it smells of bergamot and citrus—Viktor.

When I open the door, Viktor's standing by the table where there are two place settings, glasses of sparkling water, and a lit candle in the center. Soft music plays from Viktor's phone.

Viktor's in the middle of lifting cloches off the plates. "I hope you like Sea Bass."

"Fish is one of my favorite meals."

The food is exquisite. I close my eyes and savor the flavors. All the while, Viktor watches my every move.

"What?" I ask with a smile.

"Sorry." He actually blushes. "I didn't mean to stare. I was just." He stops. "Nevermind."

"Just what?"

"Nothing."

It's the push and pull we've been playing at the past few weeks. Viktor's usually guarded and tense. Every now and then, he drops his guard and allows me a glimpse at the man behind the walls, but it never lasts for long. He quickly puts those walls back up, and I find myself on the outside once again. We finish dinner in awkward silence, and Viktor wheels the makeshift table outside our door.

"I'm going to take a quick shower," he says.

While he showers, I relax on the bed and pull out my phone. I see a missed text.

Natalie: How was your visit with Irina and Lana?

Me: We had a good time. Lana knows.

Natalie: It's usually hard to keep stuff from her. How did she take it?

Me: She was concerned about our age difference, but other than that, she seemed okay with it. She warned me that Dad was going to blow a gasket. Hopefully, we can keep this from him for a while longer. I'm not ready for that conversation yet.

Natalie: That's walking a fine line. The longer you keep it from him, the more betrayed he'll feel.

Me: I didn't think about it that way. We'll tell them soon, I promise. Guess what?

Natalie: What?

Me: Viktor surprised me with a trip to the Santa Monica pier. We ended up staying here overnight so we could go to the aquarium tomorrow.

Natalie: That sounds like fun.

Me: Viktor just finished his shower. Gotta run. TTYL.

When Viktor comes out of the bathroom, he's wearing nothing but his boxer shorts, and wow, he looks mouthwateringly delicious. Parts of my body I feared would never work correctly have sprung to life.

He doesn't say anything as he walks across the room to the bed, where he sits next to me.

"I like the way you look in my shirt."

"I like the way you look out of your shirt." I trail my fingers down his exposed chest, letting them go lower and lower until his hand captures mine.

"Amelia, I don't want to rush this."

"Right." I pull my hand away and sit up, turning my back on him. "We should've taken a room with two beds."

"Amelia."

"I get your hesitation. Your disgust because I'm not a virgin. I've been raped by more men than I can count. I don't have any idea how to be in a relationship or how to please you in bed." Tears fill my eyes. "If you're worried, I'll get you sick. I won't. When I was at Jelena's Hope, they made sure I didn't have anything." Viktor walks around the bed, stopping in front of me. "And I'm on the pill, so I won't get pregnant."

"Look at me," he orders, but I refuse. He stoops down to my level and takes my face in his hands. "What happened to you was not your fault, and I'm not disgusted by you in any way. I don't ever want to hear you say that. Those bastards took your body without your permission.

They may have taken the physical signs of your virginity. But in my eyes, until you willingly give yourself to a man, you're still a virgin."

He uses his thumbs to wipe the tears that are streaming down my cheeks. "I want you, Amelia. I want you so damn much, but I don't want your first time, our first time, to be rushed. You need to be sure this is what you want."

"Viktor," I murmur. "I've never been more sure of anything. I want to be with you."

He stands to his full height and walks over to the window. "You can't say that. You don't know me."

"Then, tell me." I follow, standing behind him. "I want to know everything about you. Show me. Let me see who you really are."

He turns around. "I like to be in charge, and I'm not gentle."

"Are you into that BDSM stuff too?" I've never been interested, but if that's what I need to learn to be with Viktor, I'm willing.

"No. But I do like certain things in the bedroom." He runs his hand over his head. "You're so young, and you've been through so much."

"That's in the past. It's over." I take a step closer to him, our bodies nearly touching. "This is now. We're now." I reach my hand out to touch his face. "Teach me how to be with you."

"I can't say no to you, Amelia."

In one move, he lifts me, and I wrap my legs around his waist. His lips are on mine. The kiss is intense and full of need. Both our needs. He doesn't break our connection as he walks to the bed, where he slides me down his front, setting me on my feet. "I'll be as gentle as possible," he says as he grabs the hem of his shirt, pulling it over my head. His eyes scan my naked body. "You're beautiful. Perfect."

He takes a step closer, and the back of my knees hits the bed. I lay back, propping myself on my elbows. I can't take my eyes off his body and the erection tenting his boxers.

"Lay back."

When I do, he spreads my legs, baring me to him. No one's ever given me a choice. I've only ever known violence. No man's ever looked at me with the same mix of lust and love that's on Viktor's face. It's an internal struggle, and I fight the urge to close my legs and hide my nakedness.

"Don't go there, Amelia. You're here with me." He lowers himself to his knees, and feathers kisses up first one leg and then the other. "If you're uncomfortable, tell me to stop. We will not do anything you don't want. Okay?"

When I don't respond, Viktor stops abruptly.

"Amelia, you have a choice in what we do or don't do. Let's try this again. This time, I need you to use your voice." He looks at me expectantly. "We will not do anything you don't want. If you're uncomfortable, all you need to say is stop."

"I understand, and I don't want you to stop."

He rewards me with a stunning smile and returns to kissing my leg, moving to my inner thigh, and then his tongue finds my center. I've never had a man's mouth on me. The feeling is unlike anything I've known. Viktor explores each part of me before his tongue finds my clit. He teases it gently with his tongue. I squirm from the intense pleasure, but he steadies me with his hands on my hips. Then, he increases the pressure, sucking and nipping at the sensitive area.

An unfamiliar sensation begins to build from somewhere deep inside. Sounds of pleasure escape my mouth. Then, he adds his fingers, moving them in and out while his tongue flicks my clit. My back arches as the feeling inside grows stronger.

The sensations are so overwhelming. It feels like I no longer have control over my body, and I experience a moment of panic.

Viktor must sense my fear. "That's it, *moya zirka*. Don't be afraid. Let it happen."

He nips my clit once more, and I shatter in his arms. An orgasm washes over me, taking control of every nerve ending in my body, and I cry out in pleasure. Viktor doesn't stop. He continues his licking and sucking, drawing out the intense pleasure. Just when I don't think I can handle it a second longer, he stops.

"You taste exquisite and look beautiful when you come for me," he says as he stands and positions himself over me.

I can't speak. My senses are overwhelmed by the high I've just experienced. Then, he kisses me, letting me taste my essence on his lips.

"Was that your first?"

"Yes."

"It won't be your last." He smiles. "Are you sure you're ready?"

"Yes, please. I want to feel you inside me."

He leans back and takes his rigid length into his hand. Then, he slowly breaches my entrance and stills.

"Are you okay?

"I've had men inside me, but never willingly. All the way back to Seth, no one ever asked or cared if I was okay. Instead, they derived pleasure from my pain. My past and present collide. I swallow over the lump in my throat, trying my best to not be overcome with emotion. "Yes. I'm okay."

I hold onto his arms as he slowly pushes himself further in. His piercing blue gaze locks onto mine. His eyes say what words don't—I'm not alone. We're here together, and he'll never hurt me.

Viktor's my rock as I fight against the horrific memories trying to claw their way into the forefront of my mind. I can't let them win. They have no place in this moment.

Once he's fully sheathed inside me, he stops again. This time, lowering his forehead to mine. He's allowing my physical body to adjust to the new sensations.

Then, ever so slowly, he begins moving his hips. The gentle friction reignites my senses, and I feel that same tingling building up again. Viktor lowers his head, kissing me passionately. My hands roam his chest, shoulders, and arms, reveling in the feel of his toned muscles that flex with each move.

This is the first time I'm willingly giving myself to a man. I want to experience every move, feel every sensation to its fullest, and commit them to memory. Viktor never stops touching or kissing me. Never breaks our physical connection.

"Come for me again," he says, his voice deep and gravely.

"I don't know how," I whimper.

His hand goes between us as he rubs my clit, bringing me closer and closer.

"Just like that. Don't be afraid. I'll catch you when you fall."

His reassurance was what I needed to let go. To allow pleasure to take over my body, knowing I'm safe to fall apart in his arms.

Viktor keeps his movements still slow and gentle, but I feel the strain in his muscles. He's holding back.

I cup his cheek in my palm. "It's okay. You don't have to be so careful."

"I don't want to hurt you."

"You could never hurt me. I want to feel you—all of you."

With my permission, Viktor picks up the intensity of his movements. With each thrust, my body welcomes him deeper. I didn't think it was possible, but I feel another orgasm building.

"Come with me, moya zirka."

He thrusts one more time, and I let go. Viktor follows me over the edge. His body pulses inside mine. I'm overwhelmed by both the physical sensations and emotions of the moment. The feeling of our bodies and hearts joining together. Tears stream down my face.

"Did I hurt you?" Viktor asks nervously and tries to move off me.

"No. You didn't." I hold him as tight as I can. "Please don't move yet. Let me feel you for another minute longer."

He lowers his mouth to mine and gently kisses my lips. "I love you, Amelia Solonik."

Viktor

Her words burrow deep inside me to a place of vulnerability I hide from most people. But instead of keeping her out, I let her in.

I've only told one other woman I loved her, but she couldn't return my affection. The hurt and loneliness that resided deep inside didn't abate.

But tonight, Amelia's love fills the deep void I've carried with me for years. For the first time in my life, I feel like a whole man. A man worthy of the love Amelia's so freely giving.

Carefully, I withdraw from Amelia's body and position myself next to her. I keep my arm wrapped tightly around her, and she nestles herself against me. She lays her head on my chest, and I rub lazy circles on her back as we bask in the afterglow of what we've just shared.

At some point, we fall asleep, our bodies entwined with one another.

The sun shining through the window wakes me, and for the briefest of moments, I fear last night was nothing more than a dream. But then, I feel her breath on my chest. Amelia's still here in my arms.

"Good morning," she whispers, her voice sleepy.

"It's the best morning." I smile.

"Is it now? Why?"

"Because you're here, next to me."

"I think I can make it even better."

I'm already hard as she pushes herself up, straddling my body. I steady her as she lowers herself over my erection. Her head falls back with a quiet moan, and I take the opportunity to appreciate every inch of her perfect body.

When she opens her eyes, I see the fear. Her body tenses. "What do I do?"

"Move yourself up and down. Like this."

With my hands on her hips, I lift and lower her gently.

"This is so much more intense. I feel you everywhere."

She continues the movement on her own. As she experiments with the pace, I slide my hands up her abdomen to her breasts and roll her hard nipples between my fingers. Then, lifting my head, I take one into my mouth, sucking and nipping. She mewls in pleasure.

"I'm so close already."

I want to come with her. I lift my hips, pushing myself deeper. She fumbles with the new rhythm. I hold her hips, taking control of the pace.

"You feel so good, Viktor."

"You feel us, *moya zirka*. We're perfect together." I thrust hard. "You were made for me. You. Are. Mine." As soon as the words leave my lips, I come hard. Her orgasm squeezes my body, drawing out our shared pleasure.

She lays forward on my chest. "I am yours. Always."

As much as I want to spend the rest of the day in bed worshiping her body, we have to get up. I purchased tickets to visit the aquarium this afternoon.

"Shower with me." I take her hand and lead her into the bathroom.

After I adjust the water, I step aside to let her enter first. We stand under the rainhead shower, letting the warm water fall over us. I know we should get on with the shower, but I can't help myself. I lift her, and she instinctively wraps her legs around my waist. I back her up against the tiles as I slide into her. She holds onto my shoulders as I take her hard and fast.

"Oh my God, Viktor. You feel—"

"Is it too much?"

She squeezes her legs tight. "No. Don't stop."

The pulsing of her body sets off my orgasm. My muscles tense as I spill into her. I hold her tight against me until her breathing returns to normal. Then, I carefully lower her until her feet touch the shower floor.

Amelia reaches around me to grab the body wash, squirting some into her palm. Then she washes my body. Her petite hands rub over my chest and down my sides. Amelia lowers herself to her knees as she tenderly washes my legs and my cock, which is hard and ready to take her again.

When she's through, I help her to her feet and take my turn washing her. Our caring actions transform a regular shower into an intimate and profoundly connecting experience.

Amelia

Last night and this morning were more than I could've ever hoped for. My past experiences with sex have been unwilling and violent. They were full of pain from forceful taking.

Viktor was none of that. He was gentle and giving. I've never had a man's mouth explore my most intimate areas. I've never been granted pleasure. And when he finally penetrated me, it wasn't to gain some sick power over me. It was a consensual joining of two bodies—two souls.

Viktor told me he likes to be in control in the bedroom. That he's not gentle. Which makes last night even more special. Everything he did was for me. He set aside his own wants and needs to ensure my first time was perfect.

I was afraid to open my eyes this morning. Scared when I did, I'd realize everything was a dream. But it wasn't. Viktor's arm was still wrapped around me. My legs tangled with his, and my head on his chest, listening to the steady beat of his heart.

"I almost don't want to go back home," I say as I finish toweling off after our shower.

"Don't think about it right now. Let's focus on enjoying today." He passes me my clothes, which thankfully dried overnight. "Are you hungry?"

"I'm starving."

"I'm sorry. I shouldn't have been so selfish."

"I'm not sorry. I enjoyed every second." I smile. "I hope we do it again."

Viktor wraps his arms around my waist and pulls me up against him. "I can promise you we'll do it again. But right now, we're going to eat."

We found a cute little café with outdoor seating, where we enjoyed a delicious lunch. Now, we're at the aquarium learning about the area's wildlife and the aquarium's efforts to ensure the watersheds in the region remain a clean and healthy environment.

Viktor's like a little boy at the touch tank. He can't contain his smile when a hermit crab crawls over his hand, and he's surprised by the softness of the chocolate chip starfish. He's shocked to learn there's something called a sea cucumber and that some people consider it a delicacy.

Before we leave, we aquadopt a Swell Shark pup. On our next trip back, we'll be able to schedule a private feeding with our adopted animal. Then, we do some souvenir shopping before walking back to the car.

"Thank you for today."

"You don't have to thank me."

"I don't have to. I want to."

"I intend to give you the world, Amelia."

"All I want is you."

"I don't deserve you."

I hate that he feels unworthy of love. "You deserve every good thing in life."

And I plan to prove that to him.

Amelia

Viktor and I decide to celebrate Thanksgiving by ordering pizza and cuddling up on the couch to watch movies. We're halfway through *Son-in-Law* when Viktor's phone rings with a video call request.

"It's Natalie," he says, tapping the green button on his screen connecting the call.

"Happy Thanksgiving," Natalie says. "I hope we didn't interrupt your dinner."

"We didn't do the whole turkey thing. We ordered pizza."

"Pizza for Thanksgiving?" Alex asks, shocked.

"You forget, neither of us are born and bred American," Viktor says with a smile.

"How are you feeling, Nat?"

"Nauseous."

"Being pregnant doesn't sound appealing at all." I scrunch my nose.

"It's all worth it when you get that new baby."

"I guess."

"Rose has been asking to talk to you both," Natalie says. "Hang on while I get her."

She lays her phone down, and our view switches to the ceiling while they try to corral their daughter. I hit the mute button. "Are you okay with this?"

"I am." Viktor grabs my hand. "What's more important is if you're okay with it?"

"Alex and Natalie mean a lot to both of us. I want them to be a part of our lives. As long as you do."

"They're like family to me, but I know Natalie and I have a complicated history," Viktor says. "I don't want you to be uncomfortable."

"You were Natalie's rock when her life was in ruins. I know what you mean to one another and that you'll always have a special bond. I'd never ask you to change that."

Viktor cups my face in his palm before kissing me. "Your compassion and understanding amaze me, *moya zirka*."

"We've got her," Alex says, the camera view returning to them.

I take us off mute.

"Hi there, Rosie-girl. Auntie Melia misses you."

"I miss you too, Auntie Melia." Rose's voice melts my heart.

"Guess who's here with me?"

"*Dedushka?*"

"Nope, even better." I turn the phone, so she can see Viktor.

"Friker," Rose squeals.

"*Privet, printessa. Ya skuchayu po tebe.*"

"*Ya tozhe soskuchilsya,*" Rose answers.

"Wow, her Russian's coming along really well." I'm impressed.

"She picks it up so easy," Natalie says. "I wish I could do it as well as she does."

"I wish you guys could come out for a visit."

"We can try to plan something after you're back from Christmas break."

I look at Viktor. "I'm not going home for break. The band has a few shows over the holiday."

"Have you told Max yet?" Alex asks.

"Nope." There's a lot I haven't told him yet.

"I'm assuming he doesn't know about the two of you yet?"

"We're not in a rush for that conversation," Viktor says.

"You two are set on this relationship?"

Viktor puts his arm around me. "Yes."

"You have our full support," Natalie adds.

"Thank you. That means the world to us."

Natalie shows us her ultrasound photos. The baby looks like something from an alien movie, but I tell her how adorable they are anyway. Regardless of its current alien status, in a few months, it will be my adorable little niece or nephew.

"It's been great talking to you, but we have to get going," Viktor says. "We're in the middle of a movie marathon."

"We'll plan a get-together soon."

We say our goodbyes and get back to our movie.

The weekend goes by way too quickly. We spent most of it exploring one another's bodies. But today, we have to go back to the real world. We're meeting the guys at Mr. Hart's office to discuss the contract Death Rat's been offered.

I spent hours last night trying to decide what to wear. As usual, Viktor said everything looked great. After the fifth outfit, he was done with the fashion show. He scooped me up and carried me to his room, where he spent the rest of the night showing me how much he prefers me without clothes. The memory makes me smile.

It took a bit, but I decided to go with my denim skirt and a black tank top that exposes my mid-drift. I pull my hair back into a ponytail and put some make-up on. Then, I grab my black Chucks and am ready to go.

As usual, Viktor's ready to go before me and is waiting on the balcony.

"Ready?" I ask as I step outside.

"I am, but you're not."

"What do you mean? I love my outfit." I give a quick twirl.

He pulls me onto his lap. "Every man in that room won't be able to take his eyes off you, which will bring up violent urges in me."

His overprotectiveness and jealousy are a turn-on. "But the only man in the room I care about is you."

"Can I convince you to put on a different outfit? Something that covers some more skin?"

"Nope." I hop off his lap. "Now, let's go, or we'll be late."

Viktor

As I suspected, all eyes are on Amelia when she walks into the meeting room. Mateo gets up from his seat and gives her a hug.

"You look great." He doesn't hide his perusal of her body.

"Um. Thanks." She walks around him to an empty chair. I take a seat beside her.

Mateo's father, the band's attorney, sits across from me.

"It's nice to see you, Amelia," Mr. Hart says.

"You too, sir."

"Amelia, this is Jennifer Carlisle. She's the attorney for Zapped Euforia."

"It's very nice to meet you."

"You too," Jennifer says, turning her attention to me. "And you are?"

"Viktor."

"Are you Ms. Solonik's personal counsel?"

"Yes."

Amelia squeezes my leg under the table. I grab her hand and thread my fingers with hers.

"Now that we're all here. Let's get started." Jennifer picks up a stack of papers. "Please take a copy and pass them around. Mr. Hart, you've already had the opportunity to go over these. Are there any changes you'd like made?"

"No. Everything's been written up as we discussed. Death Rat." He stops and clears his throat. "Will be the opening act for Zapped Euforia for the duration of their nationwide stadium tour. There will be a total of twenty shows."

"When does the tour start?" Viktor asks.

"It kicks off the first weekend in May."

"That's before the spring semester is over."

"Will that be a problem?"

"No, it won't," Amelia answers before I have the chance to speak.

I give her a questioning glance but don't say anything. How's she going to manage school, the spring recital, and traveling with the band? Unless. No. She wouldn't consider quitting school, would she?

"Mr. Hart, can you review the contract details before we make a final decision?"

"Everett, please. And certainly."

Over the next twenty minutes, he explains each detail of the pending contract, including show dates, travel expenses, and compensation.

"Do you feel this offer is in the band's best interest?"

"It's a fair offer and an incredible opportunity for them." He looks at the boys and Amelia. "If you're all comfortable with this, we can sign today."

They offer a resounding yes. Despite my reservations, Amelia joins the rest of the group in signing the contract.

"Congratulations," Jennifer says as she gathers her things and stands. "Rowan Ford, Zapped Eupforia's rep, will be in touch with you in the next few weeks."

"I'll see Ms. Carlisle out," Everett says. "I'll be back in a few minutes."

Once they leave, the boys start high-fiving each other and hugging Amelia.

"This is our big break, guys," Quincy says. "Next tour, we'll be the headliners."

The five of them chat excitedly, making plans for an updated set list and a rehearsal schedule. From the sound of it, most of Amelia's holiday break will be filled with band activities.

Everett Hart returns to the room, closing the door behind him. "Congratulations. You've all worked very hard for this. I'm proud of you. My secretary's making copies of your press schedule. There are photo shoots, interviews, and several other events scheduled over the next few months."

"Interviews, for what?" Mateo asks.

"Press interviews to hype up Death Rat for the tour."

"Cool."

"We need to leave," I whisper to Amelia. "There are a few things we have to discuss."

"If there's nothing else, we have to be going," Amelia addresses the room, then we excuse ourselves.

It's a quiet walk back to the car. I'm trying to keep my temper under control—something that's proving rather difficult at the current moment.

"You're mad," Amelia says once we're on the road.

"Mad? I'm more than mad." I grip the steering wheel tighter. "How do you plan on finishing your semester and going on tour?"

"I'm not going back to school in the spring."

Amelia

"That's not an option," Viktor says through gritted teeth.

"Excuse me?"

"You're not dropping out of school." He raises his voice.

"I'm the one who gets to decide that, remember?" I cross my arms. "What am I going to do with a degree in classical music other than maybe teach?"

"What's wrong with teaching?"

"Nothing's wrong with it. But I don't want to teach." I turn slightly in my seat. "Being in a band was never on my radar. Heck, there's a lot in my life right now that was never on my radar. But I love the direction I'm headed."

"What if this band thing doesn't work out?"

"I'll figure that out then."

Viktor's silent for several minutes. His hands relax on the steering wheel, which is a good sign. I understand this decision seemed sudden, but it's something I've been thinking about for a few days.

Sparrow texted last week with a heads-up about the tour dates. I didn't say anything right away. I wanted the chance to think through

299

everything on my own. When the subject came up today, I already knew my answer.

Playing in this band has been a dream come true—a dream I didn't even know I had. But one I'm not ready to walk away from. I'm confident Viktor will come around. My parents? They're going to take some more convincing.

Viktor still hasn't said anything when we pull up at home. Unfortunately, the rest of the conversation is going to have to wait. I have an online class in ten minutes.

I grab my earbuds and laptop and head out to the balcony. There's no reason not to enjoy the afternoon sunshine while I'm in class.

My thoughts drift while the professor lectures. If I can take more classes online, I can possibly stay in school part-time while we're touring. That might smooth things over with everyone. But is that what I want?

Life's going to be crazy with rehearsals, shows, and traveling. I want to make sure there's time for Viktor and me to spend together as well. If I stay in school, that's going to significantly decrease my free time. I decide to stick to my plan of dropping out. Everyone else will have to get used to it.

Before I know it, class is over, and I'm bringing my laptop back to my room. Viktor stops me on the way.

"I packed us a picnic. How about we have an early dinner by the water?"

"That sounds perfect. I just have to put this away first."

This is a good sign that he's ready to talk. I hope he sees things my way. I'm going to need as many people in my corner as possible.

Viktor

While Amelia's in class, I keep busy in the kitchen. Cooking gives me something to focus on besides my anger. Amelia made a major life decision, something that will affect us both, without even mentioning it to me. If this is going to work, we need to have better communication.

My timing is perfect. I finish packing the cooler just as Amelia steps into the kitchen.

"I've packed us a picnic. How about we have an early dinner by the water?"

"That sounds perfect. I just have to put this away first."

It only takes a few seconds before she's ready. She grabs the bag, I take the cooler, and then we head to the beach. After we get the blanket laid out, Amelia opens the cooler and sets out our food. It isn't anything extravagant. We're having tuna sandwiches and a salad.

"I'm sorry for not telling you about the tour dates and my decision to quit school," she says. "There's no excuse. I was wrong."

"If we're going to be together, we have to talk about these things before making a decision."

"I was afraid you'd say no."

"Amelia." I take her hand. "I'll always be in your corner. But I'm not going to lie. I'm starting to worry about how your parents will handle all this."

"Me too. It's going to be a shock, but they'll get used to it."

"What idea are you referencing? Us or quitting school?"

"Both." She gives me a small smile.

"You're going to have to tell them about holiday break soon."

"I'll call them tomorrow," she sighs. "I'm not looking forward to it."

"We'll call it a warm-up for when we tell them about us."

"Hey guys," Amelia says, looking over my shoulder. "What are you two doing here?"

I turn around and see Sparrow and Mateo walking toward us.

"You forgot your copy of the contract," Mateo says. "And I thought maybe we could talk."

I know Mateo wants to talk to her about what happened at the party.

"Sparrow and I can take this stuff back up to the house," I suggest. "If that's okay with you."

Amelia nods.

I lean close to her. "I'll be watching from the house and can be here in seconds if you need me." Then, I stand and grab the cooler. "Come on, Sparrow, there's extra sandwiches in the house."

Amelia

"Here's your contract." Mateo hands me a manilla
envelope.

"Thanks." I set it down on the blanket next to me.

"We can't keep ignoring what happened."

"There's been a lot going on." I shrug.

"I went too fast. I realize that. I know something bad happened to you," Mateo says. "Will you tell me what it was?"

This is something I've worked tirelessly on in my sessions—telling my story. I knew it'd eventually come up in conversation with someone at some point. But I also knew no matter how much I prepared for this moment, it wouldn't make it any easier. Ania has stressed that I'm in control of what details I share. Not everyone is entitled to know everything.

"I was fifteen when my parents died. Within a matter of hours, I became an orphan and a foster child."

Most people would think that was the worst part of the story, but it only goes downhill from there.

"While I was in foster care, I was raped." Mateo listens quietly. Although the circumstances were different, our stories share a lot of similarities. I skip the parts about being trafficked. It's not something I feel comfortable sharing with him. "I ran away and lived on the streets. Eventually, I met Max and Irina. They're good people. They've given me a home and a family. I was lucky."

"Lucky? Shit, Amelia. There's nothing lucky about any of that."

"I'm not saying my story was all rainbows and unicorns. My past will always taunt me, but I do my best to not let it rule my life. I'm in a good place now." I glance toward the house and see Viktor and Sparrow sitting on the deck.

"Sparrow told me you know about my past."

"I do."

"You and I are so much alike." Mateo gets on his knees. "We're made for each other."

"Mateo—"

"Wait." He puts up his hand. "I know you aren't in love with me right now, but I think if you give it some time, give us some time, I'll prove that I'm worthy of your love."

"You don't have to prove anything to me. You're worthy of love." I take a deep breath. "But time isn't going to change anything. I'm in love with someone else."

"Don't tell me. You think you're in love with Viktor?" He lets out a frustrated breath. "You have to realize he's way too old for you. What could you possibly have in common?" He takes my hands in his. "My family has money. I can give you the world, Amelia. You just have to let me."

"I'm so sorry. I don't want to hurt you."

"Then don't." His grey eyes fill with tears. "Give me a chance, please."

Mateo's pleas are sincere. I have no doubt about that. I don't want to hurt him more than he's already hurting. But I can't give him what he's asking.

"Please try to understand. There's nothing wrong with you. You're a nice guy. But all we'll ever be is friends."

Tears are now pouring down his face. "If you give us some more time, I'll show you—"

"Viktor and I are together."

"There's no way he can make you happy," he spits out the words.

"I get it if you need some time and space. I want to stay friends."

Mateo stands up. His sadness has shifted to anger. "A friend, that's all I'll ever be to you. Well, that's not enough for me," he yells. "I need you to love me, not him." He points toward the house.

Viktor and Sparrow both jump from their chairs.

I get to my feet. "Mateo, please calm down. You're a nice guy. You'll find someone—"

"I don't want *someone*. I want you." He grabs my hand. "Come with me. Let me show you."

"Let me go." I try to pull my hand away.

"I want to take you out. Show you that I'm the right man for you, not Viktor. He's twice your age. He can't make you happy. He—."

"Take your hands off her." Viktor comes from nowhere and pushes Mateo away from me. He holds my trembling body close to his. "Can't you see you're scaring her?"

"I'm sorry, Amelia," Mateo cries. His anger is gone, replaced once again by grief. "I don't want to scare you. I just want a chance. Can you give me a chance?"

I tuck myself into Viktor's side and cry.

"Mateo, come on." Sparrow tugs on his arm. "It's time to go."

"Sparrow, tell her. Tell her I'm not going to hurt her."

"She knows that."

"Then why won't she love me?" Mateo grabs Sparrow's shirt. "Why won't she love me?"

"You can't force someone to love you. I know that all too well," he says quietly. "Come on, let me take you home."

As Sparrow leads Mateo away, he keeps repeating, "Why won't she love me?"

I may not love him the way he wants me to, but I do care about him. I don't like seeing him hurting.

"He'll be okay," Viktor reassures me.

"Are you sure?"

"It might take him some time to process everything. But I'm sure."

Viktor

Watching a distraught Mateo being led away by Sparrow is a gut-wrenching sight. I've been in his shoes and understand the heartache he's experiencing. Loving someone who doesn't love you back is a hard road to walk. But Mateo's young, and he has a strong support system. I'm confident he'll be okay.

Amelia's shaken up by the whole situation. Once they're out of sight, I scoop her into my arms and carry her into the house. She keeps her head tucked against my chest as I walk past what used to be her room and lay her on my bed. I lay beside her and open my arms, allowing her to curl up next to me. I kiss the top of her head but make no move to do anything more. Amelia needs the intimacy of the moment to feel safe and cherished.

Amelia's ringtone wakes me up, and I slide the phone from her pocket. The clock on her lock screen shows it's nine p.m.

"Amelia, wake up." I shake her shoulder gently. "It's your father."

"What?" She blinks her eyes a few times as she wakes up.

"It's Max. You better answer it." I pass her the phone.

She puts the call on speaker. "Hello?" Her voice is groggy.

"*Moya malen'kaya ptichka*, did I wake you?"

"I was watching television and didn't realize I fell asleep."

"Are you feeling well?"

"Yes," she says and sits up. "I've been studying for finals and had a big paper, that's all."

"And that is why I am calling. Your semester ends next Tuesday, correct?"

"Um. Yeah." She looks at me, her eyes wide.

"I will have the jet at LAX early Wednesday morning."

"There's something I need to tell you," she says hesitantly.

"Go ahead."

"I'm not coming home for the holiday break."

We hold a collective breath and wait for his response.

"I see. And why not?"

"I have some big performances coming up in the spring. Several of us decided to stay back to rehearse over the holiday break." She's walking a fine line with the truth.

"Your mom will be disappointed."

"I know, and I apologize. But this is really important to me."

"I applaud your dedication to your craft."

Amelia lowers her head. I know she feels guilty for not telling him the whole truth.

"Is Viktor around? I want to speak to him."

"Yeah, he's right here." She takes the phone off speaker and passes it to me. "Dad wants to talk to you."

"Hey, boss. What's up?"

"Did you know she was not coming home for the holiday?"

"She mentioned it to me, yes. But she requested I allow her to tell you." And right now, I'm questioning if I should've insisted she tell him the whole story.

"I see." Although I can't physically see him, I can hear the gears turning in his head. "These kids she is rehearsing with. Have you done background checks on them?"

"Yes, boss."

"And they are, okay?"

"They're good kids."

"I am expecting you to keep her safe."

"Yes, sir. She's never out of my sight."

Amelia smiles at me, and I see mischief dancing in her eyes. What is she up to? My silent question is answered a second later when she slides out of bed and takes off her clothes. My body responds immediately, and I struggle to keep my composure.

"Is she doing well otherwise?"

"She's doing terrific."

After her sexy strip tease, she crawls across the bed and works at the button on my jeans.

"She's adjusted to California life just fine."

I lift my hips so she can pull my pants off. My erection juts from my boxers. She looks at me and smiles before she licks across the slit where there's already a drop of pre-cum. It takes every ounce of willpower I possess not to groan in pleasure. Amelia's never done this before, and she chooses right now?

"Is there anything she needs?"

"Nope." I cough as she takes the tip into her mouth. My head drops back as she takes more of my cock.

"Is she there? I would like to say goodbye to her."

"Sure."

"Your dad wants to say goodbye," I say with a wicked grin.

She sits back on her heels and takes the offered phone.

Two can play this game, *moya zirka*.

"Hi again."

I pull her to me and take a nipple in my mouth.

She gasps. "No, Dad. I'm fine. I almost dropped the phone."

While my mouth gives one breast attention, my free hand moves between her legs and finds her already wet.

"I miss you too." Her voice squeaks. "Dad, I'm exhausted. I want to turn in early tonight." She pauses while Maxim speaks. I can't make out what he's saying. "I love you too. Give Mom a hug for me."

She doesn't wait for him to say goodbye before she disconnects the call and tosses her phone to the side.

"You played a dangerous game, *moya zirka*."

"Did I?" She bites her bottom lip and feigns innocence. "What are you going to do about it?"

Challenge accepted.

Amelia squeals when I flip her onto her back without warning. I continue teasing her clit with my fingers. Sweet sounds of pleasure slip from her lips as I worship her body.

"I want you." She tries to wrap her legs around me.

"Not yet."

She groans, and I add a second finger, sliding it into her. She has no idea how fucking sexy she is as I bring her to the edge of orgasm and then stop.

"Viktor, please."

"I love hearing you beg for me," I say a second before thrusting into her. "Is that what you wanted?"

"Oh my God, yes."

I'm not gentle as I thrust in and out. "Tell me to stop if it's too much."

"No, please don't stop." She pants.

I take her mouth, needing to be connected to her in as many areas as possible. She holds onto my shoulders and meets me thrust for thrust. Her body begins to tense—her orgasm is close. I see the nervousness in her beautiful brown eyes that often happens. The loss of control she feels at that moment is a struggle for her.

"That's it, *moya zirka*. I've got you. Let go." I thrust hard and deep, and she shatters beneath me. "Fuck, Amelia." Her body tightens around me, and I release with a forceful, shuddering climax deep within her.

Amelia

I've spent the last week cramming for my finals. As happy as I am that the semester's over, I know when I leave the campus today, I won't be returning. It's bittersweet saying goodbye to this short chapter of my life, but I'm also excited about what lies ahead.

Christmas is only two weeks away. Growing up in Australia, Christmas was during our summer, so I was used to a warm weather holiday. However, living in Russia for the past few years, I quickly got used to a cold holiday season. Somehow, the snow made everything feel more Christmas-y. Now, I'm back in a warm weather climate for Christmas, and I'm finding it challenging to stir up the holiday spirit.

We're driving home when I ask, "Can we get a Christmas tree?"

"Of course. You don't have to ask."

"I didn't know how you'd feel about it."

"Do you want an artificial tree or a real tree?"

"I'd love a real one." I have many lovely memories of childhood Christmases with my parents in Australia. After I was adopted by Max and Irina, we celebrated twice—the traditional Christmas for me and the Orthodox Christmas they were used to celebrating. "But we don't have any decorations."

"Sounds like we need to go shopping. You up for it today?"

"Sure."

Before we go home, we hit the stores and pick up lights, ornaments, and tons of decorations for both inside and outside the house. The next stop is a Christmas tree lot where we pick out the most beautiful Frazier Fur I've ever laid eyes on. I take pictures while Viktor ties it to the top of the car. I've learned nothing in life is permanent, so I try to capture every memory in photos.

It's been a long day, and neither of us feels like cooking. So, we order Chinese take-out. We're sitting on the living room floor, eating at the coffee table, trying to decide the best place to put the tree.

"How about we try it in front of the windows?" I suggest

While I clean up from dinner, Viktor lifts the seven-foot tree and sets it in front of the windows. Standing back, I examine it from all angles.

"It blocks the view of the ocean."

"How about the corner over there," Viktor suggests.

"I feel bad putting something so beautiful in a corner." I crinkle my forehead.

"It's not like we're hiding it." Viktor chuckles. "It'll be visible as soon as you walk into the house and won't block the view outside."

"Let's try it and see."

He lifts the large tree again and carries it across the room, where he sets it down in the corner. After he straightens the tree in the stand and makes sure it's secure, he steps out of the way.

"What do you think?"

"I think I love it." I smile.

Viktor strings the lights on the tree, wrapping them around each branch to ensure an even distribution. When he finishes, we hang the ornaments together. While I make popcorn to string, Viktor puts lights around our windows. In a matter of a few hours, we transform our house into a Christmas wonderland.

Viktor

THE HOLIDAYS BRING UP A LOT OF MEMORIES FOR AMELIA. She's been struggling with missing her birth parents. Since my parents died, I've only celebrated Christmas one time with Natalie and Rose. With both of us having a hard time getting into the Christmas spirit, I thought I'd plan something fun for us to do. A way we can begin to make happy memories. So, while I'm outside hanging lights, I make the necessary arrangements.

When I come back in, I find Amelia sitting cross-legged on the sofa, stringing popcorn. I grab a handful from the bowl and sit next to her.

"Hey. That's for the tree, not your stomach," Amelia scolds me.

"It's for eating too." I feed her a piece. "I made plans for us for the next few days. You're going to need to pack a bag."

"Where are we going?"

"South."

She freezes. A look of terror blankets her face.

"What's wrong?" Amelia doesn't move or answer. With one word, I've triggered her panic. I take the needle and string from her hand and drop them into the bowl, which I put on the coffee table. Then, I turn her to face me. "Amelia, you have to talk to me."

"Mexico." The word is barely audible.

"No, *moya zirka*." I pull her onto my lap. "I would never bring you to Mexico. We're going to San Diego for a few days."

It takes a minute, but she finally relaxes in my arms.

"I'm sorry," she whispers. "I ruined your surprise."

"Don't apologize. Nothing's been ruined. You still don't know what we're doing there." I plant a quick kiss on her lips.

"I guess we need to finish this popcorn garland if we're to pack tonight." She points to a second needle next to the bowl on the table. "Let's get moving."

We're both still learning her triggers. And thanks to Ania, I'm also learning better ways to help ground her when she panics. I don't want anything we do to cause her stress.

The drive to San Diego should only take about two hours, but this west coast traffic is worse than New York. It ends up taking us nearly three and a half hours before we pull up to the resort located on Coronado Island. We're met by the bellhop who takes our luggage. The valet is right behind him, waiting to park our car. With Amelia's hand in mine, we go to the check-in desk to get our key cards.

We're staying in a luxury beachfront villa that reminds me of the one I stayed in while I was in Grenada. The open plan features a high-end kitchen, a sitting room with modern furniture, and a fireplace. The wall of floor-to-ceiling windows offers an unobstructed view of the ocean.

The separate bedroom boasts a California King facing the ocean-front view. A set of French doors open to a private balcony with loungers and a hot tub. The ensuite bathroom boasts a marble shower big enough to fit several people.

"Wow. This place is incredible.."

"You deserve only the best, *moya zirka*." I wrap my arms around her.

"I don't care where we are as long as we're together."

Amelia's the daughter of a man with an endless amount of money. Yet none of that seems to matter to her. Unless she's forced, she doesn't buy extravagant things. That makes it even more special to bring her to these places because she truly appreciates the beauty of everything around her.

"So," She turns in my arms to face me. "What are our plans for tonight?"

"Tonight, we're staying in."

"Oh?"

"I have plans that involve only you and me tonight." I push a stray curl behind her ear. "But let's not waste the day. Want to go to the beach for a while?"

"Absolutely."

We may live on a beach, but I don't think either of us would pass up a day on the sand by the water. We'll miss oceanfront life when it's time to leave Long Beach for her tour.

Amelia

I DIDN'T THINK A BEACH COULD BE MORE PRISTINE L THAN the one we live on, but it is. The sand here literally sparkles in the sunlight, and the water is the most beautiful shade of cyan. I could lie here, entranced by the hypnotizing sound of the waves lapping at the sea's edge, and I'd never tire of the sound.

Coronado Island offers the best of both worlds with its magnificent sunrise and sunset views. And right now, we're being treated to a sunset show as the sky turns shades of pink, orange, and yellow. Just like our first night in California, we stay on the beach until the sky turns dark and the stars come out. Then, we make our way back into our villa.

Viktor doesn't know, but a few weeks ago, I bought lingerie. It's a black lace chemise with a matching thong. While I was held at Moreno's, I was forced to wear lingerie that was humiliating and degrading. Thinking about it brings back the memories of being raped. I bought this with the hope of taking back something else that was stolen from me. I've had it tucked away in my drawer, trying to get the courage to wear it.

Thankfully, Ania can't tell my parents anything we talk about. She's been a constant source of support for me when it comes to this new relationship. I told her about the lingerie and my fears surrounding it.

Replacing the traumatic memories with new, happy memories is something we've been working on. She said I'd know when the right time was, and I think tonight's it.

"I'm going to take a quick shower." I grab my pj's with the lingerie balled up inside.

"Do you mind if I order dinner?"

"Please do." I smile and disappear into the bathroom to wash away the sunscreen and sand.

After drying off, I look at the options for getting dressed. I can put on my usual pair of sleep shorts and Viktor's T-shirt, or I can overcome my fear and wear the lingerie. I stand in front of the mirror wrapped in a towel, weighing my options for what feels like an eternity. Finally, I reach out and grab the lingerie.

Tonight's the night. Then, with one last deep breath, I open the bathroom door. Viktor's lounging on the bed, looking at something on his phone. He looks up when I close the door.

"Amelia," he says my name almost reverently and sits up. "Wow. You look— Umm. You look incredible." He sets his phone aside and motions for me to go to him.

"You like it?" I ask as I walk around the bed and stand between his spread legs.

"Like it? I more than like it." He puts his hands on my hips and pulls me closer to him. "I love it."

My heart starts beating furiously. Voices from the past push their way to the surface. Flashes of faces—Seth and the men in Moreno's compound flood my senses. They're laughing with one another as they talk about what they're going to do to me. Hands grab the fabric, tearing it from my body.

Someone bends me over and kicks my legs apart. A hand wraps around my neck, holding me down. The men take turns violating my body. Some, one at a time. Others take me in different places at the same time.

"No. Stop, please," I yell. "Get away from me." I kick and punch at whatever is in front of me, desperately trying to stop the attack. I don't want to be hurt anymore.

Strong arms wrap around my waist, and I fight harder. We begin to fall, and I brace myself. I'm expecting to hit hard, but my landing is cushioned. The arms don't let go even as I continue struggling. I fight with everything I have until, finally, I break free. I scurry away on my hands and knees. I pull my knees to my chest to make myself small and hide between the bed and the wall, hoping not to be found.

Viktor

I DON'T KNOW WHAT HAPPENED. ONE SECOND, AMELIA WAS with me. The next, she was screaming and fighting against an invisible enemy.

"It's me, Amelia," I say while holding onto her. "I'm not going to hurt you."

"Let me go. Stop. Please," she screams, tears pouring down her face.

She's unable to see or hear me. Amelia's lost in her memories where she's fighting for her life. She kicks and punches with all her might. I'm not worried about getting hit. I'm concerned about her hurting herself. I keep my arms wrapped tightly around her as I desperately try to reach her and calm her.

"*Moya zirka*, stop fighting. You're safe," I say, sliding us down to the floor. That only seems to make her fight harder.

My heart shatters seeing the terror on her face. Reluctantly, I open my arms and let her go. I don't know what else to do. The second she's free, she crawls away from me as fast as possible and hides between the bed and the wall.

I stay on the floor where I am for a few minutes. I'm struggling to make sense of what's happening and what I can do to get through to her. Wetness coats my cheeks as she continues to cry.

"Go away. Please don't hurt me."

My beautiful girl, I'll never hurt you. But how do I reach you right now? How do I bring you back to me? Slowly, I stand up and walk across the room.

"*Moya zirka*, it's just me, Viktor," I say quietly and sit on the floor beside her, but I don't reach out. "No one's going to hurt you. You're safe here. Come back to me, please."

The scene is heartbreaking. Amelia curled up, her knees to her chest and her arms wrapped around her legs. She's sobbing while repeatedly begging not to be hurt. I'm afraid to touch her. Scared to send her back into fighting mode.

"Sweetheart, can you look at me?" She doesn't lift her head. "What do I do?" I think back to when I was a boy and would wake from nightmares. My mama would sit in my bed and sing to me until I fell back asleep.

So, that's what I do. I know how much Amelia loves "Just Give Me a Reason." She sings it at all her shows, and she added it to my playlist. I didn't realize it that first night, but when Amelia sang those words, she was singing to me. She already had feelings for me, but I wasn't there yet.

Although my voice is nothing like my angel's, I hope the words penetrate the fear that's taken her away from me and speak to her heart. Amelia's not broken. Our hearts are meant for one another. Amelia taught me how to love again—we're one another's destiny.

When I get to the chorus, I hear her voice, ever so softly, singing with me. That's my girl, fight through the darkness. My tears fall unbidden, watching her slay her demons and return to me. I stop singing and listen to her finish the song.

"Viktor?"

"Yes, *moya zirka*. I'm here."

"Hold me, please."

When I open my arms, Amelia climbs onto my lap and lays against my chest. "You're safe. I've got you." I close my arms around her in a protective embrace. "You're safe. I promise no one will ever hurt you again."

Amelia

Then, somewhere in the distance, I hear a different voice. A comforting voice—a song. Little by little, it gets closer. As it does, it chases the bad things away until all that's left is this new voice. Viktor.

It all comes back to me.

I'm here with Viktor. He'll never allow anyone to hurt me.

"Hold me, please," I beg.

He opens his arms, and I climb onto his lap and press my head against his chest. The sound of his steady heartbeat is calming. The feel of his arms around me is grounding.

"You're safe. I've got you. You're safe," he murmurs. "I promise no one will ever hurt you again."

"I'm sorry. I ruined tonight."

"Do not apologize. You're okay, and that's all that matters to me."

We stay huddled together on the floor until we hear a knock on the door.

"That's our dinner. Is it okay if I answer it?"

I nod.

Without letting me go, Viktor gets to his feet. He sets me gently on the edge of the bed. "Stay in here. I'll be right back."

While he's gone, I grab a robe from the bathroom and slip it on. Then, I get my phone and text, Ania. It's morning in Russia, and I know she usually starts her day early.

Me: Are you awake?

I get a response right away.

Ania: I am. Are you okay?

Me: Not really. Can I call you?

I don't get a chance to pull up her number before my phone rings. I touch the green circle connecting the call.

"What's wrong?"

"I had a panic attack," I say. "It was like I was right back in the room with those men.

"Are you ready to—" Viktor stops when he gets to the doorway. "I'm sorry. I didn't know you were on a call." He turns to walk away.

"Please stay."

"Are you sure?" he asks.

"Yes."

Viktor sits next to me, and I explain to Ania about the flashbacks I started having when I came out of the bathroom. "I know what I was experiencing, but I don't know what was happening in reality. All I remember is hearing Viktor singing to me."

"May I ask Viktor to tell me what happened?"

I nod. I'm scared to hear it, but at the same time, I need to know.

"As Amelia said, she'd just come into the bedroom. I told her how beautiful she looked and called her over to me." He stops and looks at me for permission to continue.

I nod, letting him know it's okay.

"When I reached out to touch her, she started screaming."

Viktor continues telling Ania how I yelled and fought him physically. How he held me, but I got more agitated. He didn't know what to do, so he finally let me go. It wasn't until he began singing that I came around.

"You had a trauma reaction."

"I feel like I lost all the ground I've worked so hard to gain." A tear drips down my face.

"You stumbled, but we've talked about that. It's okay, and something I anticipate will occasionally happen," Ania reassures me. "Now, we're going to devise a plan to minimize how often it happens until it doesn't happen at all. And we'll give Viktor some more tools to help if it does."

"Viktor knows a lot of my story. He knows I was raped. But I haven't told him what happened that night."

"Is that something you're comfortable doing now?"

"It's not something I ever look forward to talking about. But if I don't, it'll continue to come between us. To have power over me. I don't want to give it that much power anymore." I turn slightly on the bed, facing Viktor. "Moreno had a few *special* clients he'd bring to the house. Sometimes, one at a time, but more often, he'd have a party. There'd be a group of men. Those nights were awful, but not the worst." I stop and take a breath. "The worst was the night you came to rescue Natalie and Alex. There were five guards. The power went out, and they knew something was up. One of them grabbed me and brought me into Moreno's panic room. The other four guards followed us. They didn't care about their boss's orders anymore. They laughed as they talked about what they were going to do to me."

"I tried to get out, but the door wouldn't open. One held me still while another took his knife and cut off the black lingerie I was wearing." I close my eyes, reliving the horror of that night. "They started by taking turns with me. But as they grew more aroused, they grew bolder. If there was a hole, they made sure one of them was filling it. My body tore from their violent intrusion. I thought they were going to kill me."

Viktor's beautiful blue eyes look tortured as he struggles to hold my gaze.

"I fought. I fought so hard."

"It's my fault," he says.

"It's not your fault. The people to blame are those men and Moreno. And they're all dead. If it wasn't for you, they would've killed me."

Ania allows us to process at our own pace. Then, she reaffirms what I told Viktor, that none of what happened was his fault. Once we're ready, we'll make a plan to move forward.

She suggests wearing lingerie a few times without doing anything physical so I can get used to wearing it and associate it with new, positive memories. She encourages Viktor to check in with me frequently to gauge where I'm at and if we need to stop.

"Amelia, I think it would be beneficial for you and Viktor to establish a safe word or gesture. You need to feel empowered when you're in a vulnerable situation," Ania explains. Then, she gives a final piece of advice. "For now, try a color other than black. Something that isn't associated with the past."

By the time our emergency session is over, Viktor and I are both feeling more confident moving forward.

"Why don't you get changed, and then we'll eat," Viktor suggests.

I stop on my way into the bathroom. "I'm sorry for ruining your plans tonight."

"Seeing you terrified was hell for me, but I'm sure it was worse for you reliving that nightmare." He walks over to me. "Please don't apologize. We're here. We're together, and you're safe. That's all that matters to me."

Taking his face in my hands, I stand on tiptoes and kiss him. "I love you, Viktor."

"And I love you, *moya zirka*."

Amelia

Last night started in the worst possible way. It was no surprise that I was raped, Viktor already knew that, but he didn't know the specifics. Especially from that last night. I've been afraid to tell him. Scared that when he found out, he'd run in the other direction. But that's not what happened. If anything, telling him strengthened our bond.

"Are you ready to go?" Viktor pops his head into the bathroom, where I'm trying to get my unruly curls up in a bun.

"As soon as I get my hair to cooperate, yes."

Viktor stands behind me. Our reflections stare back at us. "You're beautiful, no matter what your hair does."

"You're sweet but crazy." I laugh and finish securing my hair. "I'm ready."

We're going to see the San Diego Parade of Lights. It's something I've learned is a holiday tradition here. Viktor drives us back over the Coronado Bridge to the pier. It's supposed to be the perfect spot to watch the water parade.

While he drives, I take pictures of this incredible five-lane bridge and the other beautiful sights as we make our way up the coast of Southern

California. We pass a marina filled with boats of all different sizes, and I smile, thinking about the dinner cruise we took when we first moved here.

"Look at the ship," I exclaim as we pass the USS Midway Museum. "How in the world does something that big even float?"

"It's pretty impressive."

Viktor glances at it quickly and then turns into a parking lot on the pier. It seems like an odd place to watch the boat parade, but I'm sure Viktor knows what he's doing. As I get out of the car, my phone rings. It's Sparrow.

"Hello?"

"Hey. Do you have a minute?"

"Sure. What's up?"

"It's Mateo."

The tone in Sparrow's voice makes my heart stop. "Is he okay?"

"Not really. God, I don't know how to say this, Mel."

I put the phone on speaker so Viktor can hear, too. "You're scaring me, Sparrow."

"The day after he flipped out on you at your house, he overdosed."

"What? Why didn't anyone call me?"

"The first few days, he was in bad shape. They weren't sure he was going to make it. Once he crossed the major hurdles and woke up, I was going to call you, but he asked me not to."

A mix of emotions hits me all at once. Fear. Sadness. Guilt. "I didn't realize things were that bad."

"None of us did. Mateo learned how to function while he was high or drunk."

"I don't know what to say." I'm concerned for Mateo and Sparrow. I know how much he cares for Mateo.

"Mateo finally hit rock bottom. He told his mom he needed help, and his parents arranged for him to go to a rehab center. He's been there about a week."

"Have you talked to him?"

Sparrow's voice cracks. "No one's allowed to contact him until he's fully detoxed."

"I'm sorry. I didn't mean for this to happen."

"His overdosing isn't your fault," Viktor adds.

"Viktor's right, Mel. None of us is responsible for Mateo's actions."

"If we don't go, we're going to be late," Viktor says quietly.

"Sparrow, can I call you tomorrow?" I don't want him to think I'm blowing him off. "Viktor brought me to San Diego. We're about to watch the Parade of Lights."

"I'm leaving for Aspen tomorrow. I'll text you after we get settled. Don't worry about Mateo. He's safe now. You go and have fun. You're going to love it."

"Thanks for letting me know about Mateo."

The call ends, and I close my eyes, trying to wrap my head around everything Sparrow just told me. "Wow."

"That was a lot. Are you okay?"

I turn my head to look at Viktor. "Are you sure this isn't my fault?"

"*Moya zirka*, Mateo had substance abuse problems long before he met you. His actions are his and his alone." Viktor takes my hand in his. "Hopefully, he takes this opportunity seriously."

"I hope so, too."

"Do you still want to do this tonight?"

I sit back up. "Yes."

"Let's go then." Viktor smiles.

In true Viktor style, nothing about tonight is done halfway. We aren't just watching the Parade of Lights from the shore. We're taking a dinner cruise in the harbor to watch the parade.

This year's theme is A Tropical Christmas, and the lights are spectacular. The owners have taken the theme to the extreme. There are inflatable palm trees and Santas in Hawaiian shirts. When I think it can't get any better, the next display is even more impressive. There's a whole island on one of the boats. I wish the parade could go on all night, but eventually, it ends, and our boat sails back to the pier.

"Thank you." I thread my arm through Viktor's as we walk back to the car. "This was one of the best things I've ever seen."

"I'm glad you liked it, *moya zirka*." He slides his arm around me. "I love making memories with you."

Viktor

The unexpected phone call from Sparrow left Amelia and me a bit shaken. The good thing is Mateo is safe and in a place that can help him get well. I offered to take Amelia back to the hotel if she wasn't up to our date. I can't lie. I was glad she didn't take that option. The Parade of Lights was an incredible spectacle to watch, but what I found even more special was how Amelia's eyes sparkled as the boats slowly sailed past.

"I think we should get a boat," I suggest as we drive back to the resort.

"Us? We don't know anything about sailing."

"We could learn."

"You're serious? You want to get a boat?"

"Yes. Then we can go out on the water whenever we want."

"Okay, Captain Vik." She giggles.

I make a mental note to check out both boats and sailing lessons.

Amelia fell asleep about fifteen minutes after we started driving.

"*Moya zirka*." I run my knuckles gently down her cheek. "Time to wake up."

"I didn't realize I fell asleep." She stretches and then unbuckles her safety belt. "You should've woken me sooner."

"You looked too pretty."

She smiles as we enter our villa. "You're a silly man."

"You call it silly. I call it head over heels in love."

"Whoever you're in love with is one lucky girl." She bats her eyelashes at me.

"Is she now?" I step closer to her.

"Yes." She takes a step backward.

"Maybe I should show her just how lucky she is?" I grab her by the waist, pulling her against me.

"I think she'd like that."

I lift her, and she wraps her legs around my waist. I attack her mouth as I walk her into the bedroom and kick the door closed behind us. She slides down my body. The friction only makes me harder.

"Are you okay? Do you want me to keep going?"

"Yes, please."

"Raise your arms," I command.

When she does, I pull her shirt over her head and toss it to the side. Her shorts follow a second later. Amelia stands in front of me in her pink lace bra and panties. I'm in awe of how perfect she is.

"You're overdressed." She smiles seductively as she toward me. Sliding her hands up my chest, she pulls my shirt over my head. I remove my pants and kick them off to the side.

"Better?"

"Much."

"Lie down." Amelia lies on her back with her head on the pillows. "Can we try something different?"

"Like what?"

"Stay there." I go into my bag in the closet. I'm a little nervous about how she'll react to my idea. When I return, I have a small silver vibrator and a bottle in my hand. I hold them up for her to see. "I'd like to watch you make yourself come for me. You can say no if you're uncomfortable." I don't want to push her too far out of her comfort zone.

Without speaking, she shimmies her panties down her legs and drops them onto the floor.

"Is that a yes?"

She nods.

I take a step closer to her. "*Moya zirka*, you know I need more than that."

"Yes. I want to try."

"Open your legs." I can already see her arousal, but I still apply a generous amount of lubrication. Then, I pass her the vibrator.

She turns it on and pushes the button several times, familiarizing herself with the different vibrating patterns before lowering it between her legs. She gasps when it makes contact with her clit. While she explores and finds her rhythm, I push my boxers off, freeing my erection. Then I join her on the bed, sitting on my knees between her spread legs. Leaning forward, I pull the cups of her bra down, exposing her breasts to me. Her nipples are hard and begging for attention.

"Oh my God," she moans in delight.

As much as I enjoy teasing her, I let go of her nipple with a pop and sit back on my heels. I squirt some lube in my hand and slide it up and down my erection while I watch her pleasure herself. Her eyes lock onto what I'm doing. "Do you like this?" I ask.

"Very much." She clicks the button on the vibrator, turning it up to the highest intensity. "This feels so good."

"I want you to come for me."

She closes her eyes.

"Open your eyes. I want you looking at me when you come."

Her eyelids flutter open, and her gaze locks on mine. "I'm getting close."

I don't want to come yet, so I switch my attention to Amelia and slide two fingers into her opening. Her body readily accepts them as I pump them in and out. "Are you ready?"

She nods.

I push my fingers in and curl them. As soon as they find her G-spot, she explodes. Her body squeezes my fingers as a gush of wetness coats my hand.

"What was that?" she asks, her eyes wide in panic.

"That was a fucking good orgasm," I smirk.

Without wasting another second, I crawl over her and slide my erection into her welcoming body. I take the vibrator out of her hand and press it on her overly sensitive clit. Her back arches as another orgasm rips through her body.

"Do you think you can give me one more?"

"I don't know," she pants. "It feels so intense—"

I lean forward, pressing our bodies together to kiss her. Then, I pull out.

"Please don't stop," she begs.

"There's not a chance that'll happen. Turn over."

She rolls over onto her hands and knees. Without warning, I slam into her.

"Oh God, Viktor."

"Tell me if you want me to stop."

"Don't stop, please."

Holding her hips to keep her steady, I pull back and thrust in as far as possible. My rhythm is fast and hard. Her breathing increases as she chases another orgasm.

I'm close, but I want her to come with me. I grab the vibrator that's lying next to her and press it to her swollen clit. Amelia's orgasm is almost violent in its intensity. Her arms give out from under her. I drop the toy and use my arm to hold her up. I thrust into her one more time before I follow her over the cliff. Our shared climax seems to last forever.

When the pleasure finally wanes, I pull out slowly. "That wasn't too much, was it?"

"No," she says and wraps herself around me. I was nervous at first. I've never done anything like that. But when I saw the way you looked at me and how turned on you were, that gave me the courage I lacked." She signs in contentment. "I like exploring new things with you."

"I'm glad." I hold the woman who's become my entire world against me tightly.

"So." She pushes up on her elbow. "I planned something for us tomorrow. I wanted it to be a surprise, but since I don't have my license yet, I have let you in on it."

"Okay." I grin. "What's your plan?"

"I'll tell you tomorrow." She reaches over and kisses my cheek.

Amelia

"You wait here. I'm going to put the address into the GPS." I'm doing everything possible to keep our destination a secret for as long as possible.

"Whatever you say, boss." Viktor laughs.

I hope he enjoys this and doesn't think it was a childish idea. When I was growing up, I wanted to be a zookeeper. My parents took me to the Australia Zoo several times a year. In one of my photo albums, there's a picture of me with Steve Irwin taken a few months before he passed away. Being a good steward of our planet and wildlife has been instilled in me since I was a child.

Before they adopted me, Mom and Dad learned of my love for animals. They brought me to the Leningrad Zoo, the oldest zoo in Russia. That place has quite a history. Dad's not a fan of animals and wouldn't let me get a pet, but each time we went, he adopted an animal at the zoo in my honor.

I was even happier when they told me Jelena's Hope would incorporate pet therapy into their services.

"All done." I pop my head into the villa. "We're good to go."

It's a short ride from the island to downtown San Diego. Before too long, signs for the zoo start popping up on the sides of the road, and Viktor begins laughing.

"What's so funny?" I'm sure he thinks going to the zoo is a stupid idea.

"After you fell asleep last night, I bought zoo tickets. I wanted to bring you before our trip was over." He glances my way. "I guess great minds think alike."

"I guess they do." He doesn't know that there's more to this surprise trip than I've told him.

Fifteen minutes later, we're parked in one of the zoo's parking lots and heading for the main entrance.

"We need to go to the will call. The Christmas lights won't come on until this evening, so I made some other plans for this afternoon."

"Oh?"

"I guess I can let you in on them now. We're going to be taking a private safari. I hope that's okay."

Viktor stops walking and turns to face me. "No one's done anything like this for me in a very long time."

"I want to give you the world, too."

Right there, in the middle of the sidewalk, he kisses me. And not just a peck on the cheek. A passionate display of affection.

"What did I do to deserve you?" he whispers. I go to answer him, but he puts his finger to my lips.

"Next," the lady behind the window calls.

"That's us."

After I give the woman my name, she makes a call and points to a bench where she says our tour guide, Dante, will meet us in about ten minutes.

The rest of the afternoon and early evening is spent on the adventure of a lifetime. If I didn't know we were in California, I'd swear we were somewhere on the African savannah. As we drive, we're treated to sightings of giraffes that come right up to the vehicle. Dante hands us some Acacia leaves to feed these gentle giants, who gladly wrap their tongues around the offered treats. We continue on and observe elephants, rhinoceros, cheetahs, and so many more animals who wander freely.

Part of our afternoon includes a sit-down lunch with Dante. While we eat, he gives us in-depth information on the various habitats and the zoo's efforts in conservation and protecting the futures of the animal species they're privileged to host.

The last stop on the safari includes a very special up-close encounter with several rhinoceros. He explains that the animals are never forced to interact with safari guests, but today, we're in luck. These pre-historic-looking creatures wander over to the vehicle and allow us to feed and touch them. It's an unbelievable privilege that neither Viktor nor I will forget.

"This isn't part of the usual tour," Dante says. "But when I heard you were originally from Australia, I thought you might enjoy a taste of home."

I'm shocked when he drives us to the Walkabout Australia part of the zoo. He leads us behind the scenes, where we get a firsthand look at what the zookeepers do daily to provide a safe, natural environment for the many endangered Australian animals housed here.

While we talk, a female employee enters the room with one of their animal ambassadors, an echidna named Orange. Although we aren't able to hold her, it's a thrill to see an animal I'm so familiar with.

Before we leave the area, we're brought back outside to a staff-only area.

"We're gonna sit here for a few minutes and see what happens." Dante leads us to some large rocks. "Here she comes."

I can't believe my eyes. A wallaby hops over to us and allows us to pet her. Several minutes later, a female kangaroo also makes her way to us.

"She has a joey," I say quietly so as not to scare her.

She eyes Viktor warily as she hops past him and stops between the tour guide and me.

"You can pet her if she'll let you. Put your hand out."

Slowly, I move my hand and place it in front of her with my palm up. She lowers her head to check out my hand. I'm shocked when she allows me to touch her fur. She sits in front of me and doesn't move.

"It appears as though Polly likes you," Dante says with a smile. "She letting you see her joey."

"Is it a boy or a girl?"

"It's a little boy who, up until recently, didn't have a name."

"He has a name now," Viktor says. "His name is Mel."

"What?" I ask, shocked.

"While you were in the restroom at lunch, Viktor arranged for this extra part of the tour," Dante says. "It happened very quickly, but Viktor arranged to adopt Polly and her joey. The director also agreed to name the baby after you."

I look at Viktor, too stunned for words. "This was supposed to be my surprise to you."

"I added a little something extra, that's all." He shrugs.

We feed Polly some vegetables. When she's through visiting, she hops away.

"This has been a wonderful treat." My voice cracks from trying to hold back my tears. "I miss Australia so much. Thank you both for this." I swipe at a tear that escapes.

We finish up just as the sun's beginning to set. Hand-in-hand, Viktor and I take a slow walk through the zoo. As darkness settles in, the lights turn on, transforming the zoo into a Christmas wonderland. Performers and musicians take their places, entertaining the passersby. It's magical.

What's even more special is that Viktor's let his guard down. I've enjoyed seeing him smile and hearing him laugh. He hasn't been scanning the horizon for some unknown threat. He's been present in the moment with me. The safari and seeing the animals up close were fun, but seeing him so carefree is the best part of my day.

Before we leave, Viktor insists we stop in the souvenir shop. We buy some stuff for ourselves and a stuffed animal to send to Rose. We also adopt two more animals. A gorilla and an African elephant.

"We're going to have adopted animals all over the world if we keep this up." I giggle as we walk back to our car.

"It's like leaving a piece of us everywhere we go. A kind of legacy."

"I like that idea." I enter the car and watch as Viktor walks around the front and slides into the driver's seat. "We're helping to make a positive difference in the world."

And in the end, that's all one can hope to do—leave things just a little better for future generations.

Amelia

bittersweet. I have so many wonderful memories, but with those memories comes a reminder of everything I've lost. I know it's the same way for Viktor. Our mini vacation was exactly what we needed. Getting away and making new holiday memories has helped relieve some of the sadness we've both been struggling with.

On our way home, we stop at a small store to grab a few fresh groceries. We're unpacking the bags when Viktor finds the surprise I snuck in.

"What's this?" He holds up a little plastic bag.

"Mistletoe." I smile. "You should hang it up so we can try it out."

"Where do you want it?"

"How about over there." I point to the doorway that leads to our balcony, knowing we'll get to use it often.

Viktor secures it to the doorframe and then opens the doors. "Come here. We need to try it out. Make sure it works."

"Do we now?" I cross the room slowly.

As soon as I'm within his grasp, he puts his hand around my waist, pulling me against him. "I think the mistletoe's working too well." I drag my fingers up the outline of his erection. "What do you say we remedy this?"

Lust swirls in his blue eyes as he leans down and kisses me. My hands move to unbuckle his belt.

"What the fuck is going on?"

I jump back. "Dad? Mom? What are you doing here?"

My father storms across the room. "I believe I asked a question."

Viktor takes my arm and pulls me behind him. "Calm down, Max. Let's talk about this like rational adults."

"Calm down?" he yells even louder. "What were you doing to my daughter?"

"He wasn't doing anything *to* me," I say as I try to step out from behind Viktor's protective stance. "It was consensual."

"Hush, Amelia. I want to hear it from him." Dad pokes a finger into Viktor's chest.

I look over Dad's shoulder and see Pyotr and Igor rush in. Mom stands back, a look of shock on her face.

"Well, I am waiting for an explanation," Dad says. "No. I do not want to hear what you have to say. It does not matter. You are fired."

"You can't do that," I argue.

"I can, and I did. Get your things and get the hell out of here."

"Stop. Please." I hold onto Viktor's arm. "I don't want him to leave. Can't we take a few minutes to calm down and talk?"

"There is nothing to discuss."

"Mom." I hurry across the room to her. "Can you tell Dad to calm down and talk to us?"

"Your father is in charge. I will not go against his wishes."

Although I'm standing in the room with three of the people I love most, I've never felt so alone. I'm confused and scared. I don't know what to do.

"I'll go pack my things," Viktor says and turns to walk away.

I rush over to his side. "If he leaves, I leave too."

"No." Viktor doesn't hesitate with his response. "You need to stay with your family. I won't let you lose them over me."

"I don't want to lose anyone." Tears cloud my vision. "Why do I have to choose?"

"You aren't choosing, *moya zirka*." Viktor cups my face in his palm. "The decision's already made."

I'm paralyzed by fear, anger, and hurt as I watch Viktor walk down the hall and disappear inside his bedroom.

Spinning around, I look at my father. "You're not really going to let him leave, are you?"

"Yes." He takes a step toward me. "You are young. You do not know what you want. He has no business going anywhere near you. Once he is gone, you will see I am right."

"No, I won't. I hate you," I yell and run to my room, slamming the door. I don't care what he says. Nothing is going to change my mind.

Me: Please don't leave.

Viktor: I have to.

Me: Stay and fight for us.

Viktor: For now, that's not the right choice.

Me: So, you're giving up?

Viktor: No. I'm giving Maxim some space before I try to talk to him. Right now, he wouldn't hear anything I have to say.

Me: I'm going with you then.

Viktor: Walking away without you by my side will be the hardest thing I've ever done. But it won't be forever. I love you, *moya zirka*.

Me: I love you, too.

My heart's shattered into a million pieces. How am I supposed to do this without him? I pull up Natalie's contact and hit the green call button.

"Hello?"

"Natalie, I need your help." I manage to get out between sobs.

"What's wrong? Where's Viktor?"

"Mom and Dad showed up. They caught us together."

"Oh, honey."

"Dad freaked out. He kicked Viktor out. He won't listen to either one of us."

"We figured he wasn't going to take the news well. I'm sure walking in on something unexpected made it even worse."

"What do I do?"

"First, you need to take some deep breaths and try to calm down. Where's Viktor right now?"

"In his room packing. He's leaving."

"I know it's not what either of you wants, but for the current moment, it may be for the best. Max isn't going to calm down if Viktor's there. He needs some time and space."

"But what about me? What about what I need?"

"Right now, you need to be strong. For you and Viktor. I'm sure this is killing him, too."

"I hate Maxim, Natalie."

"You're angry, but I know you don't hate him."

"I do."

"I won't argue with you because there were times I felt the same way about my parents—especially when they forbid me from seeing Alex. I know from firsthand experience this isn't going to be easy. Max isn't going to want to hear anything about you and Viktor. Don't push. Give him some time to process the information."

"What if that doesn't help?"

"We'll cross that bridge if it comes to that." Natalie's quiet for a moment. "I know this is hard, but if you and Viktor are meant to be, it'll work out."

I hope Natalie's right because I won't give up being with Viktor no matter what Maxim says.

Viktor

IN A MATTER OF SECONDS, MY WORLD CAME CRASHING DOWN around me. Maxim gave me no warning he and Irina were coming to visit. It's not like he's required to clear it with me, but he always gives me a heads-up. The fury on his face. I've seen that look directed at other men but never at me. And especially never toward Amelia.

The pain in her eyes when she begged to come with me was too much. I almost said yes. She's eighteen and doesn't have to stay. But that would've only enraged Maxim more. There's no way he'd let me out of the door with her. If we were to have gotten out together, he'd hunt us down and kill me—he may still kill me.

Right now, I'm trying to spare Amelia as much of the anger and violence I'm sure is heading my way. I finish packing my bag and return to the living room, where Irina's sitting on the sofa. Max is on the balcony talking with Pyotr and Igor.

"Boss. I'm leaving now."

Maxim doesn't turn around or show any signs of acknowledging my presence. His lack of action cuts deep. Maxim's been like a father to me for most of my adult life. I knew he wouldn't take the news about Amelia and me well. I have to believe if we had the chance to tell him rather than him walking in on us, it might've gone over a bit better.

When it's clear Max isn't going to respond, Igor looks up at me and nods.

I walk over to Irina. "I don't expect you to side with me or even speak to me. I need you to know I love Amelia. I would never do anything to harm her."

Irina looks up. Her dark blue eyes are filled with tears. "I think I've known that since I saw you and her together." She glances behind her to Max, whose back is still turned. "Please understand. My hands are tied."

"I understand." I hear Amelia's door open, but I don't look back. I'm afraid if I see her, I'll lose my self-control and do something we'll both regret. So, instead, I hurry to the door and leave.

With each step away from the house, breathing becomes more difficult. My heart physically hurts, and I wonder if it will fail. "I'm coming back for you, *moya zirka*," I whisper.

I stop at the coffee shop a few blocks from our house. I need to find a hotel for a few nights. Once I find a room, I text Amelia so she knows where I'll be staying.

I may only be a half mile away from her, but I may as well be on the other side of the world. Being without Amelia feels like a piece of myself is missing. I'm lying on the bed, trying to figure out what to do next, when my phone rings.

"Hello?"

"Natalie told me," Alex says. "Are you okay?"

"No."

"Amelia's no better."

Hearing that is what bothers me most. I don't want her to hurt.

"How do I fix this?"

"Max needs a few days to wrap his head around everything. But I'm sure he'll come around." Even as he says it, I hear the uncertainty in his voice. He's no more sure of that than I am.

"Alex, I can't lose her. As long as she wants me, I refuse to walk away from her."

"I know."

Amelia

I DIDN'T SLEEP LAST NIGHT. INSTEAD, I SAT UP AND contemplated packing my things and leaving. The only reason I didn't is because I'm afraid for Viktor's life if I do—that's too high a price.

Unfortunately, things aren't going to get any better today. I still haven't told my parents about Death Rat, and now time's run out. We have practice in less than an hour.

Me: Can you pick me up for rehearsal?

Sparrow: Of course. Where's Viktor?

Me: It's a long story. I'll tell you on the way to Quincy's. Text me when you get here. Do not come to the door.

Sparrow: Why not?

Me: My father, the Russian mob boss, is here.

Sparrow: Enough said. I'll text you when I get there.

I take my time getting ready in my room. The less time I spend with my father right now, the better. Then, with a deep breath, I turn the handle and pull my door open. Mom and Dad are both in the kitchen. Mom's cooking while Dad's sitting drinking coffee.

"Good morning, Amelia," Dad says. "Sit and eat."

"I can't. I have somewhere I need to be." My phone buzzes. When I check, it's Sparrow. He's outside.

"Where are you going?"

"Music rehearsal."

"Will you be at the school?" Mom asks.

"No. It's at a friend's house. I have to go. He's outside waiting."

"Outside waiting?" Dad sets his coffee down. "He will need to come to the door like any decent young man."

"Seriously?" I cross my arms. "We're not dating. There's no need for the formalities."

"It is obvious you are not dating anyone your own age," Dad quips. "Before you leave this house, I will know who you will be with and where you will be. And Igor will accompany you."

I roll my eyes as I pull out my phone.

Me: My father's being a jerk. Can you come to the door?

Sparrow: Um. Yeah.

I half expect Sparrow to drive away rather than having to come face to face with Maxim, but a minute later, the doorbell rings. I pull it open and find a terrified-looking Sparrow.

"Don't worry, it's not you he's mad at," I whisper. "Dad, this is Sparrow. Sparrow, these are my parents."

"It's nice to meet you both." He puts on a brave face.

"Have you eaten yet?" Dad asks.

"No. Amelia and I were going to grab a bite to eat on the way to Quincy's."

"Quincy?"

"He's the lead—"

"We have to go, or we'll be late." I interrupt and grab Sparrow's arm, hoping to make a quick exit.

"The lead what?" Mom asks.

"There's something I need to tell you, but first, you need to promise not to take your anger out on Sparrow."

Dad raises an eyebrow.

"I told you I had music rehearsals over the holiday. That much is true, but it's not for school." I take a deep breath. "I'm in a band, and we're going on tour this summer." While I'm at it, I may as well tell them the rest. "I'm also not returning to school in the spring."

Mom stops what she's doing and spins around to face me. Dad

pushes back his chair so fast it nearly falls over before turning to face me. When he does, that same look of fury I saw yesterday is again there.

"You are not returning to school to play in some band?" Dad asks.

"Sparrow, you should go ahead without me."

"I think that would be a very good idea, young man," Dad says flatly. "My daughter and I have much to discuss."

"Are you going to be okay here?" Sparrow asks quietly.

I nod. "Tell the guys I'll be there Friday for the show."

"Will do." Sparrow looks back and forth between my father and me. "It was nice meeting you both." He turns and hurries out the door.

"Irina, please excuse us. We will be late for breakfast."

"Yes, Sir. I'll keep it warm."

"Let us go for a walk," Dad says, heading for the door.

He doesn't say a word as we walk through the warm sand down to the water. However, I can feel the anger rolling off him in waves bigger than the ocean's. Once we get to the water's edge, Dad stares at the sparkling crystal water.

"I know there's a lot I've been keeping from you, and I'm sorry you had to find out this way." He remains silent. "I was planning on telling you, but to be honest, I was struggling to find the words."

"Being open and honest is the one thing we have asked for, and it is the one thing you have not done since you came here."

When he finally looks at me, the disappointment in his eyes is almost too much. It takes me a few seconds to compose myself.

"I'm sorry," I say. "I'd like the opportunity to explain what I was thinking."

"Go ahead."

"How about we sit." I point to the lounge chairs Viktor and I keep down here. "This is probably going to take a while."

He follows me over and takes a seat.

"Where do I start?"

"How about the beginning," Dad suggests.

That's where I start—the beginning. How when we first got here, I started having panic attacks again. And how Viktor began attending sessions with me to learn how to help me manage them. Then, I move into meeting Mateo.

"Viktor ran a background check, and everything looked good on paper. Even still, he never let me go anywhere alone with him."

"That is what I pay him for."

"Well, sometimes background checks aren't enough," I say, unafraid to meet his penetrating stare. "Mateo's how I got involved with the band. He wanted to be more than just friends."

"But you did not?"

"I tried, but I didn't care for Mateo as anything more than a friend."

Dad listens while I tell him about the day Mateo showed up here and how Viktor had to jump in.

"I found out a few days ago that when Mateo left, he overdosed and almost died."

"How did Viktor miss a drug addiction?"

"No one knew how bad Mateo's problems really were. He was a functional alcoholic and drug user."

"And where is this boy now?"

"He's in a rehab facility. He wants to get his life together before Death Rat goes on tour."

Dad's eyes open wide. "Death Rat?"

"That's our band."

"You are in a band that calls themselves Death Rat?"

I can't help the giggle that slips out. "We just signed a contract to be the opening act for Zapped Euforia on their summer stadium tour."

Dad looks at me, confused.

"Do you know how big of a deal that is?"

"No, I do not."

"It's the chance of a lifetime."

"What about school?"

"I'm not going back. I've already decided that."

"Because of this tour?"

"Yes. The tour starts the first weekend in May. Between now and then, we have some shows, rehearsals, and press events," I explain. "I don't want to pass up this opportunity. Anyway, it's a done deal. The contracts are signed."

"Contracts can be bought out."

"But this one won't be. I'm going on tour, Dad. And I'd really like your support." I stop and search his face for a reaction but find none. "We have a show this Friday. I hope you and Mom will be there."

"Igor will need the information to clear the place."

"Viktor's already done that. He cleared the list as soon as we got it."

"I do not want to hear that man's name."

"You're going to have to because I'm in love with him."

"That is not possible. You are a child, and he is a full-grown man. You are not in love with him." He balls his hands into fists. "Viktor had no business touching you—something he will reap the repercussions of."

"If you lay a finger on him, I'll never forgive you."

"Amelia, please. Whatever you thought was going on between the two of you was wrong. It cannot be allowed to continue."

"You're wrong. Viktor's kind and respectful. He didn't touch me until he was sure I'd thought it through and was confident I knew what I was getting into."

"Touched you? He better not have—"

"We've had sex."

"No. That is impossible."

"Why is it impossible?" I jump up. "Do you think I'm so damaged that I can't make a decision about my own body? Or that I'm too broken to fall in love?"

Maxim

AMELIA STORMS OFF, AND I GO AFTER HER. WE ARE NOT finished with this conversation.

"Amelia, stop. That is not what I was saying."

She spins around, and I see fire in her eyes. "Then, please explain it because that's sure what it sounded like."

"You are not damaged or broken." I reach out to take her hand, but she pulls it away. "And I know you can make decisions about your body. But Viktor is much older. He has more experience. He has no business being with you."

"Yes, he's older, and yes, he's been with other women. Viktor and I have talked about it all. But his past and who he's been with has nothing to do with him and me now." Amelia takes a deep breath before continuing. "Viktor knows all about my past as well. He knows the horrible things that were done to me—stolen from me. I didn't think a man could look past all that. But he did. Viktor loves me." Her hand goes over her heart.

"Do you know what that means to me? Viktor was the first man to show me kindness and tenderness. He didn't take from me. I willingly gave myself to him."

"You will not see him again."

"You can't stop us from being together."

"I can, and I will. Viktor is going back to Russia."

"He's a grown man, remember? He doesn't have to follow your orders."

"If he wants to remain alive, he will."

"If you want me to remain your daughter, you'll have to learn to accept us together. If you force me to choose. I choose Viktor." With that, she turns and walks away.

I watch until she disappears inside the house. I am a man who is used to being in control. To people following my orders. How did things go so wrong with Amelia? Obviously, I am not going to get through to her, but I know someone who will. I pull my phone out and call Svetlana.

"Hi, Papa," she answers. "How's everything in sunny California?"

"Terrible."

"I see."

"You know about Amelia and Viktor, do you not?"

"I do."

I feel betrayed by the amount of secrecy from my daughters.

"And you did not tell me?"

"No, I didn't. That was for Amelia and Viktor. When they were ready."

"Well, they had no choice when we walked in and found them kissing. I am just glad we got here when we did. She was about to—"

"They're in love," Svetlana interrupts me.

"That is ridiculous."

"We knew you wouldn't be happy, but you're going to have to get used to it. They have the real thing going on."

"I will get used to no such idea. If Viktor goes near her again, I will kill him myself."

"Be reasonable, Papa." Svetlana raises her voice. "You can't go around dictating who she can love."

"It will not be him."

"Papa, it's already him. You'll lose her if you harm him or try to keep them apart."

"I do not know how you can be so okay with this. Amelia is just a child."

"No, Papa. Amelia hasn't been for a very long time."

Svetlana and I do not often see eye-to-eye, but considering her views on men as of late, I was confident she would be on my side. But no, of course, she must oppose me. Before I end up in a fight with her, too, I say my goodbyes and disconnect our call.

I am the boss. The one in charge. I always have the answers, but this time, I find myself searching for guidance. "What am I going to do?"

Amelia

Tonight's the last show until after the holidays.
Mom and Dad are in the audience, albeit reluctantly on Dad's part. I'm
sure he's only here to tell me how much he hates it and that I have to
quit. To make matters worse, they sent Igor to babysit me backstage. At
least Viktor acted like a normal person. Igor's standing there stoically
with his legs spread and arms crossed.

Viktor: I'm outside the stage door. Who did Max put backstage?

Me: Igor.

Viktor: Come let me in.

Viktor doesn't have to tell me twice. I won't pass up any opportunity to spend time with him. I push the door open, and the sight of him
takes my breath away. Viktor's wearing tight jeans and a blue T-shirt that
makes the depth of color in his eyes even more striking.

He's barely through the doorway when I launch myself into his
arms.

"I miss you so much."

"*Moya zirka.*" He holds me tight. "I miss you, too."

"Viktor, what're you doing here?" Igor appears behind me.

"Please don't tell my father."

Igor's currently in a stare-off with Viktor and ignores my plea.

"I have strict orders to tell the boss if Viktor shows up," he finally says without breaking eye contact.

"Yury," Viktor says calmly.

I look between the men, not understanding who Yury is.

After a few seconds, Igor's shoulders drop. "Don't get caught, or my head's on the chopping block too."

"We'll be in the green room," Viktor tells Igor, then takes my hand and leads me through the busy hallway. Once we're inside the room, Viktor locks the door.

"Who's Yury?"

"Don't worry about that right now." Viktor sits on the sofa. "Come here. I need to feel you."

I straddle his lap and wrap my arms around him. "I don't know how much longer I can go without you."

My lips meet his, and the erection jutting from between his legs makes me wish I didn't have to be on stage in five minutes.

"Are you going to stay for the show?" I ask between kisses.

"I can't. It's too dangerous. If Maxim or Pyotr comes backstage, we'll be in for bigger problems than we already have."

"How much longer do we have to be apart?"

"I don't know."

"Amelia, are you in there?" Sparrow calls from the other side of the door.

"I want to ignore the world and stay with you."

"Me too. But we can't do that." He stands up and sets me on the floor in front of him. "This show's important. You need to get onstage."

"Amelia," Sparrow calls again.

I unlock the door and crack it open. "Is it still only Igor out there?"

"Yeah. Come on. We need to get on stage."

"Text me later." Viktor kisses me. "You didn't see me," he says and makes his way to the stage door.

I bring my finger to my lips and watch until he's gone.

"Your dad still won't let you see him?"

"No."

Sparrow throws his arm around me, and I rest my head on his shoulder. He and I have become very close since the night of the party. It's like I finally have the older brother I always wanted.

"Everything's going to work out. I'm not sure how, but it will." He gives me a quick peck on the cheek. "Now let's get out there and give this audience one hell of a show."

This is the first concert Viktor's missing. Even though I know Viktor's not here, I can't stop myself from scanning the audience for him. He's always front and center with a gorgeous smile on his face, except for tonight. Tonight, my parents sit in his place. It's not that I'm not happy they're here. I guess I'm selfish. I want them and Viktor to be here.

The light's come up, and I'm forced to stop feeling sorry for myself. Since Mateo's still in rehab, Tristan's stepped up for lead guitar and vocals. He loves being the center of attention and is currently hyping the audience up—not that they need much help. News of our upcoming tour has already increased our popularity. I can't believe we've gone from playing small local bars and clubs to being set to go on a major stadium tour in such a short time. I'm realizing a dream I never knew I had.

We're on our last song, "Just Give Me a Reason." Since Mateo and I sang this duet the first night, it's become so popular that now, we close each show with it. Since Mateo left, Sparrow and I have been performing it together. He steps up to the mic.

"Our final song of the evening is very special to both Amelia and me." He glances back at me. "We'd like to dedicate it to the two people who've stolen our hearts."

He grabs his acoustic guitar and sits on the stool next to the piano. My emotions almost get the best of me several times during the song, but somehow, I manage to make it to the end before the tears fall. While the audience is applauding, Sparrow wraps me in a hug.

"We'll get them both back. I promise."

Maxim

AMELIA'S AN ACCOMPLISHED MUSICIAN of that I had no doubt. Until tonight, I have only heard her play classical pieces. But it is clear her talent extends far beyond that.

"Max," Irina says and touches my arm softly. "I think you need to give her this. She looks happy on the stage."

"Yes. She does." I place my hand over Irina's. "But no daughter of mine will be in a group called Death Rat."

"You'll tell her we support her with this?"

"That is what you would like us to do, is it not?"

"Very much."

I lean over and kiss my wife's forehead. "Then, that is what we will do."

"And Viktor?"

"I will not discuss him."

A well-dressed man walks toward where Irina and I wait for Amelia.

"You must be Amelia's parents," he says. "I'm Everett Hart, Mateo's father and legal counsel for Death Rat."

"I am Maxim Solonik, and this is my wife, Irina. It is a pleasure to meet you." I extend my hand. "How is your son doing?"

"He's doing better, but he still has a long road ahead of him."

"We wish him the best." Recovering from an addiction is never easy on the person with an addiction or their family. Unfortunately, we see it a lot at Jelena's Hope. "I would like to discuss the name of this band with you."

"Death Rat." Everett chuckles. "I don't know where the kids came up with that, but it'll grow on you."

"No, it will not. If Amelia is to remain with this band, the name will have to change."

"That's not up to us. And Amelia is already under contract."

"I will buy out her part of the contract." I am not playing games, and I am not joking. "Either the name goes, or Amelia does."

"What did you guys think?" Amelia comes bouncing out of the stage door.

"You amaze me, *moya malen'kaya ptichka*," Irina says and hugs our daughter.

"What about you, Dad?" she asks hesitantly.

"You were superb, Amelia." I smile proudly at my daughter. Our relationship has been on shaky ground since we arrived. I hope this helps bridge the gap between us. "As I was just telling Mr. Hart, If you plan on staying with this group, the name will have to change."

"You can't be serious."

"I am very serious."

"This is ridiculous. It's one thing to try to control my relationship—"

"Amelia." The young man who came to pick her up the other day touches her arm. "Changing the name isn't a big deal. Actually, I think it's a good idea. The three of us never liked it anyway. It was something stupid that came up in a random name generator."

"For real?" She smiles.

"Yep. How about the four of us talk about it and come up with something else." He turns to Mr. Hart. "Would you be able to run it by Mateo for us?"

"He's still in the blackout period. We can't communicate with him for at least another week. But I'm sure he'll go along with whatever name change you come up with," Mr. Hart says. "Let me know what you pick something, and I'll make sure it gets switched on all the legal documents."

"Are you sure, Sparrow? You don't have to do this."

He puts his arm around Amelia. "I'm positive. We aren't going to lose you over a silly name."

She rests her head on his shoulder, and I make a mental note to speak with my daughter about this young man. The two appear comfortable with one another, and he is much closer to her age than the alternative.

"Then, we have a deal," I say. "Looks like you are going on tour, Amelia."

The drive back home is quiet and fraught with tension. Amelia stares out the window as if we are not in the car. Irina and I exchange glances several times, but neither of us attempts to get our daughter to talk.

After an agonizingly long drive, Igor turns into the driveway and puts the vehicle in park. Amelia does not wait for the ignition to turn off before she jumps out and runs into the house.

Our relationship feels strained, much like when she first came to live with us. I do not like it.

"Irina, please get Amelia," I say as we enter the house. "I would like to speak with her."

"Yes, Sir."

"I will be on the balcony."

It takes a few minutes for Irina to return with a clearly unwilling Amelia by her side.

"Thank you, *moye schast'ye*." I turn to Amelia and motion to the chairs. "Please sit." I grab a chair and move it so I am facing her. "Tomorrow is Christmas Eve. "What would you like to do?"

"Nothing. I don't feel like celebrating."

"That is not like you."

"I was planning on spending the holiday with Viktor."

"Amelia," I warn. "We have already taken care of that situation."

"No, we didn't. You kicked Viktor out and refused to even discuss the subject."

"I do not want to have this same argument again."

"Neither do I. I'd like to have a conversation where you also listen instead of barking orders at me like I'm one of your men."

"Is that what you think?"

"Yes," she says matter-of-factly.

"And you, Irina?" I glance back at my wife.

"Do I have permission to speak freely?"

"Yes, you do."

"Amelia, understandably, your father and I were shocked when we walked into the house and saw you and Viktor," she says calmly. "We had no idea anything was developing between you two." Irina looks at me. "Well, I had a suspicion but brushed it off as nothing."

I look at my daughter, but she refuses to make eye contact with me.

Irina continues, "You must try to see it from our perspective. The age difference between you and Viktor is concerning. He has much more life experience. He's more settled, and I'm assuming looking to settle down with one woman."

Irina touches Amelia's hand. "You are just beginning to live your life. You deserve to experiment with dating. You need time to learn what you're looking for in a partner. You shouldn't be tied to one man."

"I've tested those waters and quickly realized they're not for me. I'm not tied to one man out of coercion or desperation—I chose only one man." Amelia looks at Irina. "Why is it so difficult to believe that Viktor and I want the same things?"

"What about that young man, Sparrow?" I interrupt. "He seems nice and very interested in you."

Amelia laughs. "Sparrow is one of my best friends. And he's gay."

"I see." That did not work out as I had hoped.

Amelia

"I KNOW YOU BOTH THINK I'M TOO YOUNG TO BE WITH Viktor. But you fail to remember that I haven't lived a *normal* life. From the day my parents died, I was forced to grow up real fast." I swallow over the lump in my throat. "Did you know my father was ten years older than my mother?"

A look of shock registers on Dad's face. "I was unaware."

"They were soulmates. Everyone who met them recognized it." I swipe at a tear that escapes. "It was only right they died together. They wouldn't have been able to live apart."

"That does not mean it is okay for you and Viktor, who is fourteen years older, to be together."

"Why not? Who decides that? Who makes up these rules?" I look between my parents. "It's not what most people do. So what? You and Dad don't have the most traditional or what most would call a *normal* relationship. But you respect and love each other. Don't I deserve the same thing? To be loved by a good man?"

"Your father and I understand what you're saying, but honey, Viktor's lived a hard life."

"That makes two of us."

"He has a dangerous job. Your life would be at risk being with him." She takes Dad's hand. "We don't want that for you."

"I know what Viktor does. We—"

"You do not know the full extent of Viktor's job. If you did, you would not be arguing about this with us."

"Yes, Dad. I do. Viktor and I talked about it—all of it. I know what he's done and will have to do in the future. He expressed his concern for my safety. Heck, he fought me on this. He didn't want to put me in danger."

"That is the first sensible thing I have heard since I arrived here."

"If I recall correctly, he does these things at your command." I meet my father's stern gaze. I'm not afraid of him, and I refuse to back down. "I'm going into this with my eyes wide open."

"My answer is still no. That will not change."

I get up, walk to the balcony rail, and look out into the darkness. "And if I continue seeing him?"

"If Viktor goes against my orders, he will face the consequences."

I know they're concerned for me. But how do I get them to see I'm not a child? Just like I understand who and what Maxim is, I also understand who and what Viktor is. I have complete faith that he'll always protect me—with his life if necessary. And I would do the same for him. That's what love is.

"Now, Christmas, what do you want to do?" Dad asks again as if he hasn't heard a word I've said.

I turn around slowly. "I want to see Viktor. There's no reason for him to spend the holiday alone. Even you couldn't be that cruel." My words come out harsh.

"Amelia," Dad warns.

"You'll all be here to ensure we don't do anything you wouldn't approve of."

"Fine. I will allow him to spend Christmas Day with our family."

Me: Dad will be calling you tomorrow. He's letting you come over for Christmas.

Viktor: Igor just texted me to let me know.

Me: I can't wait to see you. I love you.

Viktor: I love you, *moya zirka.*

Viktor

I DON'T KNOW WHAT AMELIA SAID, BUT SOMEHOW, SHE GOT Maxim to relent and let me spend Christmas Day with them. I'm not holding out any hope that this is anything more than an obligatory holiday invite. There's no way he's backing down and giving us his blessing.

Regardless, I can't wait to get there. I miss her so much. My life with her had a purpose. When she looked at me, her eyes were filled with nothing other than pure love—for me. Somehow, Amelia penetrated the walls I built around my heart and quickly became my whole world.

I don't know how we're going to get Maxim to change his mind. What I do know is he better be prepared for a fight because I'm not giving her up.

I grab the two gifts I have for her and go down to the lobby. Igor texted a few minutes ago, letting me know he's outside.

"Merry Christmas," he says when I get in the car.

"Yeah, something like that." I fidget nervously with the gifts on my lap. "What am I walking into today?"

"Amelia's been trying to convince the boss to accept you two. There's no chance of that happening." He glances at me.

"How long are they staying?"

"They're leaving tomorrow. I'll be staying behind until Max finds a new security team for her."

"Fuck." I run my hand over my head. "It wasn't supposed to happen this way."

"What were you two thinking?"

"We didn't plan it. It just happened."

"What are you going to do?"

"It's not like I can stop loving her. I'm not willing to walk away from this. I have to find a way to get through to him."

"Good luck with that."

"I'm gonna need it," I mumble. "How's Yury?"

"He's good." Igor's face lights up. "He flew in yesterday. We plan on seeing each other after the boss leaves."

"I'm happy for you."

"Weren't we supposed to do a double date?" Igor grins.

"I heard something about that."

I follow Igor into the house and immediately feel the tension in the air. Just a few days ago, this was my home with Amelia. Today, it feels like I'm an unwelcome stranger until Amelia, who's setting the table, looks up.

"Merry Christmas," she says, a smile gracing her beautiful face.

The temptation to wrap her in my arms is strong, but I have to resist. I'm not exactly welcome here as it is. "Merry Christmas."

"Viktor," Maxim says my name.

"Thank you for inviting me."

"It was only because of Amelia's insistence that you not be alone for the holiday."

"I understand." I set my gifts under the tree.

"Dinner's ready," Amelia calls from the kitchen. "Igor. Pyotr. That means you, too."

From the outside looking in, we'd appear to be a happy family as we gather around the table for the holiday meal. Igor and Pyotr sit to my right and left. Amelia sits across from me.

Irina makes Maxim's plate. After he's been served, we take turns passing the serving platters as we make our plates.

"Natalie gave me her lasagna recipe." Amelia's brown eyes meet mine. "I hope you like it."

"It is delicious, *moya malen'kaya ptichka*," Maxim says. "You have done an excellent job."

When we got here, Amelia had no cooking skills. One of her goals was to be able to cook meals for us. She's been practicing for months. She watches me expectantly as I take a bite.

"It's delicious," I compliment her. "I know you could do it."

"Thank you," she says quietly.

"Since we are all here, it is a good time to inform everyone of our plans," Maxim says, obviously meaning to interrupt us. "Irina and I will be returning to Russia first thing in the morning. There are several projects we need to wrap up before the new year. Pyotr will be accompanying us. Igor will remain here until Amelia's new security detail is put in place." Then, he turns his attention to me. "I expect you to arrive at my estate in forty-eight hours."

"You can't force him to go back to Russia." Amelia comes to my defense.

"He is still my employee and under my protection. If he expects to continue as such, he will do as he is told."

Amelia sets her fork down. "My friends used to whisper about you behind my back. They talked about what a cruel and heartless man you are. Maybe they were right all along."

Maxim's relationship with Amelia is important to him. It's clear from the shocked look on his face that her sharp words affected him.

"It's okay, Amelia. Your father's only doing what he feels is best for you."

"No, it's not—"

"Let's not fight during our meal," Irina interrupts."

"My wife is right. Today is for celebration."

Amelia looks at me, and I see her firey temper ready to explode. I give her a slight shake of my head. Having this fight today will not accomplish anything other than causing more hurt. We'll have time to come up with a plan after her parents leave.

Trust me, *moya zirka*. I'm not letting you go.

Amelia

AFTER MOM AND I CLEAR THE DINNER DISHES, WE JOIN everyone in the living room. I grab Viktor's gift from under the tree.

"This is for you." I hand him the wrapped box. "If I knew you guys were coming here for Christmas, I wouldn't have mailed your gifts."

"It is okay. Spending time with you is present enough," Dad says.

I resist the urge to roll my eyes and turn my attention back to Viktor. "Go ahead and open it."

Viktor carefully tears the paper open and lifts the lid off the box. For the first time today, some of the sadness disappears, replaced by a smile. "I love it. Thank you."

"What is it?" Mom asks with genuine curiosity.

Viktor holds the gift up to show her. It's a silver photo frame with a selfie of us from our first night here. The frame is engraved with the words *Her Nightingale.*

"That's beautiful." Mom smiles.

"I have something for you too." Viktor sets the box on the table and grabs the presents he brought. He passes me the first one.

"This paper is too pretty to tear." Carefully, I work at the tape, trying to preserve the vintage-looking gift wrap. I gasp when I see what's inside. "Are these?"

"Yes," Viktor says quietly. "They're the Matryoshka dolls *Babusya* and I made for Mama and Papa." Viktor's voice cracks.

I take my time opening them one by one. They're exquisite. "I don't know what to say."

"You don't have to say anything. I hope you like them." He quickly wipes a stray tear.

"Viktor," I say softly, longing to comfort him. "I'll treasure these always."

"There's one more." He hands me a small gift.

"I don't need anything else."

"Open it." He smiles.

I tear off the paper and find a small jewelry box. When I open it, I can no longer hold back the tears. "I don't know what to say."

"What is it?" Dad asks.

I turn the box so he can see the silver chain with the star made from diamonds.

"That is quite an extravagant gift."

Ignoring Dad's comment, I ask Viktor, "Will you help me put it on?"

Turning around, I lift my hair. Viktor's hands tremble as he puts the delicate chain around my neck and does the clasp.

"How does it look?" I turn and ask him.

"It's perfect, *moya zirka*."

"Isn't it beautiful, Mom?"

She examines the necklace. "It's lovely." She turns to Viktor. "It's a very special gift."

"Amelia's a very special young woman."

Mom can't hide the softness in her eyes. But when I look at my father, his eyes are still cold and heartless. I know his line of work often requires him to do things others consider violent and cruel. But, he's always done a good job of keeping that part of himself separate from the man he is at home—until now.

Many of my Russian friends believe my father is nothing but a cold-blooded killer. They don't know or care to understand what he does and why. But I know. I'm alive today because of my father and his efforts. He and his men, including Viktor, kill. They snuff out the lives of men, if they can even be called that, who steal and destroy innocent people's lives.

I've defended him on many occasions. I've lost friends because I've defended his actions. It never bothered me because I believed my father was doing the right thing—I still do. I choose to turn a blind eye to the methods he employs because his mission is important. The traffickers don't care who gets hurt. They prey on those who are weak or vulnerable. My dad works endlessly to wipe them from the face of the earth.

But this past week, I've witnessed another side of him. A cruelty I didn't believe he was capable of. He's taken the anger and hatred he usually reserves for the animals he hunts and turned it on his family.

He's come just short of threatening Viktor's life for what? Because we fell in love? Only someone with no heart would do that.

Amelia

"ARE YOU SURE YOU WON'T COME HOME? EVEN JUST FOR A few days?" Mom asks for the hundredth time this morning.

"I'm positive. I need some space away from Dad." Who's outside on the balcony going over his orders for Igor.

Dad wanted to leave Pyotr with me, but there was no way he'd let me see Viktor. My father's still concerned with my comfort level around men, so it was easy to convince him to leave Igor. Especially after Viktor told me he and Igor have an agreement and that at least until the new security detail arrives, we'll be okay.

"Amelia, you know he only wants the best for you."

"I thought I knew that. But after this week, I'm not so sure."

"Please don't say that. You and he have come such a long way. I don't want to pry, but have you considered discussing this situation with Ania?

The conversations in my therapy sessions are private. I'm hoping by divulging some information, my parents will see how serious Viktor and I are about each other.

"Ania knows about Viktor."

"Oh," Mom says, surprised.

"I told her about my feelings for him long before he knew. Ania and I discussed the pros and cons at great length," I explain. "Then, after a particularly difficult night when I had a major breakdown, he sat in on an emergency session. He wanted to learn how to help me avoid a full-blown panic attack and how best to help me if I have one. We've also done several sessions together, working through some of my issues with intimacy."

"You and Viktor have had sex?"

"Yes."

Mom takes a deep breath. "I didn't realize you two were that serious."

"If you listened to me and if anyone let Viktor talk, we could've explained all this together."

"May I tell your father this information?"

"If it's going to help him change his mind, you can tell him. But he better not go after Viktor because of it." I'd never forgive my father. "Mom, this isn't just infatuation or a crush. I love him. And he loves me. We want a future together."

"I saw the way he looked at you yesterday. I do believe he loves you very much."

"Then please convince Dad to back off."

"I'll talk to him, but in the end, it's his decision."

Dad and Igor walk back into the house. "It is time to leave, Irina."

Mom leans over and gives me one more hug. "I love you, and I'll do what I can," she whispers.

"Thank you."

"Amelia," Dad says. "I do not want to leave with this negativity between us."

"All you have to do is agree to accept Viktor and me together."

"That I cannot do."

"I hope you both have a safe flight," I say and start walking to my bedroom.

"Maxim, please don't leave things like this," Mom begs.

"Irina, do not overstep."

Once I'm in my room, I pull out my phone to text Viktor.

Me: They're leaving now. I'll let you know when Igor gets the message that their plane has left.

Viktor: I can't wait to see you.

Viktor

YYURY AND I ARE WAITING AT A COFFEE SHOP A FEW BLOCKS from the house. We're excited to see our loved ones, but neither of us is willing to take the chance to go there until we know Maxim is safely in the air and on his way back to Russia.

When I was invited to the house for Christmas, I naively held onto the hope that perhaps Max was coming around, even slightly. I was wrong. He only did it to appease Amelia for the day. Now I'm facing the inevitable, I'll have to return to Russia in less than two days. That doesn't mean I'm giving up. My return to Russia is for one reason—to change Maxim's mind about us.

Amelia

Igor assures me he watched Dad's jet leave the ground. You and Yury can come over as soon as you're ready.

Me: We'll be there in about ten minutes.

"Ready to go?" I ask Yury.

"I was born ready." He grins.

With our bags in hand, we walk from the café to the house.

"Wow," Yury says when we get there. "This place is incredible."

"Max only buys the best."

Before we get all the way up the sidewalk, Amelia bursts through the door.

"I missed you so much." I drop my bag as she launches herself into my arms. "Don't ever leave me again."

My world rights itself when I wrap my arms around her. I want to give her the assurances she seeks, but I can't until after this trip to Russia.

Hopefully, I'll be successful at convincing Max. But if he still refuses, I'm going to have to call in a few favors of my own to ensure Amelia and I are protected. Because I'm coming back to get her one way or another.

"Get a room, you two," Igor jokes as he bypasses us to greet Yury.

"Let's take this inside," I suggest.

Once we're safely in the house, I make the introductions.

"Amelia, this is Yury. Yury, this is Amelia."

"I've heard a lot about you," Yury says as he gives her a hug. "I'm glad we're finally getting to meet."

While Igor takes Yury to their room to get settled, Amelia and I go onto the balcony.

"There's something you're not telling me," Amelia says once we're alone.

"What do you mean?"

"You're giving in and going back to Russia, aren't you?"

Fuck. I don't want this to ruin the short time we have together. "Can we not talk about this right now? I want to focus on us."

Igor pops his head out the door. "We're going to spend the day at the beach. You two enjoy yourselves."

Amelia and I stare at one another. No words are exchanged until they leave.

"I need you, *moya zirka*."

"You have me. You'll always have me." She takes my hands and leads me to our room. "I've missed you." Amelia slides her yoga pants off. Then she pulls her shirt over her head. She's not wearing a bra or panties.

"You were walking around bare under your clothes with another man in the house?" I growl.

"Igor?" She tilts her head. "Let me let you in on a little secret. He's gay." She smirks.

"I don't care," I say as I rip off my shirt and unbutton my jeans, pushing them and my boxers down in one move. "I don't want another man even accidentally getting a glance at what's mine."

"I love it when you get possessive."

"Do you now?" I advance toward her, grab her waist, and put her over my shoulder.

Amelia laughs and pretends to punch my back. "Put me down."

I slap her ass. "As you wish, my lady."

Gently, I toss her onto the bed. She pushes up on her elbows and watches me as I spread her legs and devour her pussy.

"God, I've missed you," I say between licks. Then, I add two fingers fucking her while my tongue attacks her clit.

"Viktor, it's too much," she pants.

"Come for me. I want to hear you scream my name."

I increase the intensity of my fingers and suck her clit. She calls my name as her body explodes. Then, she grabs at my arms, trying to pull me up.

"Do you need something, moya zirka?"

"I need you."

"Where?"

"Inside me. Please, Viktor."

"I love it when you beg for me." I line myself up with her opening and push myself inside in one forceful action. "Is that better?"

"Mhm. More, please."

"I'm not going to be gentle. But if it's too much, all you have to say is stop." I may be possessive, but I never want her to feel like she's a possession. She must always feel empowered and remember she has a voice that'll be heard and respected.

"Okay." Her voice is breathy.

My hips move in a punishing rhythm. "You. Are. Mine. Do you hear me, Amelia? Mine."

"Yes, Viktor." Her tiny hand cups my cheek. "I'm yours. I've always been yours. I'll always be yours. You'll never be alone again."

Amelia doesn't know how much power her words hold. They took root in my heart, binding me with her. There's no force on earth that can separate us.

I fuck her harder and deeper until the lines of where one of us begins, and ends are no longer clear. We're one as our bodies climax together.

Amelia

Viktor and I spent the day making up for lost time. As much as I want to spend every second we have alone, we also need to eat. We're sitting in the kitchen, deciding whether we'll cook or order take-out when Igor and Yury come back from the beach.

This is the first time I'm seeing Igor without my father around. He's usually uptight, like all the other men my father employs. I like this version of Igor much better.

"Did you kids have a good afternoon?" Igor asks, a knowing smile on his face.

"It was acceptable." Viktor shrugs.

I slap his arm, and we share a laugh. "Have you two eaten yet?" I ask as they join us at the table?

"No. We were going to see if you want to go out for dinner?"

Viktor and I look at each other before we answer in unison. "Sure."

Viktor calls Bay Front, our favorite go-to restaurant, and makes a reservation for an early dinner.

"So, what's the plan?" Igor gets right to the point.

"I have no choice but to return to Russia."

Every muscle in my body tenses while Viktor's speaking. "I don't want you to go."

"I don't want to either, but there's no other option."

"He's right. If he doesn't confront your father on his turf, there's no chance of resolving this."

"My father made it clear he isn't changing his mind. I don't see the point of you going."

"*Moya zirka*, it must be done."

"And when he still refuses?"

"I'll deal with that if it happens." Viktor takes my hand in his.

"Yury and I will stay with you while Viktor's gone."

I give him a small smile. I've gotten to know Igor better over the past few days, and although I'm glad they'll be here, I'm worried for Viktor.

"Let's not overfocus on that tonight. I have another twenty-four hours before my flight leaves."

Twenty-four hours. That's it? My next breath is hard to take. I can feel the panic clawing at me, seeking to drag me into its deep abyss. Fight it, Amelia. Don't let the fear win. Instead, I do what I'm taught and focus on the things around me. My hand in Viktor's. The men talking. Take it one breath at a time until the panic abates. I'm okay, and Viktor will be too.

We arrive at the restaurant a few minutes early. Every head turns as we pass the other diner's tables. I can only imagine what they're thinking. One younger girl with three much older and drop-dead gorgeous men. I hear some of the whispers and almost laugh out loud. Eat your heart out, ladies. These three are spoken for.

We're seated on the back patio that overlooks the bay. In my opinion, this is the best seat in the entire restaurant. It's the best time, too. The sun's just beginning to drop below the horizon. The sky is painted vivid shades of purples and pinks.

"I'll be right back." Viktor excuses himself from the table.

"Did Viktor tell you it's his birthday Sunday?" Igor asks.

"New Year's Day?"

"Yep."

"No, he didn't." Our server arrives at our table to take our drink orders. "We're here celebrating my boyfriend's birthday." The server takes note and promises an after-dinner surprise.

The food's delicious as always, and the company's even better. It's a nice reprieve from the stress of the past few days. The four of us get along so well. It's easy to forget who these men are and what they do when we're sharing these ordinary moments together.

While we talk, I learn that Igor and Yury have been together for nearly ten years. However, their relationship and Igor's sexuality have always been a secret.

"I'd like us to go public. I want to marry him. But Igor's worried we won't be accepted." Yury takes Igor's hand in his. "And that he'd lose his job," he says quietly.

Before this week, I would've said that's a crazy thought. But after seeing how my father treated Viktor when he found out about us, Igor's worries may be legitimate.

"You'll always have a safe place with us," I reassure them.

"Thank you, sweetie," Yury says with a smile. "We both appreciate that."

"How often do you see each other back home?"

"Not very much," Igor says sadly. "When Yury lived in St. Petersburg, we could see each other more. But, since he's moved back to Ukraine, it's much harder to sneak away."

"Why do you keep working for Max when that's the very thing keeping you apart?"

"Your father saved my life." A haunted look comes over Igor's face.

He's interrupted when several servers head our way with a cake in hand and singing Happy Birthday. Viktor's eyes grow wide in surprise. I grab my phone to record the moment.

"How did you?" Viktor asks and then looks at Igor, who shrugs.

After we leave the restaurant, we go back home, where we spend the rest of the evening playing a highly competitive game of Monopoly. The game continued until three a.m. when Viktor was declared the winner.

"Can we go to bed now?" I yawn.

Viktor scoops me up from where I sit on the couch. "Goodnight, everyone."

"Don't worry," Igor calls. "We'll clean up the mess."

"Leave it. I'll get it in the morning," Viktor calls before closing the bedroom door behind us.

Viktor

THIS IS THE LAST TIME I'LL SEE AMELIA FOR A WHILE. I keep saying it'll be a few days, but in reality, I don't know how long it'll take to get through to Maxim. But right now, I don't want to think about that. I want to focus all of my attention on Amelia.

"Lie down," I say.

Amelia crawls onto the bed, and I straddle her. My hands start at her hips and slide her shirt up her body. She puts her arms out over her head as my hands continue their path, taking her shirt off. After tossing her shirt off to one side, I hold her arms above her head with one hand and lean down to kiss her.

Her lips are soft as they welcome mine and open, allowing my tongue access to her mouth. The kiss isn't hurried. It's languid and full of unspoken emotions. It tells the tale of impending separation and heartache.

I let go of her arms and pull my shirt over my head. I need to feel her. To memorize the feel of her body beneath mine. Amelia runs her hands down my chest and abdomen. She works to open the button on my jeans. I help her slide them and my boxers off and then help her shimmy out of her leggings.

She's on full display for me in her dark purple bra and panties.

"You're perfect." I make no effort to move. Instead, I take in every inch of her beauty. "I don't deserve you."

"Don't say stuff like that." Amelia puts her finger to my lips. "You, Viktor Dobrow, deserve all the love in the world."

Reverently, I slide her satin panties down her legs, then reach behind her to unclasp her bra. I toss it to the floor with the rest of our clothes. I lean down and take one of her pert nipples into my mouth. She mewls in pleasure. I take my time lavishing attention on her breast before moving to the other side and doing the same.

Amelia runs her hands up my back, pulling my face back to hers. Our mouths collide. This time, the kiss is filled with a sense of desperation. We both know time's running out.

"Please, Viktor. Make love to me." Amelia's plea is barely above a whisper.

I guide my erection inside her and begin moving slowly and gently. I don't want to rush this. Don't want to miss a single touch. This, tonight, needs to last until we're together again.

Our hands explore every inch of one another. Our bodies rock in perfect synch. Our hearts beat as one as we chase a shared climax. Her body begins to pulse around mine, triggering my orgasm. As we share this most intimate of moments, Amelia's tears pour down her face.

"Please don't cry, *moya zirka*," I beg between kisses.

"I don't want to let you go. I don't want us to be over."

"We're not over. We'll never be over."

Viktor

QUIETLY, I PACK A BAG WHILE AMELIA'S STILL SLEEPING. MY flight leaves tomorrow afternoon. Igor plans to stay with Amelia while Yury drives me to LAX.

I've been downplaying this trip. I don't want Amelia to worry any more than she already is. But I can't lie to myself. I'm not looking forward to this trip. Not only because I'll be apart from Amelia, but I'm sure what we saw from Maxim when he was here was nothing compared to what's going to happen when I get to St. Petersburg.

"Are you packing already?" Amelia asks.

"I am." I walk to the bed and sit next to her. "Did you sleep well?"

"I guess so." She sits up. "Are you sure—" Her sentence is interrupted by the ringing of her phone. "It's my father." Amelia accepts the call and puts it on speaker. "Hello?"

"I did not wake you, did I?" Maxim asks.

"No, I've been up for a little bit."

There's a long pause.

"Amelia, I do not like how we left things between us."

"Neither do I."

"I know you want me to give my blessing for you to have a relationship with Viktor. But I cannot."

"Why are you being so unreasonable? You know Viktor. You trust Viktor. So, how is he not a good choice of a man for me?"

"You are little more than a child. He is old enough to be your father."

"Age doesn't matter. I told you about my parents."

"You did, yes. But moya malen'kaya ptichka, please try to see this from where I am looking. I want you to meet a boy your age. Someone who is not involved in this business. With Viktor comes danger. Danger, I do not want you in."

"Aren't I in danger just by being your daughter?"

Maxim hesitates before answering, "Yes."

"Then I don't understand. How's being with Viktor any different?"

"He is actively working. He will have to be gone on jobs." Max pauses. "One day, he may not come back. You will be left alone."

Amelia looks at me with tears in her eyes. "I understand, and I accept that risk."

"I do not."

"Dad, I'm going to see him with or without your blessing."

"Viktor is due back here tomorrow. Since I know he is most likely listening to this conversation, let me make myself perfectly clear. If you and Viktor try to see one another after tomorrow, I will no longer be responsible for what happens to him."

"Please don't do this," Amelia begs.

"My decision is final."

"Goodbye, Dad." Amelia hangs up the phone. Her hands are trembling, and tears stream down her face.

"Don't go, Viktor. Please."

"I have to." I wipe the tears from her face. "I'll be back. I promise."

"No, Viktor, you won't. Dad's not going to let you come back."

"I have to face him."

"He's going to let the Albanians take you." She's getting more frantic by the second. "Don't go back there. We can run away together. Igor will help us."

I take her hand in mine. "What about your tour?"

"I don't care about the tour. The only thing I care about is you." She drops to her knees in front of me. "Please. Let's pack our things and go. Right now."

"*Moya zirka*, don't do this." She folds in on herself, falling deeper into a panic attack. I get on the floor with her. "Stay with me, Amelia. Don't let the fear win." But she no longer hears me. Instead, she's alone, lost in her panic.

There's a knock on my door. "Everything ok in there?" Igor calls.

"No."

The door cracks open. When Igor sees the state Amelia's in, he rushes into the room. "What's going on?"

"She's having a panic attack."

"What the hell do we do?"

"First, you need to calm down."

Igor goes to reach out to her.

"Don't touch her. You'll make it worse," I say as calmly as I can. "Amelia, baby, listen to me." Despite Igor's presence, I begin to sing quietly. She doesn't respond right away. I keep singing, praying I break through the walls she's erected.

Finally, her crying begins to subside. I put my arms out, and Amelia collapses against me. "It's okay, *moya zirka*. I've got you." I look up at Igor, who's watching over us with tears in his eyes. "Everything's going to be okay."

"I'll leave you two alone," he says quietly and leaves the room, closing the door softly behind him.

We stay on the floor until she feels more secure. Then, we take a long, hot shower together before joining Igor and Yury in the kitchen.

Amelia

Yury loves to cook, and he's really good at it. He makes sure the four of us sit down together for all our meals—like we're a real family. This morning's no different. He's cooked breakfast, and we sit down to eat, but things are not okay. Viktor's leaving for the airport tomorrow. Yet the guys talk as though nothing's wrong. I sit quietly, not really listening or eating. I'm just pushing the food around on my plate.

"Are you all going to keep pretending Viktor's not leaving?" I finally speak up.

"That's not what we're doing, Amelia. This is the life we're used to. Things like this happen. We take it one day at a time."

"Dad's not going to let Viktor come back." I look between the men. "Don't you all see that?"

"Amelia, I need you to trust me," Viktor says.

"I do trust you," I reply and set my fork down. " But I don't want you to go. I can't do this without you."

He takes my hand in his. "I'm going to call Alex and Natalie. Maybe they can come out and stay with you until I get back."

"Okay," I say softly.

Viktor pulls up Alex's contact and puts the phone on speaker.

"Hello?" Alex answers.

"It's me."

"Is everything okay?"

"We're in a bit of a rough spot right now."

"Lana called. She told us what happened."

"I have a flight back to Russia. I'm leaving today," Viktor explains. "Is there any chance the three of you can fly out here and stay until I'm back?"

"Natalie's in the other room with Rose. They just finished up a session. Hang on while I get her."

Yury and Igor clear the breakfast plates while we wait.

"You should try to eat." Yury encourages me.

"I'm really not hungry. I'm sorry."

He leans down and kisses my forehead. "Let me know when you get hungry, and I'll make whatever you want."

"Sorry about that," Alex says when he returns

Natalie tries to quiet Rose, who's chattering away in the background.

"I filled Natalie in on what's happening."

"Can you guys come out here?" Amelia asks.

"Of course. Alex's looking for a flight right now. How long do you think you'll be gone?"

"I'm hoping only a few days."

I can't sit here and listen to this. I don't know if everyone is putting on a brave face for my benefit or what. They can't really believe my father's going to let Viktor come back in a few days.

If Viktor leaves me tomorrow, he'll never come back.

I can't listen to the rest of the call, so I go out onto the balcony. It's a stormy day, and angry waves crash onto the shore. They look and sound like I feel.

"They got a flight at six this evening. They're going to fly into the Long Beach Airport," Viktor says as he joins me on the balcony. "Yury probably won't be back by then, so Igor will pick them up."

"Thank you." I wrap my arms around him. "I still wish you wouldn't go."

"The last thing I want to do is leave you, but I have to do this." Viktor sits down and pulls me onto his lap. "If I don't go back, Max will hunt us down. We'll always be on the run, looking over our shoulders. You deserve better than that."

"He's never going to change his mind."

"It's not going to be easy, but please trust me. I'll make this work for us."

I rest my head against his chest, listening to the steady beat of his heart. There are no more words left to say.

"It's time to leave," Yury says quietly from the doorway.

"I'll be right there."

I lift my head and gaze into Viktor's blue eyes. His lips meet mine for a passionate kiss. He pulls back and tucks a curl behind my ear. As much as I don't want to, I force myself to stand.

"I can't say goodbye."

"Then we won't say it."

With a final kiss, he turns and walks away from me. I wanted to be strong, but I can't. "Please don't go," I cry and try to go after him, but Igor grabs onto me.

Viktor stops with his hand on the doorknob. "I'll be back as soon as possible," he says without looking back.

Then, he walks out the door.

"Let me go." I struggle to get out of Igor's grasp. "I have to stop him."

"He has to go."

"No. I need him to stay." My body shakes from the depth of pain and fear I'm experiencing.

Amelia

IGOR SHOULD BE HERE WITH ALEX AND NATALIE ANY minute. I've picked up one of Viktor's habits, pacing back and forth while I wait for them to get here. It's been forever since I've seen them, and right now, I really need their support.

The sound of a car pulling into the driveway interrupts my cadence, and I rush to the window. "They're here."

I rush over to unlock the door and throw it open. Natalie's already on her way up the steps. "Oh my gosh, this house is amazing." She gushes.

"Hello to you, too," I joke.

"Hi, sweetheart." She gives him a hug. "It's been too long."

"It has. You look great." Natalie's a few months pregnant and is just starting to sport a tiny bump.

"Thank you." She runs her hand over her abdomen.

"Auntie Melia." Little arms wrap around my leg.

"Hello there, big girl. I've missed you," I say as I pick her up and pepper her face with kisses, making her giggle.

"How are you holding up?" Alex asks.

"Not well. I still wish he didn't go."

"I know, but this is something he has to do."

"I guess." I shrug. "Are you guys hungry? Yury made a bunch of appetizers."

"I sure am." Igor kisses my cheek on his way to the kitchen. "He'll be okay."

We make our way to the kitchen and pick on the light snacks that are artfully arranged on our serving platters. While we're eating, Yury comes back from dropping Viktor off. He joins us at the table.

Everyone's chatting away as if this is a typical night. The only thing I can focus on is that Viktor's on his way to what I'm sure isn't going to be a fun time. I smile and pretend I'm having a good time, but my mind and heart are on a plane heading to St. Petersburg.

It's not long before Rose starts to get cranky.

"It's been a really long day for her," Natalie says. "We're going to have to call it a night."

I show them to my old bedroom, where they'll be staying. Igor's already brought their luggage in and set up the portable playpen for Rose to sleep in.

Then, I head to our bedroom. It's cold and lonely here without Viktor. I'm not ready to sleep, so I take my cell, sit on our private balcony, and wait for a call to let me know Viktor's arrived safely.

Viktor

Leaving Amelia sobbing in Igor's arms nearly shattered me. Every fiber of my being screamed to turn back, to hold her, to promise her everything would be okay. But I couldn't. I had to force myself to walk away, to board the plane to St. Petersburg, even though it felt like I was tearing out my own heart.

Now, I'm halfway through the eighteen-hour flight, and sleep is impossible. Every time I close my eyes, I see Amelia's tear-streaked face and hear her desperate pleas for me to stay. The memory claws at me, relentless. Desperate for distraction, I try to focus on the conversation I'll have with Maxim. But it's no comfort. Every scenario I run through ends the same way—with me either dead or wishing I were.

Snow is beginning to fall as the plane touches down in Russia. I quickly grew used to the climate in California and didn't miss winter at all. Dimitri's supposed to be picking me up. I search for him but don't find him anywhere.

Me: I'm here. Where are you?

Dimitri: In the car waiting.

I make my way to the main doors and scan the area for the car. I spot him on the far side of the parking lot. Dimitri and I have been on shaky ground for a while. The situation in Grenada didn't help anything. The fact he sees me freezing my ass off as I trek through the parking lot and he doesn't even attempt to drive closer is all I need to let me know he's still pissed at me.

When I get to the car, I'm shivering. I didn't pack any winter gear when we moved to California. I'm paying for that now.

I open the passenger side door and climb into the black SUV. I've never been so thankful for heated seats. My hands are so cold, they're numb. I hold them close to the vent to warm them.

"Did you forget it's winter?"

"No. I don't have my winter things. I left them all here."

"Oh. That's too bad," he says with mock sympathy. He's enjoying seeing me suffer.

Dimitri pulls out of the parking spot, and we make our way to the main road.

"I never got a chance to thank you for bailing me out. I wouldn't have made it out of Grenada alive if you didn't show up."

He doesn't answer. Doesn't give me any hint that he's even listening.

"I know I screwed up."

"Screwed up? You took off without telling anyone where you were going."

I was in a bad place. I put not only my life but the lives of others in danger.

"We've been brothers for most of our lives. It would've been nice to at least know you were alive."

"I didn't think you'd care."

"Oh yeah. I forgot. I have no feelings."

"I needed some space to clear my head."

"You nearly got yourself and Jessica killed."

"I realize that." I close my eyes, knowing how lucky I am that Dimitri showed up when he did. "I thought going to visit *Babusya* would help. I had no idea she was sick," I say quietly. "Her death only made things worse. I didn't care if I lived or died."

"Did you ever think that other people might give a shit?"

"No." It's not a great answer, but it's the truth.

Dimitri doesn't respond again until he pulls into Max's garage.

"And now? Have you decided to live?"

"Yes." Although I'm not sure how long Maxim's going to let that happen. "I have a lot to live for."

"Amelia?"

"You know?"

"Everybody knows. Max was livid when he came home."

We get out of the car. "How is he now?"

"Still out for blood." Dimitri snickers. "By the way, he's waiting for you in his office. I'll put your bag in your room."

He walks away, and I'm left to face the boss alone.

Viktor

DIMITRI MAKES A RIGHT AND HEADS TOWARD THE GUARDS'
wing while I go straight to Maxim's office. Pyotr is on duty outside the
office.

"Good to see you, Viktor."

"You too. I'm told the boss is waiting for me."

"He is. You can go in."

I've never been afraid to enter Maxim's office—until now.

"Dimitri said you wanted to see me right away."

"Sit," Maxim says without looking up.

Hesitantly, I walk to the leather chair across from his desk and take a
seat.

"You are being reassigned. Starting today, you will be stationed
here," Max explains. "You will report to Yevgeniy."

"That won't be necessary. I'm resigning."

"That is unacceptable." He stands and rounds the desk. "The
assignment was not a request."

I stand, meeting him head-on. "The only reason I returned was to
discuss my relationship with Amelia. I'm in love with your daughter.
When I leave here, I'm going back to her."

The words are barely out of my mouth when Max's fist connects with my face.

"The hell you are," he yells. "Whatever you think you had with her is over. Do you understand me?"

"No, boss. It isn't." His fist connects with my face again. "What we have is real, and I'm not willing to walk away from her."

Max may be an older man, but he keeps himself in good physical shape. His fist connects with my face again, and blood spatters on the floor. I don't try to block or defend myself, knowing he needs an outlet for his anger.

"You will stay the fuck away from my daughter."

"I can't do that, boss." He can physically punish me however he wants, but I refuse to turn my back on Amelia.

"You do not have a choice. She is off-limits."

Fists rain down on me, relentless and punishing, each blow brutal. He lands one squarely against my torso, and a sharp crack reverberates through the room. Pain explodes in my chest, stealing the air from my lungs. My knees hit the floor, and I'm left gasping, unable to draw a single breath.

"I should have let the Albanians kill you. It is not too late. One phone call is all it will take.

"I'm sorry," I cough, trying to catch my breath. "Neither of us planned this."

"You are a grown man. She is an eighteen-year-old child."

"Amelia isn't a child. She's a grown woman who's free to make her own choices."

"I do not want to hear you speak her name," Max roars. "Stay the fuck away from my daughter."

"You're going to need some more time to accept that we're together. I understand that."

Another barrage of punches and kicks rains down on me. I curl into myself, trying to shield vital areas, but there's no true escape from the onslaught. Max's fury pours out with every strike, each blow a brutal reminder of the price I have to pay. I grit my teeth against the pain, knowing this is the only path forward.

The office door flies open and cracks off the wall.

"What the hell?" Dimitri yells. "Max, you're going to kill him."

"That is my plan." Maxim doesn't stop his assault on me.

"Boss, stop," Pyotr yells as he pulls Max away.

"Get the fuck off me." Max struggles to get out of his hold.

"You don't want to do this." Pyotr tries to reason with him.

"The fuck I do not," Max argues. "If you value your life, you will let me go."

Pyotr ignores Max's threats.

"Since when do we turn on our own men?" Dimitri faces off with his uncle.

"Since he touched my daughter."

"I get it. You're mad."

"Mad? Is that what you think, nephew?" Max's voice booms. "I am beyond mad."

"Okay, you're beyond mad. But Viktor's one of us. He's family."

"He is no longer family. He is dead to me."

His words hurt worse than any one of his physical strikes.

"Come on. Get up." Dimitri helps me from the floor. "Uncle, you don't mean that."

"Do not tell me what I mean or do not mean, Dimitri." Max points at me. "He touched something that did not belong to him."

"Amelia is not a piece of property," I snap back. "She made a choice."

"She is too young to know better." Max takes another swing at me, but Dimitri jumps in front of him.

"Boss, Amelia's an adult. She's old enough to make her own decisions—even if they're ones you disagree with."

"Are you taking his side?"

"I'm taking Amelia's side since she's not here to speak for herself," Dimitri says calmly. "I get it. You want to kill him. But what about Amelia? If you take away her voice. If you refuse to let her have a voice, you're no better than Moreno or any of the men who've hurt her."

Silence.

Dimitri struck a nerve.

"Get him out of my sight." Max storms out of his office. Pyotr follows behind him.

"Are you okay?" Dimitri turns to me.

"I'm pretty sure he broke at least one rib." Breathing is harder than it should be.

"Let's go." Dimitri helps me walk. "We'll have the doc take a look at you."

I lean on him for support. "You shouldn't have gotten in the middle of that."

"Should I have let him kill you?"

"He wouldn't have killed me."

"How about you just thank me for saving your ass again."

"Thank you for saving my ass again," I say mockingly.

"You owe me." Dimitri grins. "And I plan on cashing in on that debt."

Amelia

I'M LYING ON MY BED WHEN MY PHONE BUZZES NEXT TO ME. Viktor's name lights up the screen, and I answer immediately.

"How are you?" I ask, my voice tight with worry.

He exhales, the sound weary. "Your father called me to his office as soon as I arrived," he begins, recounting everything that happened.

My stomach churns as he finishes. "Three fractured ribs? Viktor, that's not okay," I exclaim, sitting up.

"It is," he replies. "Max needed to vent his anger, and this was the only way."

"He didn't have to hurt you," I argue, my voice rising. "I hate him for this, Viktor. I really do."

"No, you don't," he counters gently. "You're angry and upset right now, but deep down, you know your father loves you."

I pace the length of my room, my free hand clenching into a fist. "That's not love," I snap. "Love doesn't do this to people."

"He was protecting you," Viktor says, his tone maddeningly calm. "In the only way he knows how. I don't blame him for it."

I stop in my tracks and glare at the floor as though he's standing there. "I don't know how you can forgive him so easily."

"I understand him," he says. "If I were in his position, I'd probably do the same thing."

His words hit me like a slap. "How much longer are you going to be gone?" I ask, desperate to change the subject. It's been two days, but it already feels like an eternity.

"I'm not sure," he admits, his voice softer now. "Hopefully, not much longer. Dimitri just came in—I need to handle something. Can I call you later?"

I swallow hard, the ache in my chest growing. "Yes," I murmur reluctantly.

"I love you, *moya zirka*."

"And I love you," I reply, my voice trembling.

We hang up, and I hold the phone against my chest. I can't believe my father physically attacked him. I'm furious and debate calling him to tell him exactly what I'm thinking. The only thing holding me back is Viktor. I fear my father would retaliate by hurting Viktor more.

Instead, I decide to ask Natalie if she'd intervene.

It's just the three of us here right now. Alex gave Igor and Yury a few unofficial days off. They went to a nearby hotel to ring in the new year alone. I find Natalie sitting on the sofa, a movie on pause. Alex is on the phone out on the balcony. It looks like they're having some downtime while Rose takes her afternoon nap.

"What's wrong?"

"Everything," I say and sit on the ottoman across from her.

"What's going on?" Alex asks as he comes back into the room.

"My father broke three of Viktor's ribs."

"Oh my God." Natalie brings her hand to her mouth. "Is he okay?"

"He said he's fine." I sigh. "Dad told Viktor he's dead to him. I think that hurt more than the broken ribs." Alex and Natalie exchange a worried glance. "Natalie, I need your help. Dad will listen to you if you talk to him."

"I don't know—"

"Please, Natalie."

"What do you think, Alex?" We both stare at him expectantly.

"Give me a little time to figure something out," Alex says. "Meanwhile, we have a New Year to celebrate tonight."

"I don't feel like celebrating."

"I didn't ask," Alex smirks. "Go take a shower or whatever you need to do to get ready for a party." He tilts the ottoman, forcing me to get up.

"What's wrong with your husband?"

"He likes to be in control." Natalie winks.

"You two can celebrate. I'll keep Rose tonight."

"Nope. We're all celebrating together," Alex insists.

I roll my eyes at him. "Whatever you say, boss," I say in my best sarcastic voice.

"That's better. Now go." Alex points down the hall.

There's nothing for me to celebrate. I was planning a quiet evening in my room where I could feel sorry for myself. I guess that's not going to happen now.

Alex

"YOU REALIZE SHE'S NOT IN A PARTYING MOOD?" NATALIE asks, her brow furrowed in concern.

"She will be," Alex says confidently, a hint of a smirk playing on his lips. "Dimitri called. He just put Viktor on Max's jet a few minutes ago. If all goes well, he'll be here just before midnight."

Natalie's eyes widen. "Max changed his mind?"

"No," I interject, lowering myself onto the couch beside her. "Max is still determined to keep them apart. But Dimitri was worried about Viktor's safety if he stayed there. So, he went behind Max's back and got Viktor on a plane home."

Natalie's expression shifts from surprise to unease. "Oh. What's going to happen to Dimitri when Max finds out?"

"He'll be fine," I reassure her, picking up my phone. "I have an idea."

Her gaze sharpens. "What kind of idea?"

I don't answer; instead, I tap the call icon. After a few rings, Max's deep voice filters through the line. "Alexander. To what do I owe this?"

"Max," I say, keeping my tone light. "I didn't wake you, did I?"

"No," he replies, his voice heavy with exhaustion. "I have not been sleeping much lately. Is everything well there?"

"Yes," I say casually. "The girls are getting ready for tonight. Meanwhile, I'm trying to tie up some loose ends at Jelena's Hope NYC before the New Year."

There's a pause before Max speaks again, his voice softening. "How is Amelia? I am sure she has heard what occurred here."

"She did," I admit. "She's upset, as you might imagine."

Max sighs audibly, the weight of his guilt palpable. "I do not know what came over me. The thought of Viktor with my little girl... I could not control the rage I felt."

"Amelia isn't a little girl anymore," I remind him, keeping my tone even.

"That is what everyone keeps saying," Max says gruffly, "but I do not see it."

If I want my plan to work, I can't risk antagonizing him. I shift gears, opting for a softer approach. "I get it," I say. "I have a little girl too."

· · ·

Finally, a hint of approval creeps into Max's voice. "Finally, a man with some sense."

"The reason for my call," I say, steering the conversation in a new direction, "is about Jelena's Hope. We've outgrown our residential units. We had to turn away the last two calls we received."

"We are going through the same growing pains here," Max notes, his tone thoughtful.

"Would you be able to meet me in New York to look at some new properties? I'd like to move on this quickly."

"How is the end of next week?" he offers.

"That would be perfect. Thanks, Max."

As I hang up, I feel a sense of relief wash over me. Getting Maxim on board was the biggest hurdle—now I need to pull the rest of this together.

Natalie looks at me skeptically. "Are you planning on bringing them both to New York?"

"I am," I reply, my jaw tightening slightly.

"Do you really think that's a good idea?"

I shrug, the weight of uncertainty settling over me. "I don't know. But I have to try something. If we can get them on neutral ground, maybe we can make some progress—without the violence."

Natalie arches an eyebrow. "I sure hope you know what you're doing."

"So do I," I admit with a faint smile.

Amelia

I'VE BEEN TRYING TO REACH VIKTOR FOR HOURS, BUT MY calls keep going straight to voicemail, and my texts remain unread. Frustration twists in my chest, but I refuse to speak to my father. Instead, I scroll through my contacts and call Lana.

"Good morning," Lana answers, her tone light. "Or should I say good evening?"

"Sorry for calling so early," I say quickly. "I've been trying to reach Viktor, but he's not answering his phone."

There's a pause before she responds. "I'm not sure where he is," she admits. "If I see him, I'll tell him to call you."

"Thanks." I hesitate, my voice faltering. "Lana, was he okay the last time you saw him?"

She exhales audibly. "He looked a little roughed up, but he'll live."

My heart clenches. "What got into Dad?"

Lana lets out a bitter laugh. "You do know who our father is, right?"

"Yes," I say, my voice quieter now. "But I didn't think he'd hurt one of his own men."

"Dad will stop at nothing if he believes it's to keep us safe," she replies matter-of-factly.

I shake my head, anger bubbling beneath my worry. "I'm not in danger with Viktor. I don't understand it."

"He still sees you as his little girl," Lana explains, her voice softening. "And Viktor is Dad's employee. He knew the boundaries and didn't respect them."

"The boundaries?" I ask sharply. "Don't I get a say in these so-called boundaries?"

"In Dad's eyes? No."

"Can you talk to him?" I plead. "Try to make him understand?"

Her tone shifts, turning guarded. "We're not really speaking to each other right now."

"Lana, what's going on with you?" I press gently. "I know something's up."

"I'm just trying to figure out what's next for me," she says vaguely.

She's not telling me everything. But I know if I push too hard, she'll shut me out. "Well, if you ever decide you want to talk, I'm here. I'm a good listener."

"Thanks, Melia," she says, her tone warming slightly. "I have to run. Happy New Year."

"I'll try," I murmur before the call disconnects.

I toss the phone onto my bed and sigh, running a hand through my damp hair. At Alex's insistence, I'd showered, but if he's hoping for a dress-up event, he'll be disappointed. Sweatpants and a T-shirt are as fancy as I'm getting tonight.

After tying my hair into a ponytail, I slip my phone into my pocket and head to the living room.

"It's about time you joined us," Alex greets me with a wide grin. "I had some food delivered."

I glance toward the kitchen counter, where an impressive spread of appetizers and finger foods is laid out. "That's enough food for an army. Are we expecting company?"

"I am eating for two," Natalie teases, rubbing her growing belly.

"Auntie Melia! Want some?" Rose toddles over, holding out her half-eaten peanut butter and jelly sandwich.

"Thank you, princess." I kneel to her level and pretend to take a big bite. "Your turn."

Giggling, she takes another bite before scampering off to her daddy, who scoops her onto his lap.

Natalie passes by, a plate in her hand, and gives me a pointed look. "That'll be Viktor and your baby one day."

"Not me," I say quickly. "I don't want kids."

"You'll change your mind."

Her words settle over me like a heavy cloud. Realizing I'm not in the right frame of mind to be around everyone, I head toward the door. "I'm going down to the beach for a little while."

"Want some company?" Alex asks, his grin fading slightly.

"No, thanks," I reply softly. "I just need some time alone. I won't go far."

Alex's expression turns serious. "Keep your phone with you," he says firmly.

"I will," I promise, stepping outside into the warm night air.

With the moonlight as my guide, I walk along the water's edge. The old year is quickly coming to a close, while the new year and all its promises are at the cusp of being born. The tranquility of the beach allows me the opportunity for reflection.

Life guarantees one thing: change. But the ocean, the constant I've come to love, remains steadfast. No matter the chaos that unfolds, the waves remain unaffected. They roll in, crashing against the shore in their steady, rhythmic dance. One after another. Day after day. Predictable. Safe. Calming.

It's a stark contrast to the storm raging inside me. Just days ago, my life felt perfect—more perfect than I ever dared to dream. Then, in the blink of an eye, everything crumbled. Facades shattered. People revealed their true colors. I went from feeling protected in the arms of the man I love to standing alone, vulnerable, and exposed.

The ache in my chest is overwhelming, a suffocating weight I can't seem to escape. The ocean soothes me in a way nothing else can, but even its steady rhythm isn't enough to quiet the pain in my heart.

Opening my music app, I select my favorite playlist. Music plays softly as I lie down on the cool sand. The sky is full of millions of twinkling stars that transcend time and space. Somewhere up there are two stars that can never be separated—unlike Viktor and me.

I don't realize how long I've been lying here until I get a text alert.

Natalie: It's almost midnight. Will you come ring in the New Year with us?

Me: I'll be right there.

I try calling Viktor once more, but there's still no answer. Standing up, I wipe the sand off my clothes and start back toward the house.

Viktor

"Thanks for picking me up," I say to Igor and Yury. "Looks like we'll make it just in time."

I don't know how Dimitri pulled it off, but Max's jet was fueled and ready to fly me back to California. The universe must have been cheering me on because not only did we have the help of a tailwind, but Dimitri also arranged for us to land at the Long Beach Airport.

"Does Max know you're here?" Igor asks.

"I'm sure he does by now. Dimitri was going to speak to him after the jet was safely out of Russian airspace," I explain.

Right on cue, Igor's phone rings.

Yury checks it since Igor's behind the wheel. "It's Maxim."

Igor glances at me in the rearview mirror. "Answer it. But put it on speaker, please."

"Hello?" Igor answers, his tone carefully neutral.

"My nephew tells me my jet has landed in California with Viktor on board," Max says, his voice sharp and authoritative.

"That's what I've been told. I'm on my way to pick him up now," Igor replies, keeping his tone steady.

"Where is my daughter?"

"She's at home," Igor responds quickly, already anticipating the next question. "The doors are locked, and the security system is armed. I won't be gone long," he reassures him.

"I am trusting you to keep him away from Amelia."

"If I may speak freely, boss," Igor ventures carefully, "I think this is a good call—an olive branch if you will. Amelia's a sweet girl, but she's uncomfortable being alone with me. Having Viktor around will help ease some of her nerves."

There's a pause before he speaks again, his tone colder this time. "He is not to be alone with her."

"I understand, boss," Igor says, his words laced with dutiful respect. He's walking a fine line now, fully aware of the risks. "When will her new team arrive?"

"I am hoping it will be soon," Max admits, a rare note of frustration slipping through. "Unfortunately, it is taking more time than I would prefer to assemble a qualified team."

"Okay, no problem."

"I am trusting you to keep my little girl safe," Maxim says firmly, his protectiveness unmistakable.

"Amelia's a capable young woman," Igor replies with quiet sincerity, "but I'll guard her with my life, sir."

The call ends, and Igor exhales a relieved sigh.

"Thank you for doing this," I say.

"It's for a good cause," Igor says with a small smile. "You both deserve to be happy."

With it being close to midnight, there's not much traffic. Even still, the ride feels like it's taking forever. Finally, we're pulling up to the house. I rush inside and find Alex, Natalie, and Rose watching Times Square's New Year's Eve festivities.

"You made it." Natalie gives me a quick hug.

"Barely." I look around. "Where's Amelia?"

"She's on the beach," Alex says, "We've been keeping an eye on her."

I step onto the balcony and spot her lying on the sand. My beautiful girl.

"She's been lost without you," Natalie says as she comes to stand next to me.

"Are you sure I'm doing the right thing?"

"Viktor, you have so much love to give. I know because, for a few months, I was the recipient of that love. I'm ashamed to admit this, but After Alex came back, I wanted both yours and Alex's love," she admits. "It took a long time for me to see that it was unfair to everyone. Especially you." She looks up at me.

"You deserve to have a woman look at you and see their whole world. Someone who'll love you with the same all-encompassing love you give. Amelia is that woman. You're everything to her."

"I was afraid of how you'd feel about her and me. That you'd disapprove because of our age difference or that you'd think the feelings I had for you weren't real because I moved on."

"I'm not going to lie. I was shocked." She chuckles. "But I never questioned your feelings for her or me." Natalie touches my arm. "What you and I shared was beautiful and very complicated."

"That's putting it mildly."

"Circumstances beyond our control threw us together. I know you loved me, and I loved you. I always will. Love doesn't go away. But what you and I had wasn't the same all-encompassing love Alex and I share— what you and Amelia share."

"When she looks at me, she sees only me. Wants only me."

"That's exactly how it's supposed to be. As hard as I tried, I wouldn't have been able to give you that. In life or death, Alex and I will always be connected."

"I knew that."

"And yet you were willing to sacrifice what you deserved to be with me."

"I made a promise to Alex."

"And you honored that." Natalie looks out into the darkness. "I see the way you look at Amelia and the way she looks at you. Your heart recognized its soulmate."

"Even though I'm so much older than her?"

"Age is irrelevant. Your hearts and souls are connected. You were made for each other."

"Thank you, Natalie." I hug her. "I think I'm beginning to understand how lucky I am."

"It's about time." Natalie smiles.

"Hey, you two." Alex joins us on the deck. "There's only fifteen minutes until midnight. Amelia needs to come back for her New Year's surprise."

"I'll text her now." Natalie's fingers fly across her screen. It's only seconds before she gets a reply. "She's on her way."

"Let's ring in the New Year, baby girl," Alex says, and we walk into the house together.

"I'm going to wait in our room. I don't want her to know I'm here until midnight."

Amelia

"Igor. Yury. What are you guys doing here?" I'm surprised to see them. I thought they were ringing in the New Year alone.

"We wanted to spend the holiday with friends," Yury says.

There's less than five minutes until the ball drops. Natalie passes champagne flutes out to everyone.

I look around the room. Rose is passed out on the couch. Igor and Yury are together. Natalie's wrapped in Alex's embrace. But I'm alone. The man I wish was by my side is on the other side of the world.

The ball slowly starts to fall, and everyone counts aloud. "Five, four, three, two, one."

"Happy New Year, *moya zirka*."

Everything disappears as I spin around and find Viktor a few steps behind me, a champagne flute in his hand and a huge grin on his face.

"Viktor? Are you really here?"

He takes a step toward me. "I am."

I close the distance between us and throw my arms around him, spilling champagne in the process. His breath catches.

"I'm sorry." I try to back away. "I forgot about your ribs."

"You're not going anywhere." He holds me tight with one arm.

"Your face." She gently touches the bandage over my eye. "Did you need stitches?"

"Yes, but don't worry about it." He holds up his glass. "Here's to a happy and prosperous new year."

We clink glasses, and then our lips meet for a kiss.

"Happy Birthday," I whisper between kisses. "I wasn't able to get you anything."

"You're all I want."

"You already have me."

"And I plan on having you all night," he growls in my ear, making me squirm.

Alex clears his throat, "Did you two forget you're not alone?"

Viktor kisses me once more before we exchange New Year's toasts with everyone. I don't know what I did to deserve these wonderful friends—my chosen family. But I'm so thankful for them.

"Look at the time." Viktor pretends to check his non-existent watch. "It's time for us to go to bed."

"Smooth, Dobrow," Igor jokes.

I want to crawl under a piece of furniture and hide from embarrassment.

"Sleep tight." Alex laughs.

Viktor takes my hand and leads me out of the living room. As we walk away, I hear Yury say, "Well, it's past our bedtime, too."

"I really wish the rooms were soundproof," I mumble as we go into our room.

Viktor

Once we're in our room and the door's locked, I waste
no time removing my shirt. My movements are stiff because of the pain.

Amelia gasps when she sees my chest. "I thought your face was bad.
What did he do to you?"

I didn't stop to think about what her reaction would be. My chest is
covered in bruises, and my ribs are taped tight.

"I'll be fine."

She steps closer and places her tiny hand on my chest.

"Does it hurt?"

"Only when I breathe."

"You need to lie down and rest."

"No, I need to be with you."

"I don't think so." Amelia puts her hands on her waist.

"It's my birthday wish." I smile.

She pauses as though she's considering my appeal. Then, she reaches
out and opens my jeans. She pulls them down, followed by my boxers.
I'm already hard for her.

"We can do this on one condition."

"I like bossy Amelia," I chuckle. "What's your condition?"

"You need to be on the bottom so you don't put stress on your ribs."

"That's a condition I can agree to."

She steps out of my way so I can lie down. I appreciate the sacrifice she's making tonight. Amelia's often insecure about being on top, so the significance of what she's doing is not lost on me.

"I think my birthday boy deserves a little show."

Carefully, I put my hands behind my head. Every movement is painful, but I try not to show that on my face.

Amelia takes out her phone and puts on music. She sways her hips to the seductive song that plays. As she does, she hooks her fingers in the waistband of her sweatpants and slowly slides them down her legs. When they're off, she tosses them to the side. She's bare underneath— something that usually infuriates me, but right now, I don't care. I'm entranced by this sexy, brave woman in front of me.

When she turns to face me, she's biting her lower lip. A move that gives away her insecurities.

"You don't have to do this," I remind her.

"I want to. But I don't feel very sexy doing it."

"Amelia Solonik, you are very sexy."

A smile spreads across her face as she crawls over me. If I'm not careful, I'll come before she touches me. Amelia sits back on her knees and pulls her shirt off. Her bra follows. She maneuvers her body between my legs until her mouth is centimeters from my cock. Then, she glances up at me through her thick lashes.

Her next move seems to go in slow motion. Without breaking eye contact, she drags her tongue from the base to the tip of my cock. My eyes roll back in pleasure as her tongue circles the sensitive tip before teasing my slit. Amelia looks up and licks her lips.

"You taste delicious, Mr. Dobrow." She runs her tongue across my tip once more.

"If you keep doing that, I'm not going to last."

"No?" she teases. "So, if I do this." She opens her lips and lowers her head, taking me all the way in before sliding back up slowly.

"Amelia," I growl.

"Yes?" Without warning, she takes me in her mouth again. She glides her mouth along my length while her other hand massages my balls.

"You need to stop."

She ignores me and continues her sensual movements.

"I can't hold back much longer," I grit out. "I'm going to come in your mouth if you don't stop." And I don't want to do that.

Amelia told me how she was forced to take men in her mouth. She described the helplessness of being unable to breathe as they forced their length down her throat. She's expressed fear that I wouldn't want her if she wouldn't do this for me. I reassured her that I would never ask or expect her to do anything she was uncomfortable with and that she could never be a disappointment to me.

She looks up at me. Her brown eyes dance with delight as she opens her mouth and takes me in again. My hips buck up of their own accord. She takes all of me—everything I have to give her. With a final thrust, I come in her mouth. Amelia doesn't falter as she swallows everything I have to give. When my cock stops throbbing, she sits back on her heels, a satisfied look on her face.

I don't say it aloud, but I'm so proud of Amelia. My brave girl's just conquered one of her fears. Taken back something that was stolen from her and made it her own.

"You're going to be the death of me. Get up here." She crawls up my body and situates herself over my still-hard dick. I take her by the waist and guide her down my length. "I missed you, *moya zirka*."

"Promise me that you'll never leave again."

As much as I want to make that promise, I can't. "If I leave, I'll always come back to you."

Amelia nods. She understands what my job is and what assurances I can and can't give her.

Without warning, she starts moving. My world is thrown off its axis by the sheer pleasure of being inside her.

"Touch yourself."

Amelia slides her hand down her front and between her legs. Her head falls back with a moan.

"That's it, *moya zirka*," I encourage her. "Fuck, you're amazing."

Despite the stabbing pain in my chest, another orgasm is building. "Are you ready to come for me?"

"Yes. I'm—" Her sentence is interrupted by the orgasm that rips through her.

My hips thrust wildly. Once. Twice. "Fuck. Amelia." Blackness creeps into the corners of my vision from the force of the orgasm mixed with the pain in my chest. I try to hang onto consciousness. Despite my efforts, everything goes dark and silent as I lose the battle.

Amelia

"Viktor." I gently shake his shoulder, but he doesn't respond. "Viktor, wake up. You're scaring me." I knew it was too soon. I shouldn't have let him talk me into this. What do I do now?

I dig through the pile of clothes on the floor for my sweatpants and T-shirt and get dressed quickly. Before I leave the room, I pull the covers over him. Even though I don't want to disturb anyone else, I have to. Viktor still isn't waking up.

I knock on the bedroom door. "Igor," I call, not too loudly. I don't want to wake up the whole house.

It takes a minute before he answers the door. When he does, he's wearing only a pair of shorts. "What's up?"

"I'm sorry for bothering you. Viktor passed out, and I can't wake him up."

"Shit." He rushes down the hall and into our room. "Viktor." He shakes him more aggressively than I did.

I stand back, frightened by my unresponsive boyfriend.

"What happened?" Yury asks when he gets to our room.

"Um. Well, we were—"

My sentence is interrupted when Viktor begins to come to. I rush over to the bed.

"Is everything okay in here?" Alex appears in the doorway.

Yury fills him in while Igor and I tend to Viktor.

"Welcome back," Igor says with a smirk.

"What happened?"

"You passed out after you—"

"Stop," Viktor interrupts.

"You're lucky you didn't injure yourself any further," Igor says. "You have three broken ribs. You need to be resting, not fucking."

"Watch your mouth." Viktor glances my way before sliding himself to a sitting position with a groan. "I'm fine. You can all go back to bed."

"I'm serious. You need to take it easy." Igor looks at me. "I don't care what he says. The answer's no."

"Got it. I'm sorry for bothering everyone."

The men exit the room, leaving Viktor and me alone.

"You shouldn't have gone to Igor."

"You wouldn't wake up." I rest my head on his shoulder. "I was scared and didn't know what else to do. Are you sure you're okay?"

"I'll live."

"We aren't doing that again until I'm certain you're healed."

I don't have the strength to argue with her. The exhaustion from my injuries and the long flight are hitting me hard. "I'll let you win this one."

Amelia climbs out of bed.

"Where are you going?"

"Stay there. I'll be right back." She disappears into our bathroom.

It's not like I have much of a choice. I don't think I could follow her if I tried. When she returns, she has a wet washcloth and a towel in her hands. With great tenderness, she washes my body and then helps me slip on a pair of pajama pants.

"Do you need anything else?"

"You. Next to me."

Amelia climbs into bed and pulls the blanket over us.

I was only gone a few nights, but I'd grown used to her next to me. One night without Amelia is too many.

Tonight, I fall asleep with my world in my arms.

Amelia

AMELIA

It was so much fun having everyone here this week. For a little while, I didn't think about everything with my father. Instead, we were able to focus on spending quality time with Alex, Natalie, and Rose.

Viktor's so good with Rose. He's still having difficulty with movements, but somehow, he's managed to get on the floor with her to have a tea party. He's even wearing her princess tiara.

"I hate that you guys are leaving today."

"Me too," Natalie says. "It doesn't feel like we had enough time, but we have to get back to Jelena's Hope NYC."

While Viktor was sipping tea with Rose, Natalie filled me in on Alex's plan to get Viktor and Max together in New York next week. I'm scared that Dad's going to flip. That he's going to hurt Viktor again or worse. Natalie assured me that there would be enough security to keep any more violence from happening. I'm not totally on board, but I don't see we have any other choice.

"Princess Viktor," Natalie jokes.

"What?" he asks, pretending to take a sip from a little pink teacup.

Rose lets out a belly laugh.

"How about you and Amelia come out to visit us for a few days next week?" she asks. "Rose, do you want Friker and Auntie Melia to come to our house?"

I have to give it to her. Natalie's good. She knows Viktor can't say no to Rose.

"Friker, can you come see me at my house?" Rose jumps onto his lap. "Pwease?"

"What do you think, Auntie Melia?" he asks.

"I'd love that."

Viktor grabs Rose and holds her in the air. "I guess we're going to New York City, then."

Viktor and I drive to Long Beach Airport for Alex and Natalie's flight.

"We'll see you two in a few days," she says. "Try not to worry. We'll figure this out."

"I hope you're right."

Natalie gives me a reassuring smile before walking over to Viktor, who's holding Rose and chatting with Alex.

"We're going to need to take her with us." Natalie reaches out, but Rose turns away and wraps her little arms around Viktor's neck.

"Printessa, you need to go with your mama. I'll see you very soon." He tries to pry Rose's hands from his neck, but she whimpers.

My heart aches watching this scene unfold. Even though Viktor hasn't spent much time with her since he left, she's still very much bonded with him.

"Rose, we have to go home so you can get your toys ready to play with Friker," Natalie says. After a moment of indecision, Rose lets go, and Viktor passes her to Natalie. She rests her head on her mama's shoulder while big tears fall. "Don't cry." Natalie soothes her daughter.

The boarding call for their flight plays over the speakers.

"That's us," Alex says. "We'll see you soon." He and Viktor exchange a quick hug. Then, he turns to me. "Hang in there, okay?"

"I will." We hug each other goodbye.

Viktor and I hold hands while we watch them go through security, and they disappear from our sight.

Amelia

ALEX AND NATALIE FLEW OUT A FEW DAYS AGO, AND LAST night, Yury flew back to Ukraine. We went from a full house to just the three of us. The quiet won't last for long. Tomorrow, Viktor, Igor, and I are flying out to New York, where I'm afraid sparks will fly.

I've finished packing and am going outside to collect the day's mail while the guys are in the house discussing the new security team that's currently in St. Petersburg on trial with my father's men. If they get the final approval, he'll be sending them here sometime next month.

I open the mailbox and pull out the stack of mail. Most of it's junk, but one envelope catches my eye. It's from Mateo. I sit on the step and carefully open the envelope.

Dear Amelia,

I know I'm probably the last person you want to hear from, but I'm writing anyway. By now, Sparrow has probably told you what happened and where I am. I want you to know that I've been sober for three weeks. It's not much, but it's a start. I see my therapist every day, and we're working through my issues. Part of that work is making amends to the people I've hurt. You are one of those people.

The last day I saw you, you shared some of your story with me. I never got the chance to tell you mine. I'm adopted, too.

My biological mom was an addict. I never knew who my father was. After she overdosed, the Harts adopted me. They're good people—they don't deserve the shit I've put them through. I've never felt like I really belonged anywhere.

Summer was the perfect daughter—smart, accomplished, and always doing the right thing. And me? I'm the kid from the wrong side of the tracks, always screwing up. Sparrow was the only person I ever felt I could trust.

Until I met you. You only saw me. And by some stroke of luck, you liked me.

Amelia, you're so easy to love. You're good, kind, and everything I'm not. For a while, my world felt right, or at least I could pretend it was.

But I was so messed up—drugs, alcohol, all of it. I couldn't see straight. I wanted a future with you, but deep down, I knew you were right not to want me. I was as much of a screwup as my bio mom. The only difference was that no one knew what I was doing—or so I thought.

I messed up. I hurt the only people who cared about me. Everything that happened is my fault, and I accept that.

I'm sorry.

Those two words don't feel like enough, but they're all I have right now. I can't promise I'll never mess up again. Honestly, I can guarantee I'll screw something up at some point.

I accept that you're with Viktor. He's a lucky man. I won't lie—I'm jealous. But I know he'll protect your heart.

I plan to do everything I can to earn your trust and friendship back—if you'll let me. I don't expect an answer right away. I know this will take time.

I want to be better—for the tour, yes, but more importantly, for myself.

I've come to realize there are people who care about me in ways I didn't fully see before. That's something else I need to work through.

I can't have phone calls or visitors, except for family, for another two weeks. But when I can, I hope you'll be one of them.

Sincerely,

Matteo

I wipe the tears from my cheeks. I didn't expect this, but I'm glad to hear Matteo's getting the help he needs. He's a good guy. My phone dings with a text.

Sparrow: Did you get a letter from Matteo too?

Me: I did. It sounds like he's doing a lot of soul-searching.

Sparrow: It does.

Sparrow: He knows.

Me: He knows what?

Sparrow: How I feel about him. Once he was three weeks sober, he was allowed to start having contact with his family. His dad asked that he also be allowed to talk to me since we've been like brothers.

Me: That must've been a difficult conversation.

Sparrow: It was. I didn't know if I should tell him or not, but I decided there wouldn't be a better time.

Me: What did he say?

Sparrow: He wasn't as shocked as I thought he'd be. He didn't close the door on it completely.

Me: That's a good thing, right?

Sparrow: We'll see.

"There you are," Viktor says as he comes to sit next to me.

Me: I have to go. We're flying to New York City tomorrow.

Sparrow: Have a great trip.

"Why are you crying?"

I show Viktor the letter from Matteo. He's as surprised as I am. But we both agree it's a good sign.

Matteo has a long road ahead of him, but he seems to be working in the right direction.

Amelia

VIKTOR'S ALARM BLARES IN THE SILENCE OF THE MORNING. Viktor sits up and throws off the covers. I roll over and put my pillow over my head, trying to ignore it.

"Let's go, sleepyhead." Viktor takes my pillow. "We have a plane to catch today."

"Can't I sleep just a little longer?"

"Nope," he says, far too awake for me. "We have enough time to take a shower, eat, and get to the airport."

"Fine." I sit up and swing my legs over the side of the bed. "As long as I can have coffee."

"That can be arranged."

After a hot shower, Viktor and Igor pack the car, and then we're off. We stop to grab a late breakfast and a coffee at the drive-thru. My stomach is twisted in knots, making it hard to enjoy the coffee I was craving.

I'm terrified we're going to have a repeat of whatever went on between them in Russia. Viktor refuses to discuss it with me, but he's wearing the evidence on his body. The stitches are out, and the bruises are starting to fade, but his ribs are still healing.

As much as I want to get there, I want to turn around and go home just the same.

The flight goes by way too quickly, and we find ourselves in a rental car on the way to Alex and Natalie's.

Me: What time are my parents supposed to get here?

Natalie: About two hours.

Me: I'm so nervous I might throw up.

Natalie: Try to relax. There will not be any fighting. I promise.

I wish I was as confident.

"Is everything okay?" Viktor asks. "You don't look so good."

"I'm just a little nauseous from the car ride."

"You don't usually get carsick." Viktor looks concerned.

"It's probably because I didn't really eat. I'm sure I'll be fine once I have some food." I give him a reassuring smile.

Viktor turns into the underground parking. For better or worse, we're here. We have a few hours to get settled before the fireworks begin.

Viktor

AMELIA'S VERY PALE. SHE SAYS SHE'S OKAY, BUT I'M NOT buying her story. I can tell when she's nervous. We're not alone, so I don't push her to talk.

"You two go on up," Igor says. "I'll grab the bags."

"You sure?"

Igor nods and goes to the trunk while Amelia and I make our way to the elevator. I take her tiny hand in mine. It's trembling. When the elevator doors close, I turn her to face me.

"What's wrong? And don't tell me it's that you're nauseous from not eating."

"I'm feeling overwhelmed, and I'm trying to deal with it."

"I'm here." I put my arm around her. "You can lean on me."

"Thank you," she says quietly and tucks herself against me.

The elevator doors open, and Rose comes barreling at us.

"Friker. Auntie Melia," she squeals.

I step out of the elevator and squat down to her level to catch her. She wraps her arms around my neck as I stand up with her.

"My little *printessa*." I kiss her chubby cheek. "I told you I'd come to your house."

"Can we have a tea party?"

"We need to let Friker and Auntie Melia get settled in first, honey," Natalie says as she catches up to her rambunctious toddler. "Did you have a good flight?"

"We did," Amelia answers and gives Natalie a hug.

"Are you okay?"

"Just a bit nervous."

"We're going to have a great visit," Natalie says reassuringly.

"Come on in and make yourselves at home. Are you hungry?"

"Amelia isn't feeling well." I pretend to go along with her story for now. "She says it's because she hasn't eaten." After I say the words, I experience a flashback. When this happened with Natalie, she was pregnant. Could Amelia be pregnant?

"Auntie Melia." Rose reaches her arms out, and I pass her over. "Do you want my *wunch*?"

"Thank you, princess. If I eat your lunch, your belly will be hungry." Amelia tickles Rose's tummy, making her laugh. "How about we go with mommy, and I can get my own lunch?"

"Okay." She gives Amelia a big smile.

That has to be it. Once we're alone, I'll bring it up. A smile spreads across my face at the thought—I'm going to be a father. With that realization, I follow the girls into the kitchen.

We've barely taken our seats when the elevator chimes, announcing someone's arrival.

I glance toward the sound, my curiosity piqued, but the sight that greets me stops me in my tracks. Stepping out of the elevator is Igor, followed closely by Pyotr, Irina, and Maxim.

"You're early," Natalie says as she hurries to greet them.

"Did you know about this?" I ask Amelia quietly.

She nods, a guilty look on her face. Suddenly, everything makes sense. What the hell was I thinking? Amelia takes her birth control religiously. She's not pregnant. She was nervous because she knew Maxim was coming.

Alex enters the room, followed by Timur and Sasha. He freezes when he sees everyone.

"Max and Irina got in early," Natalie says with a tight smile.

"I see that."

"What is *he* doing here?" Maxim asks, disdain dripping from his every word.

"This was my idea," Alex says, stepping between Max and us. "Viktor didn't know anything about it."

"Then, you have much explaining to do, Alexander."

Natalie moves to stand next to Alex. "There's going to be some ground rules to this visit." She puts her hands on her hips. "There will be no yelling or fighting. Rose is here, and she loves each one of you. I don't want her scared or confused seeing everyone she loves arguing."

"Then you should take her out," Max snips.

"This is her house. That isn't going to happen." Alex stands his ground. "What will happen is we're going to sit and discuss this like rational adults." He looks between Maxim and me. "There's been enough hurtful words said and violence unleashed."

"Irina, we are going home." Max turns to walk out.

"No, Maxim. We are not." Irina's voice doesn't waver.

Maxim looks like he's going to explode. It isn't like Irina to ever go against her husband's orders.

She touches his arm. "Maxim, this has gone on long enough. Our daughter loves both you and Viktor. She's stuck in the middle, and it's hurting her."

Max looks at Amelia, who now has tears in her eyes. I take her hand in mine and stroke it gently with my thumb. The room is bathed in uncomfortable silence. The men on both sides stand at the ready for whatever comes next, but no one moves or makes a sound.

"I was just about to take Rose to the park. Would you go for a walk with us, Max?" Natalie asks.

Max doesn't answer. His icy stare is locked on me.

"Rose, ask *Dedushka* if he'll come and push you on the swing."

"*Dedushka,*" Rose says and goes to Max, taking his large hand. "Will you *pway* with me at the swings?"

His body visibly relaxes. "How can I say no to *moya vnuchka*?" Max lifts her into his arms. "But *he* better be gone before we get back."

No one moves while Natalie still bundles Rose up in her pale pink snowsuit, an adorable pink hat, and matching mittens.

"I think we're all ready to go."

We watch as Natalie opens the stroller and Max buckles Rose in. Then, the three of them leave for the park with Timur in tow.

"What the hell are you trying to do?" I ask Alex once they've left. "Maxim already made his point loud and clear. And I'm really not up for a round two."

"That's why I arranged this," Alex says patiently. "Threats and violence are not going to fix this. You and Maxim are better than that." He looks at Irina. "And I believe Amelia deserves this to be solved peacefully."

"I agree with you, Alexander," Irina says. "But I sure hope you know what you're doing." She motions between Amelia and me. "Maxim hasn't been able to reconcile this."

"Are you against us too?" Amelia asks nervously.

"It's taken a little bit to wrap my head around it." She smiles. "But I've known Viktor for many years. I trust him with our lives and your life. You couldn't have chosen a better man to fall in love with."

"Why can't Dad see that, too?"

"Because neither of you was honest with him. He feels betrayed."

"Why does he keep carrying on about the age difference then?"

"Your age difference bothers him, but it's also the easier thing for him to be mad at. He's a proud man and doesn't admit his hurt easily."

"I understand that. We were trying to figure out how and when to tell him." I take Amelia's hand in mind. "I love your daughter. I would never do anything to hurt her."

"I know. And hopefully, we can get Maxim to see that, too."

Natalie

IT'S CHILLY OUTSIDE, BUT THAT'S OKAY. WE TRY TO VISIT the park at least once a week, especially on a mild day. Rose's need to run and play doesn't go away just because it's winter.

Maxim pushes Rose's stroller as we walk down the sidewalk. Anger is rolling off him in waves, so I don't force conversation. I glance behind us to make sure Timur isn't lagging too far behind. The look he gives me doesn't help my confidence right now.

"Did you know your husband planned this little get-together?" Max asks.

"I did."

"And you went along with it?" He looks at me with a raised eyebrow.

"I did, yes."

We walk the last block in silence. But when the park comes into view, Rose gets very excited.

"*Dedushka* swings. *Pozhaluysta?*" she asks.

"Her Russian is coming along very well."

"She has such an easy time switching back and forth." I smile proudly. "Timur, Katia, and the kids have been a huge help. They usually only speak Russian to her. She catches on so naturally."

"It is easier when they are young." Max unbuckles Rose and sets her on the ground, and she runs to her favorite swing. When Max and I catch up, he puts her in the swing and fastens the safety harness. Then, he pushes her gently. "I suppose you are planning to lecture me about Viktor and Amelia."

"I wasn't planning on a lecture. But I was hoping we could talk about it."

"There is nothing to talk about, Natalia." He pushes Rose a little higher, making her giggle. "He will return to Russia once Amelia's new security team is in place."

"I agree that she needs a new security team."

"I knew you were more sensible than that husband of yours."

"You didn't let me finish," I say, earning a disapproving look from Max. "Viktor will always protect her with his life. That'll never change. With them together, though, Viktor may be distracted. It's safer, more sensible, to have someone who is only there for her security needs."

"I think you have misunderstood. Viktor will be leaving."

"Can I *pway* in the sand, mommy?"

"Of course." Max takes Rose out of the swing, and she runs over to the sandbox. I grab the sand toys I keep in her stroller and put them next to her. "Tell Mommy if you get too cold, okay?"

Rose nods and goes right to work shoveling sand into her bucket. Max and I sit on a nearby bench.

"May I speak freely?"

"Of course, Natalia."

"Do you remember how my parents hated Alex?"

"That is something hard to forget."

"They tried everything to keep us apart. And Max, that hurt. It almost completely ruined our relationship." Even though they get along now, those memories still hurt. "Alex and I were forced to sneak around and lie to the people we cared about most."

"That was a different situation. Your parents are very small-minded."

I don't respond. I simply stare at him. His words aren't untrue, but right now, Max fits into that definition, too. It takes several minutes before I see the recognition in his eyes.

"You think I am being small-minded?"

"I do. It may not be for the same reasons as my parents, but you're doing the same thing to Amelia that my parents did to me. You're forbidding her to be with the man her heart chose to love. If you don't fix this now, you'll alienate your daughter."

"But his age, Natalia. Now, he is thirty-three to her eighteen."

"She's almost nineteen, but I understand your concern. However, you need to remember Amelia has not lived a typical life. She was forced to grow up far earlier than she should've. She's experienced horrific things and has come out the other side a strong and confident young woman."

"They did not come to me." Max looks at me, tears in his eyes. "I am her father. He should have come to me first."

Now, I realize what the heart of the matter is. It's less about anger and more about hurt—something there's too much of right now.

"I can't imagine the shock of walking in and seeing them together."

"She was in his arms. They were—." Max stops, the sadness replaced by a mask of anger once again. "I cannot talk about it."

"They never intended to hurt you."

"Viktor betrayed my trust. And still, he has not apologized or taken responsibility."

"Have you given him the chance?" Max goes to speak, but I hold up my hand to stop him. "He went to Russia intending to make things right. But from what I understand, he wasn't given a chance to speak. You beat him like he was one of the criminals you go after." I put my hand over his. "That's not the Maxim I know."

He nods but says nothing.

"I spent nearly a year with Viktor. He showed me nothing but love and tenderness even though I was unable to give him anything in return."

"He lives a dangerous life, Natalia."

"Did you worry about Rose and me being with him?"

"Of course not. He loved you and would never let anything—" Max stops mid-sentence.

"Viktor loves your daughter." I look over at Rose. "When Alex came back, it nearly destroyed Viktor. In a matter of a few hours, he went from having a family to being alone. The day he said his goodbye to Rose nearly broke me." A tear slips down my face. "At the time, if I could've chosen both Alex and Viktor, I would have."

"You can. Polyamory is real," Max offers with a smile.

"It is, but it's not for me. Alex is my soulmate. And as much as I cared about Viktor—loved Viktor, my heart always belonged to Alex. Viktor knew when I looked at him and kissed him, it was always Alex I imagined in his place." That's still difficult to admit aloud.

"Viktor was willing to accept being my second choice. I'll forever be grateful for every day we spent together. But he deserves to be number one in someone's life. When Amelia looks at him, she's not wishing he was someone else. Viktor is her heart."

"Mama. I'm cold," Rose calls as she climbs out of the sandbox. I wipe the sand off her snowsuit while Max gathers her toys.

"Let's get you in your stroller. When we get home, I'll make you some hot chocolate, okay?"

"Yummy." Rose claps her mittened hands.

"Why did they not come to me sooner?"

"You can be a bit intimidating." I smile. "They weren't purposely hiding it from you. It was all new. They were trying to make sense of their feelings for each other before they could tell anyone else."

"They told you?"

"Not at first."

While we walk, I explain to Max how Amelia was talking to me about someone she met who she was interested in but who wasn't interested in her. And how I assumed it was a boy at school.

"The night she called me and told me she was in love with Viktor, I almost fell over." I laugh, remembering the conversation. "But once the shock wore off, I knew her heart was safe. Not only that, but Viktor would finally get the love he deserves."

"Natalia, I am afraid. I do not want my daughter to be hurt if he decides she is not what he wants. Or worse. If he is killed doing a job I send him on."

"I understand. No parent wants to see their child's heart hurt. But something tells me she is his forever." I slip my arm through his as we're walking. "And if the unthinkable ever happens, we'll all be there to help her through. But this division and fighting are what's hurting her now. She only wants your love and support. They both need that from you."

Maxim's silent again for a few minutes. "Your words make sense," he says, finally.

"Does that mean you'll give them your blessing?"

Max stops walking. "They both owe a debt of gratitude to you, Natalia." He kisses my forehead. "I will give them my blessing as long as Viktor continues to respect my daughter."

I let out a big breath. Part of me was terrified I wouldn't be able to get through to him, and we'd have a repeat of what happened between them in Russia.

I'm glad we're back at our building because the air is turning chillier by the minute.

"Thank you, *Dedushka*." I stand on my tiptoes to kiss his cheek.

The elevator opens, and we step in.

"But you are not to tell them I have conceded." Max gives me a wicked grin, and we share a laugh.

"As long as no punches are thrown."

"There will be no violence, but I would like to see them squirm just a while longer." Max looks around the front of the stroller. "It appears our conversation has bored *moya vnuchka* right to sleep."

"I might keep you around. It's getting more and more difficult to get her to nap."

"I remember those days. They were very tiring."

Alex is waiting in the foyer when the elevator arrives. Timur must've told him we were on our way.

"Rose is asleep? It's a miracle." He chuckles and looks between Maxim and me, but I give no hint of how things went. "I'll take her and put her in her crib," he says hesitantly.

Max and I join everyone in the living room. Amelia looks at me, and I shrug. I feel bad not letting them know everything's okay, but it's important that Max is able to do this on his own.

Maxim

I did not intend to give in, but Natalia's words made too much sense. I remember well the devastation she experienced when her family would not accept her and Alexander. Yet, I have done the same thing to my daughter.

I never intended to hurt her. I hoped if I said no, Amelia would back down and find someone else. But she has not. Natalia is correct. This between Amelia and Viktor is not just a fleeting thing.

The age difference is concerning. But I must remember Amelia has not had a normal upbringing. Her childhood was stolen from her, and she was forced to grow up at a very young age. At eighteen, she is more mature than most young ladies.

Her history also explains why she is attracted to someone like Viktor. He is a good man—a kind man. He has fought against evil for his entire adult life. It only makes sense that Amelia is drawn to him. Her heart knows it is safe with Viktor.

I have turned a blind eye to what was happening. Refused to hear the truth in their words.

The room has been silent since we walked in. I sit next to my wife. "Do not stop talking on my account. Please continue." Everyone's eyes are wide. They are not sure what to make of me right now. Alex returns to the room and sits next to Natalie. My men all stand at the ready. They are waiting to intervene at any given second.

"I apologize for bringing you both here under false pretense," Alex says.

I hold my hand up. "Please, let me speak first."

Alex sits back, allowing me to address the room.

"Amelia, I know things have been strained between us the past few weeks. I take full responsibility for that." I look at Viktor. "I apologize for my behavior when you were at my home. Reacting out of anger and using violence was unacceptable."

"I accept your apology." Viktor visibly relaxes.

"Amelia, I must apologize to you as well. I will never forget your fear of me when you first came to us. I worked hard to prove to you that what I do for a job would never cross into our home and family. In a matter of a few minutes, I destroyed that trust."

Tears pool in her eyes. I get up and go over to her. I lower myself to her level and take her hands in mine. "I am so very sorry for breaking my word to you. Because of what I did, you see me as a monster. If I could go back in time, I would. I never again wanted to see that fear in your eyes when you looked at me. But I deserve it."

I lower my head and try to get my emotions under control. It is no use. Tears are already falling. "How do I fix this? How do I get my daughter back?"

"I forgive you," she says, her voice cracking with emotion. "You did scare me, and I have lost some of the trust I gave you. But it's not gone for good. Every day is a new chance to wipe the slate clean and move forward." She squeezes my hands. "I love you, Dad. Even when I was angry and thought I hated you, I still loved you."

"I do not deserve your forgiveness." Those are not just words meant to sugarcoat this situation. They are my true feelings. I have acted like the monster she once believed I was. I have shown her that I can be just as scary as the men who took her, yet she still loves me.

"Don't say that. You made a mistake. I hope this is a turning point and you're ready to accept Viktor and me as a couple?"

"It is still not easy for me to see you with Viktor. And it is not because I do not trust Viktor. On the contrary, I trust him with your life." Expressing my emotions is not easy, but it is the only way right now. "I am hurt that you hid this from me."

"And I apologize for that. We were planning on talking to you. We had to figure it out for ourselves before explaining it to you."

"I understand that now." I pause. "The age difference and Viktor's job are also a concern. Being in his life will put you in danger."

"Before I agreed to the adoption, you told me about your life. You wanted to make sure I fully understood what I was agreeing to. You are the one who told me I'm in danger by being Amelia Solonik. Yet, I still chose to be your daughter. I just had to get used to a different life. One in which I trust you to keep me safe." She pauses and wipes the tears from her face. "I've accepted the potential consequences of being your daughter, and I accept the same being with Viktor. I trust both of you to keep me physically safe. I trust Viktor to keep my heart safe."

I look at Viktor and speak directly to him. "Today, I have realized my actions are hurting Amelia. I have been a hypocrite, accusing you of hurting her when I was the one doing the damage. I am ashamed of my behavior."

"I understand your concerns, boss. Like Amelia said, we were planning on talking to you about the change in our relationship. We weren't expecting you to show up at the house. I'm sorry that's how you found out. That was never our intention."

"I know that now."

"Maxim, I love your daughter. She's entrusted her heart to me, and I treasure that. I will do everything in my power to keep her safe."

Looking at them together right now, I see the love between them. "You have my blessing to be together."

Amelia lunges off the sofa, nearly knocking me over, and wraps her arms around me. "Thank you, Dad. You have no idea how much this means to me."

I hold my daughter. This young woman who was chosen for us and who chose us. "You are precious to me, Amelia. I wish you only love and happiness."

Amelia

I pull back so I can see his face. "You and mom have given me the world. You've reminded me what it means to be loved unconditionally. I will always love my birth parents, but I'm so grateful that fate brought me to you when I needed you the most. And you chose me to be your daughter." She softens her voice. "And I'm thankful you're finally accepting Viktor and me."

I go to my mom and hug her. "I love you very much."

"And I you, *moya malen'kaya ptichka*," Mom says and kisses my cheeks. "It's sometimes difficult as a parent to accept that our child is no longer a child. No longer dependent on us for everything. That she's transitioned into a beautiful and capable young woman. It can make a parent scared to be no longer needed."

"Growing up and falling in love doesn't mean you lose me. I'll always need you and Dad." I look at Viktor. "The only thing that's changed is now I have one more person who loves me."

"It has been difficult being your parent," Dad says. "Not because you are difficult, quite the opposite. You have been easygoing and never challenged us." He takes his seat next to mom.

"I have always felt that we missed out on so much of your life. That somehow, we needed to make up for that time—for all the wrong that was done against you. I have been so focused on correcting the past that I failed to see you growing up and moving forward. I want to hold on so tightly, but moya malen'kaya ptichka, it is your time to spread your wings and fly."

Dad's eyes are a mix of sadness and pride. Knowing that sharing his feelings is not comfortable for him makes this all the more special. I knew he loved me, but until right now, I didn't understand the depth of his love.

"Thank you, Dad. I will make you proud of me." I walk back to Viktor and take my seat next to him.

"Amelia, I am already proud of you."

I can't speak because I'm crying once again. Viktor holds me close.

The silence is broken by Alex's laughter. All heads turn his way. "I know this was my idea, but I was scared to death it would backfire and we'd have a disaster on our hands." His comment makes everyone laugh.

Rose's soft talking comes through the baby monitor. "She's up just in time," Natalie says.

"May I get her?" Viktor asks.

Viktor adores Rose. He's been head over heels for that little girl from the day she was born. He still talks about the first year of her life, when he was her father. His eyes hold a mix of pride, joy, and pain.

"Of course."

"What's this I hear about you not returning to school?" Alex asks when Viktor leaves the room.

"Wow. Good news travels fast." I chuckle. "Our group was offered a contract to go on tour with Zapped Euforia. The tour will start before the semester is over."

"Can't you arrange something with your professors to at least finish out your first year?"

"If it was just for the tour dates, I'm sure I could do that. But we're going to have rehearsals, press events, and so much other stuff. I wouldn't be able to give my full attention to either one," I explain. "So, I chose the band."

I glance at Dad, whose body is stiff with tension once again.

"I know it isn't the choice most of you would've preferred I made," I say and look at my father. "There have been too many things in my life that I didn't have a say in. This decision is mine, and it's one I feel good about. I hope you'll all support me."

"Of course we will," Natalie says. "I'm starving. Let's order some dinner, and you can tell us all about it."

Viktor

I'M HIT WITH AN ONSLAUGHT OF MEMORIES AS I WALK THE familiar hallway to Rose's nursery. I used to look forward to being the one to get her when she woke from a nap. We'd sit in the rocker and cuddle while I whispered all my dreams and hopes for her future.

When I open her door, Rose sits in her crib, talking to her teddy bear.

"Did you have a good nap, *printessa*?"

"Friker," she exclaims, dropping the teddy bear in exchange for standing up and reaching her arms out to me.

Ignoring the pain in my chest, I lift her from the crib, and just like when she was little, Rose rests her head on my shoulder. Instinct takes over, and I sit in the rocking chair. She stays cuddled against me while I rub her back gently.

"Friker misses you very much."

"Me too. Are you staying with me again?"

"No. Auntie Melia and I are just visiting."

"Oh." She sticks her bottom lip out in a pout.

"Don't be sad, *printessa*. We can still talk on the video, and you can come to visit us again."

"I *wike* you here." She rubs my bald head with her little hand. "Mama shows me TV of Friker and baby Rose."

"You're still baby Rose, silly girl."

"No. I big girl Rose."

"Oh, I see." I chuckle. "My baby Rose is all gone." I pretend to pout.

"Friker is silly." Rose giggles.

Movement catches my eye. Amelia's standing in the doorway watching.

"You can come in."

"I didn't want to interrupt."

"Auntie Melia." Rose wiggles from my lap, and I set her down. She runs over to Amelia. "Can we *pway* tea party?"

"I think we need to have dinner first."

Rose rubs her tummy. "I hungry."

"Me too." Amelia grins. "Let's go potty, and then we'll go eat."

Rose takes Amelia's hand. The sight of them together fuels a yearning deep inside. I never thought about having children until Rose. When everything fell apart, I thought that dream was gone forever. Seeing Amelia and Rose gives me renewed hope. I can see Amelia and me with our own little girl one day.

I'm still sitting in the rocking chair long after Amelia and Rose leave the room.

"Viktor." Maxim's deep voice startles me.

"Yeah, boss?" I jump to my feet and groan from the sudden movement.

"I wanted to speak to you alone." He closes the door behind him.

"Okay." Worry builds once again. I know what he said earlier, but I'm still apprehensive. Is this when he asks me to leave quietly?

"I do not feel my public apology was sufficient."

"It was more than sufficient. We're good now."

"No. I am not good. When my nephew brought you to me many years ago, you were not healed from the loss of your parents. I took you in not only as an employee but as family. I grew to love you like a son." Maxim pauses. "I have practiced self-control in all aspects of my life until the day I hurt you. I am ashamed of my behavior as a boss, a Dominant, and a man."

"Max—"

"Please, let me finish. I neglected to see Amelia as an adult. I still viewed her as the frightened young girl who came to live with us." I see the pain in Max's eyes as he recalls those days. "Those first weeks were some of the hardest in my life. Not since my Jelena was taken have I felt utterly useless. Nearly every night, she would partially wake terrified from a nightmare. Tears covered her face as she screamed and fought an invisible enemy—relived the hell she had been forced to live. Amelia was inconsolable.

Some say I do not have a heart, but I know they are wrong. Because each night, my heart was ripped from my chest watching the pure terror Amelia experienced. Those memories will never fade. They not only overshadowed her healing but also blinded me to her growing self-confidence and maturity. To the fact that she is no longer a little girl. She is a woman who is free to make her own choices—to fall in love."

"I know how much you love her and how much she loves you." I'm forced to sit from the pain in my ribs. "You need to know that we weren't trying to deceive you."

He holds up his hand, stopping me.

"Amelia does not trust easily. It makes perfect sense that her heart found yours. You have much love to give, and you deserve to be loved in return." Max takes a deep breath. "Your age difference also clouded my thoughts. I was unable to see past a number. I failed to recognize two hearts that were made for each other."

"Boss, I tried to fight it. To push her away. Love was the last thing I was looking for."

"But love found you. My little girl's heart is safe with you. I know you will treat her with the love and respect she deserves. And I am certain she will return that love to you."

"I never thought I'd get over losing Natalie. When we were together, I knew that even though Alex was gone, he was still very much there. He was all she saw—all she wanted. I was content to be the runner-up. After Alex came back, and I know this makes me a horrible person, I wished he didn't. I wanted to keep Natalie and Rose."

"Viktor, that only makes you human."

I stand back up. My breath catches from the pain, and I wrap my arm around my ribs. "But when Natalie told me she was pregnant again, something inside me changed. I realized it was time to stop pretending and dreaming of the what-ifs. To stop torturing myself. I had to let her go."

"You will always have a special bond with her," Max interrupts. "Love never fully goes away."

"You're right. I will. Natalie and I have discussed it. And more importantly, Amelia and I discussed it. Grigor was instrumental in teaching me how to honor those feelings and then how to put them away so I could move forward." I smile and shake my head. "Never did I imagine Amelia would be part of my moving forward. She took me by complete surprise."

"She is quite the force sometimes." Maxim chuckles.

"That she is. Boss, I'm sorry for not coming to you right away. God." I run my hand over my head. "My world was turned upside down."

I explain about the night Mateo came to the house drunk and how Amelia had a panic attack.

"Then, she kissed me. I pushed her away. Told her there was no way there could ever be anything between us."

"Stop. The boy came to the house drunk, looking for Amelia? I thought you checked him out."

"I did. Like I said, on paper, everything was good. Mateo's not a bad kid. He had a rough past and lost his way. Right after Thanksgiving, he attempted suicide."

"Does Amelia know this?"

"She does. She got a letter from him the other day. He's three weeks sober and making amends with the people he hurt. The letter meant a lot to her. Although she's not been allowed to speak to him, she's relieved knowing he's beginning to find his way." I return to the story, picking up when she kissed me. "The more we tried to stay apart, the more we were drawn together. I didn't know what to think except that you'd kill me." I laugh and then grab my ribs and groan from the pain.

"Nothing has ever felt so right. Something that scared us both because we didn't know how to tell you and Irina. But I guess fate did that for us."

"Yes, it certainly did." Max leans against Rose's changing table. "Amelia is still young. She may change her mind about this in a few months. Are you willing to go through another loss?"

"If it means having the chance to love her and the possibility of having a forever with her. Yes."

"I only ask one thing."

"Okay?"

"Do not rush her to marry and have children. Allow her time to grow up and to experience more of life before she becomes a wife and mother."

"I won't push her into anything she's not ready for. You have my word."

I reach my hand out to shake Maxim's, but he pulls me in for a hug instead. He pats me on the back and then realizes his mistake. "I am sorry. I did not think."

"It's all good. I'm happy we've fixed this between us."

"As am I, son."

Amelia

Our time in New York City went by too quickly. We would've loved to stay longer, but I was due back in California to start our rehearsal schedule.

We've already had several interviews and have had to field too many prying questions on Mateo's whereabouts. I wish people would drop it. He's struggling enough. He doesn't deserve to have his name dragged through the mud. I didn't know, but Mateo also has Type 1 Diabetes. So the group's official statement is Mateo suffered a medical emergency due to a pre-existing condition and is in the hospital for stabilizing treatment. Our hope is that if we don't make a big deal about it, the extreme curiosity will fade.

Today's rehearsal is at an actual recording studio. We're recording our first demo song that will be going out to local radio stations. There's a guy here who's using recordings from previous concerts to mix Mateo's voice into the songs.

"Sorry I'm late," Sparrow says as he bursts into the room out of breath. "I was a little tied up with something."

Sparrow's been attending video therapy sessions with Mateo. His therapist knew the significant role Sparrow played in Mateo's life and asked him to be involved in some of their sessions. Sparrow's revelation about his feelings for Mateo has only strengthened the decision to have him involved. The guys are trying to explore what, if anything, it means to Mateo. Other than me, no one else in the group knows about it.

"Something of the female variety?" Tristan jokes.

"Yeah, something like that." Sparrow comes over and gives me a quick hug. Although we've seen each other a few times, we haven't really had the chance to talk since I got back from New York. He doesn't know everything that happened. "How are you holding up?"

"Much better. We'll talk later."

"Sounds good." He turns to the guys. "Let's get to work."

It took about a million tries to get a clean copy of our single "Dangerous Vibes." Nerves played a significant role in all our screw-ups.

"Do you two mind if we record your duet?" Nick, our new agent, asks.

"I'm fine with it if you are," Sparrow says.

I look to Viktor for his approval. "It's up to you."

"Sure. Let's do it."

After we signed the contract for the tour, we started working on doing more of our own music instead of cover songs. The "Just Give Me a Reason" duet has been replaced with "Written in the Stars." It's a beautiful ballad Sparrow wrote about star-crossed lovers who stumble through the night, missing one another—missing a piece of their heart. Until their worlds finally collide.

While we sing, Viktor stands outside the window of the sound booth. His gaze never wavers from mine while I sing the magical lyrics, my soul being laid bare at his feet. I don't know how Sparrow did it, but somehow, he reached into both our hearts and pulled out the most intimate and private of emotions. It's a powerful song that I'm sure will become a fan favorite.

"Great job today, everyone," Nick praises us. "We'll work on the edits and mixes. I'll give you a call when they're done."

Tristan and Quincy hang by Nick and pepper him with questions. They're both very interested in the inner workings of how everything comes together.

"How's everything going with Mateo?" I ask Sparrow quietly.

"He's a little over thirty days sober."

"That's awesome. Can you tell Mateo how proud I am?"

"I will."

"Is everything else between you two okay?"

"It's complicated." Sparrow holds the door to the studio open, allowing me to go through first.

Viktor follows behind us. "I'll get the car. Take your time here."

Sparrow and I sit on the bench in the hallway.

"Mateo knows how I feel about him and that I've felt that way for a long time. He's not totally turned off by it."

"That's a good thing, right?"

"Kinda." Sparrow rests his head back on the wall. "Mateo's attracted to girls but said that a part of him is also interested in me as more than a friend. But he's not ready to act on anything."

"Keep being there for him. That's all you can do."

"Enough about me," Sparrow says, changing the subject. "How was your trip to New York?"

"Viktor and my father were surprised, to say the least. When Dad walked in and they saw each other, I was terrified. But somehow, Natalie was able to get through to Dad. He ended up apologizing and giving us his blessing." I smile, still shocked at the way everything worked out.

"I'm so happy for you." Sparrow puts his arm around me, and I rest my head on his shoulder.

"You'll get your happy ending too. I'm sure of it."

"We'll see."

"Look at these two lovebirds," Tristan jokes as he and Quincy come down the hall. "Where's Viktor? Does he know you two are so cozy together?"

"Viktor doesn't mind sharing me with Sparrow." I give him a quick peck on the cheek and stand.

"Will he share you with us too?" Tristan waggles his eyebrows.

"No chance. Let's go, Sparrow." I grab his hand. "Viktor might be okay with sharing, but I'm not." Sparrow and I share a laugh as we walk toward the doors.

Just as he promised, Viktor has the Audi pulled out front. He's leaning against the car, wearing dark sunglasses, his arms crossed over his chest. My heart rate picks up, and my stomach flip-flops when I see him.

"We didn't know you loaned Amelia out." Quincy's laughing so hard he barely gets the words out.

Viktor lifts his sunglasses. His blue eyes zone in on Quincy. "What the hell are you talking about?"

I rush over and put my hands on his chest. "I let them know you share me with Sparrow." I smile sweetly.

His body relaxes under my touch. "Oh, that. Yeah. Sparrow and I have a private arrangement." The corner of his mouth turns up slightly. "You need a ride, Sparrow?"

"I have the car today. I'm good." He hugs me and plants a kiss on my cheek. "I'll call you later."

Quincy and Tristan elbow each other, laughing. I roll my eyes at them.

"I'll see you two next week."

"See ya, Mel," Quincy says.

"You know I was just kidding, right? I hope I didn't offend you," Tristan says in a rare moment of seriousness.

"It's all good with me. It's him you have to worry about." I point at Viktor and walk to my side of the car, leaving Tristan face-to-face with Viktor.

"Yeah, well. I'm heading out. See ya around, Vik."

Viktor gets in the car and turns to face me. "Sharing you is completely out of the question. You are mine, Amelia."

Viktor

THIS GIRL BETTER NOT BE GETTING ANY IDEAS THAT I'M willing to share her. I want to kill anyone who dares to look at her. The thought of them touching her makes me want to do it with my bare hands.

"Relax," she giggles. "They saw me sitting with my head on Sparrow's shoulder and were giving him a hard time."

"You're lucky."

"You're the lucky one. You get me all to yourself."

"You're damn right I do." I put my hand on her leg and slide it up to the top of her thigh, teasing her.

"I like it when you go all caveman on me."

"You do?" I glance at her with a raised eyebrow.

"I think it's pretty hot."

"It doesn't scare you?" I've been hesitant to let Amelia see how possessive I feel. Knowing her history, I didn't want to trigger her or make her feel like she was nothing more than a possession to me.

"I know who you are," she explains. "You're not *them*. Your possessiveness isn't about manipulation or coercion."

"What the hell?" My attention is drawn away from our conversation when I turn onto our street and see two unfamiliar cars in our driveway.

"Who is it?"

"I don't know." I pull the car over a few houses away and come up with a quick plan. "You're going to get in the driver's seat and keep the doors locked. I want your phone out. If I don't give you the all-clear in five minutes, you're going to drive to the police station and call your dad."

"I don't have my license yet." Amelia's been behind the wheel a few times, but she isn't comfortable driving and hasn't wanted to take her driver's license test.

"I don't care. We'll deal with the consequences later. My only concern is your safety."

Damn it. Right now, I wish Max hadn't taken Igor back to St. Petersburg. I haven't forgotten the lesson about not doing things on my own, yet here we are. I'm about to not only walk into an unknown situation without backup, but I'm also leaving Amelia alone with the hope she stays safe.

I force myself to get out of the car and wait for Amelia to come to the driver's side.

"Why can't I come with you?"

"I will not put you at risk." I grab her by the back of the neck and pull her in for a kiss. "Get in the car and lock the doors. If anyone approaches the car, you will not hesitate. You will drive away. Okay?"

"Viktor—"

"I won't be focused if I have to worry about you. Promise me you'll drive away."

"I promise."

I watch her get into the car and lock the doors. She follows my instructions and shows me her phone. I reward her with a smile before turning and walking toward the house. Am I doing the right thing? Should I have stayed with her? Should I have made her drive away? I have to stop second-guessing my decisions and focus my attention on whoever is in our house.

Once I get to the sidewalk leading up to our front door, I take the gun from the waistband of my pants. I'm not sure what I'll find when I get to the house, but I know I'll be ready.

Quietly, I walk up the steps. The door's open, and people are inside talking. It's clear there's more than one person, but I'm not sure how many. Standing out of sight, I shoot a quick text to Dimitri.

Me: I need you to access the cameras in the house. Someone's in there.

Dimitri: On it.

Seconds that feel like hours tick by before I get his response.

Dimitri: Have you checked your email lately?

Me: What the hell does that have to do with anything?

Dimitri: Boss sent you an email last week letting you know that Amelia's new security team would be arriving today.

I open the email program, and sure enough, there's an email sitting there. He should've known I don't regularly check my inbox. That's why he usually texts.

Me: I see it now.

Dimitri: Should be a team of three. One female. Two males.

Me: Thanks.

Sliding the gun back into my waistband, I make my way back down the sidewalk to the car. Amelia unlocks the doors, and I get in the passenger seat.

"What's going on?"

"It's the new security team. Pull the car up to the house."

"Dad didn't tell you they were coming?" Amelia asks as she parks behind the cars in our driveway.

"He emailed," I reply and hold up my phone.

She laughs. "Like you ever check your email."

"I guess I'm going to have to start."

I hold the door for Amelia, allowing her to walk in first. The three people sitting at our table jump up when they hear us come in.

"Viktor?" The female asks.

"Yes." I know Maxim approved these people, but my guard's still up.

"I'm Indigo. These are my partners, Chase and Bode." She looks next to me. "And you must be Amelia. It's a pleasure to meet you." Indigo offers her hand to Amelia.

"How did you get into our house?"

"Your father had us programmed into the ID system."

"It was nice of him to tell us," Amelia mumbles.

We've already gotten off to a rather uncomfortable start, and I'm about to make it worse. "Have a seat. We're going to go over the boundaries and how this will all work."

"With all due respect, sir. Mr. Solonik has already briefed us on our assignment."

"It's me you'll be reporting to day-to-day, correct?"

"Yes, sir."

"Good." I pull out Amelia's chair and look pointedly at the new team. "Now, take a seat."

"We were told Ms. Solonik will be going on tour?" Chase asks.

"That's correct. The tour kicks off in May, but we'll be moving to Los Angeles in late April."

"How long is the tour?" Bode asks.

"The last show is in August," Amelia answers.

"You must be excited." Indigo smiles.

"Excited and nervous."

"I can't wait to hear you."

"While we're at home, we do not want our privacy interrupted." Viktor directs the conversation back to the guidelines. "The house has a security system, and I'm here. Your presence is not required."

Bode sits up straighter. "That isn't what Mr. Solinik—"

"As I previously said, Mr. Solonik is not here. I am."

"Yes, sir."

"Where will they sleep?" Amelia asks quietly.

That's a detail I haven't figured out. This house is luxurious, but it's not set up to have extra people living with us. Having Igor here was different. Amelia and I both knew him and were comfortable having him around. He also had Yury, so they were off on their own for much of the time. I need to come up with a solution quick.

Amelia

VIKTOR DOESN'T WASTE TIME LETTING THESE NEW PEOPLE know who the boss is. Indigo isn't intimidated by him. I think I'm going to like her. In contrast, the two men sit with wide-eyed stares while Viktor barks orders at them. Their fear works for me. Dad screened them, so I know they're okay, but they're also men. I don't know them, and I don't trust them—trust must be earned.

I'm a bit shocked at how quickly Viktor went from the tender man I know to this intimidating man who's all business. I know he's experienced and good at his job, but I've never witnessed this side of him. If I didn't know him, I'd be scared too. Instead, I'm able to sit back and relax, knowing Viktor's got it under control. He details the distance they must remain from me, especially the men. And places they're forbidden to follow me.

While he's giving his instructions, I realize the one thing that hasn't been discussed is our sleeping arrangements. The three bedrooms are all next to each other, and I'm not comfortable knowing there will be other men that close.

"Where will they sleep?" I ask quietly.

For a brief second, Viktor looks at me like a deer caught in the headlights, but he quickly regains his composure.

"Indigo, you will have the first bedroom on the right. It's Amelia's old room. Chase and Bode, you'll sleep downstairs. Tomorrow we'll rearrange the game room. There's already a pull-out sofa in place. We can bring the furniture from the guest room down. That should work." Viktor turns his attention to me. "Are you comfortable with those arrangements?"

"I am. Thank you."

"The overnight shift will be on a rotation. I believe Mr. Solonik provided you with that schedule." The newcomers nod. "I see no reason to alter that. Where it's not necessary while we're here, it's something we will put into practice, so we all have a chance to get used to it and work out any kinks."

I think we've done enough business talk for tonight. My stomach agrees, which is evident by how loud it growls. "Is anyone hungry?" I ask.

"Do you want to order out?"

"I'd like to cook. Is that okay?" I'm not the world's best chef, but I'm trying.

"If you'd like to." Viktor smiles appreciatively.

I look to our new housemates. "Do you have any allergies or anything you really don't like?"

"Nope. Not picky at all," Chase says, and the others agree.

"Okay then." I head into our walk-in pantry with the intention of finding something manageable for me to cook.

Instead, my over-reactive nervous system decides to make an appearance. Thoughts rapidly fire in my head. They said they weren't picky, but were they only trying to be polite? What if they hate everything I make?

The familiar waves of panic start to seep into my consciousness. I reach out and touch some of the boxes and cans on the shelf. My eyes want to close, but I resist recognizing I need to stay in the moment—stay grounded. I refuse to let fear win. After taking a few controlled breaths, my heart rate slowly returns to normal. I'm proud of myself. I've managed to avoid a full-blown panic attack. Even just a few months ago, that was something I wouldn't have been able to accomplish on my own.

"Did you get lost in here?" Viktor asks from the doorway.

"I needed a minute."

"Are you okay?" He steps closer.

"I am now. But I don't know what to make."

Viktor scans the shelves. "We have breaded chicken in the fridge." He grabs a box of pasta. "How about that chicken parmesan and pasta you made a few weeks ago?"

Sparrow's dad's a chef and has been teaching Sparrow how to cook since he was little. Now Sparrow's passing those lessons on to me. He was over a few weeks ago, and we made this meal together.

"I'm pretty sure I can do that."

Viktor grabs a few boxes of cut pasta, and I grab some cans of sauce.

"Can I help?" he asks.

"No, thank you." I want to prove I can do this on my own. That I can do something to care for Viktor. "Why don't you go entertain our new guests." I look over at the table where the new arrivals sit.

"I'll bring them out on the balcony." He leans down and gives me a quick kiss. "If you need help, just give a yell."

Viktor escorts our guests, or whatever I'm supposed to call them, outside. Then, I busy myself in the kitchen. I have to text Sparrow a few times, but overall, I think I did okay. While the food's in the oven, Sparrow and I chat back and forth.

Sparrow: Did Nick text you the pics of the tour buses?

Me: I saw a text from him, but I haven't had a chance to look at it yet. We had some unexpected visitors.

Sparrow: Is everything okay?

Me: Yeah. It's my new security team. It's weird having three new people around.

Sparrow: Having people follow you everywhere must get annoying.

Me: Most of the time, it's okay. It's harder when it's new people. How's Mateo?

I'd rather not dissect the intricacies of being Maxim Solonik's daughter. Sparrow never pries, but I know he's curious about exactly what my Dad does back in Russia. And why it requires me to have so much personal security. It's not something I really like talking about, though.

Sparrow: Next week, he'll be sober for sixty days. He's getting discharged, then.

Me: That's awesome. I'm sure you're super excited.

Sparrow: Part of me is. The other part is terrified. We haven't seen each other since I told him, and he's still unsure how he feels. I'm afraid it's going to be awkward and that I screwed up our friendship.

Me: I'm sure that's not true.

The fire alarm blares over my head, and I nearly fall off my chair. I spin around and see the smoke pouring from the oven. How did I not notice it sooner?

Viktor's already at my side, pulling the oven door open. I grab the hot pads, pull the tray out, and set it on the stovetop. Once the smoke clears, I see the blackened chicken.

"I ruined it." I toss the hot pads onto the counter.

While Indigo's on the phone with the security company, giving them the passcode and letting them know it was a false alarm, one of the other guys manually turns the alarm off. I flop on the kitchen chair, embarrassed.

"Are you okay?" Viktor gets down to my level. "Are you hurt?"

"Only my pride." I can't believe I screwed up dinner. "I was texting Sparrow. I must've forgotten to set the timer."

"It's okay. We can order something."

"I know, but that's not the point." I wave my hand at the still-smoking tray. "I wanted to prove that I can cook and care for you."

"*Moya zirka*, there's no doubt in my mind that you can care for me. Whether or not you can cook doesn't matter."

"It does to me." I look into his sparkling blue eyes. "What kind of woman can't cook dinner for her man?"

"We will cook together. I don't ever expect you to do everything. Cooking, cleaning, and raising our children. They're responsibilities we'll share."

Raising our children? Viktor's never mentioned children before. The thought scares me. I don't have time to focus on it because Viktor's taking my hand and pulling me to my feet.

"Come on. Let's take our new guests out for a meal."

Amelia

WHEN I WAKE UP, I SPOT AN ENVELOPE ON VIKTOR'S PILLOW. I open it and pull out the notecard.

Moya zirka,

Happy Valentine's Day. I had to go out and do something. Indigo's in charge while I'm gone. Take some time to pamper yourself. You'll find a red dress and heels in the closet. Be dressed and ready for six. I'll be there to pick you up.

I bring the note to my chest. What's he planning? Reaching over to the nightstand, I grab my phone.

Me: Do I get any hints?

Viktor: Good morning to you, too.

Me: It's actually good afternoon. But you didn't answer my question. Do I get a hint?

Viktor: We're not leaving the state.

Amelia: Haha. You're so funny.

Viktor: Go eat and have a relaxing afternoon. I'll see you later. Love you.

Amelia: I love you, too.

Indigo and I spend the afternoon on the balcony, getting to know one another. She's in her mid-thirties and is ex-military. She served with

Michael, which is how Dad found her. Apparently, he reached out to Michael, hoping to find well-trained and trustworthy people.

"How do you like living in California? It must be a big change from St. Petersburg?" Indigo asks.

"It was a difficult transition. I'm glad Viktor was here, or I don't think I would've lasted a week."

"He seems like a nice guy."

"He is." I smile. "But don't tell anyone else. I don't want it to ruin his tough guy reputation." Indigo and I share a laugh. She's quickly becoming a friend.

The past few weeks have been interesting. At first, it felt like we were always in each other's way—that we were tripping over each other. I was uncomfortable having three virtual strangers in our house. I called Dad more than once, begging him to change his mind, but he refused.

I tried pleading my point with Viktor, but I didn't get anywhere there either. Viktor wants to be able to focus on us as a couple. He said he couldn't do that and act as my primary security. That being in a relationship can compromise his abilities. And how he'd never forgive himself if harm came to be because he refused to expand my security team.

It's been a bit of trial and error, but we've finally worked it all out and have found a comfortable rhythm. Hopefully, that will carry over to our living arrangements while I'm on tour.

The dress Viktor bought for me is stunning. It's a deep red form-fitting dress that sits off my shoulders and stops several inches above my knees. Using the full-length mirror, I check out myself from different angles, admiring how the dress accentuates my curves.

It's almost six, so I slide my heels on and make my way out to the living room. Viktor should be here any minute.

"You look gorgeous," Indigo says when I enter the room. "Viktor picked it out." I smile and give her a twirl.

"That man is sure head over heels for you." She grabs the small gift bag from the table.

"Thank you for keeping it for me."

The door opening interrupts us. Viktor strides in, wearing a black suit and a tie that matches my dress. In his hands is a bouquet of red roses. His eyes are locked on me as he crosses the room.

"I'll leave you two alone. Enjoy your evening." Indigo makes a quick exit.

"You look stunning, *moya zirka*." He kisses me. "These are for you."

I take the bouquet from his outstretched hand. "They're beautiful."

"They don't hold a candle to you."

"Give me a minute to put these in water."

"Leave them on the counter. Indigo will take care of them. We have someplace to be."

"Wait. I have something for you." I hand him the bag.

He takes out the small box inside and gives me a quizzical look. "What is it?"

"Open it."

He tosses the bag onto the couch and opens the box. There's silence while Viktor reads the paper inside.

"You bought a star?" He looks up.

"I'm sorry if you think it's a dumb gift."

Viktor takes another step, closing the distance between us. "There's nothing dumb about it."

"If you look under that paper, I bought two stars next to one another. They're named after us.

"*Moya zirka*, this is the most perfect gift anyone's ever given me."

I wrap my arms around his neck and pull him to me. Our lips meet for a passionate kiss that ends far too soon.

"If we don't leave now, we're going to be late."

"Or we could just change plans?"

"Nope. Let's go." He takes my hand and leads me out to our car.

Viktor

Amelia's quiet in the car. I know she's trying to figure out where we're going. Fortunately, it's not too far, so she won't have to wonder for long. Amelia sits up when I make the final turn into the parking lot.

"Are we having dinner on the Queen Mary?" Amelia asks, her eyes sparkling with excitement.

"We are. And we're spending the night on board."

"I don't know what to say."

"This is the last time we'll get to be alone for a while. I want to make the most of it."

We get out of the car, and I grab the bags I packed this morning while she was still sleeping. It doesn't take long to check in and arrange for our bags to be delivered to our room. With her hand in mine, we make our way to the restaurant.

I reserved a table by the windows overlooking the bay. We've grown to love being by the water and will miss it while she's touring, so I'm taking every opportunity to enjoy the views while we can. Over the next two hours, we share a decadent meal and each other's company.

"Do you want dessert?"

"Not anything they have here." Amelia bites her lip.

"We need to go now."

The security team does their best to stay out of our way, but we still don't have the privacy we used to. If we're anywhere other than our bedroom, there's always a chance someone can walk in. I miss it being just Amelia and me.

The walk to our room is excruciating. Amelia doesn't realize how sexy she looks in that little red dress. We're barely inside the door when I lose what little self-control I have.

I kick the door closed behind us as my mouth attacks hers. Amelia's already sliding off my suit jacket. Reaching behind her, I open the zipper on her dress. I step back and watch as she allows the fabric to slide off. It lands in a puddle at her feet.

Amelia stands before me in a strapless red lace bra and matching panties.

"Once again, you're very overdressed, Mr. Dobrow."

"I think we should remedy that." While I unbutton my shirt, Amelia starts to take off her heels. "No. They stay. Get on the bed."

I think I see uncertainty in her eyes for a brief second, but it quickly disappears. Amelia turns around and walks to the bed. She gets on all fours and crawls to the center of the bed, pausing to look over her shoulder. "Like this?" she asks with a flirtatious smile.

"Just like that. Now lay down and spread your legs. I want to see if you're wet for me." With her legs open, I see the wet spot on her panties. She's enjoying this as much as I am. "Touch yourself."

Amelia slides her hand down the center of her breasts, inching it down her abdomen. She stops when she reaches her panties. Teasing me, she puts a finger under the elastic of the waistband and then pulls it out.

With my shirt hanging open, I walk to the bed and lean over, placing my hands on each side. She arches her back, and the lace of her bra rubs against my bare chest.

"Are you trying to tease me?" I ask in a low, deep voice.

"Maybe." She bats her eyelashes.

I reach between us and tear the delicate panties from her body. "These won't be a problem now."

I push off the bed and watch as she teases her wet folds with her finger before it disappears inside her entrance. She moans in pleasure while she fucks herself with her finger.

Without taking my eyes off her, I finish undressing and toss my clothes to the side. My cock's hard and ready to sink into her body. Amelia watches as I stroke my length.

"Do you like watching me, Amelia?"

"Yes." Her voice is breathy. "Very much."

"Make yourself come for me."

Her fingers alternate between circling her clit and pumping in and out of her body. She doesn't take her eyes off me as I continue touching myself. As she climbs closer and closer to her orgasm, her breathing becomes more rapid, and mewls of pleasure escape her lips. She's a goddess lying before me, uninhibited and unashamed of her sexuality.

"That's it, *moya zirka*. You're almost there," I encourage.

She circles her clit once more. Her back arches from the bed, and her hand stills as pleasure flows through her body.

"Fuck, Amelia. You're so damn gorgeous." I'm in awe. "I love when you come for me."

"I need you, now."

Amelia's plea barely leaves her lips before I'm on top of her sliding my cock into her wet center. Being sheathed inside her is like coming home. Her body was made for mine.

I pull the cups of her bra down, allowing her breasts to spill out. Leaning down, I take one of her hardened nipples into my mouth, suckling and teasing her. Leaning closer, I whisper, "I want to take you hard and fast, okay?"

She nods.

"Nodding your head doesn't work." I still my movements waiting for her to answer.

"Harder, please. I want to feel every inch of you."

I nip at her earlobe. "Your wish is my command." I grab her hips to steady her body while I thrust deep inside her.

Amelia's body begins to squeeze my cock as her orgasm takes over. I thrust two more times, and then I follow her over the edge. I still, allowing myself to spill into her body.

"Happy Valentine's Day," she whispers.

"It's the first of many more to come, *moya zirka*."

Amelia

Valentine's Day was the last day of what I now consider my *normal* life. Since then, everything has been on hyper speed.

Mateo was discharged two weeks ago. Sparrow brought him over a few days after he was discharged. He looked good—healthy. And more importantly, he seemed content.

As far as his relationship with Sparrow—it's complicated. They're still exploring what, if anything, is between them. Neither is in a rush to make any decisions, but it's obvious something's shifted. They aren't outwardly affectionate with one another. I don't know how to describe it. They seem comfortable being near each other. I'm rooting for them and hope they can make a relationship work.

Our rehearsal schedule has been getting more intense. It's great having Mateo back. It feels like the band is whole again. We also have an official new name. None of us wanted to rename the group without Mateo. Some of the vendors weren't happy, but it was a battle we were willing to fight. Once he was discharged, finding a new name was the first thing on the list. Death Rat is no more. We are officially—Beautiful Division.

Mr. Hart handled the legal end, and Nick worked his magic on the merchandise. Yesterday, we received a shipment of samples. It's surreal knowing fans can buy T-shirts, hats, hoodies, CDs, bandanas, and a bunch of other things with our pictures and names on them.

Speaking of concerts, tickets have already gone on sale. Some of the packages include a meet and greet with us. And they're selling out. I can't believe this is even my life.

"How's the packing coming along?" Viktor asks as he walks into our room and sits on the bed.

"I think I'm just about done." I look around. "I can't believe we're leaving tomorrow."

Our tour buses are ready and waiting for us in Los Angeles. We're driving up early to check them out and ensure they're exactly as we ordered. As long as all is well, we'll be moving into them.

The next few weeks, we'll be traveling from L.A. and Hollywood to do some radio and television spots. We're booked pretty solid until the tour kicks off in L.A. the first weekend in May.

"Are you having second thoughts?" Viktor sits on the bed next to me.

"Not second thoughts, no." I sit next to him. "We've made so many memories here. It's bittersweet leaving."

"Once we have a better idea of what life's going to look like, we can discuss buying our own house."

"Our own house?"

"That is if you want to spend your forever with me."

"I couldn't imagine not waking up next to you every day." I climb over his lap, straddling him. "I don't want to think about my life without you in it."

He pulls me close to him and kisses me. It's unhurried but so full of emotion that it brings tears to my eyes.

I never imagined falling in love and never with a man like Viktor. But now that we're together, I'm never letting him go.

Amelia

WE ARRIVE AT THE CAMPGROUND IN UNIVERSAL THEME Park, which will be our home for the next few weeks. Four buses are waiting for us. Nick points out who's going to each one. Quincy and Tristan head off to check out their new digs. Mateo and Sparrow are up next. Then, Viktor and I. Lastly, my security team.

"Ready to check out our new mobile home?" Viktor jokes.

"I guess." I'm not super excited about this, but when I step inside, everything changes. "Can you believe how incredible this is?" I ask Viktor excitedly. "Living on a bus didn't sound appealing, but this is beyond anything I imagined."

"I think we'll be pretty comfortable on here." Viktor sits on the couch across from a fireplace. He hits a button, and a television screen rises from the mantle area. "Not bad." He smiles.

We continue the tour. There's a full kitchen complete with granite countertops. Past the kitchen is a hallway. Behind a door on the side, I find a washer and dryer. The door across from the laundry leads to the bathroom.

"The shower looks big enough for two."

"I can't wait to try it out." Viktor grins.

The last room is the bedroom. I didn't think it was possible, but we have a king-size bed. On each side is a night table with a small lamp.

"I think this room is going to be my favorite," Viktor says when we enter the bedroom. He lays down on the bed. "Come here. Let's see how it works."

I crawl onto the bed beside him. It's surprisingly comfortable, and I don't want to get up. I'm so tired already that I could fall asleep right now. Unfortunately, I have rehearsal in a half hour, so there's no time to rest.

It's only been a week, and already, my head's spinning from traveling back and forth from L.A. to Hollywood. We've done several morning talk shows, one late-night show, and some national radio broadcasts. Each time we show up at a studio, there's a line of fans outside wanting selfies and autographs. It's overwhelming and is giving my security team a run for their money.

Viktor's continually reminding me I'm not required to say yes to anything I'm not comfortable with. But I don't like saying no to people who've waited for hours to see us. So, I try to spend just a few seconds with as many people as possible.

"This is nothing compared to what you'll experience on tour," Nick says. "There will be meet and greets before each concert, and fans will always try to sneak into the tour bus area."

"I need specs on each venue so we can arrange for Amelia's security," Viktor interrupts.

"The venues will have plenty of security." Nick attempts to reassure him.

I already know that answer isn't going to work, but I sit back and watch the scene play out.

"Amelia has her own security." Viktor sits up straighter. "How soon can I expect to have the information?"

"I'll email you by the end of the day." Thankfully, Nick doesn't try to argue with Viktor.

Knowing fans are anticipating seeing us helps with our excitement level during rehearsals. Today's session is one of the best we've had so far. Having Mateo back makes the group feel whole again. Mateo and Tristan split the lead vocals between them. It's a whole new look and feel for us, but I think it's great.

"You guys are on fire," Griffin, the lead singer from Zapped Euforia, says.

"Hey, Grif. I didn't see you there. You like the new setup?"

"I think it works great." He puts his arm over Tristan's shoulder. "We don't have to hear this one all the time." He laughs. "You guys really have it all. There's Mr. Plays to the crowd here." He points to Mateo. "And Mr. Broody Musician over there." He points to Sparrow. "Then you have the girl who will break all the guys' hearts." He flashes me his mega-watt smile that drives all the girls crazy.

I glance at Viktor, who's sitting in a folding chair next to our stage. His focus is zoned in on Griffin.

"There's only one heart I'm interested in." I walk over to Viktor and sit on his lap. "Are we done for today?"

"You guys sound great and look super comfortable on the stage," Nick says from the back of the room. "I think you're ready."

"Hell, yeah, we're ready," Tristan calls.

"I'm giving you guys the rest of the week off. Rest up because this will be the last downtime you'll have until the end of the tour."

Viktor

As soon as the email from Nick arrives in my inbox, I send it off to Dimitri. He'll test each venue's security systems and will get the details of the tour bus areas. It's a relief knowing Dimitri's handling the details. That leaves me free to spend some quality time with Amelia before the tour kicks off. Part of that quality time includes a surprise party for her birthday.

Between her schedule and Maxim's, coordinating this surprise party hasn't been easy. It took a bit of doing, but I finally received a text a few hours ago confirming Max, Irina, and Lana have arrived safely and are staying at a local hotel. Unfortunately, Alex and Natalie couldn't fly out. She's too far along in her pregnancy for traveling.

Amelia's official birthday isn't until next week, but I wanted to have it early since we'll already be on the road. She thinks we're just going out to dinner.

"You look stunning," I say when she comes out of the bedroom wearing a satin emerald green skater dress.

"Do you like it?" She spins, and the skirt of the dress floats around her.

I get up from where I'm sitting on the couch and pull her to me. "You're beautiful no matter what you wear."

"Thank you." She smiles as she takes in my outfit of black dress pants and a white button-down shirt. "You don't look so bad yourself."

"Are you ready to go?"

"I am."

When we get out of the car, she looks around. "No security detail tonight?"

"I gave them the night off." She doesn't need to know they've gone ahead and are already at the venue.

"Perfect," she says and slides into the car.

While we drive across town, we talk about the upcoming concert.

"I'm so nervous," she explains. "We've never played to audiences like this."

The tour has stops at stadiums across the U.S. The first concert is at Dodgers Stadium here in L.A. The venue holds over fifty thousand people, which is small compared to some of the venues they'll play.

"Everyone's going to love your music," I reassure her. "And I'll be front and center for each show."

"You have no idea how much that means to me."

I make the turn into the venue's parking lot. One of the guys in Zapped Euforia told me about this place. I've only seen pictures of it, but at first glance, it isn't going to disappoint.

Amelia looks out the window and then back at me. "What is this place?"

"It's called Spellbound. I was told it's a great place to eat."

"It looks like something straight out of a fairy tale."

Offering my hand, I help her out of the car. We walk toward a stone cottage, which is the main building. Inside is decorated with rustic hand-carved furniture set up around a fireplace. It feels more like we've entered someone's home rather than a party venue.

We're met by an older couple. "I presume you are Mr. Dobrow?" the man asks.

"I am."

"It's nice to finally meet you in person. I'm Oliver, and this is my wife, Josephine."

"This is my lovely girlfriend, Amelia."

"Our birthday girl," Josephine says with a smile.

Amelia looks at me, a bit confused.

"I know your birthday isn't until next week, but since we'll already be on the road, I thought we'd celebrate early."

"You amaze me." Amelia slips her hand into mine.

"If you'll follow us," Oliver says.

He leads us to the back of the cottage and through a set of French doors. I thought the inside was gorgeous, but the outside puts the place over the top.

Several stone cottages are spread out around the inner courtyard. Trees and flowers give the place a natural feel. More hand-carved tables and chairs are set out on inlaid bricks. Each table is draped in white linens with live flower centerpieces. Twinkling lights are strung around the area, and lanterns hang from various branches. The sound of flowing water draws my attention to the far side of the courtyard, where there's a large pond with a waterfall.

"Your restaurant is magical," Amelia says as she looks around.

"Ah, the magic is just beginning," Oliver says and walks away.

He stops outside one of the other cottages and opens the doors. Then, he steps aside, allowing our guests to begin filtering into the courtyard.

"Viktor," Amelia says, bringing her hands to cover her mouth. "How did you do this?"

Amelia

Not only am I standing in the most enchanting garden I've ever laid eyes on, but everyone I know and love is here.

"Happy Birthday, *moya malen'kaya ptichka*," my father says and kisses me on both cheeks in a traditional greeting.

Mom hugs me. "You didn't think we'd miss your birthday, did you?"

"I didn't know we were celebrating my birthday tonight." I look at Viktor, who's standing off to the side, grinning from ear to ear.

Quincy, Tristan, Mateo, and Sparrow are here, as are the guys from Zapped Euforia. Movement in the shadows catches my eye, and for a brief second, I panic until the figure steps out.

"Lana," I squeal and run over to my sister, wrapping my arms around her. "I can't believe you're here."

"Mr. tall and broody over there can be pretty persuasive." She smiles and leans in close. "I think he's got it bad for you."

We both laugh.

"I'm so glad you're here." I turn around and address everyone. "I'm so glad you're all here."

After the initial shock passes, we're seated for the meal to be served.

I grab Viktor's hand under the table. "You didn't have to go through all this."

"*Moya zirka*, there's nothing I won't do for you."

Dinner's nothing short of exquisite. We're served a mix of American and Russian dishes—my favorites of both. It's nice to be able to relax and enjoy everyone's company.

"Are you and your guests ready for cake?" Josephine asks Viktor.

"We are."

Josephine signals to Oliver, who's standing where the servers have been coming in and out. He nods and opens them. Two servers carefully exit, carrying my cake.

"Oh, my word," I exclaim. "It's a piano."

The cake, which is more like a piece of art, is a grand piano. The servers set it carefully on a display table. Everyone gathers around, snapping pictures. After I get my photos, I step out of the way and return to our table. Viktor watches me for a moment before coming over.

"Are you okay?"

"I'm so overwhelmed. This is more than I could've ever asked for."

"I intend to make all your dreams come true." He wraps his arms around me and holds me close.

"You're every one of my dreams come true." I bring my hand to his cheek.

"It's time to sing to the birthday girl," Mateo interrupts us.

"We'll be right over." Viktor places a soft kiss on my lips.

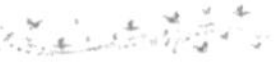

The party's finally winding down, which is good because I'm exhausted. The only people left are my family and us.

"How long are you in town for?"

"We're staying for your first concert," Mom says. "We go home the next day."

"Really?"

"We would not miss it," Dad adds with a proud smile.

When we left New York, I was happy that Dad and Viktor made up and gave us his blessing. However, Dad rarely mentions our relationship, and I find myself filtering what I say. Making up so there's peace and really being happy for us are two different things.

However, tonight Dad's acknowledged we're a couple several times. I overheard him talking to Foster, the drummer from Zapped. Dad was telling him how, at first, he wasn't sure of us as a couple, but now he couldn't be any more pleased. This is the first time we've all been together, and things feel normal. I couldn't be any happier.

Amelia

"I'm going to throw up." I pace back and forth backstage. "I can't do this."

"Listen to me, Mel." Mateo puts his hands on my shoulders. "This is just like any other show."

"Except that there are fifty thousand people out there." I point toward the stage. "And the most we've ever played to is a couple hundred."

"Alright, so that's a little different." Mateo smiles. "But other than that, it's exactly the same. We can perform these songs in our sleep."

"Maybe I should've asked Viktor to stay."

Viktor was backstage for the pre-show meet and greets. Then I sent him to take his seat with my family. At first, he put up some resistance, but I reminded him he was not part of my official security team anymore. Eventually, he gave in.

"Everything okay over here?" Indigo asks.

"Mel's freaking out a bit."

"What can I do to help?" she asks, concern etched on her face.

"I need to get some fresh air. Can we go outside for a few minutes?"

"We go on in fifteen," Mateo adds.

"I'll be there." Indigo leads me out the backdoor. I slide down the wall and sit on the ground. "I can't do this, Indi."

She squats down to my eye level. "I didn't think you were the type to give up so easily."

"This is too much. I don't know what I was thinking."

"I suppose it was something about how much you enjoy music and performing."

"That's pretty close." I pull my knees to my chest. "But I didn't think about stadiums full of people."

"What scares you most about it?"

"What if I screw up?"

"You might, but you'll keep going."

"What if everyone hates us?"

"I've been backstage all night. I highly doubt that's going to happen." She pauses and searches my face. "What if you don't screw up? What if everyone loves you, and you grow your fan base? What if you're the headliner on the next tour?"

Indi's always calm under pressure, and she gives excellent advice. This isn't the first time she's taken my negative what-ifs and turned them into positives.

"Those are all good points."

"Let's take a few deep breaths."

I inhale and exhale slowly until I feel centered. Then, I get myself up to my feet. Indigo follows me.

"You've earned your place here. Hold your head high and go kick ass."

I don't know what I imagined fifty thousand people to be like, but whatever I thought didn't cover it. The energy in the stadium is palpable while everyone sings along to our most popular songs. It's beyond my wildest dreams.

We've played almost our entire set. There's only one song left.

As Sparrow and I take center stage to sing "Written in the Stars," the audience goes silent. Sparrow opens the song on his acoustic guitar. As soon as he starts playing, cell phone flashlights turn on all around the stadium. Looking out across the audience, it looks like thousands of stars twinkling. Tears spring in my eyes.

I look down to the front row, and like everyone else, Viktor's on his feet. His gaze is locked on me. I smile and mouth the words *I love you.*

When we finish the song, the audience erupts in applause. Mateo, Quincy, and Tristan join us at the front of the stage for our bows. We exchange hugs with each other. The tour photographer takes pictures of us with the audience as our background.

At this moment, my life feels complete. My family is here supporting me. I am in love with a wonderful man. And I have the career of my dreams.

Viktor

WE'VE BEEN ON THE ROAD FOR A LITTLE OVER A MONTH. Today, we're somewhere in North Carolina. Things are so fast-paced the towns blend together. That's where Nick comes in. He makes sure we all know where we are from one day to the next.

It's all worth it, though. Amelia's positively radiant. She shines like the star I already knew she was. I'll travel anywhere. Live anywhere. As long as we're together.

Today's her first day off since the tour started. Last night, we shut our phones off so we could sleep in. When I wake up, Amelia's still sound asleep next to me, her leg thrown over mine. Carefully, I reach over to my night table and grab my phone, powering it on.

As soon as everything's loaded, I see several text messages from Alex. I know Natalie's due any time now, so I hurry to read them.

Alex: Are you still awake?

Five minutes later.

Alex: I'm guessing not. It's almost 2 am. Natalie's water broke. We're heading to the hospital.

I stop reading and shake Amelia gently.

"Amelia. Wake up."

She groans.

"You need to get up. Natalie's water broke."

"It did?" Her eyes pop open. "Did she have the baby?"

"I don't know. I didn't want to keep reading without you."

She pushes up on her elbow to read my screen with me.

Alex: I don't know how you did this with her. She's in so much pain, and she's refusing pain meds.

A half-hour later.

Alex: It's a boy. I have a son. Michael Alexander Montgomery.

Alex: He's so small. 5lbs. 3oz. and 16 inches. But he's perfect and healthy.

The following texts contain pictures of the baby. The sweetest one is of Rose holding her new little brother.

"Oh my gosh. He's adorable," Amelia gushes. "Can we try calling them?"

I hit Alex's contact, and the phone rings.

"Hello?" he answers.

"Congratulations and Happy Birthday." Amelia and I say in unison.

"Thank you."

"I hope we didn't disturb you."

"You didn't. Misha just brought Rose home. You're on speaker now."

"Congratulations, Nat. Michael's gorgeous."

"I can't believe he's here. I wish you two were here, too."

"I wish I knew where we were," Amelia says and giggles. "All this traveling gets confusing."

"I'm sorry I didn't get your texts earlier. We had our phones off so we could get some sleep."

"It's all good," Alex says. "It wasn't last night, but it is now."

"Natalie was stubborn and refused pain meds again?" I chuckle.

"It was awful, but she was amazing."

I stay silent for a moment, remembering just how helpless it felt watching her suffer, knowing there was relief at the press of a button. Relief, she refused. Seeing that precious baby at the end was worth it all, though.

The sound of a baby crying interrupts our conversation.

"We'll let you two go. It sounds like you have your hands full."

"We can't wait to see you guys," Natalie says.

"Did you get the tickets?" Amelia asks.

"We did," Alex answers.

The crying gets louder.

"We'll talk to you both soon."

We say our goodbyes and disconnect the call. Amelia taps my screen, bringing pictures of the baby back up.

"Just look at him," she coos. "He's so tiny and perfect."

"He is." I watch as she flips through the pictures again. "I can't wait until we have babies of our own."

Her finger freezes mid-motion, and she looks up at me. "What do you mean?"

"I can't wait to see you pregnant with our baby." I push a stray curl behind her ear. "A little boy or girl with your red hair."

Amelia sits up and turns to face me. "I don't want children."

"Not yet, of course. But someday."

"No, Viktor." She shakes her head slowly. "I don't want children at all."

She doesn't ever want to have children. Her words are like a punch to my gut, knocking the air out of me.

"Maybe you'll see things differently in a few years."

"I've known since the first night Seth snuck into my bedroom that I didn't want to be a mother. Being taken by Moreno only solidified my decision."

"Your life is different now. I'd never allow anyone to hurt you or our baby."

"I believe you mean every word, but even you can't control everything. There are no guarantees in life."

"Can we agree to table this discussion for another time?" I have to hold onto hope that she'll eventually change her mind.

"No. My answer isn't going to change."

I never thought being a father was in the cards for me. A man like me doesn't get to have a wife and kids—a happily ever after. But then I experienced Natalie giving birth to Rose, and I got the chance to raise her. Even for just a short time, and that changed everything.

After getting a taste of being a father, I knew I wanted that again.

This time with a woman who was mine—who I'd spend my forever with.

"Amelia." I reach out to her, but she backs away.

"I need to get some air." She jumps out of bed and hurries out of the room.

I don't follow her. We both need a few minutes to gather our thoughts before we talk again.

Amelia

I'M GLAD I SLEPT IN SHORTS AND A T-SHIRT LAST NIGHT because I'm able to get out of the bus quickly. My sandals are by the door. I slide my feet into them and go outside. Wherever we are today, the sun is shining brightly.

Chase is standing outside my bus. "Where are you going?" he asks.

"For a walk." I don't stop to chat.

"Ms. Solonik," he calls, but I don't turn around. "Amelia, wait."

I need a few minutes alone. I hurry to get away from him, but the buses are parked in a fenced-in area. It usually doesn't bother me, but today, I feel like a caged animal.

"Ms. Solonik, you can't wander off like this," Chase says when he catches up to me.

I spin around and nearly explode. "I'm locked in a fenced-in area. It's not like I can actually go anywhere. Go away, please."

"I apologize." Chase turns and hurries away.

He doesn't go as far as I would like, but at least he gives me some space.

"What's going on?" Sparrow pops his head out of his bus.

"I'm sorry. I hope I didn't wake you."

"We're up." He steps out and closes the door behind him. "I heard you yelling. Is everything okay?"

"No." Tears spring from my eyes.

"Hey." Sparrow walks over and puts his arms around me. "I've got you. You're okay."

His words are soothing, and his arms are comforting. He allows me to cry without pushing me to talk until I'm ready. Once the tears stop, he leads me to a spot behind his bus where there are some picnic tables set up.

"Are you ready to talk about it?" Sparrow asks as we sit down.

"Viktor wants a baby," I say bluntly.

"Now?" he asks, his brow furrowing.

"No. Sometime in the future," I reply with a shrug.

"That's reasonable," Sparrow says cautiously, trying to gauge my reaction.

"I don't want one."

"You're only nineteen," he says, his voice soft but insistent. "You'll change your mind eventually."

I shake my head, my voice firm. "I've seen how evil this world can be. I won't ever change my mind."

Sparrow leans forward, his expression a mix of concern and diplomacy. "I don't think it's something you need to decide on today. Give it some time."

"Yeah, you're probably right. Thanks for the talk," I mumble, standing up abruptly and turning to leave.

"Mel, wait," Sparrow calls after me, his voice filled with concern.

But I wave him off without looking back and keep walking.

When I get back to the bus, Viktor is up, standing at the small counter, making lunch for us.

"You're right on time," he says with a smile, but it doesn't reach his eyes.

We sit at our tiny table and eat in silence. I hate this tension between us, but I don't know how to fix it. I can't give him false hope, and I also can't agree to something I don't want.

When we finish eating, I silently gather our plates and put them in the dishwasher. My chest tightens as dread seeps in—I know what I have to do.

"I think we need some time apart," I say quietly.

"What?" Viktor stands up so fast his chair scrapes against the floor. "Let's pretend I never said anything."

"We can't do that," I reply, shaking my head.

"We can do anything we want." Viktor walks over to me, his voice desperate. "Having children isn't important."

Even as he says it, I see the sadness in his eyes. It's a lie he's telling himself—and me.

"That's not true," I whisper.

"It is. It was a stupid thought," he says, his voice cracking. He reaches out to me, but I step back, raising my hands to stop him.

"Your thoughts and desires aren't stupid," I say, my voice firm despite the ache in my chest. "And I won't let you give up on something you want."

"I want you, Amelia," Viktor says, his voice breaking.

"But you also want to be a father," I reply softly. "If you stay and I won't give you that, you'll resent me—resent us. I won't let you do that."

"Amelia, please," he whispers, his desperation cutting through me like a knife.

"I'm going to get dressed and meet the guys outside," I say, my voice cracking. "I have to be at a band meeting in a few minutes. I'll stay with Sparrow and Mateo until you can find a flight home."

"*Moya zirka*," Viktor pleads, his voice raw. "Please don't do this."

"I have to," I whisper, tears threatening to spill.

I hurry to our bedroom, close the door behind me, and lock it. Only then do I let the sobs escape.

I get dressed and pull my hair into a ponytail. I couldn't care less what I look like right now. When I'm ready, I take a deep breath and open the door. I'm both relieved and saddened to find the bus empty. Holding back tears, I start walking to the stage door at the back of the stadium. Chase learned from earlier and gives me enough space but still follows behind me.

When I get inside, I hear voices coming from down the hall. I get to the room and see I'm the last to arrive.

"You look like hell," Quincy says.

Sparrow and Mateo make space between them on the sofa. I sit between them, and Sparrow puts his arm around me. I rest my head on his shoulder.

"What's wrong?" Tristan asks.

"Mel and Viktor had a disagreement," Sparrow answers for me. "Let's get started."

I don't know what Nick talked about because I couldn't focus on anything other than my heart breaking. The last thing I want to do is be apart from Viktor, but I can't let him give up on a dream just because I don't share it. He deserves better than that.

"Enjoy the rest of your day off," Nick says, ending the meeting.

Quincy, Tristan, and Nick walk out together, leaving me alone with Mateo and Sparrow.

"What happened?" Mateo asks. "Did he hurt you?"

"No. He'd never do anything like that." I wipe my face. "We had a big difference in opinions on our future."

Mateo's phone dings. When he checks it, a smile lights up his face.

"Are you two okay here? I need to take care of something."

"Go on. We're good." Sparrow says.

"You still good to find somewhere to stay tonight?"

"Yep."

I look between them, knowing I'm missing something, but no one stops to explain.

"Awesome. I'll see you two later." Mateo hurries from the room.

When the door closes, I look at Sparrow. "Care to tell me what that was about?"

"Mateo met someone."

"I thought you two were—"

"We are. This is a girl."

"A girl?" I'm confused.

"Mateo's bi. He met a girl a few cities back. They've been talking, and he invited her to spend time with him."

"How do you feel about that?"

"I'm not sure right now. It's all really new." He shrugs slightly. "Back to you. Are you sure time apart is what's best for you and Viktor?"

"No. But it's what has to happen. I can't ask him to give up on something as big as wanting children. That's not fair." I swipe at the tears that are once again falling. "But that doesn't mean it doesn't hurt."

"I'm so sorry, Mel. I know how much you love him."

"Do you need a place to stay tonight?"

"I do."

"Why don't you stay with me? I'm going to be alone."

"You sure?"

I nod.

My heart's shattering into a million pieces. I don't know how to do this. How do I go on when a part of my soul is missing?

Viktor

WHY DID I SAY ANYTHING ABOUT A BABY? I SHOULD'VE KEPT my mouth shut. Look at the mess I've made. My world has been thrown off its axis. Amelia asked me to leave. I don't want that, but I swore I'd always respect her wishes and not push her into anything she didn't want.

Before she comes out of the bedroom, I walk out of our bus. I have to stop and talk to her team and then try to find a flight out of here. Where to? I don't know.

Chase's standing by the bus when I go outside.

"I'm not going to be here today. Please keep an extra eye on her."

"Sure thing."

I head over to the team's bus and knock on the door. Indigo answers. "This is a surprise."

"Can I come in?"

"Sure." She steps aside. "Is everything okay?"

"No," I say as I sink down on the sofa.

"Can I get you a coffee?"

"No thanks." I drop my head into my hands. "I'll be heading out today. I need to make sure you're capable of handling Amelia's security without me."

"We are." Indigo sits next to me. "May I ask what's wrong?"

I sit up. "Amelia and I are taking a break to figure some things out." That's the most I can admit to right now. To say we're over for good would break me.

"I'm sorry to hear that. I won't push you to talk, but I'm a good listener if you need one."

"I want children. She doesn't." It's as simple and as complicated as that.

"She's young. I understand why she's not ready for them right now."

"Amelia's had a rough life. She doesn't want children, ever," I reply. "She asked me to leave. I can't push her to let me stay. I need to know that your team will keep her security tight."

"You have my word. We'll keep her safe."

"Can I stay here while I make arrangements for a hotel?"

"Stay as long as you need."

"I'll be out of here as soon as I can." I can't be this close to Amelia and not be able to go to her.

"I'm going to take a shower. Make yourself comfortable."

Indigo walks to the back of the bus, and I pull my phone out to book a hotel room. I'll figure out where I'm going from there. The venue offers a driver if we need to leave the area, so I shoot a text asking them to have a car ready.

Amelia has a band meeting soon, so I watch for her to leave the bus. Once she's out of sight, I make my way over and grab my bag. I thought I was done packing and leaving. The emotions are familiar and are accompanied by a tremendous feeling of loss. One I hoped to never feel again.

A text alerts me that my ride's outside waiting for me.

Before I leave, I write a note.

Moya zirka,

I don't know how to walk away from you. How to turn my back on us. You're everything to me, Amelia. My life is empty, meaningless, without you. I'll do anything to change this. I love you.

~Viktor

I set the note on the table and take a final look around before I walk out the door.

The night drags on as I sit in the hotel room alone. Somehow, no matter what I do, I always find myself alone.

Me: Is it okay if I stay at the lake for a while?

Alex: Sure. What's going on?

Me: Amelia and I are taking some time apart.

Alex: Do you want to talk about it?

Me: No.

Alex: When you do, I'm here.

I book the next available flight to Missouri and arrange for a rental car to be ready when I get there. Hopefully, spending some time at the lake will give me the clarity I need to figure this shit out—to get my girl back.

Amelia

Sparrow and I are sitting on the couch watching some sappy romance movie. Why? I have no idea because it's not helping either of us to feel any better. My phone rings, interrupting our pity party.

"It's my sister."

"I'll pause this."

I take a deep breath and connect the call. "Hey, Lana. What's up?"

"Mom told me Viktor called to let Dad know he has some business to attend to. That he's going to be gone for a while."

"Mhm."

"Want to tell me the truth?"

"We had a disagreement." I swallow over the lump in my throat. "I asked him to leave."

"What could possibly be that bad that you made him leave?"

"Babies." The line goes silent. I wait a few minutes and then check to make sure the call's still connected. "You there?"

"I am," she says. "You want a baby, and he doesn't?"

"It's the other way around."

"He knows you're young. What the hell is he asking you to have a baby for?"

"He didn't. He said in the future. But I don't want kids—ever."

"And he couldn't get past that?"

"I can't ask him to give up something that important. That's not fair."

"That's not for you to decide."

"Was whatever the reason why you left Brandon something for you to decide?"

Even after all this time, Lana still hasn't opened up about why she left Brandon. And as much as she denies it, she's still in love with him.

"What happened was out of both of our control," she says quietly. "Don't make the same mistake I did. Don't let this come between you two."

"It already has."

Lana encourages me to reconsider. That if Viktor's willing to stay together despite wanting kids, I should go with that. But I can't. I refuse to be selfish and ask him to stay with me when I'm unwilling to give him the children he wants.

I've watched him with Rose. He's tender and patient. He's content. I should've seen this coming. I guess I just ignored the warning signs. But having children isn't a dream one simply gets over. I'd never be able to live with myself for keeping this from him.

After we hang up, I rest my head back on the couch and let out a big breath.

"Mel, maybe you should call Viktor," Sparrow says softly, his expression cautious as he tests the waters.

"Why?" I ask, lifting my head slightly.

"I think maybe you two should talk more before you give up," he suggests.

"There's nothing to talk about," I say, shaking my head as I sit up straighter and force myself to meet his eyes. "Do you mind if we save the rest of this for another night? I'm tired, and we have a long day ahead of us tomorrow."

"That's fine," Sparrow replies, though the concern in his voice lingers.

I stand up and head toward the bedroom, but when I glance back, I realize Sparrow hasn't moved. He's still sitting on the couch, his hands resting on his knees.

"Aren't you coming to bed?" I ask, pausing in the doorway.

"I'm going to sleep on the couch," he says, his voice casual, though his posture is rigid.

"You aren't going to be comfortable out here," I protest, crossing my arms. "It's not a pull-out."

"I'll be fine," Sparrow insists, leaning back into the cushions as if to prove his point.

"There's no reason you can't share the bed with me." I step closer and grab his hands, tugging him gently to his feet. "I don't think I'm in any danger with you. Wrong body parts, remember?" I add with a chuckle, trying to lighten the mood.

"You're so funny," Sparrow says with a grin, though his eyes briefly flicker with hesitation.

"There's no reason for either of us to be alone," I say, my voice soft but firm.

"You sure?" he asks, his tone serious, as if giving me one last chance to change my mind.

"I'm sure," I reply with a small smile, squeezing his hands before leading him toward the bedroom.

Other than Viktor, Sparrow's the only other man I trust enough to fall asleep when I'm alone with him. "I'm positive."

I thought having company would help me feel less alone, but I was wrong. I feel Viktor's loss so strongly tonight. Unwanted tears begin to fall. I try to stay quiet, so I don't disturb Sparrow. But he's already sliding his arm under me, pulling me close.

"It'll be okay," he says and kisses my head.

I cry myself to sleep.

Amelia

Over the past few weeks, we've made our way up the east coast. Tonight, we're playing Madison Square Garden. I'm excited because Alex and Natalie will be here any minute. Timur and his wife Katia are accompanying them to keep the kids on the bus while we're at the concert.

I peek my head out the door for the millionth time, but there's still no sign of them. Closing the door, I resume my pacing. Time seems to be going backward.

"Relax, Mel," Sparrow says. "They'll be here."

"It's getting late, and I haven't seen them in forever," I murmur, glancing toward the road. A car's horn blares, drawing my attention. My heart leaps. "They're here."

I throw open the bus door and sprint outside. Natalie steps out of the car first, and I rush over, wrapping her in a tight hug.

"Thank you so much for coming," I whisper, my voice thick with relief.

She squeezes me back. "We wouldn't have missed this for anything."

"Hey, kid," Alex says as he pulls me into a quick hug. "How are you holding up?"

I exhale shakily. "It's been hard. Have you heard from Viktor?"

Alex's expression turns serious. "We talk every day."

"Is he okay?" I ask, my voice dropping to a tentative whisper.

He hesitates, then sighs. "To be honest, no."

"Auntie Melia!" Rose's voice breaks the tension as she bounds toward me.

I crouch to scoop her up, spinning her in a playful circle. "Hey, big girl. I've missed my favorite niece."

She giggles and points excitedly toward the car. "I'm a big sister now. See?"

I follow her gaze as Natalie turns around, cradling a tiny bundle in her arms. She approaches, her face glowing.

"Auntie Melia," she says softly. "Meet your nephew, Michael."

My breath catches as I peek at the baby. "He's so small."

Natalie laughs, pulling the cotton hat off his head to reveal a fluff of unruly hair. "Look at this."

"Oh my gosh." I laugh, reaching out to gently touch the tufts.

"That's one reason I keep a hat on him," she admits with a giggle. "His hair's always wild."

I can't help but grin. "He's absolutely perfect." Hugging Rose closer, I glance toward the bus. "Come on inside and get settled. I have to be at the stadium for a meet-and-greet soon."

Bode steps forward to open the bus door, and Alex helps Natalie climb the steps with Michael. Timur takes Rose and carries her inside. Katia trails behind and pulls me into a firm embrace.

Her voice is low but concerned. "You don't look well. Your usual sparkle is missing."

"It's been difficult."

"I know you and Viktor aren't together right now," she says gently, searching my face. "I don't know what happened, but I urge you to work it out."

"I wish it were that easy," I reply, my tone tinged with exhaustion.

Katia's eyes soften. "Sweet girl, relationships require compromise on both sides. When the love you share is real, like I know yours and Viktor's is, you can't let anything stand in your way. You both need to fight for it."

I shake my head. "This is a big issue. There's no compromise."

"There's always room for compromise," she insists before stepping onto the bus.

I take a deep breath and follow her inside. Sparrow's already showing everyone around.

"We'll leave you all to settle in," Sparrow says, reaching for my hand. "Amelia and I need to be backstage in less than five minutes."

Alex waves us off with a reassuring smile. "Don't worry about us. I think we've got it handled."

"I'll send someone to get you closer to showtime," I promise before Sparrow and I exit the bus.

In comparison to some of our other venues, Madison Square Garden is small, only holding about twenty thousand fans, but their enthusiasm was over the top. Despite my depressed mood, I think it was probably one of our best concerts this summer. We finish our songs, take our bows, and exit the stage. One more concert in the books.

Although I've loved being on tour, I'm glad it will wrap up in a few weeks. I'm exhausted emotionally and physically. I'm looking forward to some time off to rest and regroup. I'm about to push the door open to leave the stadium when Sparrow calls me.

"Mel, wait a second."

I turn back. "What's up?"

He shifts his weight awkwardly, rubbing the back of his neck. "I'm not going to be staying on your bus tonight."

"You're more than welcome to. Alex and Natalie are heading home."

. . .

Sparrow hesitates, his tone nervous as he explains, "Mateo asked me to spend some time with Aspen and him."

I study him for a moment. "How do you feel about that?"

He shrugs, looking down at his shoes. "I'm not sure yet. There's a lot... but I want to give it a chance."

Placing a reassuring hand on his arm, I soften my tone. "If anything changes and you need a place to stay, just come over."

"Thanks," he murmurs, leaning in to press a quick kiss to my cheek before walking away.

When I open the door to the bus, Alex, Natalie, Bode, and Indigo are waiting outside. Natalie immediately lets out an excited squeal.

"You were amazing," she gushes, her eyes sparkling. "I can't believe this is your life now. You're a rock star."

I laugh softly, brushing off her enthusiasm. "It's still just me."

"Just you? Don't sell yourself short," Alex interjects. "Look at everything you've accomplished. You should be proud of yourself."

"I just happened to be in the right place at the right time."

Inside, the bus is quiet. Timur and Katia must have already put the kids to bed. I hesitate, glancing at Natalie and Alex. "I hate for you guys to have to wake them. Why don't you stay here tonight? I can sleep on the couch, and Timur and Katia can move to Indigo's bus. They've got an extra bed."

"Are you sure?" she asks, her voice cautious. "We don't want to inconvenience you."

"I'm positive," I insist. "Honestly, it's kinda selfish. I want to spend more time with you guys before we leave tomorrow."

Natalie glances back at Alex, who gives a slight nod of approval. "It's a yes, then."

"Thank you," I say sincerely. Opening the door, I call Bode over. "Can you bring Timur and Katia to Indigo's bus? Let them know they'll be staying there tonight."

"Yes, Ms. Solonik," Bode replies dutifully.

"It's just Amelia," I remind him with a playful smile, the habit starting to wear on me. "For the millionth time."

He chuckles sheepishly. "Sorry, Amelia. It's hard to get used to."

"It's all good," I reply, offering a smile before heading back inside.

Timur and Katia say their goodnights and follow Bode to Indigo's bus. I sink onto the couch with a deep sigh, the weight of the day pressing down on me. Natalie sits beside me, her warmth a comfort. Across from us, Alex grabs a snack and settles at the table.

"How many more shows do you have?" Natalie asks, tucking a strand of hair behind her ear.

"Six," I answer, my tone weary.

"What's your plan after the tour?" Alex asks.

"I'm not sure," I admit, pausing to take a sip from my water bottle. "Viktor and I were still trying to decide what we wanted to do. Now, I need to figure that out on my own."

Natalie reaches over, giving my hand a comforting squeeze as I continue, "I was wondering if maybe I could stay at the lake for a little while to sort things out?"

"You're welcome to stay as long as you want," Alex responds without hesitation, his tone full of reassurance.

"Thank you."

Michael's cries echo through the baby monitor, breaking the moment.

"The baby beckons," Natalie says with a tired but affectionate sigh as she starts to stand.

. . .

"Can I get him?" I ask quickly, already getting to my feet.

"Absolutely. But he'll probably need a diaper change."

"I can handle that," I reply, my voice lightening. I hurry off, thankful for the distraction. I walk into my bedroom and find a sleeping Rose in the center of my bed. Michael's in his travel bassinet. I don't want to wake Rose, so I keep the lights dim and then reach down to lift the baby.

"Hi there, precious boy." I kiss his soft cheek. "I'm your Auntie Melia."

He stops crying and watches me closely.

I grab his diaper bag from the closet. "How about we change your diaper, and then we'll go to your mama?"

I'm amazed at how tiny but perfect his features are. Both of his feet fit into the palm of one hand. I successfully get his diaper changed without waking Rose. Then, I snap his sleeper back up and cradle him close to me. Carefully, I sit on the edge of the bed. "I know we're just meeting, but I already love you very much." His tiny hand grabs onto one of my fingers while he coos at me.

Looking at this tiny bundle, I understand Viktor's desire to have a child of his own. It's not that I'm unaffected or hate children. On the contrary, I adore them. They're innocent and curious. A miraculous representation of the love between two people. It's those same reasons that make me not want them.

I've seen the worst this world has to offer. Moreno didn't only take adults. I witnessed what Moreno and the sick men he entertained liked to do to children. The little lives that were tortured before mercy was shown, and they were put out of their misery.

Moreno might be gone, but there are many more just like him. My father works hard to stop as many trafficking rings as possible, but they'll never be entirely eradicated. How can I justify bringing a baby into this world knowing that?

Holding Michael, I can't help but daydream about him being mine and Viktor's. Would he have my red hair and Viktor's blue eyes? Would he be a she—a little girl who would steal her daddy's heart?

Just because I didn't have anyone looking out for me doesn't mean it would be the same for a child we'd have. As long as Viktor and I are alive, he'd never let anything happen to them. And if the worst happened and we were taken away too soon, my family would be there to protect our child. The past wouldn't have a chance to repeat itself.

What about the evil that's out there? Viktor's only human. He can't be everywhere and see every possible danger. Is that a risk I'm willing to take?

"I don't know what to do. I wish I had the answers." Michael wiggles and pushes his bottom lip out in a pout. "Is your belly hungry?" I kiss his tiny nose. "Let's get you to your mama so you don't wake up your sissy."

Amelia

Even though I knew I'd see Alex and Natalie again in a few weeks, saying goodbye to them was hard. I cried as they drove away, knowing this time I was really going to be alone.

Things seem to be working out between Mateo, Aspen, and Sparrow. He hasn't given too many details, but he also hasn't returned to being my roommate. The three of them spend their free time together. I'm happy for him, but I'm sad for me. The past few weeks have been incredibly lonely.

I'd hoped time would heal the ache in my heart. Instead, I think it's only gotten worse. Viktor texts me daily to tell me he loves me and that he'll wait forever. That not having children isn't a deal breaker for him. I've picked up the phone countless times to call or text him back but didn't go through with it.

Once I got past my pride and brought it up to Ania, she helped me talk through the whole subject of children rationally. She advised me not to make future decisions based on past trauma.

We've had some tough sessions. Ania encouraged me to respect Viktor's decisions, whatever they may be. That he gets to decide what he can or cannot live with, not me. Not respecting Viktor's opinion and taking away his voice, his right to choose, was exactly what was done to me. And it's wrong.

After our sessions, I spent a lot of time alone with my thoughts. I took everything I'd always thought and all the things Ania and I discussed and made a decision. But I haven't talked to Viktor yet.

Ania encouraged me to reach out and talk to him. But I can't. I'm embarrassed. I behaved like a spoiled child and sent him away the first time we didn't agree on something instead of being an adult and talking through it.

"What do you think?" I turn away from the mirror and show Sparrow the new tattoo on my upper back.

His eyes widen as he leans in for a closer look. "Did it hurt

"Not really," I reply casually, a small smile tugging at my lips.

"It's beautiful," he says, admiration evident in his voice as he studies the intricate design.

I glance over my shoulder at him, my smile broadening. "I love it," I say with quiet conviction, the excitement evident in my voice.

Getting this tattoo was something I'd been planning for several months —before Viktor and I broke up. The problem was we were on tour and didn't stay in one place long enough to do much of anything. I knew our last show would be in Kansas City and that we'd be arriving a few days early.

A few months ago, I found a local tattoo shop and scheduled an appointment. The plan was to get this one before tonight's show. It was supposed to be a surprise for Viktor. My heart sinks at that thought.

I haven't heard from him since we left New York. I guess he got sick of hoping and waiting for me to respond to his messages. I waited too long to come to my senses. I can't blame him for finally realizing what I said was true—he deserves to have every one of his dreams come true.

"Send him a text, Mel," Sparrow encourages me. "It's never too late."

"I was a jerk and never responded to his texts begging me to talk to him. I fear it's too late now."

"Love doesn't just go away."

"Tell me about it. You don't think my heart's still breaking?"

I've been paralyzed by fear and embarrassment. Because of that, I might've lost the best thing that's ever happened to me.

Viktor

"YOU NEED TO GIVE HER SPACE," GRIGOR SAYS FIRMLY, HIS tone steady but empathetic. "Amelia's had a traumatic past. The things she's gone through are things most people can't even begin to comprehend. And that's not a bad thing—it just means she's carrying a heavy burden."

I run a hand through my hair, frustration bubbling to the surface. "I don't want her to think I deserted her."

"She asked you to leave. To give her space, right?"

"Yes."

"And she hasn't responded to any of your attempts to contact her?" he presses, his tone more pointed now.

"No," I admit, the word coming out as little more than a whisper.

"Then," he continues gently, "I think you need to respect the boundaries she's put in place. Leave the ball in her court. If she wants to contact you, she will. And if not..." He hesitates for a moment, his voice dropping to a softer tone. "You'll have to face that it's over."

The words hit me like a blow to the chest, and I swallow hard, fighting the urge to argue. I can only nod, the weight of his advice settling heavily on my shoulders.

I know what Grigor's saying is the right thing to do, so I stopped texting her. That doesn't mean I haven't picked my phone up and typed them out. I've done that more times than I can count. Each text begging her to call me. But I didn't send them.

Instead, I took my therapist's advice and backed off. Amelia's boundaries must be respected. I also decided to use this time to honestly consider Amelia's point of view. I didn't want to admit it, but she had a valid point. I couldn't just pretend I didn't want children. I needed to take time to really consider if not being a father is something I can live with. When she first brought it up and asked me to leave, I reacted. But she was right. I needed to think it through.

The other night, I pulled up her playlist and listened to the songs. "Just Give Me a Reason" came on. I've heard her sing that song a million times, but this was the first time I really listened to the words.

If I didn't know better, I would've sworn the song was written about us—for us. Two people who've each experienced the worst of what the world has to offer. They have battle wounds and think they're damaged beyond repair. But then they meet each other. Their souls connect and heal every fractured part of their hearts. I put it on repeat and listened to it until I memorized every word.

Although I've enjoyed my quiet solace at the lake, I'm equally as happy that Alex and Natalie flew in two weeks ago. Natalie wanted to make sure the kids had happy memories of summers spent at Finn Lake. It also allows Charlotte and Stanley to spend time with their grandkids. They try to spend as much time as they can at their cottage over the summer.

I've been able to spend a lot of time with their family, too. Which is where I am right now. Alex and Natalie needed some groceries, so I offered to sit with the kids. When Rose was a baby, I had our routine down to a science. But this whole two-kid thing is serious business. Meeting the needs of two little ones is certainly not for the faint of heart.

Rose is well-behaved, but she's a busy toddler. She's curious about everything. And Michael, he's an infant. He can do no wrong, but it's an immediate need when he's hungry or his diaper requires changing. It's been a very long hour. I'm sitting on the floor watching Rose do a little wooden puzzle while I give Michael a bottle when I hear their car pull in.

"Mama. Daddy." Rose runs to the door.

I can't get up as fast as I'd like while balancing a baby. By that time, Rose is already turning the handle to open the door. I'm at a distinct disadvantage.

Natalie's the first one in. Rose wraps herself around Natalie's leg. As soon as Michael sees his Mama, he decides the bottle is no longer acceptable—his cries alert everyone to that fact. Natalie sets the bags she's carrying down and takes the baby.

"Thank you so much for watching them," Natalie says as she tries to make her way to the couch with one child in her arms, the other hanging onto her leg.

"Come here, Rose." I attempt to extricate her from her mother's leg. "Let's let mama walk."

"I'm used to it." Natalie shakes her head.

"I'll go help Alex with the bags." I turn to go to the door. "Thanks for letting me watch them."

"I should be the one thanking you. It was a treat to go out alone."

"I'm glad I could help."

I leave her to feed her baby and head outside, where Alex is unpacking the groceries from the trunk.

"You're still in one piece. That's a good sign."

"They're good kids. I love spending time with them."

Alex stops what he's doing and looks at me. "It sounds like there's a but coming."

I lean against the car. "You and Natalie and the kids are my family. Over the past few weeks, I've realized that the part of me that loves children is fulfilled when I spend time with Rose and Michael."

"Ah, we're talking about Amelia."

"We are."

"What are you thinking?"

"With them in my life, I don't think I'd ever feel like I gave something up."

After everything that happened between Natalie and me the year Alex was gone, I was afraid our friendship was ruined. Before I left, he told me he forgave me, but I assumed those were just words to send me off.

It took me too long to understand he honestly wasn't angry at me. He didn't blame me for anything that happened between Natalie and me. Hell, I still don't understand it. All I know is I'm thankful for his friendship and support. Especially now.

"I've been doing a lot of soul-searching since I've been here. I didn't want to believe Amelia was right. That the best thing for us was time apart."

"I'm not following," Alex says.

"Amelia was right when she said I couldn't pretend I never brought up wanting kids. And I couldn't just write off wanting them in the future. Having this time apart allowed me to weigh the possibilities for my future. Gave me the clarity I needed to make a decision I'm comfortable with."

"I guess I'm glad we were able to help." Alex chuckles.

"I'll help you get these in." I reach into the trunk and grab the last few bags. "Then I have to go. I have an important errand to run."

Amelia

"Can you believe this is it? The last show?" Tristan asks.

"It's been one hell of a ride," Quincy adds. "What's everyone's plans for after?"

"I need to take a few weeks off. There are some important things I have to do. After that, I don't know."

"Just the group I was looking for," Nick says as he strolls into the green room. "We need to chat before things get going here tonight."

"What's up?" Matteo asks.

"We received an offer from Crimson Flame Music to record a full album in preparation for a tour next year with Beautiful Division as the headliner."

The room is quiet while we let Nick's words sink in.

"A recording deal and a tour?" I'm sure I misheard him.

"I forgot another small detail. Beautiful Division has also been nominated for a Grammy in the Best New Artist category, and they'd like you to play at the awards ceremony." Nick grins.

"Nominated for a Grammy?" Sparrow asks in disbelief.

Nick nods.

Once the reality of what he said hits, the celebrating starts. Never in a million years would I have imagined my life taking this turn. If it's a dream, I never want to wake up.

"Mr. Hart has the contracts. He's going through them now. We'll meet in a few weeks to go over the details. But guys and girl," Nick smiles. "I couldn't be more proud of you and more excited for your future."

We stay tucked away in the green room, talking excitedly about what's coming for us. Sparrow has been writing songs, so we already have some new music to record. Our celebration comes to an end when the pre-concert meet and greet starts.

After all the pictures and autographs are done, there are only a few minutes left until we take the stage. I pull my phone out to text Natalie.

Me: Are you guys here yet?

Natalie: We are. Front row center stage.

Me: Perfect.

Then, I do something I've been terrified to do.

Me: Can we talk?

It only takes a second for me to see he read the message. The little bubbles pop up on the screen, indicating he's texting back.

Viktor: Sure.

Me: I'm about to go on stage. Can I call you after the concert?

Viktor: I'll be waiting.

"Mel, it's go time," Sparrow says as he walks past me, heading for the stage.

"I'm right behind you."

The stage is shrouded in darkness as I take my place behind the keyboard. The familiar recording announcing Beautiful Division plays through the sound system, and the crowd goes crazy. We start playing our first song just as the lights come up.

It's become a habit for me to search the audience even though I know Viktor won't be there. I spot Alex and Natalie, but it's what's next to them, rather who's next to them, that shocks me most. My parents and Lana are here too.

I don't know if it's possible to smile even bigger than I already was.

Knowing they're all here to support me and celebrate the last show is more than I could've asked for. The only thing that would make it even more perfect is if Viktor was here.

Viktor

Yesterday, I went to the local animal shelter. I walked the concrete aisles looking at all the dogs waiting for their forever home, not sure what I was looking for. I trusted fate would step in and show me which dog was the right one.

I stopped at a few kennels, and although the dogs were cute, I didn't feel a connection. I was about to give up hope when I came to the last cage. A golden brown pup was huddled in the corner, clearly terrified.

"What's the story on this one?" I ask the shelter worker who's accompanying me.

"This little girl's about four months old. One of our volunteers found her abandoned on the side of the road. She was only about eight weeks old and cold and dehydrated," she explains. "It was touch and go for a good while. But she's a fighter."

"How could someone do that to an innocent animal?"

"You'd be surprised at the things we see."

Unfortunately, I probably wouldn't. I've been witness to the evils of society against their own species. I can only imagine the unconscionable acts committed against animals.

"She's spayed and has her vaccines. All the tests we've run show she's healthy. But as you can see, she's terrified. We've had people interested in her, but her trust issues scare them away."

"Can I meet her?"

"You can try, but you probably won't have much success."

"Do you have treats?"

"I'll be right back." She disappears for a few minutes and returns with a baggie containing several small treats.

"Thanks."

She pulls out her keys and unlocks the door, allowing me to enter the dog's space. "I'm going to close this so she doesn't try to escape. Take as much time as you want. I'll be in here cleaning up."

Once the puppy and I are alone, I sit down slowly, keeping my back against the wall and leaving enough space between us so she doesn't feel threatened.

I sit quietly, allowing her to get used to my presence in her space. She doesn't move from her huddled spot in the corner.

"I'm told you've had a rough start in life," I murmur. "I don't blame you for being scared of people."

Her ears move as I whisper to her, so I know she's listening.

"I know how scary trusting people can be." I take a small piece of treat out of the bag and gently toss it over to her. She looks between me and the treat several times. "It's okay. That's for you."

Although hesitant, she lowers her head, sniffs the treat, and then picks it up.

"That's a good girl," I quietly praise the puppy. "I know another girl. Her name's Amelia. You remind me of her when she and I first met." I take another piece of treat, this time tossing it so it lands a few steps away from her. "She had bad things done to her and was scared too."

The puppy stares at the treat. She wants it but isn't sure if she should move from her safe corner.

"It's okay. I won't hurt you."

The puppy doesn't move. I'm sure she's trying to decide if it's worth risking her safety to grab the treat. Eventually, she ventures forward and grabs the treat but quickly returns to her corner.

I continue to whisper to her and give her treats. Each time, she inches out, grabs the treat, and hurries away.

"I'd like to bring you home with me. You'd be safe. No one would hurt you ever again." She tilts her head as if trying to understand what I'm telling her. "How about you try coming a little closer?" I put a treat on the ground within my reach.

The puppy cautiously inches toward the treat. This time, when she takes it, she doesn't go back.

"That's a good girl," I say quietly. "Do you think you and I can try to get to know one another? Maybe become friends?" I hold out an open palm with a piece of treat in it.

Even though she's trembling, the puppy takes the treat from me.

"Very good, Nadiya," I say softly. "Nadiya means hope. You give me hope for the future." She wags her tail for a fraction of a second. I smile at her and offer another treat from my hand. "You like your new name, don't you, sweet girl?"

She takes the treat from my hand. Then, her barriers fall away, and she hops onto my lap. Her tail's wagging a mile a minute as she licks my face.

"I don't know how you did it," the shelter worker says with a big smile.

I stand up with the pup in my arms. "I'd like to adopt her."

I was able to get cleared to bring Nadiya home early this morning. Before I left the shelter, I also made a sizeable donation. If it were up to me, I would've taken every animal there and given it a home, but that's not realistic. The next best thing I could do was ensure there were enough funds to provide high-quality care.

On the way home, we stopped at the pet store to purchase food, bowls, a leash and collar, a bed, and more toys than one puppy could ever want. The shelter's getting a large delivery of supplies along with a note letting them know whenever they need more, to place an order, and the cost will be covered.

It took much longer than I thought, which is why I'm late getting to the concert. Who knew a puppy would take more work than a human child?

"She's adorable." Indigo gushes over the puppy that's slathering her in kisses.

Looking at her now, you wouldn't believe she's the same pup who was cowering in a corner less than twenty-four hours ago.

"Are you sure you're okay with watching her? She's not house-broken yet."

"Go. Nadiya and I'll be just fine. Won't we, little girl?" Indigo ignores me while she showers Nadiya with love.

Knowing my new little girl's in good hands, I head over to the concert venue, hoping that my plan is not about to backfire on me.

Amelia

WE'RE IN THE MIDDLE OF "WRITTEN IN THE STARS" WHEN Sparrow quickly motions for me to look backstage. I glance over my shoulder and nearly lose my place. Viktor's standing there. I look back to Sparrow, who shrugs as if he's as surprised as I am by his presence.

My hands tremble through the rest of the song. Every emotion I've buried for the past few weeks bubbles to the surface. By the end of the song, tears are streaming down my face.

The rest of the guys join us at the front of the stage to take our final bow. Sparrow thanks the crowd for their support and tells them to be sure to follow us on social media for all our updates.

After we exchange hugs and the photographer finishes her on-stage pictures, we make our exit.

Viktor's striking blue eyes meet mine, drawing me to him.

"You're here." My voice wavers as I step closer, struggling to believe he's standing in front of me.

"I am," Viktor replies simply, his tone steady but his eyes betraying a depth of emotion.

"We need to talk," I say softly, glancing away to collect myself.

"Yes, we do." His voice is calm, but there's an intensity behind it that makes my heart race.

Without another word, Viktor places his hand on the small of my back and guides me through the crowd that's milling around backstage. The weight of our unspoken words hangs heavy in the air as we walk to my bus in silence. When we arrive, I freeze in surprise—Indigo is inside, sitting on the floor with a small, wiggling puppy.

As soon as the puppy sees Viktor, it abandons Indigo and sprints toward him, its tiny tail wagging furiously.

"Did you miss me, Nadiya?" Viktor asks as he kneels to stroke her head.

"She did fantastic," Indigo chimes in, getting to her feet. "I'll be outside if you need me."

Viktor straightens and gives her a curt nod. "Can you ensure we have privacy?"

"Will do, sir," Indigo replies before slipping out the door.

Turning back to me, Viktor gestures toward the couch. "Let's sit. We have a lot to talk about."

We settle on the couch, the little puppy curling up near Viktor's feet. She's utterly enamored with him, and it's clear the feeling is mutual.

I take a deep breath, the words I've rehearsed threatening to spill out. "Viktor, I—"

"Let me go first, please," he interrupts gently, his voice low but firm.

I nod, clasping my hands tightly in my lap.

"The past few weeks have been hell without you," he begins, his gaze locking with mine. "But you were right to ask me to leave. I needed the time and space to think about my future." He pauses to shoo the puppy away from his shoelaces, handing her a chew toy instead. "I didn't know where to go, so I asked Alex if I could stay at the lake."

The puppy, bored with the toy, bounces over to me and places her tiny paws on my leg. I scoop her up, cradling her in my arms. "Is it a boy or a girl?" I ask softly, running a hand over her silky fur.

"She's a little girl—Nadiya," Viktor says, a proud smile touching his lips. "Her name means hope."

"She's precious." I stroke her gently, my heart warming as her tiny eyes flutter closed.

Viktor watches us for a moment before continuing. "While I was at the lake, I gave my future a lot of thought. About what my life might look like—with children and without. I also spent time with Alex, Natalie, and the kids. And I realized something important." He pauses, his voice catching. "My future is empty without you. Having children or not—that's not what matters most to me."

"But I've seen you with Rose," I whisper, the words tumbling out. "I've seen the longing in your eyes."

"I do love Rose and Michael with all my heart," he admits, his voice tender. "And they'll always be part of our lives. We can shower all the love we have to give on them—and on Nadiya."

I glance down, realizing the puppy has fallen asleep in my arms. "She's had a rough life, hasn't she?"

Viktor nods, his expression darkening slightly. "She was abandoned as a young pup, left for dead. When I went to the shelter, I found her cowering in a corner. The worker told me that, despite being a puppy, her fear kept her from getting adopted. She refused to connect with anyone—until yesterday." He reaches over to gently pet her head. "I saw her fear and knew I had to stay as long as it took to earn her trust."

Tears prick at my eyes. "How could anyone do that to an animal?"

"She needed someone to see her," Viktor says, his gaze never leaving the puppy. "I went there to find a dog for us. I know how much animal welfare means to you."

I smile at the thought. We've symbolically adopted animals at every zoo and aquarium we've visited. This feels like the next step.

"We both have painful pasts," Viktor continues. "And if we never have children of our own, I'm okay with that. There are other ways we can show love and make a difference. Starting with Nadiya. We'll give her a life full of love and safety."

"Stop, please," I whisper, cutting him off.

The hopeful look in his eyes vanishes instantly. "Amelia?" he asks cautiously.

I carefully set the sleeping puppy on the floor, then stand and pull off my T-shirt. Viktor's gaze never wavers from me as I turn around to reveal the tattoo on my shoulder.

"I got this done a few days ago," I say quietly.

He rises from the couch and steps closer, his fingers tracing the delicate lines of the tattoo. The image is a watercolor Nightingale made of music notes.

"It's a mix of the both of us," I explain, my voice breaking. "You're my Nightingale."

"And you're my melody," he murmurs, his voice thick with emotion as he leans forward, his lips brushing my shoulder where the ink marks our bond.

"I did a lot of soul-searching while we were apart, too." I look up at him. "I'm scared to bring a child into this world because of my past. But I realized if I let trauma dictate my future, all those evil people would win. I don't want to have a baby right now, but I don't want to close the door on ever having children."

"I don't want you to say that because you feel you have to. We have Nadiya, and there are plenty more animals who've had traumatic pasts. We can change a lot of lives."

"And I'm for adopting as many as we can care for. But if one day we decide we want to add a baby to the mix, I'm okay with that too." I reach out and take his hand. "When I looked at my future, there was also nothing without you."

Viktor pulls me against him. "I love you, Amelia."

"I love you more, Viktor." I stand on my tiptoes, my lips meeting his.

There's nothing gentle about our kiss. We pour all of our emotions into it. Viktor lifts me, and I wrap my legs around his waist. He starts walking back toward our bedroom.

"You will not keep me from my daughter." My father's voice booms from outside the bus, startling Nadiya awake. She runs behind Viktor.

"Sir, she's asked for privacy," Indigo argues.

"If you do not move, you will find yourself out of a job," he yells.

The bus door flies open as I scramble to grab my shirt. It's too late, though. Dad's already on the bus. I hold the shirt up, trying to cover myself.

"Amelia. Viktor." Dad looks between us, his eyes wide with shock. "I did not know you were here."

Indigo rushes in behind him. "I tried to stop him, sir."

"It's okay, Indi." Viktor gives her a kind smile.

I manage to step behind Viktor and use his large frame as a cover to put my shirt on. Once I'm presentable, I stand next to Viktor.

With the situation a bit calmer, Nadiya peeks her head from behind Viktor's leg before deciding it's safe. She runs over to my father, rubbing herself up against his legs. Dad's not a huge animal lover, evidenced by the dissatisfied look on his face at the mess Nadiya's making of his black suit pants.

"What is that?" Dad asks, pointing at the dog.

"This is our new little girl, Nadiya," Viktor introduces the dog proudly.

"Why?"

Viktor and I look at each other and laugh. "I've always wanted a dog, and now I have one." I stoop down and tap my leg. Nadiya runs back to me. "In her young life, she's only known abandonment and loss. Viktor and I are going to show her that not all people are bad." She licks my face, and Dad scrunches his nose. "We're her family now, and we'll give her all the love a puppy could ever need."

"I am guessing this means you two have made up?"

"We have." Viktor puts his arm around me. "And we made you a dedushka." Viktor grins.

As hard as Dad tries to keep a straight face, he loses the battle and begins to laugh. When Nadiya runs to him this time, my father leans down and pats her on the head.

"*Ty schastlivyy malen'kiy shchenok.*"

"She is lucky and very loved."

Viktor

THE REST OF AMELIA'S FAMILY, ALONG WITH ALEX AND Natalie, pile onto the bus. I was hoping for some alone time to reconnect with my girl, but that'll have to wait. Everyone's hungry, so we order pizza and celebrate the end of the tour. It's well after midnight before everyone starts to leave.

"I'm going to walk them out. I'll be right back," I say, grabbing my jacket.

"I'll wait here," Amelia murmurs, stifling a yawn as she sinks deeper into the couch.

As I step outside with Irina and Max, Irina looks over at me with a curious expression. "Do you know Amelia's plans now that the tour is over?" she asks, her tone measured.

I shrug slightly. "I'm not sure. We planned to stay at the lake for a week or two to unwind."

Max nods thoughtfully. "We are in town for a few days. I would like to spend some time with her."

"I'm sure that'll be fine," I assure him. "We'll call you tomorrow and make some plans."

Satisfied with my answer, they exchange goodbyes and head off toward their car. I watch as they drive away before Alex steps up beside me, clapping a hand on my back.

"I'm glad everything worked out for you," Alex says, his tone warm and genuine.

"That puppy's so sweet," Natalie says. "I can't wait for Rose to meet her."

"My little *printessa* is going to love her new furry cousin."

"I have a feeling she's going to want a puppy of her own now," Natalie says.

"There's plenty of dogs in need of a good home," I reply with a knowing grin.

"I don't think I'm ready to take on two kids and a dog," he adds, shaking his head.

We share a quiet laugh before Alex and Natalie climb into their car. I watch them drive off, their taillights fading into the distance. Turning back, I head inside the bus.

The scene inside warms my heart. Amelia is fast asleep on the couch, her breathing soft and even. Nadiya is curled up behind her, nestled into the curve of her back.

After carefully setting up the puppy in her crate for the night, I return to the couch. For a moment, I watch Amelia as she sleeps. Her peaceful expression and the way her hair spills across the pillow make my chest tighten with emotion. I slide my arms under her, gently lifting her up.

She stirs slightly, her eyes fluttering open. "I was hoping this wasn't a dream," she whispers, her voice groggy but laced with emotion. "I was afraid I'd wake up, and you'd be gone."

"It's not a dream, *moya zirka*," I murmur. "I'm right here."

Her arms tighten around my neck as she relaxes against me, a small, contented smile playing on her lips. I lean down and press my lips to hers to show her how real this is. My tongue seeks access to her mouth, which she readily allows. I don't break our connection as I carry her to our bedroom, where I rid us of our clothing and worship her body, bringing her to orgasm several times.

"Please, Viktor. I need you," she begs.

I line myself up with her opening and push inside. My eyes close from the intensity of the emotions. Amelia's my heart and soul. Without her, my world is dark and empty. I never want to experience life without her by my side again.

I move slowly, trying to prolong our shared pleasure. Hoping to make tonight last forever. But my self-control is slipping. I increase the speed and intensity of my movements. I want more—need to be deeper.

Pulling out, I flip Amelia onto her hands and knees. She looks at me over her shoulder and bites her bottom lip.

"Are you okay with this?"

"I am," she breathes.

Her consent is all I need to thrust back into her welcoming body. Her head drops as she mewls in pleasure. I hold onto her hips as I drive into her over and over. Her body begins to tense beneath mine. I know she's close. I reach around to her clit and rub my thumb over her sensitive area. The first waves of her orgasm begin, and she calls out my name. Then, I'm falling over the cliff with her. We soar on the wings of ecstasy until the last waves of pleasure subside, and we float to the ground.

Amelia's body collapses underneath mine. Not wanting to put my full weight on her, I roll over and lie next to her. She rests her head on my chest, and I hold her close.

"I'm sorry for the way I behaved. I shouldn't have shut you down so quickly," Amelia says quietly.

"I forgive you, *moya zirka*. We both need to learn how to communicate better." I rub her back gently. "The important thing is we figured it out and are here now."

"I never want to be away from you again."

I'm woken by the buzzing of my cell phone. Amelia's still sound asleep, her head on my chest and her leg tossed over mine. I reach over and grab my phone.

Charlotte: We're having a surprise party for Natalie tomorrow. We'd love for you and Amelia to be there.

Me: We wouldn't miss it. Just tell me when and where.

Charlotte gives me the address. When I look it up on the internet, I see it's at Water's Edge Bed and Breakfast. It's an odd place for a party, but I understand that it might be the only place to keep it a secret.

I set the phone back on the nightstand. I'm not in a hurry to go anywhere, but then I hear Nadiya whining. Carefully, I slide out from under Amelia and throw on a pair of pants and a shirt so I can take the puppy out for a walk.

Amelia

Yesterday, Viktor got us a rental car so we could drive to Northmeadow. My father's making arrangements for our Audi to be delivered to the lake house since we'll be spending a few weeks there.

I'm not due to be in California until mid-October. I'm looking forward to spending time alone with Viktor in one place.

This tour was incredible, and we were only the opening act. Knowing we'll be doing it next time as the headliner is unbelievable. But as fun as it was, waking up in a different city and state every day became tiresome. It'll be nice to be in the same place for a few weeks.

Today, we got up extra early. Viktor's finishing loading the car with all our stuff while I pack a doggie diaper bag for Nadiya. We have a nearly three-hour drive ahead of us. Traveling with a puppy is going to make the ride even longer since we'll have to make multiple stops.

"Are my girls ready to go?" Viktor asks when he comes back inside.

"I just finished packing her stuff."

Nadiya's running around the bus, dragging her leash behind her. She's so excited even though she doesn't know what's happening.

"Let's get on the road." Viktor grabs the puppy's leash, and I take her bag.

We make our way out to the car, where Viktor buckles Nadiya into her puppy car seat. I do the important thing—take pictures of Viktor and our fur baby.

The guys left for home yesterday, and my parents and Lana flew down to Northmeadow two nights ago, so it's just us and my security team left. Thankfully, Dad gave them a few weeks off. We'll meet back up with them in California when we go back.

Viktor's already started looking for someplace for us to live since we told Dad it was okay to put the Long Beach house on the market. We'll spend most of our time in L.A., so we're looking for something closer.

It's a good thing we left early. We had to make more stops than we anticipated. For the most part, Nadiya did great on the drive, and four hours later, we're pulling up at the cottage. Natalie texted that she and Alex were spending the day with her parents, so they're not at the lake right now.

There's about an hour until the party, so we unpack the car and try to get everything settled inside before we have to leave for the bed and breakfast.

"It's a pretty cottage. But you didn't even hang up a picture?" I ask as I look around.

"Why would I?"

"To make it feel like a home."

"This place was only for work."

I walk over to the windows overlooking the lake. "Do you think Natalie and Alex would let us decorate it some?

"I don't think they'd have a problem with that." Viktor comes to stand behind me. "We can work on that tomorrow if you'd like."

I rest my head on his chest. "This view is beautiful. I might not ever want to leave."

"We'll make sure our new house has a view of the ocean."

"I'd love that, but I was also thinking about something else."

"What is it?"

I turn around to face him. "What if we had a place that had some land, and we could take in more rescue animals?" I study his face for a few seconds, hoping for a reaction. "I know we won't be able to be there all the time. Maybe we can hire someone to help care for the animals."

Viktor's mouth turns up in a smile. "You have the biggest heart of anyone I've ever met."

"Is that a yes?" I ask hopefully.

"Absolutely. That would be a great thing for us to do."

Standing on my tiptoes, I wrap my arms around his neck and plant a kiss on his lips. "Thank you."

"As much as I want to bring you to bed right now, we have to leave for the party."

"We'll have something to look forward to later."

The ride to the bed and breakfast is short. I couldn't figure out why Charlotte was having her party here, but now I see why. It's a beautiful place full of charm and character.

The three of us get out and walk around the house. The party's being held outside by the lake. Nadiya immediately spots my father and starts whining and pulling on her leash. Somehow, she charmed him, and they became best friends. I drop her leash and let her run to him. He stoops down, giving her lots of love, and takes her leash.

There's a bunch of people here that are unfamiliar. I'm assuming they're Natalie's friends from Northmeadow.

"I'm so glad you both made it." Leo comes over to us.

"So are we."

"Make yourselves at home. Charlotte texted. They'll be here in about five minutes."

Everyone's milling about inside a white gazebo that's decorated with lanterns and large, colorful hanging flower baskets.

"Congratulations on the tour and the record deal." Brandon, Lana's ex, comes over and gives me a hug.

"Thank you." I look over his shoulder and see Lana watching us. "Has she spoken to you at all?"

"A curt hello. But I'm not letting her leave without getting to the bottom of this."

It's been two years, but he's clearly not given up on them. I'm glad. Brandon's a genuinely sweet guy, and it's obvious he still loves my sister.

"Let me know if there's anything I can do to help," I offer.

"I will."

We make our way over to my parents. Dad insists that Nadiya stays with him and Mom. It makes me laugh, considering he couldn't wrap his head around the idea of why we got a dog just a few days ago.

While we wait for Natalie to get here, we stop and chat with Star and her sub, Jackson. Dimitri, Jessica, and Lana join us. It's so nice to see everyone in the same place. We're talking to Sam and Luna when Leo announces that Alex and Natalie are pulling in. Her parents told them they were coming here for an early dinner.

Everyone quiets while we wait for them to come around the building. As soon as they come into view, the group shouts a collective "Happy Birthday."

Natalie brings her hands to her mouth. "I don't know what to say." She enters the gazebo and looks around at everyone gathered here.

Leo steps over to Natalie and gives her a hug. "Your mom was instrumental in making this happen."

"Thank you both." Natalie looks between her mom and Leo. "I can't believe everyone's here. How did you do this?"

"Leo and I have an announcement to make." Anthony steps up next to his husband. "We'd like to tell everyone that we're now the proud owners of Water's Edge Bed and Breakfast."

Congratulations and applause come from all the guests. Rose sees Viktor and squeals as she runs over to him. He lifts her into his arms, planting kisses on both cheeks. Rose giggles in delight.

"We thought it very fitting for our first event to be a birthday party for Natalie. Especially since we would've never found this place without her."

"You guys bought it?" Natalie asks, shocked.

"We did," Tony says proudly. "To be fair, it was Leo and Charlotte who brought the idea up."

"We fell in love with the area when we were here for Natalie's wedding," Leo adds. "Mrs. Wilson let us know she was looking to sell the place so she could retire, and we were looking at getting out of the city and slowing down. So, we took the leap and purchased it." Leo motions to Natalie's mom. "Charlotte has been instrumental in helping us make some changes."

Charlotte and Leo have become very close. I think it has something to do with her regret over how they treated their son, Michael, before he passed away. Regardless of how or why, it's been a beautiful thing to see.

"Let's sit and eat," Anthony suggests.

I take Michael from Natalie so she can eat her meal uninterrupted.

We spend an enjoyable afternoon and evening with our friends and family.

It feels so good to be home.

Viktor

Yesterday, we spent a wonderful afternoon with our friends and family. Nadiya was a big hit and fit right in with this eclectic group. But I'm equally as happy to be back at our quiet cottage. Just Amelia and me spending time together.

Tonight, like almost every night since we got here, we sit on our deck, a fire burning in the fire pit, while we watch the sun setting over the lake. Nadiya lays on her doggie bed next to us. It's quiet and relaxing.

The silence allows me to reflect on my life over the past few years. I've gone from a man who thought he had everything with Natalie and Rose to a man who found himself lost and alone.

There was a time when I didn't care about life. I actually wished I wouldn't be alive to see the next sunrise. I couldn't see it then, but the best part of my life was still to come. Thankfully, fate and my friends intervened.

Something happened to me that day in my bedroom when Amelia kissed me for the first time. Even though I pushed her away and gave her every reason we couldn't be together, I knew it was no use. The walls I'd erected around my heart crumbled. I knew there was no way I'd be able to resist this woman. Amelia's love is pure. When she looks at me, I'm all she sees. And for the first time in my life, I can admit that I deserve the love she gives me.

There's a lot on the radar for us. Amelia's career in the music industry is starting to take off. We'll be doing much more living from her tour bus.

We've also started taking the first steps toward opening Hope Ranch. A place for abused and neglected animals who need rehabilitation and love. Earlier today, we sent emails about some properties with plenty of land. We're also looking for staff who are well-versed in abused animals to help us with this endeavor.

Amelia owns my heart.

When I look at her, I see my forever.

I'm not sure what the future holds for us. What I am certain of is that whatever comes our way, we'll face it together.

Craving More Viktor and Amelia?

The story doesn't end here! Unlock an exclusive, never-before-seen bonus epilogue and discover what's next for Viktor and Amelia.

Scan the QR code to join my VIP Readers and get instant access to this special bonus content—completely free!

Don't miss out on the next chapter of their unforgettable love story!

Ready for the next captivating chapter? Dive into *Shattered Dreams* and discover Svetlana and Brandon's powerful story—where broken hearts begin to heal and love finds a way.

Acknowledgments

To my husband, Dominant, and best friend George. I can't say thank you enough for everything you do to make my books gor-geous. I wouldn't want to be on this crazy adventure with anyone else. I love you with all my heart.

To all my kids: Thank you for always being my biggest cheering squad. I appreciate all your support. I love you guys.

To my readers: From Booktok to Instagram. Twitter to Face-book. And everything in between. Each one of you is so very important to me. Starting this journey, I was scared that no one would bother to read my books and even if they did, they'd hate them. You have all showed my so much love and support. I treasure every message and email from you. Thank you all for your support. I love you all!

About Tara

Tara Conrad is the author behind sizzling and passionate love stories that ignite the senses. Her novels celebrate the fiery intensity of desire. They're known for having a blend of deep emotional connections, relatable characters, and captivating plots that ensnare readers from the very first page to the last.

Tara's married to her soulmate and Dominant, George. They are about to celebrate their 30th anniversary and are more in love today than yesterday. George encouraged Tara to start writing, and with each passing day, she's more thankful for his insistence that she tell her stories and his partnership on this journey. There's no one else in this world she'd ever want by her side. He is her happily ever after.